INTO THE
HEART OF THE COUNTRY

INTO THE HEART
of the
COUNTRY

A NOVEL

Pauline Holdstock

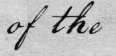

HarperCollins
Publishers Ltd

Into the Heart of the Country
Copyright © 2011 by Pauline Holdstock.
All rights reserved.

Published by HarperCollins Publishers Ltd.

First Edition

No part of this book may be used or reproduced in any manner
whatsoever without the prior written permission of the publisher,
except in the case of brief quotations embodied in reviews.

The author gratefully acknowledges the support of the British Columbia
Arts Council during the early stages of writing this novel.

HarperCollins books may be purchased for educational, business, or sales
promotional use through our Special Markets Department.

HarperCollins Publishers Ltd
2 Bloor Street East, 20th Floor
Toronto, Ontario, Canada
M4W 1A8

www.harpercollins.ca

Library and Archives Canada Cataloguing in Publication
information is available upon request

ISBN 978-1-55468-634-6

Printed and bound in the United States
RRD 9 8 7 6 5 4 3 2 1

For my family

*Under the skin of the earth deep in its rocky
bones all dreams are one. The dreams of the dead are
but one dream in search of the blood that courses through
the body's veins flooding the dark chambers of the heart
and lighting them with its fire.*

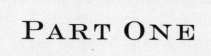

PART ONE

Molly Norton's Dream

NO ONE TOLD ME THE VASTNESS OF THE land. That when a person walks out the horizon is always farther and still farther and no amount of walking will bring it near. When I was a girl the horizon was the place the Wêcîpwayânak came from and the Kisiskâciwanak. A place a man could walk to as Samuel did and see there the Far-off Metal River and the Frozen Sea and come back and tell it. I did not expect the horizon to walk away from me. The vastness of the land was beyond my imagining. All my world was the fort. Its walls contained all that I could need and until Samuel left all that I desired. It was my home. Why would I desire ever to walk away from it? Why would anyone leave her home unless to be with her husband?

And yet I did leave and I did discover the vastness. So that it was as if my own life's purpose after all was to supply an answer to the question I believed required none. As if all my life had been only a prelude. All our lives only ever a prelude to what is to come.

But here is a question I did not think to ask. Why would a man any man leave his family and his home to come across the sea? When some new English man or boy stepped stinking from the boat to come and work in the house of my father I had no thought to ask why. It was what Englishmen did. And not just for my father Moses. It was what they had always done. From this great distance now I see their strangeness. How they came without their women these men these boys. How they came lonely and cold and rough with little comfort but the rum and the brandy they brought in their ships. They came onto the land and they clung about its edges so that it seemed they feared the land itself or perhaps its people and could not wait to see their ships again. They built houses of so many trees they could never be moved unless burned away by fire or carried away by flood and they fenced them round with palings as if they would themselves be caught and contained in a pound. Only a few were bold enough to walk out on the land. And there they were as children in need living on the pemmican of my mother's people. Wearing furs sewn fine for them against the wind. Warming themselves at night with the wives and the daughters who worked for them by day.

The rest remained in the houses they built and there they were masters. They opened and closed the gates at will and at trade they named their terms. Some of the women they took for their own. Yet when it was time for the men to return they left as they had arrived— lonely and cold. Sometimes their women wept on the shore and sometimes they delighted and danced.

And always there were more boys and more men who came like waves washing and receding at the shore. My grandfather Richard one of them. He lay down his gunpowder in the rocks and broke apart the very land for stones to build his house. And the people were drawn there like bees to a nest. And in that house my father was raised and in that same house my mother raised me. And to that house Samuel came like any other Englishman. I should have known he would not stay forever. When he took me for a wife how did I not see? Like any other Englishman he would sail away. He would turn his back on me and he would sail away as if all those stones upon stones were no more to him than an empty shelter on the trail. As if he were a man with no family of his own.

But my grandfather and my father and Samuel too are long dead and I am thinned now almost to nothing. A vapour rising from the muskeg a mist breathing up from the melt. Do you remember at the end of summer the swathes of white seed floss that float on the air across the land in the early morning? The breath of the dogs in the winter air? I am less. I am less than the high white smears across the blue roof of the world. Less than the faint haze round the moon in summer. I have thinned and thinned until on a still morning I shall vanish at the same moment that a hare will leap clear of the tongue of a fox.

It has taken many years to come to this but I have been patient willing myself back into the thin soil under the moss. Willing myself out of the steel teeth of his betrayal where for a hundred years I lay ready to gnaw at my own limbs to escape the jaws of loneliness. All my people starved and broken.

Did he know what was coming when he said *for your life Molly?* Saying my name through his clenched teeth? Surely he knew I would have gone with him into the boat. Wouldn't any wife? But he said *for your life Molly for your life*. Did he not know the journey that lay before me? And if he did not know then did he come to learn it? Did he see it when his life was over? Did he see my corpse as I have seen it cold and alone on the trail beside the frozen lake? To lie alone beside the lake in that silence on the snow that did not melt was terror worse than death. For if I were dead where were my people who should come to greet me? My sister? My grandmother? My daughter?

Yet the silence was trickery for a wind roared though it bent no sedge nor lifted any snow from the lake. It came from a great distance out of the hunting grounds. And the more I listened the more it seemed that the roaring was filled with the voices of all animals and all people who had lived—though they massed as one and I could distinguish none. At last I raised my voice to join them and the days and seasons rolled swiftly under me. The breath of the wind became my breath and I could quiet it.

I lay on a trail beside my boy where the others had left us. I had taken off the last of my clothing to speed my departure. I had given my moosehide blanket to my boy had given him too the knife and had laid myself down. If I had not curled my limbs inward I would have looked like a skinned animal for I could see the bones of my hips and my shoulders the ribs of my back stretching my hide. The knife marks on my thigh made it seem that already the animals had come to test my flesh but had turned away from the bitter taste. My boy Athîkis wrapped in the moosehide sat without moving. I laid my body in such a way that he could see the cuts—would if he were driven to find the courage to make his own.

When I had looked on all this a long while I closed my eyes on whiteness and welcomed it. A strange twinned creature I was—both in and out of this remembered world. I saw my body lying on the snow and my sight could leave my own body and see beyond to where the others lay. My aunt had not travelled more than a day from us before she too had fallen. My small cousin was holding tight still to her robe. Her fingers clutched the edge of the fur and I knew in an instant that she would lie with her mother for all time and that her fingers would hold fast long after the fur had rotted away. My mother had walked on for two days more. She had thought perhaps to find some shelter at a hollow where two pines grew close together but she had fallen just before she reached it. She was on her hands and knees and was moaning softly though there was no one to hear but she would not—I knew this for certain—go on again.

Strange to say my eyes absorbed these things without pity and did not see them with pain as they would in life. My own corpse on the snow was no more to me now than the carcass of an animal before it has melted back into the land. Nor were the little bones of my daughter's body any more or any less lying where they did on the trail behind us.

I did not enter the place where tears fall. Instead I felt the rolling of the year and began to know. If my life had no place in the seasons to come then my own days must now run backwards like a falling tide. The pull of it carried me back to the last days of my living when my mother walked away from me into the face of the storm. When my aunt too vanished in the whitened air between us. I was laying my small daughter to rest. My daughter who had refused a journey so hard and let her breath be lost to the sweep of the wind. I covered her with a blanket of snow and when I looked up the two of us my small boy Athîkis and I were alone and the world was wide. I crouched for him to climb onto my back and covered him with the moosehide. I watched my body rise from its knees and fall rise again and go on.

Fall again rise. Another watching our progress might have asked why it was I would not lie down and allow the two of us to rest. Lie down and open ourselves to death. But without breaking faith I could not. I walked on. I followed the path the others had made keeping my head down keeping my feet in the trodden snow of their tracks but never did I see them waiting as I had hoped on the trail ahead. When I came near to a small lake I saw there the bundle of skins my mother had carried for our shelter and the ice chisel my grandmother had given and I began to know why my mother had walked on. I was comforted and knew that Athîkis and I were not alone.

Those who were with us were in my heart. My aunt my mother. And the ones who had gone before them. Kôhkôhkahôw who had fished for us teaching us patience and fortitude. My grandmother with no protest or complaint suffering cold and hardship for all of us. Sharing all that she caught. Lying now where she left us. And farther back still Jane my sister bringing her husband's geese to the fort in the sweet sad time before this journey. Still farther a woman unknown to me. And she was with me too. She was strong and stood as if at my back with her hand on my shoulder to give me strength. Where she lived or where she lay in the whole wide land I had no knowledge. I knew only what Samuel had told me one night as we lay in the great soft bed that once was my father's. How Matonabbee and his friends had with Samuel come upon a woman of the Atimospikayak the Dog Rib people living alone on the shores of a lake in winter. How she had lived by cutting the flesh of her thigh to bait her line for fish. And the woman told me how to save Athîkis.

I watched myself out on the frozen lake and saw how the knife trembled in my hand. How blood fell on the snow from my bitten lip. The knife skidded from my thigh. I tried again. And then again. I

6

tried with its tip to cut out a sliver but my hands trembled so violently that it was not possible. I lay down with my face on the snow and I felt Athîkis's tears falling hot on the back of my neck.

I see how I had no place in the world. No father or mother no sister living. No passage to England with Samuel. No stone house. No lodge to return to. I lived only for the promise I had made to my sister's bones.

When I looked up the sky had darkened and the only thing to be seen was the white snow falling to cover again the face of the land. A long time it fell through that night and the day following and the next night too. In the morning it grew less and still less until an astonishing blue appeared behind it between it when I turned my face to the sky. And when I looked downward I saw that I was sleeping dropping deeper as a body sinks through water falling far below the surface where other hands take hold.

1717

THE WOMAN LYING AT RICHARD NORTON'S BACK leaned over his shoulder, tried to see his face but it was shielded with his hand at his neck, his forearm across his cheek, his eye, like a boy asleep, like the boy he was.

—Are you weeping?

He shook his head and swallowed mightily. He did not understand the word she used but he caught the tone that would mock him.

—You're weeping.

He rolled over on his back and looked towards her.

They had been travelling north out of York Factory for almost two weeks, the three of them. Governor Knight had arranged the expedition and chosen the guides—this Northern woman Iyese and the man Tudelzen, who had claimed her at once for his companion on the journey. Richard—the governor's sixteen-year-old ambassador—had no voice of his own in the matter. But Richard had voice in very little, enthusiasm, undeniable flesh-and-blood Englishness, and dispensability being the chief qualities he brought to this expedition of uncertain outcome.

They had paddled up the coast, winding through the rotting shore ice, parting great rafts of ducks that floated like dark yapping sea wrack. They pulled the canoes onto the flats each night and feasted on whatever they had caught that day. The waveys were nesting, and neither Richard nor the man Tudelzen had any trouble picking off the sentinels. They ate roast goose as long as their firewood lasted. Iyese could have a fire going and the goose drawn and dismembered and spitted on a bayonet above it before they had finished a pipe. When all the wood they had carried was burned, they ate the pemmican they had brought with them and eggs the woman gathered. She could walk in a straight line directly to a nest. And so they continued, always north. And then one night Richard had complained of the increasing wind from the bay and Tudelzen had offered the woman. Richard had heard of this hospitality and longed to experience it, but still it shocked him. Here was no shelter, no tent for privacy, their blankets of moosehide their only cover. But the man was insistent. He said his sister, Thanadelthur, had made him give his word to her before she died. Take good care of the boy Norton, she had said. She was a formidable woman, his sister. She would have been with them herself if she had not sickened. A man would not want to cross her even in death. So Tudelzen had promised. He registered deep offence at Richard's hesitation.

Richard read it plainly on his face. What choice did he have? Tudelzen said he was going to sleep in the lee of his canoe. It would be some shelter from the wind. Richard will not remember the wind. He will remember only the million stars and their glittering disinterest, their vertiginous wheeling behind the woman's tattooed face as he rolled onto his back.

Iyese laughed.

—God in heaven, he said. Then again, God. I am destroyed.

He was smiling now, shaking his head. He shuddered and heaved a great sigh.

She climbed onto him and lay flat.

She said, Do that again—and this time he understood the words and he flexed himself, making her laugh. He loved that laugh. Delight. Right up against his own agonies of desire. Already she was making him hard again. She knew exactly how to pleasure him, this woman, and he let her. It was true. Everything he'd heard about them. It was true. So he lay, floating on the sea of his desire while she navigated all its channels. He tried to stop himself from grabbing her so that he could make the pleasure last. But it was not possible. In a moment he had pushed her off and was on her, and in another minute it was over—the two of them apart again, catching their breath, her head still tipped back awkwardly on her arched neck, his fingers still deep in her hair. A sailor on the *Dering* had told him when he was just a lad that if you lie still you can get the women to ride you like a mount. The sailor had said the best of it was you could watch their whole bodies doing it. And then the men had descended into vulgarities the like of which his young ears had never known. But he did not stop them.

He understood now why men volunteered so readily for details away from the factory.

THEY PADDLED NORTH in their small canoes, negotiating the mouth of the great river by working upstream with the rising tide and waiting for the ebb to carry them over at an easy angle. Three stripped spruce poles marked the proposed site of the new post, a low point of land with a rock cliff at its back. They beached the canoes and went ashore briefly so that Iyese could get her bearings. Inland, all was an inhospitable mixture of boulder and marsh until the woods began almost a mile away to the west. Iyese walked out a short distance to the north and to the west, fixing the location and its approaches in her memory before they continued downriver. The falling tide carried them safely round the northeast point and into Button's Bay. They paddled on the next day past the mouth of the Seal River and on again until they reached the river the woman knew, the one she said would take them to the place where the Wêcîpwayânak, her own people, would be gathering before they headed west for the winter. Richard had more faith in this Northern woman now that he had lain with her—and now that the promised river had materialized. He had seen how her eyes glistened when she spoke about her people. Before they set out he had regarded her—purchased for goods to the amount of sixty made beaver—as a mere replacement for the governor's first choice. Now he no longer doubted that Iyese was equal to the undertaking. When they reached her people she would act as his mouthpiece for the Honourable Company. She would explain on Richard's behalf exactly where Churchill Factory, the new house for trade, was to be built. Richard would distribute the samples they had brought with them, the knives and the awls, the beads and the good duffle cloth. Using the words Thanadel-thur had taught him, he would recite a list of every item that would be available at the new post. He would promise the very best standard of trade. And Iyese and Tudelzen would bring him safely home.

FOR A WHILE they kept to the waterway, taking advantage of the easy paddling across its lakes, the abundant fish, but when the river became unnavigable they abandoned the canoes and continued on foot. They carried their provisions and the sleeping skins as well as all the gifts. Their progress was slow.

Without the definition of the coast Richard began to feel disoriented. That long stain of purple and orange that had stretched away across the open country to the northeast was now on his left, to the southwest. Or was it another tract of the same plants, the same lichen? That low ridge in front of them. Hadn't they crossed it before? And that chain of lakes, three together? This land as big as a world. Nothing to hold to. No human habitation. He could stand in one spot and turn full round on his heel and the horizon was unmarked. No end of this land in sight in any direction. He was cowed by the vastness and envied the birds, who might outfly it. Still he had faith in these guides and gave himself up to them entirely. They travelled on the land as if it were marked with signposts and milestones, and so long as the weather held he could feel secure, the world a known place, a legible page, at least to his companions. Even through the sleet and the first snows he did not lose confidence. But then came a storm like a raging beast and it was as if the very air had taken animal life, the wind become a wolf's breath with the power to freeze the heart in the throat, turn the blood to ice. He was not able to see in the stinging snow and when he closed his eyes against it he could no longer think clearly, was barely able to place one foot in front of the other, never knowing which way to turn, which way was forward. The unearthly howling of the wind shredded the fabric of a man's thinking. Its bitter cold wrung the flesh from the bones. He wanted only to fall to his knees and cover his head. Iyese insisted that there were trees not a day off and she refused to stop.

RICHARD'S TEETH CLATTERED in his head. He could not open his eyes. He believed that his head had been stripped of its covering of hair and skin, that no flesh remained, only his bony skull through which the wind knifed and sang. That must be why he was so cold, why his jaw bounced as if set on tiny springs. The clamour and the terror of the morning's attack had blasted all coherence from his head. He had forgotten why he was travelling, where he was supposed to be going. He hoped he had hands still, and feet.

They had been walking a long time after the weather came on, he remembered that. Turning and striking southwest towards the trees. Had he walked on the stumps of his ankles? Iyese and the man would not slow for him, he remembered that too. He had stumbled after them until he fell and covered his head. He had no idea how long he had lain in his exhaustion. He knew only that when he woke it was night. He was in the presence of many others. The smell of food and acrid smoke. A tent skin obscuring the sky. Someone offering fragrant meat. But he could not swallow and his chest hurt and he had fallen again into a sleep stronger than pain.

It was when he was in this state, more dead than alive, that the attack came. A party of Mikisiwak, eager no doubt to assuage some persistent itch, stole up through the woods intent on mischief. He will not forget the sound of shouting in the pre-dawn, panic exploding like lit powder in their midst, his heart's thunderings, screams like seabirds. Expecting every moment to be his last, he did not open his eyes. Did not see how the panic belonged to the Mikisiwak as they registered the sound of a Company musket fired by Tudelzen into the half dark.

When quiet was restored he tried to stir but felt his limbs frozen in place. The question, the sob that formed in his throat, will never leave him. To die, then, out here on the land?

For the rest of his life Richard Norton will dream this moment of his blind terror and always he will wake without being able to open his eyes. He will be lying with his knees clasped to his chest and all around will be the inhuman yells, the piercing crack of musket shot, and the shrieks of the wounded. He will have the stock of his own gun between his knees, his temple pressed to the side of the barrel.

When he did dare to open his eyes, his teeth miraculously stopped their dance. He found that the bones of his face were after all, and praise be, still covered with flesh, and that his own thatch of hair still covered his head. He had ears at last to hear the murmur of voices, his companions among them. He was luckier than the man who led the attack and now lay near him, the side of his head gaping open to the new day.

The Mikisiwak did not return again.

THE NORTHERN WOMEN dismantled the tents in the early light and packed up their belongings. No one wished to remain at the site of the attack. They said the English boy would be a problem. Tudelzen said he would have to be hauled. Weak with a quaking nausea, Richard was glad enough to lie passively on a makeshift sled and let himself be bumped over the snow, but the travelling was not easy. At the first stopping place an older woman offered to stay and care for him. She seemed not to mind the charge of nursing him back to health, and she let him lie in the tent she shared with an old man. She gave him tea made of powdered clay and white spruce bark. The old man came every day to blow into his mouth and his anus. It made Richard weep with shame, and the old man smiled because tears are good and carry away poisons.

When he was sufficiently recovered the woman—he never did grasp her name—packed up the travelling tent and the meat she had dried and led him away to rejoin the people. The old man left them in search of deer, taking Richard's ammunition with him. Richard followed the woman meekly. They walked now across a land bright with winter. He had no idea what he should be doing to serve the Company. He had his gun but no powder or shot. His goods were gone. His legs were untrustworthy. He was trying only to stay alive and not freeze to the solid ground. For five days he stumbled blindly after the woman until his spirits were lifted by the smell of woodsmoke on the air and the barking of dogs and they came to the tents. But Iyese and Tudelzen were no longer in the camp. They had moved on, taking Richard's goods with them. He was assured they would be back. They had promised to return after they had met with the main body of the people away to the west. By niski-pîsim, they said. The month when the geese come. A winter away. No one in the camp had any desire to follow and Richard had no means of persuading them. He committed himself to their care, accepted their perfunctory gifts of food, and was thankful to be in the company of hunters. A woman made him a coat and he was thankful too for that.

The winter was long, and before they met with his guides Richard fell ill again and again, his body curling around the pain that was like an iron rod thrust into the centre of his chest, his breath scraping in his throat. The woman who had cared for him before was at his side each time. She had deep reserves of patience. She knew how to manage his tremors and at night she lay against him to warm him. Though no shaman came to blow into him, sometimes Richard cried.

Out on the land Iyese and Tudelzen distributed his goods to all they came upon and spread word of the new trading post. It was March when they rejoined him exactly as they had promised and walked with him back across country, some of their friends accompanying them with sleds piled high with pelts procured along the way. They walked on through the gradually brightening days, leaving the woods and cutting across the windswept ice of the marshes to the river. The new house, Churchill Factory, thrown up hastily in the fall as soon as the supply ship had left, stood in place of the marker poles on the low point of land.

MORE THAN FOURTEEN years have passed since Richard's ordeal out on the land and the injurious sickness from which his lungs will never quite recover. The cold and the bowel-loosening fear live on for him, as a horrid dream subsides to live in ambush, or a vicious dog subdued skulks in a corner of the room. But Richard is no longer a boy and has learned how to suppress his fears. He has seen men set out and not return. He has sailed as far north as the Company's ships will dare, has glimpsed there the appalling remains of Governor Knight's own doomed expedition. He has relegated the sight of the men's skulls and bones, muddled and gleaming on the rocky headland, to the corner of his mind where the untrustworthy dog lies. He tries never to rouse it. Meanwhile he has helped to construct the rough outbuildings of the factory with his own hands. He has travelled again into the country, has learned to converse easily with the Northern men who come in now to trade and with the Mashkêgowak, the Southern men who provision the post. Over the years he has absorbed some of the complexities of the post's management, has scraped together a rudimentary knowledge of its book-keeping and stock-taking and payroll, its annual indent and inventory. And to the surprise of several old hands he has reaped reward. He has been named Chief Factor and given command of this post, this ramshackle affair on the Churchill River. He has lost no time in taking a slender young wife—he calls her Abigail—and bringing her to live with him within the house. And she has lost no time in bearing him a son. But there is more. Though Richard has never entertained a thought about the French in his life, the London Committee has. The French and their potential to do harm are always making alarming, even if figurative, appearances in the board-room of the Company. In consequence the Company has fixed its distant heart on the construction of a stone fortress at the mouth of the Churchill River, where it can protect the ships and ensure that no attempt on the Company's interests can ever seriously be entertained. Thus a new dream for Richard, this one infinitely preferable to his dream of adolescent death. This is a dream he can dream awake: an impregnable fortress where the Company's servants, with himself at their head, can conduct business in full security. It is a far cry from a smoky tent on the trail, and from the sorry cluster of chill wooden houses that is his present home. The new stone fort, five miles downriver and in the building now these several years, will be his personal triumph. It will stand for generations, its stone walls strong enough to withstand all onslaught. When he al-lows himself to gloat on his good fortune he marvels at how fate breaks its own trail across our trackless lives regardless of our fears and dreams. As a boy shivering on the winter journey, at the mercy of strangers for his every need, for his very life, he had feared to die so lost, his bones melting into the vastness of the land, his life reduced to nothing but a fleeting shadow and no stone to mark its passing. Yet here he is, the overseer of these stones upon stones that bulk and extend daily towards their own enduring destiny, and that will carry his memory within them. It will be his name that is spoken when the abiding, astonishing monument is remarked in the wilderness. And Richard dreams. He dreams his small son a man and that man walking on the ramparts, men and women peacefully encamped outside the walls. It will be a fortress fast against all comers: disgruntled or ill-willed Indians, jealous Frenchmen—and pugnacious Americans especially. He dreams himself asleep within thick stone walls that he imagines will be proof against the cold, that worst of hardships; no more waking in the morning to these logs behind his head glazed with ice an inch thick. He sleeps each night with the plans for the new fort carefully rolled and wrapped in oilskin and hanging from a nail out of reach of rodents.

But downriver the work of building is beset with difficulties, not least of which is the bumptious little Robson, sent out from England to interfere. He finds fault with everything, with the stone, the mortar, the men, Thomas Giddins, Robert Menzies, the horse. He even has a finished curtain wall demolished—to prove his point? It did go down with little resistance—and built up again with mortar mixed to his particular specifications. Richard is a little sorry now he took the horsewhip to him because in that instance at least the man did seem to be right. Still he won't give up the plans to him but persists in carrying them back at each day's end to the wooden house up the river, though Robson insists that everything would go more expeditiously if all concerned slept at the site.

Richard's young wife will not think of it. Abigail is happy at the decrepit wooden house with her small son in her arms and her own people camped outside the rotting stockade, a stone's throw from the creaky gate. Richard tells her they must eventually go down to the great fort. He promises a high stone room where they will play. He promises to fill the room with all manner of goods, which he will bring back across the sea from England. He rolls towards his wife, reaches across his sleeping son to put his hand on her shoulder. The governor's wife. The only countrywoman who will know his bed. He would like to promise she will not see another of her countrywomen in their new stone bedchamber. But he is too tired to say the words. Abigail sighs in her sleep and draws the infant closer. The stone walls of the fort rise up in Richard's sleep and tower round, a bulwark against old fears. Within their fastness he will choose his dreams. No sudden ambuscade, no bloodshed in the night. Disorder and strife, starvation and killing cold will have to roam outside biting at each other's bones, not his. In Richard's dreams the walls' mute stones represent the power of the king, the might of his country, the solidity of all that is civilized and of lasting value. Fortitude, stability, constancy—these are inherent and will stand firm against the trials of the country.

WHEN THE MEN'S dwelling house is finished and the roof of the governor's quarters is finally leaded, Richard and his family move downriver. The work of building continues. Richard's wife is rarely parted from her son unless it is to allow a niece or a nephew to take his place. The boy, christened Moses by the captain of the *Prince Rupert,* is always at her breast or riding on her back. She goes nowhere without him, spending her time in the company of her sisters and their several children who come and go at will in the half-finished fort. Richard can't help noticing that while he was preoccupied with lime and mortar and stone he lost his slender young wife. Her heavy breasts are playthings for the boy, who walks to her now and climbs onto her lap, roots into the opening of her beaded dress whenever it pleases him. Still the two of them, mother and son, continue to share his bed—except when he asks Abigail to repair to one of her sisters' tents and take the boy with her. For opportunities do arise, and a man must have his distractions after all, his small rewards for the burden of responsibility that is Prince of Wales Fort.

Abigail herself is amply provided for. She has no other obligations but the raising of the boy. Through the changes of the year she sews supple hides for his clothes and, as far as Richard can see, does little else but smile into his blue eyes and caress him. Moses learns to live like a princeling—but then all the boys of the country are princelings, free to exult the days' length and breadth, rolling like pups, trying their strength and speed, the sharpness of their eye and ear. Rarely admonished, they grow accustomed to fish in the kettle for the sweetest morsels of meat. On the day that Richard, seeing a pack of small boys playing at target on the hill of broken stones, hails the wrong child, he understands that he is in danger of losing the boy too. He finds Moses and takes him into the house. He measures his legs and his arms and the circumference of his belly, and with the next packet to York he requests that the tailor there make breeches and a jacket to size in whatever material he has on hand. Three months later, Moses' first appearance in the suit is the source of much amused interest on every side. His aunts love him more than ever. Richard takes the opportunity to announce that henceforth the boy, now breeched, is to be addressed as Master Norton. Abigail will at all times be Mrs. Norton and on no account Wîhkiminêsiw, her given name. His policy alters little. His son, left to the women, remains their darling and shows no sign of turning overnight into an English boy. Richard himself makes the possibility only more remote when, in recognition of a past distraction, he agrees to take a recently orphaned Northern boy into his family. The child, not long out of infancy, renews Moses' attachment to his mother, who allows the two of them to enjoy her encompassing warmth by turns. Moses is besotted with the younger boy. He hugs him and leads him by the hand. He would like to eat him up, he loves him so fiercely. In winter they wear identical otterskin capes over their deerskin coats. They look like small walking tents. The capes have pointed hoods that descend about their ears and shoulders. Underneath, the ends of the younger boy's sleeves are stitched tightly together so that his fingers will not freeze. Abigail does the same for Moses when he asks her. In summer she greases the little boy's skin against the mosquitos. Moses stuffs his coat into a rock pile and takes off his shirt. He steals a handful of fat from one of his aunts and polishes his own skin. He ties the ends of the breeches closed and tries to use them for an ingenious new fish net down at the water's edge. But when one day, wearing his English jacket over his bare belly, he strolls to where his mother is consoling his tearful foster brother and reaches again into the beaded dress, he closes the book on his bucolic childhood. Richard, watching from across the yard, makes up his mind. He does not have to wait for permission from the Company. He can make it all right with Captain Fowler. When the Company finds out he'll simply offer to pay for the passage. And Abigail will have the other boy. It will work out most agreeably.

1741

Moses Norton's memory of his depar-
ture from the shores of the bay will not include the
sight of his mother's face or the sound of her voice when she
discovered what her husband had done. By that time he had
been lifted up the greasy ladder to the decks of the *Sea Horse*
and taken to his father's quarters by a smiling sailor who
showed him the small hammock rigged across a corner for
him to sleep, the hanging ladder by which means he would
reach it, the lantern that would swing close to his head.

Moses at six was easily won over by such novelty.

—Nikâwiy is coming? My mother? And Matonabbee?

The sailor didn't answer but took him by the hand to
show him the galley and the country provisions they had taken
on board for the voyage back. And had he known, what could
he have replied? Your father is sitting dumbstruck in the jolly

boat just now leaving the shore. Your father is shaken, has never witnessed such an exhibition as your mother is providing. Your father never dreamed she would take it so hard.

For Abigail—Wîhkiminêsiw—is putting on a display of considerable invention. She is on the shore by the makeshift ramp that serves for now as a landing stage. She is knee-deep in the chill waters of the river, her sisters restraining her. She is naked except for the red ribbon woven into her braid, for she has torn off her clothes and rent them. It was the tearing of the clothes that so shook Richard. The strength of the woman. She took her dress and tore it with her teeth, then with brute force rent the thing in two though it was sewn from good new skin. Her face and throat are smeared with the gritty mud of the beach except where tears have made clear paths like streams. The mud is plastered on her breasts, her thighs, and she is wailing, her face turned up to the sky.

But none of this figures in Moses' memory, which will offer only what he saw that day on board the *Sea Horse* as she rose and fell at her anchor, and suggest only a vague disquiet. He sees the dull glow of the varnished panels lining the dark walls of his father's accommodation—no more than a cabinet squeezed next to the captain's quarters—the small stern light that barely admits the day; he can smell smoke and pitch, a sickening animal stench from the hold, and the bitter salt smell of men's sweat. The whole ship is alive with creaking and straining, and the wind somewhere very high is singing strange, unearthly songs he has not heard before. He cannot wait for his mother to appear, for a question is crystallizing in his mind. The sailor has shown him many passages, many different quarters, and everywhere men pass to and from their duties. Moses knows there is something lacking on this ship, something he is in need of. He will ask his mother as soon as she comes. Where are all the women? Something is making him want to cry. He does his best not to.

Richard Norton arrived on the jolly boat's last trip and attempted to look bluff and optimistic as he boarded.

The boy was locked in his cabin, a sailor told him. It seemed best. He gave him the key. Richard waited on deck with Captain Fowler until they were under way and then he went to his son.

Moses remembers the small screech of the key in the lock, something unsure about it, then the familiar sight of his father framed stooping in the unfamiliar doorway. He comes in and closes the door behind him. He picks Moses up and carries him to the stern light.

—See? We're on our way.

Moses can see nothing but a blur of grey salt stuck to the glass. He reframes the question he had formulated, asks instead, Nikâwiy? My mother?

MOSES NORTON DREAMS he is a small child again, a very small child, and yet in the dream he is not in his home where he should be, with his mother and his aunts. He is here in England in Mother Dupeer's sitting room with a heap of soft dun-coloured deerskins piled on the chaise and spilling to the floor. The dream ends abruptly and in discomfort yet Moses would begin it again in a wink, so sweet are those furs and the anticipation of delight in his belly. His dream will return to him at intervals throughout his life, most often when he is on board ship. If he wakes to the creaking of the vessel, he will squeeze his eyes shut, still trying as he is now to recapture it.

He closes his eyes at once on the green-painted panels of the room with the strange sour-smelling children in their beds. He tries to will himself back to the warmth of fur, but even with his eyes closed he is conscious of the terrifying presence of the little blood-streaked man hanging on a cross on the wall, the thin counterpanes on the cots, the striped bolsters in their scratchy linen covers. The dream refuses his summons and the memory of it though sweet is not enough.

MOSES' DAYS at Mother Dupeer's were to be the days of any boy fortunate enough to be put out to care in a household of modest but dependable means, and more than fortunate— at least so his father would have it on the day he left him there—to be in the hands of a good woman whose calling it was to improve the stock of learning of the world's boys. For Mother Dupeer also presided over a small day school that promised to raise a tradesman's son to the very brink of advancement. She offered to bring in a boy to the drawing room to demonstrate his ability. Richard Norton would have liked to decline but she had already rung the bell. A lumpen girl came in and was sent off to fetch someone called Thomas—and mind she returned with a primer.

Young Thomas grubbily appeared and the book was thrust into his hands.

—Page six, if you please.

The boy, his tongue between his teeth, thumbed for the page.

—*It is a . . . sin. / To . . . s-s-*

—*Steal*, Thomas. *Steal*. We learned *steal*.

—*Stea-l*

—Begin again, if you please.

Thomas took such a breath that his chin disappeared in his shirt.

—*It is a s-sin. / To . . . s . . .*

Mother Dupeer could have waited, given him a second or two more but she chose not to.

—This, she said, is a pupil who has been with us but one month. *Steal*.

—*Steal a pin*. Thomas let the words come in a rush, hoping to forestall a reprise.

Richard smiled obligingly.

—True words, young man. I'm impressed by your wisdom.

Mother Dupeer laughed for longer than the joke warranted. Mr. Norton would be her bread and butter for the next three years.

Thomas unexpectedly said that he could figure sums too. As well as James. But Richard Norton was content to take his word on it and did not seem to want a demonstration. Instead he clapped his palms to his thighs and stuck his elbows out in readiness to stand.

—Well! It is time to thank you, Mother Dupeer, for the instruction you will give to my son. Without you . . .

His words dwindled as he stood up and he made an awkward bow to cover their disappearance.

—My heartfelt gratitude.

When he looked up, Mother Dupeer had her freckled hand extended. For a moment, Richard thought that she expected it—surely not—to be kissed. Relieved, he saw he was mistaken and enclosed it in his own two, which seemed to please her.

Moses looked uncertainly between the adults, not relishing the freckled hand at any cost, and started for the door.

Mother Dupeer said, What's this? If you quit me your father shall have thanked me for nothing.

Moses turned. His father was laughing tolerantly.

—Moses, Moses! he was saying and shaking his head gently. Moses, Moses! You are to remain at school.

—Remain?

—Certainly.

—Where are you going? To the ship? Moses caught the swift glance Mother Dupeer cast in his father's direction.

His father hesitated and then said, Aye. To the ship. But I shall be back. In the meantime, my boy, you too will learn all manner of useful things. About pins and sins . . .

But Moses heard the words with the ears of a six-year-old, missing no false note and catching every small deception.

—When will you come back for me?

Why this panic, this sense of loss? What was he losing? There was a need. Moses could not name it.

—I shall be back, my boy, in three years' time, when the Company, God willing, shall grant me furlough. In the meantime, learn your lessons well and perhaps when I see you next you will have the makings of a young gentleman. On the brink of advancement. Now come here.

But Richard's embrace was no blessing. Moses felt its message through his arms, his shoulders, his chest. The language of Richard's embrace travelled through him but he could not read it. Yet—here is the strange thing—though Moses could not read the language, he understood the nature of its meaning, which was dark and signified only loss.

His father squeezed him again and he was left with his eyes and nose smarting from tears withheld.

MOSES ATE LITTLE for supper that night. Lying on his cot he stared a long time into the autumn dark before he slept, falling through time to become again a small child in search of his mother's comfort.

The first time Moses asked when his father was coming back, Mother Dupeer said firmly, Three long years. On the fifth occasion, foreseeing how this exercise might grow tedious, she said he was not to ask again. She herself was not at all sure that Mr. Norton had returned to Rupert's Land at all. It was her understanding that the boats left only once a year. Someone had hinted that he was still at his wife's house. But that was no concern of the boy's. And really no concern of hers as long as he paid his bill.

Though she had a voice as thin as lemon juice, Mother Dupeer was not an unkind woman. She treated Moses with the same mixture of curbed affection and unrestrained discipline that she bestowed on her own children, James, Abraham, and

Jane. The most menial chores, it is true, devolved to him as the
years passed, but when he transgressed he was tied to the very
same table leg that Mother Dupeer used for Jane. He was fed
and clothed as if he were indeed Mother Dupeer's own flesh
and blood, and were it not for the tawniness of his skin no visi-
tor would have guessed that the family housed a stranger. If,
when times were hard, he was served the rinsing of the pot
instead of broth, or had a plaster steeped in water instead of
vinegar, it was not after all observable, and since water was free
he received the same cold baths as the other children for the
improvement of his constitution.

Moses' days by and large unrolled without any great dis-
ruption. Daily he rose and went without question to perform
his obligations as a tractable boy. During the hours of school,
he took his place among the rest of the pupils and learned his
numbers and letters by rote, and thanks to—or perhaps in
spite of—Mother Dupeer's best efforts at tickling Latin into
him with a birch could by the age of nine read passages of
Ovid aloud. There were occasional fights. There were injus-
tices that stung. He learned to lie a little and to hate James,
who lied a lot. But like his foster brothers and sister, Moses
managed to keep his seat in the saddle and hurtle on through
his young life to the next holiday from his duties. In winter
he prayed for the school's tiny pond to freeze so that he could
slide on it with Abraham, and he prayed for the wondrous,
otherworldly snow that made Mother Dupeer so bad-tem-
pered but brightened the afternoon with its particular light.
In summer he ran all the way to the stream to angle for stick-
lebacks with a worm. At night he knelt on the splintery floor

and waited until an appropriately pious length of time had elapsed so that he could with decency roll into his cot.

—RICHARD, YOU ARE dreaming again.

Elizabeth Norton did not like it when her husband made incongruous noises in his sleep. She did not much like her husband, though it was not a statement she would ever air. His falling ill almost immediately on his return to England seemed to her like a grievous injustice. Other Company men stayed on in Rupert's Land until they died there, sparing their wives the hardship of nursing them. They died there of the country distemper or of a pleurisy, or they froze themselves solid on some God-forsaken stretch of ice, and then their wives, just as her mother had, received all unasked for every bit of unpaid salary with every outstanding bonus or recognition that was owed. *And* a small pension. They did not have to lift a finger. Since Richard had been home she was busy day and night with his needs. He was a poor figure of a man. She did not know how he had survived so long in harsh conditions. There was very little flesh on him and his skin was an unsavoury shade of bluish grey. And he coughed. She could not say she had slept two hours at a stretch since he had been home. And then there was his constant fretting. She was busy enough calling the doctor back constantly without his repeated requests for Napier. Perhaps the arrangement had been a mistake, but what was she expected to do? Assume the charge of his half-breed bastard? Well. But she would like to be able to say that to his face. To anyone's face. The knowledge of the boy was a burden in her heart. Well again. A good thing she had the sense not to dwell on her grievances.

Richard stirred and woke. He coughed, moving the splintery slush that had taken residence in his lungs.

—Is Napier here? He had been dozing in Elizabeth's deep armchair beside the hearth.

—No, Mr. Norton. Tomorrow. He comes tomorrow. Shall you go to bed now?

She rather hoped so, thinking she might have a little time herself in the chair before the coals died down.

—No, my dear. It will bring on a coughing fit. I'll sit up a while longer. But my feet, you know . . . If you could, my dear . . . If you would be so good.

—Of course. Though her body, her whole body, her lips, her neck, her shoulders, even the way she carried her wrists, said, I do not wish to. She got up and went upstairs. She kept a pair of muslin gloves beside the bed for the times when Richard asked for his feet to be warmed. Nothing, he said, but the warmth of human flesh could reach them. Anything other—the heat of the fire, a warming pan, an earthen bottle of hot water, even when allowed to cool—burned his skin. The pain was intolerable.

When she came down he had removed the slipper from his left foot. She pulled on the gloves and drew up a footstool. He thought for a minute she would sit and place his foot in her warm lap but instead she knelt and asked him to put his foot on the padded stool. So there it was, a parody of a precious artifact, a gift for a queen. He regarded his own foot, swollen and nacreous, the skin purplish, in places almost black, the shiny ridge where the surgeon had had to take off two of his toes. He forgave her the gloves though he had not been able ever to forgive her wearing them on the night they were married.

Thomas Napier arrived promptly next morning at nine o'clock to take his client to Hudson's Bay House in Fenchurch Street. His connection to the London Committee was well known and his familiarity with the sometimes delicate affairs of its employees was undisputed. An engraver seeing the two men get into the carriage outside Mrs. Norton's house would have had ample inspiration for a broadsheet on the Reaper at work in the City, for Napier, big-boned and tall, had a cadaverous look about him and poor Richard seemed half-dead already as he slumped against the buttoned seat.

The attorney hoped his client would last long enough to make the journey in both directions. He felt sorry for the man, who should have been in bed at home, at rest, making the most of his last days to establish peace with his Maker, not climbing into carriages on foggy November mornings to pursue some fool's errand. It might salve Norton's own conscience perhaps but was unlikely to impress his Maker, who, Napier was sure, was not to be hoodwinked so easily. And besides, from what he understood, Norton was about to ask of the Company a favour that rested on a good deal of ifs and whomsoevers and whensoevers. In his experience these projections into a future in which the author had little hope of agency nearly always came to nought.

Life—or more to the point, death—would have been a lot simpler for his client if only the wife were more cooperative. The stumbling block, the sticking point, was the son. It would not be the first time or the last that a loving husband coughing blood into his whiskers had looked into his wife's eyes and declared he had a confession to make, begged his last companion to *look after the boy. See that he's all right*. And had added feebly, *Forgive me*. Mrs. Norton was going to deny the existence of a son until her last breath. Napier could see that. He had tried to reason with her. Without going so far as to *say* that it was her duty as a good wife to carry out her husband's wishes and assume *his* obligations as her own, he thought he had made it quite clear. But the woman would not be moved. And as for undertaking a visit to the boy in order to apprise him of his affairs, he did not dare broach it. She simply refused to acknowledge the child's existence and insisted that Norton made no revision to his will. Even the payments for the child's board would be managed through Napier.

Richard Norton, by now an extremely sick man, had bowed to his wife's wishes. He had made no provision in his will—which would have been the simpler, and for him the cheaper, option—but had instead entrusted the execution of his wishes to Napier, saying he would like to know all was settled so that his mind could be at rest.

Accordingly, Napier had arranged an apprenticeship of seven years at sea upon the boy's attaining the age of nine, to be followed by a paid position in Captain Spurrell's service, and terminating with a permanent appointment on Hudson Bay. He had thought the whole thing settled. But now his client, taken with a fit of who knows what kind of conscientious torments and night terrors, had thought of something else. For some reason of his own he had been unable to entrust the commission to Napier but instead had to come all the way to town to arrange matters for himself.

The day being so unsuitable for walking, Thomas Napier consumed the time along with a bowl of punch at a coffee house while he waited for Norton to settle his affairs behind the dark blue doors of the Honourable Company of Adventurers. When he returned, Richard Norton was sitting at the bottom of the stairs, fighting for breath. Napier left him to sit while he went in search of their carriage driver. On the way home Richard said the Company had undertaken to provide for Moses' mother, if she could be found, drawing on what was due to him before the balance was sent to Mrs. Norton.

—And, he said, there was a second matter.

He gave Napier a letter with the Company seal.

—I should like you to keep this safe until the time comes to give it to Moses. It is a copy of a letter penned to the commander-in-chief at Prince of Wales Fort. Give it to Moses on completion of his apprenticeship. Let him take it to Churchill to deliver personally. I shall not be on this earth to thank you for your part in this, and so I extend my thanks to you now, sir.

—We may none of us be here in ten years' time. The attempt at levity seemed only fair to the man who was so obviously going to be the first to make his exit. But Norton was intent.

—Your successors surely can be trusted to act accordingly.

Napier stopped the carriage twice on the way back. The

day had almost done for Richard, who was so racked with coughing it seemed he might choke. The attorney was not surprised when Norton did not ask him to come inside.

Returning to his office, Napier calculated the amount for the new invoice he would have his clerk deliver to Richard Norton. Mrs. Norton, he thought, was seriously depleting her own financial resources by letting herself be ruled by such stubborn propriety.

Though Richard Norton had looked as if he might expire right there on the stairs of the head office, he held to life, such as it was for him, for several weeks more. Long enough for his conscience to acknowledge yet another last thing. He sent again for Napier, who this time was compelled to conduct his business at the bedside. Richard Norton, who had put his affairs in order and done all he could to ensure that his family was provided for, had thought of something else. He asked Napier to fetch the writing materials and dictated to him his latest request to be sent on the next ship to Prince of Wales Fort in Rupert's Land.

Napier carried the letter away with him, realizing that his client was losing all sense of time. Moses Norton would not even see those shores for at least four or five years, perhaps longer. And the whole matter seemed to be to do with yet another Indian lad. As if one weren't enough. There seemed little point in sending the letter—yet another fool's errand—off into the blue so soon. He was a very busy man.

But Richard at least was now content. He spent his days and nights dreaming—an idyllic future for his son, a bucolic past for himself. His body, all unaware of these deep delights, kept his rasping breath coming and going like a starving animal. When finally he did let go, he was deep in a dream of another place, another time. A woman at his back asks him something. He knows the words. She asks if he is weeping. He rolls over and holds her gaze in his. And holds it. His wife's gloved hand is on his brow. It is a mercy he does not feel it.

Elizabeth took her hand away and observed how his features had subtly changed. She thanked God she had been able to do her duty.

ONE MONTH BEFORE Moses' ninth birthday, he was summoned by the latest lumpen girl to Mother Dupeer's drawing room. And how the heart can leap to what it desires. He bumped walls in his haste to get there. But the figure that loomed there with the bony face and hands of a skeleton was not his father. It was from this wreck of a man, this Mr. Napier, that Moses learned he was to be apprenticed from the month following for a period of seven years to Mr. George Spurrell, present captain of the Company's supply ship that sailed yearly to Churchill. Captain Spurrell, for the rest of the year, sailed to less frigid waters. He was a most excellent captain and a fair and just man.

The attorney had a singular manner of delivering the information, trailing after it some shreds of secondary intelligence concerning Mr. Richard Norton's demise that he seemed to think of no consequence.

—For though it is not expressly written in his will, he said, your father conveyed his intent to me most clearly before he paid the debt of Nature and has amply and generously provided for you.

Mother Dupeer nodded benevolently while Moses' world juddered once before spinning on.

He looked at Mother Dupeer but she was staring at the folds of her dress. She leaned a little to brush away some invisible thread or hair. His father dead? Was he supposed to know this already? He wanted to ask a dozen questions, but Mr. Napier and Mother Dupeer were behaving as if he already knew all there was to know. He felt he ought to have known. He felt inadequate, wrong-footed.

Like ice melt in spring images of Rupert's Land came tumbling, rushing back to him from his frozen memory. As if riding a high torrent they came crowding, jostling. Here were the women. They flung back their heads and laughed. The strongest of them caught him up and carried him like a deer carcass slung round her shoulders. She had hold of his neck and the seat of his trousers to keep him there until she twisted and lightly tossed him to her sister. And then he was a feather kept aloft above their brown hands as they played with him, their eyes like moist kisses every time they caught his glance. And then he was down among them where they stretched themselves on the ground or curled for sleep, the deerskins everywhere about them, over them, and he crawling to the softest stillest woman and nudging his way in under her crooked arm, feeling her breath come down warm across his ear and his neck.

—Norton?

—Is he in a fit?

—No, no. He is himself.

He had opened his eyes, he knew he had, but the drawing

room was obliterated in white. He drew a breath, and door, window, table, and occupants appeared as if out of drifting snow, Mr. Napier drawing a breath, Mother Dupeer exhaling until Moses thought she would cave in.

—Then my father is dead?

There was a silence. Each adult waiting for the other to speak.

—Sit down, boy. Here. Mr. Napier pushed a chair behind Moses' knees. Had no one prepared this boy for the news?

—You have no family of your own now, Master Norton, but you have the family of this house. Mother Dupeer will always be a mother to you.

—And we may call Captain Spurrell your father— though not to his face.

Mr. Napier declined to smile at the unfortunate pleasantry.

Moses again felt unsteady. Had the distinct impression the woven carpet he was standing on lay not on solid boards but on a pontoon afloat.

—But I have a mother in Rupert's Land. She is waiting for us . . . for me.

Another five minutes at the most, Napier thought. Get Mother D.'s release and he could be on his way. Leave her to attend the bawling that must surely begin before the day closed.

—Master Norton, you must listen and not grieve excessively for what you hear. You must not harbour expectations that your mother will be waiting for you at Churchill. Before he left us your father sent inquiries to the fort so that your mother could be found and provided for. The Company has told me she is not to be found. She is gone, so they tell me, into the country, where, by the grace of God, her health and happiness will be preserved.

—Is she dead?

Napier tried to speak gently.

—No. I mean, Master Norton, what I say. You will not find her at the fort when one day you return. From now on you would do well to consider yourself without any tie to her or to her people.

—My aunts too gone away?

Thomas Napier knew nothing of aunts and was beginning to feel it was time for Mother Dupeer to do her part in this discussion. He sighed.

—All, yes. All of them gone together. Let us pray for their happiness.

Moses wondered if he meant right now but apparently not, for Mr. Napier was making the same gesture he had seen his father make three years ago. His hands were on his knees, his elbows pushing out. The memory brought tears to smart behind his eyes again.

THOMAS NAPIER was satisfied with his commission, having fulfilled his obligation and managed to make his escape without being snared in questions. A copy of Richard Norton's will was tucked inside his jacket. He had shown it briefly to Mother Dupeer and they had agreed to leave it be. Explaining the living presence of "my loving wife . . ." to Norton's half-breed bastard would only be an embarrassment. *He could lay claim to the fortune.* Elizabeth's very words—though what

Richard Norton left could hardly be called a fortune. But she was right, absolutely right—as women were, he found, in matters of money, where they had a habit, as men did not, of considering affairs of the purse along with those of the heart. They knew instinctively that one always has a bearing on the other. The boy, Elizabeth Norton had said, need never know of her existence—as she most heartily wished she did not know of his.

Elizabeth Norton, much as she might wish not to know, certainly did know, though how much, Thomas Napier was not sure. Would she have been surprised, imagining a union with a moll at an inn, to have seen what he had just seen? A boy with skin the colour of a lump of dull copper topped with a greasy black thatch like a mat of crow's feathers. And the eyes on him. Black as the toe of his boot and set narrow in the protection of the dark brow, the jutting cheekbones. He did not care for the look. There was no mistaking where the boy came from. No, Norton had been right to keep the boy out of sight—though why he didn't leave him in Rupert's Land where he belonged was a conundrum. Bad enough for a wife to learn about some spurious issue of the husband, worse to be presented with the living flesh. And when the flesh shows its provenance so plainly—a common savage—no, that would be insupportable.

Napier kicked at a small stone and laughed to himself to think of Mrs. Norton falling into a faint—the bewilderment on the boy's face. He turned the key to the front door of his office. Well. Good luck to the lad. Norton had done his best for him at any rate. And he'd done his part. Captain Spurrell could do the rest.

HE IS SUCH A SMALL, small child. He feels the pile of the carpet shift under his palms as he crawls. He sees the pattern distinctly. An expanse of blue and red stretching away from him on all sides, stepped diamonds and squares overlapping, and in the centre an island he must crawl across, a black shape blooming in four directions. Beyond that, what he crawls towards is not yet in his field of vision, but its smell guides him. It is heavy and musky and there is something acrid there too, like sweat, something sweet like flesh, and all of it redolent of warmth, of comfort. He stops and looks up. The heap of furs towers. Infant Moses crawls across the carpet and puts his cheek close to one of them. He listens. The breathing is deep and rhythmic. Each exhalation sends out a message of warmth. He rises first to his knees, then reaching out takes fistfuls of fur and pulls himself onto the pile. It yields to his weight but supports him. He cannot resist. He leans in and leans in letting his face be covered, smothered by the deerskin and then he plunges his face and hands into the soft dark of the pelts. He breathes their dense smell, sinking further in darkness and warmth, feeling himself lapped in safety as he pushes forward, begins to burrow and finds an opening that admits him, the breathing louder now, heady and sweet, his mouth open, the hard teat inside it now, the hot stream drilling his tongue, warming the inside of his cheeks, filling his throat. But even as he drinks a terror begins in his gut, for he knows what follows and his ribs shrink in an attempt to escape it, his removal as inevitable as death, the grasping hands as hard as bones. His empty open mouth searches and then the furs are gone and he is at the silk-draped knees of one of Mother Dupeer's callers and Mother Dupeer is shrieking.

—Moses! Her arm catches him round the ribs and yanks him towards the ceiling and in the moment before he wakes he sees the three seated ladies, their mouths making red ovals in their white-boned faces.

And infant Moses, hoisted from his bliss, pulled up naked, hangs in the dizzying air defenceless. What wakes him, what always wakes him, is the sense of vertigo, for he hangs in air while all around is a void: no sight, no sound, no smell. Even the bony hands have melted so there is only the sense of himself alone, dependent yet depending from nothing at all, ready at any moment to begin falling and never, ever to stop.

—

TO BE IN TWO PLACES in such a way was dizzying. To see myself yet not to feel heat or cold or hard soft dry wet wind or breath. Because it was so difficult I remained a long time again detached and watching from a great distance. Not watching my corpse but watching the land and the seasons roll under me over me watching in the manner of a small child with amazement but with acceptance too—both absorbed and absorbing. For how long? I cannot tell you. Months years generations can pass in this way so mysterious is the land with its flickering embroidery its human beadwork appearing and vanishing on the surface—composing as it does its strange pattern of pain and love.

And so I watched unblinking hearing the roaring of all the living and the dead hearing the silence until I knew that if I could visit my death and the days of my dying I could visit also my life. I knew there was more pain. There was my father. There was my sister dying. There was Samuel leaving. There was goodbye. There was walking away from the fort tense with the fear of a French bullet in the back. There was the sight of the poor people in their extremity and there was the disease that fed upon their starving bodies. But with the passage of time I escaped even those places for it was not those days I wanted to live again. I sought instead for joy and I summoned my spirit to my youth.

Drifting high I saw the water. I saw how the hand of a giant scooped our land as a cupped hand spoons the contents of a deer's stomach and how the sea flowed in to fill the space. There is no far bank like a river. If you were to stand in the centre of this inrushed sea you could turn and turn and the land would spin around surround you at the horizon with just a small gate to come in and go out like a deer pound. I saw the place where my home the stone fort stood on the point. It stands there still. Little more now than a raised scar as if a great knife had sliced it from the surface of the rise where it was built. Only the roots of the stones showing. Tooth stumps in an old mouth. Birds sometimes visit. *Otâpiskâkanêsis* the lark and *athâk* the sparrow. *Nânipêko-pithêthis* and *wâki kotêsiw* sandpiper and curlew. They build their nests among the fallen stones where the dry grasses whisper and they circle calling calling as they rise. Sometimes the shadow of a hawk sends the swarming mice scurrying for a crevice or a crack blasted in the heavy stone. Sometimes *sihkosiw* the weasel is nimbler still and the feast is his. And I can see how even a fort a strong place—it too—rolls under with the seasons.

And it was a strong place. Built for soldiers. High walls so wide that men could walk upon them shoulder to shoulder. High wide gates that could be dragged shut jammed fast against assault—if it hadn't freshly snowed. Sometimes left closed in winter for many days so much trouble it was to clear away the snow from the curved sweep of their path. Thick and squat were the buildings inside the ramparts. Walls of heavy stone. Dark roofs pulled down low like the hats of the Company's servants. Windows like mistrustful eyes to watch who comes and goes. Who stays who leaves.

It is all so clear to me now. No man travels or hunts or trades but for his family. No man leaves his homeland but he returns again. The ones who came came only for the furs which were to them riches. In their own land—surely a land of scarcity if nothing runs free and all must be purchased—their families must have waited for the riches to arrive the way a family waits for the hunter and the fat carcasses that will last the winter through. The men came to our abundance leaving their kin on the other side of the water. Did they believe that to bring their women in the ships would call misfortune down and sink them all? I have seen the children of the English sent home in the ships as my father was but never their wives.

So then another thing becomes plain to me. Samuel would not have taken me back with him in the ship however long I waited. He would not have taken me a woman back across the water. Why did I not know it? It is so plain. Always he would sail back to his own land and I would remain. How did I not guess at it? The men came and they went. Of course Samuel.

But pity belongs only to the living. The long pull of the lived moment never ends for always I am drawn back and back again to the places where the headlong hurtle towards death is stilled. Where a summer day can be held unchanging while the years pass numberless as geese. I am blessed. I have known and lived more than one of those places in my life on the land. In those places I take refuge. While the seasons roll over the horizon and over again I take a breath in Samuel's arms in my mother's arms my sister's my father's. Yes his too though it is hard to understand. But even a bear that knocks down its enemies may take delight in its young and mind its claws. And what child does not delight to ride upon the back of a beast and bend it to her will? He was my father. Though he roared about the house and could blast a man with his look his eyes only welled and softened for me. What I know now is that there are two lives to be lived. One the life that is lived in the body. The other the life that returns to the held places. That breathes again where the body lived observing the joy as it was felt the pain and the peace.

1753

Moses Norton brought two things back with him from England: love and hatred of all things British. Stepping from the landing stage and setting his boot down on the stony crust of Rupert's Land he felt the pull of home—in both directions. When he turned to look, the longboat was already ploughing back through the shore waves towards the frigate that had carried him across the ocean and into the broad waters of Hudson Bay.

He swung his box on his shoulder and followed three heavily laden Homeguard women up the beach. A horse and cart stood improbably for the short haul to the fort. Governor Jacobs and two or three others were coming down the beach with stiff strides, driving their heels into the shingle for better purchase.

—Mr. Norton! The governor leaned towards the officer nearest and said something in an undertone.

—Sir! Moses put down the box and bowed extravagantly, though the effect was far from suave.

—So! Richard Norton's other boy. God save you!

Governor Jacobs was rocking with amusement at some private joke and shaking his head.

—Welcome to the house that Dick built! And now he laughed aloud. Welcome.

He clapped Moses on the shoulder and shook his hand.

—Mr. Norton, you arrive under a fair sky. Was the voyage well? Jacobs gave the question a schoolroom ring, as if his next words might be *Speak up, boy. Speak up.*

—It was, Mr. Jacobs. Governor. We had a time of it off Stromness but pretty fair winds once we were a day out . . .

But Governor Jacobs did not really wish to know.

—I'm glad to hear it, lad. Glad indeed. Now I need two men to take me out sharpish to the captain. Good. You, Marchant, and you, man, get that luggage boat launched. You see your box in place, Norton, and then you can come back down and lend a hand.

THE FORESHORE NOW was coming alive as more men from the fort and families from the camps made their way down. A swarm of memories. The children ran. The women walked over the stones in their bare feet. A few wore moccasins. He felt a peculiar relief that none would claim him for a son. When he was still an apprentice it was what he had longed for, to be claimed, to be owned. Three years in succession he had asked Captain Spurrell to make enquiries when they went ashore. Captain Spurrell's answer never varied. His mother had gone into the country, he said. She would not be back. The next year Moses did not ask. The following year he dreaded the possibility of her return. After that he did all he could to forget, concentrating his ambitions on rising like any Englishman within the Company. But for all that, and for all his eighteen years, the fringed and beaded leather some of these women wore loosed a deep response in Moses. The smell of the skins returned his childhood to him complete—as if one of the cut-and-sewn dresses had suddenly reverted to the living breathing animal and he could see its rolling eye and its flared nostril, could feel its sides heave outward to receive the air for flight.

He picked up his box again and threaded his way among them, stopping often to answer questions, receive a welcome, his mind bifurcated by time—part of it occupied in running full tilt down the beach towards the landing stage, Matonabbee behind him on short legs, falling hard onto him as he tripped in his path, his mouth filling with sandy gravel as he gasped, grit stuck up behind his upper lip, down in the pocket of his cheek, the two of them, the small boy and the smaller, laughing, drooling as they spat out the tiny stones.

Thirteen years since he tore down that slope but he could feel it as if he had just fallen. The fort, its stone ramparts up on the level ground, always looked smaller than Moses remembered. A molehill. A molehill with a white flag and chimney smoke. One of the women who had greeted him gestured to the box. When he realized she wanted to carry it he grinned. His years as an apprentice over. A man could live like a prince here. The woman swung it to her shoulder and walked. Everything he had dreamed about might well come to pass.

He followed her up the beach. She did not once turn her head or speak. In all England there was not a soul, at least not in Deptford, who dreamed of the existence of the Southern Indians or their strange tongue. He remembered the word for "river" and for "water," the words for "gun" and "boy" and "boat," but what he was hearing around him was not intelligible to his ears. "Dog" was *atim,* he remembered. And *âstam,* "come here." His mother was *Nikâwiy.* Nêkâ, he called her, but there was no face in his mind to match it. He thought he might ask just one last time for himself, in case he'd been misinformed.

—Nikâwiy? The word ridiculously foreign on his tongue. He could taste it.

The woman said something he didn't understand. She turned so that he would see the answer plainly in her eyes.

The tip of a wispy mare's tail reached the sun as Moses entered the gates. He shivered. Two or three fellows looking perfectly at ease in nothing but their breeches and moccasins came up to him as he approached.

—Mr. Moses Norton?

—It is.

The shorter man, thick-set and red-faced, seemed to be the spokesman.

—Conachie, sir. Welcome. I've been assigned to make you as comfortable as can be, Mr. Norton. Anything you require, anything you lack . . .

But Moses wasn't listening. He was observing how the ground seemed to be rising and falling under his feet as if he yet stood on the ship. He closed his eyes briefly. When he opened them the horizon spun around him, tilting—now water, now land—all without mark.

The steward had already started walking towards the sleeping quarters. He quickened his step.

—Does it come back to you now, I wonder?

—Parts of it. Yes, parts.

—How old were you, may I ask, sir, when you lived here last?

—I believe I was six or seven.

—What I thought. I remember you, you know. Running round here. You and that little Indian chap your father took a liking to. Great strapping fellow now, Matonabbee. Taller than yourself, sir. You'll see.

Conachie waved a hand towards the governor's quarters as they passed.

—Your old home, sir. You'll be missing all that. For the while.

—I asked after Matonabbee once. They said he lives on the land.

—He does. We've not seen him these two years. But he'll be in soon enough. Here we are.

Moses looked in at the door. He realized at once that his contract had said nothing about officers' accommodation.

—With the men?

—As I understand it, sir, seeing you'll be on board in the summer.

They ducked through the low door. Moses could not help thinking of a barn. Bunks in place of stalls. More room than shipboard but not much more comfort. His bed little more than a platform. Blankets and some kind of crunchy mattress. He bore down with his fist.

—Moss, that is. Some of us has our own feathers. You'll want the deerskins too. But you'll see.

Moses looked along the row.

—Most of us wash ourselves outside. When the mood takes us . . .

—In winter?

—The mood dinnae take you so in winter. But should you feel inclined, the scullery lies next the cookhouse.

And so began Moses' enlightenment.

HE WAS USED to discomfort but these conditions began to smack of the gaol. He had in his pocket his letter of appointment, obtained when his apprenticeship and his service to Captain Spurrell terminated. It was penned by a clerk in the London office and signed on behalf of Sir Atwell Lake. He had the contents by heart: *Moses Norton, having contracted and agreed with the Governor and Company of Adventurers of England to serve them and their successors for a period of three years as mate of the sloop* Churchill *of Prince of Wales Fort, is to be accorded, in consideration of his father, the late Governor Richard Norton of said Prince of Wales Fort on the Churchill River, every office and assistance in the full and prompt performance of his duties and every opportunity, if he show himself able, to advance within the Company's ranks.* Not every servant came armed with such a letter. But not every servant was the son of a former factor. Moses sensed, however, that once here on the stony shores, all things were equal.

It was not that Moses was unfamiliar with the fort or surprised at his surroundings. He'd been here almost every year with Captain Spurrell. As an apprentice, he'd slept on board for the eight days' shiptime, barred from the imagined luxuries the captain and his mate would be enjoying inside the fort, and prohibited from the unacknowledged entertainments the sailors sought outside it. Sometimes in the day he'd find a moment to walk through the encampment outside the fort, watch the women at their work, endure their teasing as he passed. At night images from his childhood would come and go with the vessel's gentle rise and fall. The smoke and the noise in the men's mess, the great fires they built kept lively with the toppling loads of willow hauled in by the women. Above all he remembered the women—his mother, his aunts. Nikâwîs. Nikâwîs. The only name he needed to know as a little lad. Any one of them would answer. Offer the same warmth, the same embrace. He remembered nourishment. In England, far from the warmth of women, the fort had assumed for him the shape of a pleasure palace with, just out of the corner of his eye, the splendid possibility of power in his father's position. In his imagination the Richard Norton who had left him at the Deptford schoolhouse was transformed into a father of an earlier time: Richard Norton, Commander-in-Chief of Prince of Wales Fort, seated comfortably by the great stove in his own quarters, a man pouring brandy for him into a warmed bowl, a woman kneeling by, handing him a pipe that left a lace of white to hang in the air above them. His memory had furnished his father's room with a brilliantly coloured carpet, with wall sconces, even a chandelier that hung above an oiled and polished table. Captain Spurrell said it was likely so—he himself had only seen the officers' mess. He said, But you'll be seeing for yourself one day. Think of that.

MOSES SAT ON THE EDGE of his so-called bed. Not a pot to piss in. Seven good years plus two he had given to Captain Spurrell. Benign bondage. The sole difference now was twenty-five pounds per annum—about as useful on these shores as twenty-five tickets to Vauxhall Gardens. He was a fish trapped by ice in a shallow pool. Everything was clear. The only mystery, to Moses at least, was why he had not foreseen his circumstances, not recognized them, before he signed, for what they were. When he went to the London office to apply for a permanent position, this was not quite the outcome he had in mind, nor quite the picture Captain Spurrell had painted when his service was over. But when the written document was pushed at him across the desk it seemed too late to say so. And what, besides, was the alternative? In England he had had no friends to call his own. Something he had acquired at Mother Dupeer's house—some whiff of the poor relation— worked against him. His self-protective silences only marked him as surly. And then there was his skin, deeply burnished as he grew older. It drew comment wherever he went. When he went back to Mother Dupeer's house, even her parlourmaid, Fitch, had remarked on it. When his apprenticeship was over he had sought out lodgings of his own, had taken the road for Deptford to the only home he knew. But Mother Dupeer did not understand why he would return. Clearly it was not something she wished to encourage. She received no callers during his stay and when her niece arrived all unannounced she sent him packing. She was, regretfully, in need of the bed. On the white stone of the doorstep, with his box already taken to the coach, Mother Dupeer had felt safe enough to return to the matter of regret. She regretted he had to leave, she regretted his stay had been so short, she regretted she had not had the opportunity to introduce him to society. And he shouldn't take Fitch's remark about being left too long in the sun as an infant to heart. And here, this will make all the difference in the world. It was your dear father's, she said, handing him a powdered wig. He had tucked it inside his jacket, not catching the lie. In his room above the stables round the corner from Fenchurch Street, he went at once to the glass and put it on. He had shocked himself. He was someone else entirely.

A man hurried in and came straight over to the foot of the bed. Moses almost knocked him down when he saw why he had come.

—From Mr. Conachie. Wouldn't want you to be without, said the man and held out a small pail. Found you one that's nae too reeky.

DISGRUNTLEMENT FOR MOSES was a short-lived luxury. The bales of skins for England stood in piles ten feet high and made a berm beside the landing stage, the sacks of goose feathers a mountain behind them, the whalebone and the tuns of train oil a wall, and none of it to be touched until the year's provisions had been brought off the *Prince Rupert* and put ashore. Every man would work until he could fall asleep standing, the procession of casks and rundlets, boxes and sacks forming a great living serpent snaking up to disappear inside the gates. No man or beast here likely to face the winter short. Moses knew the extent of the annual indent from the voyages he'd made with Spurrell. There would be oil and mustard, lard and lemons, pork, hams, raisins, and wine for the kitchens; steels and flintlocks for the armourer, pigs of iron for the smith, oak whaling for the carpenter; scissors, shirts, ice chisels, looking glasses, duffle and beads, beads, beads for the Indians; sashes and lace for their captains, barley for the poultry, beans for the horse, and powder and shot to keep every man for miles around in business. The *Prince Rupert* was a small town disgorging its material wealth, its stockings, spoons, brandy, rum, baize, and broadcloth, its fishhooks, knives, biscuits, and beef. It was at least some consolation to be able to pass the sweating men and walk on down to the boat that would carry him out to the sloop. The *Churchill* stood ready for her last voyage of the season, a round trip to York and Moose Factories to redistribute supplies assigned in error.

Down at the water Mr. Byrnes, the sloopmaster, was waiting by a small skiff, with a sailor ready to launch them and row them out. There was much to do, he said, before the weather, and a deal to do when they returned.

Once onboard the *Churchill,* Moses took his place near the wheel and did his best to look like a man in charge as the crew made ready to weigh anchor.

A sailor, mistaking him for one of the Homeguard, called out to the sloopmaster.

—That man going ashore now, Captain?

And Mr. Byrnes hissed back.

—*That man* is your first mate, Bowles. Get used to it.

Moses slipped his hand inside his jacket, pulled out the yellowed wig, and put it on. Not all of the sailors were convinced. He saw one receive a fist to the ear from the sloop-master for a remark about obeying orders. Something he'd said—Moses didn't catch it all, but the drift was enough—about damn Indian boys done up like lairds.

Well, he'd be done up like a governor one day. That would change their tune.

—You can take that off now, the sloopmaster said when they were under way.

Button's Bay drifted away behind them, the blue-grey of the low land losing colour to the vaporous air until it seemed a smudge of woodsmoke lying on the water.

—We get along. You'll see.

Ahead the open waters of Hudson Bay swelled under the aging August sun. Straggling remnants of rotting ice blown down from the north drifted in loose flotillas. A stiffening breeze pushed them on.

MOSES, THE FORMER chief factor's son, felt himself to be without a proper station in life when the work of the sloop was finished for the season. He received his orders and did his duties at the fort like any other servant. He worked for the most part alongside the Scotsmen, who seemed so at home, and yet they rarely offered him confidences or shared their jokes with him. Governor Jacobs treated him with civility, it was true, but he assigned tasks for Moses—assisting the smith or hauling water—as if he were a Company servant. He had become one of the sweating men after all. Did the governor choose to ignore the fact that his father, Richard Norton, had all but built the place himself and was governor of it while he, Jacobs, was still running up and down stairs in the London office? Did it count for nothing? Or did Jacobs too object to his Southern Indian blood? There were many others like him about the factory, children and young men and women who clearly had English fathers. But these slept outside the walls with their Indian relatives at Mr. Jacobs' insistence. It was not what Moses had expected. He could remember when he was a small lad at the fort, the slumberous women, the crying of the infants in the night. He could remember falling asleep with his mother under the warmth of the same sleeping robe. And he had heard that today at York Factory there was not a man who did not have his woman in his bed. All the women here were fully occupied with their labours for the Company—which did not extend to the nights. A group of them worked all day in one of the small storerooms that had been kept empty for the purpose. Their voices made a comforting hum if you walked by.

When the first big storm of November kept the men inside and Moses was sent to make an inventory of the pelts the women were working on for the winter clothing, he felt as if he were about to learn some great secret. The women sat together on the floor of an emptied storeroom, the piles of skins behind them.

Moses said he had come to count the pelts. The women were amused.

—We know how many: a whole heap, someone said, and they laughed.

Counting the pelts was a pointless exercise. Sorting them made sense. Piles had to be made for different purposes, that was understood. Separate piles had to be made for clothing and for bags and for footwear, then further separation into pelts suitable for coats, hoods, mittens, leggings, breeches, game bags, pemmican bags, boots, moccasins. There were many piles. But counting the skins themselves? What was the point? They would still be sewing all winter. If one pile dwindled they would have to borrow from another, make the best of it. And there were never *no* piles. New skins would always come in. One of the older women chattered at Moses, but he did not understand all she said. She tugged on his breeches, grabbed hold of his knee as he stood by, had him at last crouched down on his heels with them in the thick smells of the hides. She spoke in English for him, pausing often while the words came to her, slowly. He let her go on. A young woman opposite him was watching him intently. Moses picked up a corner of an otterskin as if assessing its worth while he listened. The older woman told him stories of his father and his protectoress, Thanadelthur, the famous Northern peacemaker, who fell sick and died before she could make him her own. It was as if she were telling tales from an old book, his father suddenly become the young traveller in a foreign land, the hapless wanderer fallen on the mercies of all whom he encountered. Moses listened guardedly. Long used to being mocked, he half-expected the barb that was contained in the end of the story.

—But she was not your mother. Not that one. No, you were not so fortunate, Mr. Norton. Only a Southern woman for your mother—one just like us.

They laughed again.

—Or—she put her arm round the oldest, least attractive—for your wife.

Moses did not look over to see if the young woman opposite was laughing. They loved above all, it seemed, to laugh.

—Thank you, no. He got to his feet amid uproar and began the count. Trying to concentrate, Moses wondered if there was anywhere, ever, that he could be treated with respect.

That the men of the fort had access to these women was without doubt. The governor himself had just had his own son christened by Mr. Haddon, the surgeon—doubtless a more welcome duty than the amputation he had performed earlier in the day. Where and when these liaisons occurred remained for Moses something of a mystery until the day he left with a hunting party.

It was late in February of that first winter and two weeks of dark ferocious blizzards and bone-splintering cold had suddenly eased. Governor Jacobs drew up a hunting party and Moses, who had not yet been out on the land, was detailed to go.

They had walked only an hour or two from the fort when they stopped and rested. Several women and three of the Homeguard Indians came up to join them in a little while and they went on. One of them, Moses saw, was the young woman from the sewing room. Like the other women she was hauling tent poles and skins, and she went on ahead. The men followed the Homeguard hunters, searching for anything that might have taken shelter in the woods. For the rest of the day they scoured the woods, stopping only occasionally for a handful of pemmican. As the sun was sinking, the smoke from the camp the women had made showed dark against the thin blue-pink of the sky.

Kettles of water hung ready to receive the meat the women cut from the day's kill. The men smoked and watched as the dusk deepened. Moses watched the men. They drank their ration of rum and the next day's too. The women ladled meat into the men's cups and suddenly it was done. The liaisons had been made. The sewing woman, Nêwositêkâpaw, was taken, he could see it. Moses had no choice. He put himself in debt to a Southern man, a Mashkêgow, for a length of cloth and a foot of Brazil tobacco, and he took a cheerful wide-hipped woman under his sleeping skin. He had never been warmer, though when she first lay down beside him he had trembled like a wounded animal. There was no man that night who was cold. He began to understand.

In the morning no one spoke about the night's pleasure. Both sides went about their separate duties as if they had slept chaste as monks and nuns. Moses could not wait to see what the next night would bring, but he was disappointed. There was no discussion or exchange. Every man retained his partner of the night before. Nêwositêkâpaw remained with her Homeguard hunter. Moses resigned himself to the broad-hipped woman. Bolder now, he was ready to spend a night of pleasure but the woman would not receive him a second time in the same night and told him to go to sleep. He began to understand that these arrangements were purely practical. They stayed on the land for a week and the pattern repeated itself. During the day the hunting was good and they might have stayed longer but the women, who would bear the burden of the game, said they could carry no more.

Before they left, the Mashkêgow man made it clear that he expected seven pints of rum in addition to the cloth and the tobacco. Moses didn't mind. He felt now as if he had comrades. Conachie's nephew Isaac regaled him on the way home with outlandish tales of his exploits among women who offered themselves gratis. It would be something to think about in the empty nights.

AS SOON AS THE RIVER ICE began to growl, Captain Byrnes made preparations to go with supplies up to Brig's Cove, where the *Churchill* was overwintered, so that they could begin to fit her for the coming season. He had had a log tent built at the back of the cove for the purpose. Moses and two of the sailors went each day to make it ready, repairing the roof where it had caved in under the weight of the snow, caulking the walls wherever they could and hauling in wood for the fire. Some river ogre, waking to the sound of distant explosions, shifted and groaned. Fissures travelled the surface as if forced by an unseen hand and water began to well from them and pool. And came the day that the ice began to move. Cakes of it tilted slowly and crawled upon each other and the water was everywhere alive. The men put down their tools and went to the bank to watch. Slabs shoved their way into the mouth of the cove and piled there. Captain Byrnes said it was a good thing, a dam against the deluge that was coming. And even as he spoke a dull roar began. Meltwater from upstream began to run then to rush over the crazed surface and then the whole river heaving with ice was in movement. The broken ice bore down past the cove, swift and unstoppable. Pans that snagged and stalled were soon whirled on in the current. In less than two hours it was over.

—Now we can get on, said Byrnes.

Sheltered from the worst of the winds and cut off from the movement of the river, the sloop was still icebound and blanketed in a winter's worth of snow. The men spent their days clearing the decks and digging out the buried booms and yards. They laid them out on the south-facing rocks for painting. They carried up the rigging and the guns from the hold and on the warmest days they tarred the stays and the shrouds. For several weeks they lived at the cove as at an outpost, sending for supplies when they needed them. Only the captain chose to return to the fort on Sundays. His officers' privileges were hard won and his place at the governor's table not so easily surrendered. Moses bore no resentment. Though he was second-in-command, he was content on Sundays to be treated like the Company servants.

—You see nothing and we say nothing, eh, Norty boy? said Bowles the first time. He had a rundlet of brandy that had escaped the overhaul of the stores.

Moses wanted to knock him flat, but he could taste it already.

—I got rum for our visitors too. That is, if you have the liking. Young Conachie might be up to see us soon. With some friends.

—I know Isaac. If he makes any trouble you'll find that brandy subtracted from your pay. Understood?

—Oh, do I understand! Sir! Not as if you're talking Indian, now is it?

His fist ached again to hit the man but he could not wait to see who Conachie would bring.

The women who came to the cove were older. They were women whose husbands readily let them go. All of them had been to the cove before, and all of them came for the same thing. Nêwositêkâpaw was not among them. In subsequent weeks Moses asked Isaac to find her. She never did come. Moses' brandy-sodden nights melted into one.

WHEN THE RIVER was fully clear and most of the debris had left the cove, a large party of canoes came down easily on the current one bright morning to trade. Loaded with furs, they sat low in the water. All of them, men and women from the north, wore the three vertical stripes of the Wêcîpwayânak. They paddled effortlessly. They had come overland and built the small canoes while they waited for the break-up of the river. The fresh-cut framework shone white. Moses saw how some of the men sat in the bow at their ease while their companions both stroked and steered. He scanned their faces. He did not know if he would recognize the man he was looking for.

When the convoy had passed, the sailors went back to their work on the sloop, listening for the sound of musket shot that would signal their arrival, the cannon that would answer. In the afternoon more of the party came in on foot, cutting across the lowlands behind the cove, hauling sleds that bumped over the old snow and dragged through the pooled melt. That night the men imagined they could hear drumming carrying up to them through the still air. Next morning when Byrnes found that two of the Orkneymen who had been sent to assist had taken themselves away in the night to join the revelry, he was glad of the opportunity to be rid of them. They had been nothing but trouble, stealing from the stores, upsetting the fresh tar, and antagonizing his men until they came to blows. He sent Moses down to the fort with a note for Governor Jacobs and a request for two replacements. Moses made a point of walking through the camp of the Wêcîpwayânak. At every step he imagined his childhood friend emerging from one of the tents, the look of astonished recognition in his eye. But he reached the fort without drawing remark. And did think that he might as well be invisible, since he had to step aside at the gate as one of them—he assumed their captain, for he was heavily tattooed—came through with a great consort of women and children behind him. It was almost a relief when Governor Jacobs said good morning.

Jacobs concealed his dismay as he read the note. He had been glad to have the men off his hands for a while. They were young and rough with something explosive and unpredictable about them that tried his nerves. He penned a note in reply and sent Moses to search out their replacements. On his way back to the cove, Moses again walked through the camp. He found the tattooed man and hailed him, putting on all the manners of an officer he could muster.

—Matonabbee? he said. I wish to know the whereabouts

of Matonabbee. The man did not understand. He called one of his wives to interpret. She shook her head. Matonabbee was out on the land, she said, gone deep into the country these two years. No one knew when he would be back.

IT WAS LATE JULY before the *Churchill* was ready and the waters of the bay were free enough of ice for the northern voyage to get under way. For Moses it could not come soon enough to escape the clouds of relentless flies. Life that had seemed pleasant at the cove had become intolerable with the onset of the biting insects. There was still painting to be done but Captain Byrnes allowed it could be completed equally well at Whales Cove, where the open country and the onshore breezes were kinder to humans.

Despite his years at sea, Moses Norton had no idea that sailing could be so agreeable. Voyages with Spurrell across the ocean and into Hudson Strait had been races against time, a pitting of wits against the deep. It was the only kind of sailing Moses knew. Running the strait in the brief interlude that the waters opened, weaving a passage through the drifting ice, often in fog so thick it obliterated everything beyond the bowsprit—and sometimes the bowsprit itself—was every time a cause for fervent prayer. Sometimes the quietness of the men on the creaking ship—broken only by the shouts of the mate from the bow, for the main-top was no use in such heavy fogs—sometimes their quiet could make a man think of ghosts. But this was altogether different. Moses had failed to anticipate the effect that the simple proximity of land, the not ever leaving it, could have upon the mind. To be sure, land for a mariner is the greatest danger, yet the prospect of foundering within sight of it cannot match or even approach the dread of being swallowed up in a saltwater grave a month away from solid ground in all directions. It was remarkably reassuring. Moses saw too how the captain could be easy, for while he was committed to returning to the factory in time for the Company ship's departure for England, he had only to curtail his voyage, to write in his book that conditions did not allow a further call, and he could return at leisure.

When that summer's voyage was done Moses did not look so unkindly on his next two years of service. He did what was required of him without complaint, only fought when he was provoked, and continued to acquaint himself with every opportunity of consorting with the women. Trading times, he learned, could be fruitful. If the season had been poor, the men, who still must have their powder and shot, sometimes offered their wives—or better, their daughters—expressly for barter. Not all the Company servants took advantage, but Moses, like some of the others, found himself sliding into debt.

Governor Jacobs had watched Moses, had seen how he always performed his duties and how discreet he was when he infringed the rules concerning the Indians. He had seen how his education had fitted him for work less menial, and he kept in mind the letter from the board. At the end of Moses' term of service on the *Churchill*, he offered him the position of his own assistant and Moses accepted.

The work was tedious. The account books in the trading room were meticulously kept, down to the last quarter inch of thread, the last pair of hawk's bells. If the books were up to date and the chief trader, Denman, had nothing for him, Moses found himself spending whole days copying letters to neighbouring posts, to the London office, even copying Captain Byrnes's journal to send back to London—and wishing himself back on board again in the summer. There were inventories and lists for every aspect of their lives within the fort: the trade, the provisioning, the transport of the goods, the maintenance of the post, its defences, the rules of conduct, the orders of discipline, the surgeon's duties. Jacobs had lists of lists and sometimes Moses imagined himself back in the schoolroom. But as Jacobs' assistant, Moses had access to the officers' mess, where he knew he belonged. In the days of deepest winter when the stove burned a cartload of wood in a day and the smith brought red hot cannonballs to hang at the shuttered windows, he was glad of his position—though the cannonballs did more to char the shutters and create smoke than they did to warm the rooms.

When the worst of the storms came screaming from the northwest, there was no prospect of work outside for days on end. Many of the Company servants spent these days as well as nights in profound sleep, undisturbed by the rowdiness of the others, who preferred the pleasures of rum. Moses Norton was expected to occupy himself as usual. Governor Jacobs could always find work for him.

He gave him, on one of these chill, smoke-racked days within the shuttered fort, a box of old correspondence to sort, compiling from it a list of any transactions that might have been overlooked in the accounts—as for instance when York or Severn requested certain items that they lacked. The letters went back several years. Among them was a letter with the signature of Thomas Napier. The first page seemed to be missing. It took Moses a moment or two to recall why the name Napier should mean something to him. The content of the document guaranteed his attention.

Now that you are in possession of the facts, I shall continue by asking you to indulge a dying man's wish, or I might include myself and say the wishes of two men at the end of their lives, and keep this missive in a safe place, executing the request it contains when such a time presents itself, or if that is not the case within your term of your office, then passing it on to your successor. This is the request, which I have set down verbatim as near as I can recollect, Mr. N.'s original note being unfortunately now lost and no one in my office being able to lay his hand upon it.

"It is with every confidence in your kind heart and goodwill that I make this petition begging you to use every means in your power to discover the whereabouts of the young man Matonabbee at Prince of Wales Fort and to impress upon the factor there my wish that he, Matonabbee, be offered gainful employment and every opportunity for advancement in the service of the Company, and that in addition he be given the opportunity to make himself known to my son Moses for his personal advancement at such time as my son, as I trust he will, take up service at the post. For your dependable assistance in this I shall be grateful to you in this life and in the life to come."

My own conscience can no longer pretend ignorance of this oversight of mine and I trust I have now done all that is necessary to rectify it.

Yours, etc.

Thomas Napier

Moses set the piece of paper aside and continued. He found nothing of equal interest and though he searched several times he did not find the upper portion of the letter.

Governor Jacobs had no recollection of it. He did not remember seeing the fragment and could not attach a date.

—But "Mr. N." would be my father?

—One would assume so.

—Then his wishes should be respected.

—Easier said than done, lad. I've no idea where to find Matonabbee. He comes in rarely.

—And yet he lived here when my father was governor. Was raised here. By my father.

—Quite so. But he wasn't living here in Isham's day. Certainly not when I arrived. Took himself into the country, I believe.

—Or was driven out.

—No, lad. He's Wêcîpwayân. A Northern man. They march to their own drum.

—But my father's wishes should still be respected.

—That goes without saying.

—Then you'll make enquiries, sir?

Governor Jacobs, with the dying breath of not one but two men at his back, had little choice.

WHEN THE STORM finally abated, Moses Norton, dressed in a beaverskin coat with mittens the size of bear's paws and a monkish hood with the fur almost entirely covering his face, set out from the fort. The sky, still low, still overcast, glared achingly. A good deal of snow had fallen. Walking, even in snowshoes, was exhausting. The tents of the Homeguard seemed to be sliced in two, their windward sides cloaked in white. No one inside had stirred. The world was put to sleep. He went only about half a mile and stopped on a low ridge. His eyes swam, drowning in whiteness. The world was without definition. He could not tell if this hollow or that rise were near or far, if it were a furrow in the snow a few feet ahead or a fold in the land miles away. He was seized with the knowledge of his aloneness on the earth. Matonabbee was out there. Somewhere in the mapless expanse. It made him dizzy. He had the same sense of falling that he experienced in his dream. It was the experience of loss, and in its wake came panic, the sense of nothing to hold to, no edge. Out here the blurring of boundaries was exaggerated, intensified. There was no border between land and sky. He turned as if nothing had happened and went back. His face was frozen in a scowl as he passed the men clearing snow around the gates, though he had intended to smile.

MATONABBEE OPENS his eyes on a sense of desolation but the content of his dream has slipped away. There is no reason for such a sickening descent of the spirit. He is travelling in the company of his countrymen. His two wives are with him, young and strong, and one of them, he is sure, is carrying his first child. It is summer. They have suffered no famine all winter. They have had good hunting and he has a fine haul of pelts to trade at the fort. He tries to remember where he travelled in his sleep, for he was travelling, or anyway walking. But he was alone. He was alone and he was walking. It was winter. The fort was at his back. He is sure of that. He was walking away from it. He was walking away from the fort and he had a destination in mind. And he had with him no hunters, no wives. He walked with purpose and his destination was his alone. Yet the dream will not tell him where he was going with such single-minded steps, or how it can be that purpose and despair can share the same road.

He can feel the warmth of his wife's skin against his back. He closes his eyes again, but the landscape remains in darkness behind his eyelids and the animals refuse to step forward. Still he senses the presence of the fort—or its absence, since he cannot see it. There is only the knowledge of it. And the weight of its stones. As heavy as the intent that propels him.

And too the dream was silent. Yes. He knows the dream was silent in a way the world can never be silent, being always tuned to the wind's breath so that even in summer when the rocks no longer moan, even when the small grasses are still, there will always be some bird cry, some insect hum carried on the movement, however faint, of its aspiration. But his dream was silent as death.

He has never before had a dream he could neither see nor hear. It fills him with a sense of loss, of loneliness. It is close to terror. There was nothing to hold on to in his dream. Nothing he wished to see. That is it. Nothing he wished to hear or taste. It was as if he was walking himself out of the world, abandoning it to exist forever in its own solitude under the clouds.

He rolls to Tháché, his wife Marten Tail, and pulls her

to him. She is asleep. He loves it when he can take her while she is sleeping. Her body is soft as a blanket to receive him, to welcome him. She brings her knees up wide beside the bones of his hips. Her breath takes on a voice deep in her throat, soft and loosely yielding. He wants to be there, to melt into it. He wants to bury himself in it. When he has taken her she lies wide awake and warm beside him, happy, while he sinks into a deep sleep that loosens its grip towards morning and brings him dreams he can understand—a scrub willow where ptarmigan hang like great fat berries, a brightly clad youth walking with great strides across the sky.

In the morning, while they are packing up to continue their long journey to the fort, he will repeat these dreams to his wife. He will have no recollection of having dreamed any other dream until many years to come, when his sons have wives of their own and Tháché is a leathern-faced grand-mother. And then it will return to him. It will fall on him like a cold shadow as he is walking, placing one foot in front of the other with purpose and with despair.

⁓

I EMBRACE THE LIVED MOMENTS as I embrace the moment of my death knowing I am beyond harm. They are life lived again. Lived as many times as I choose to return.

I can go back a child to my father's rooms. The heavy presence of wooden furniture hewn from the trees waiting to be of service to Englishmen so unhappy in their bodies they cannot sit or lie without aid. Men so unhandy they use implements to carry the food to their mouths. The walls hung with clever painted pictures of my father's homeland and with coloured cloth finely decorated. The floors too covered with thick woven cloth carpets dyed deeper and darker than blood patterned with blue as fine as juniper berries. Riches fill his two rooms. So many riches. There is not time in the day to hold and consider each one—which matters not at all for the need for any of them scarcely arises.

I can go back to my mother's house where he sent us when he left on his voyages. Where we lived life bathed in air tasting the sky in our mouths. Days of running outside the walls and playing with the animals. Nights of feasting at my mother's fire and sleeping in her tent. Everything sweeter—the water the smoky meat the spurting berries. The soft-bodied birds and their numberless voices.

But when he came back he was ravenous again for his women—my mother her sisters her cousins and us his daughters. He wanted us all and he wanted us close. We lived in his rooms. He called us his herd. There was no sleeping when he first returned. All was rutting and grunting and moans of pleasure which I mistook for pain. He had heaps of skins dumped on the floor of his dining room and in daylight my mother and the others sat there to sew the men's moccasins knot the tough thongs to frames for their snowshoes. Not I. I was forbidden the needle lest my fingers like my sister's become blunted and thickened as any man's from the constant plying. I played instead with the small animal babies I kept for companions—feeding them cow's milk and sugar clothing them in waistcoats of baize. I made them haul sleds of sticks and I adorned them with necklaces of coloured beads. One summer two great moose calves walked always at my heels until my father had them loaded on the ship for England. I wept so loudly to see them bump against the sides as they were hauled aboard that my father struck me. And then to make me smile he bought a parrot from the captain.

In the house in winter the days and nights unrolled with little to mark their passing. I slept among the warm bodies of my family sometimes waking to my father's grunting efforts. Sometimes sleeping undisturbed a flurry of small furred and feathered things continuing behind my eyelids even in sleep. In the mornings the air would be fetid for there was not any way open to the sky and no egress for the foul vapours from our many bodies. The waste of our night stood in vessels too near our noses. Yet we let ourselves grow accustomed to it and in the deep of winter we sometimes forgot the kiss of cold air on the brow.

But in the stench or in the air loved voices surrounded me voices soft as the murmur of the river. Breath surrounded me. Warmth. And I can return to those rooms in my father's house where our feet made soft slaps on the boards. To my mother and my aunts who nursed me. Always there warm and soft against me when I had need. And my cousins and my sister. Soft hands patting each other's faces. Laughter. Hidden laughter spilling everywhere like the seeds of a poppy. Shouting too and contesting and sometimes the boiling anger of my father sometimes tears—but never emptiness or waiting. Never solitude.

The lived moments are stars that wink from a dark sky. The shiptime when he my Samuel first arrived. The gates of the fort open to receive the riches. Down at the landing stage the Englishmen laughing and shouting to see their countrymen. Clapping each other on the back and making fists to contend before they picked up their loads. Some of them climbed in the longboat to go out to the ship. Bringing back more supplies bringing back more riches. They carried the loads up to the fort. And always they went down again for more. Some of the children worked alongside the Company men. It was done with great speed. A few of the Englishmen ran with their loads.

I remember the legs. I remember the movement. I remember a man who tripped over a dog and the shower of gold and silver buttons that spilled rolling and bouncing down the rock from his burst box. He kicked the barrow. The dog had fled. I remember the foreign clothing. More men now in foreign clothing than in ours. I hear again—I think I hear but perhaps I dream it—the words.

—Surely not.

And a man pale like a stone bending slightly to look me in the eye.

—Hard to tell.

Yes. I remember. My mother and my sister stood beside me down near the boats. The year of my sister's blood when my father kept her to the house. She wore the dress my father had provided. Jane—daughter of Chief Factor Moses Norton. She had not yet left to go with her Wêcîpwayân man. The green cloth of her dress was cut in two so that the lower half hung from a frame of birch wood at her hips. She could have passed almost her entire body through the neck hole of the upper half. Mother covered her breast and shoulders with a folded tartan crossed in front and behind swaddling her like an infant.

—Best leave them ladies be another sailor said and not too soon.

—So Mr. Hearne. You have found my daughters. Mark you and your men treat them for the ladies they will become.

—They are charming.

—And I'll not have them mocked.

Pale like a stone my Mr. Hearne when he came to my father's quarters. Like a stone but not still. No. Like a shining boy he appeared. Bright faced and with hair like a curled fleece. Eyes darting to every face to every man in the room to us the children who watched in the doorway. Smiling with his eyes until his mouth softened enough to show his teeth. He held his hat in one hand and twirled it with the other while he listened to my father. Like a dog he was with his hair the colour of grass straws and his eyes that said *play*.

That night my father was drunk before dinner began. Flinging his arms out. Knocking the tobacco jar onto the floor. Samuel—Mr. Hearne then—smiling and smiling. Jane brought in to sit briefly at table. I standing by my father's side. Mother watching from the door. My sister drinking yellow wine that made her loll among the platters and the cups like a fish. Samuel leaning across the surgeon and taking the point of her chin between his thumb and his curled fingers. I wanting him to do the same to me.

—A mere child yet. Wouldn't you say Mr. Purvis? Take care you do not drink up your father's wine like an old harridan.

Then he turned and smiled at me and his eyes were soft like a woman's like a mother's. But different.

—Enough said my father. That is enough of women old or young. Off to your quarters both and stay there.

Loud laughter followed us through the passageway. Someone was thumping the table with the flat of his hand making the platters knock.

1756

GOVERNOR JACOBS, TRUE TO HIS WORD, asked after Moses' childhood companion at every opportunity, and whether news of his interest got abroad or Matonabbee was simply ready, the young man did in the following year come down to the fort. And he came in style.

Two dogs were the first to appear. They came running free and barking at the dogs around the plantation. From up the river came the sound of firing. Jacobs gave the order for the twelve-pounder to answer. The men at the gates climbed onto the wall and several men followed. Governor Jacobs looked in on Moses in the trading room.

—You'd better leave that and come and see. These are Northern men coming in.

They went out and climbed up to watch from the ramparts. Conachie too came out and stood beside Moses. Two lines of canoes appeared, paddling abreast across the river.

—Twenty-three, said Conachie. Your friend could be in among them fellows.

They drew level with the fort and swung onto the beach. Four of the men, a tall youth among them, a head and shoulders above the height of the others, stepped out and walked up to the gates without a backwards glance.

—I reckon that's him, said Conachie.

The young man had bands of brilliant red painted across his eyes and cheeks and his hair tied in a long fillet on one side of his head. The men settled themselves on the ground while their companions hauled the canoes onto the beach and the women carried the furs up and placed them in the centre of the group. Two of the women stayed close to the painted youth. The man who was evidently their leader, an older, unsmiling man with the extravagantly dyed feathers of the Company tied in his hair, addressed them all in a quiet voice. Clearly these people were going to make the most of their arrival.

—That's our fellow all right, said Conachie.

He called to his son to get the pipes.

—And Mr. Jacobs says get that drummer out here too.

Isaac reappeared with his pipes and climbed up to stand on the rampart beside the gate. One of the Hospital lads came running with the kettledrum. At the opening strains of "The Dawning of the Day" one of the dogs stretched its neck to howl in response, setting off several others. Men left what they were doing to watch the entry of this party.

—We had best be ready for them, Jacobs said. He had

the ceremonial coats and hats sent out to the waiting men and went inside to put on his vest and jacket.

Moses returned inside and sat behind the writing desk in the gloom of the trading room. He thought about his own arrival at the fort, about the woman carrying his box up the beach, about his welcome gift of a chamber pot.

Outside, Matonabbee and the two other captains, following close on the leader of their party, walked through the gates to the accompaniment of "O'Donnell's Air." Matonabbee was as at ease as if he owned the very company. Or perhaps he only knew how to seem so. Moses anyway could barely see through the angle of the door. The procession halted just out of sight.

Jacobs sat in the great armchair in front of the table, leaving chairs on either side to receive the delegates. Denman was at his place behind the long table, Moses behind him.

—It's him. He's your man, said Conachie, coming in. You should come out, Mr. Norton, and make his acquaintance.

—Thank you, Mr. Conachie, said Jacobs. We'll do things in the proper manner. Have the captains come in.

IT WAS STRANGE, Moses always thought, to remain silent for so long at the start of these transactions. It made him nervous. Only Matonabbee, if indeed it was he, carried a calumet with him, the others having left their pipes the previous year in token of their good faith to return. He walked without invitation to the trading table and spread out a shining beaver pelt with a flourish, then laid the calumet in its beaded holder in the centre and took his seat. Moses could not take his eyes off him. He was wearing one of the regimental coats that had been presented outside the gates, all gold braid and orris, and a hat with a blue sash tied round the crown, the long ends trailing behind. But it was his face that held Moses' attention. The others sported the customary striped tattoos, but not Matonabbee. Three red bands of paint cut across his cheeks. His nose, Moses saw now, was painted finely in black from bridge to tip with a shape like the tail feather of a magpie. But still that was not it. What was riveting was his gaze, the ease with which it absorbed the world, and the pleasure and the satisfaction it reflected.

After a suitable pause the leader, Wâpos, signalled to the calumets on the shelf behind the table. No one had spoken. Moses got up and laid them out with a length of tobacco and all the smoking materials, then by a pantomime of nods and shakes determined which belonged to the captain. He could feel Matonabbee's eyes on him the whole time. Or perhaps he was imagining it. He gave the captain his calumet with an inch of tobacco and then he and Denman took their chairs to join the circle and the old man lit his pipe.

He smoked for a while in silence and then passed his pipe to every person present. The ceremony was repeated for each of the captains, and still no word was spoken. Denman's breathing began to sound suspiciously like a snore and the old man, whose head was bowed, was almost certainly taking a nap. They sat in silence until Wâpos finally spoke. He kept his head bowed and listened intently while Denman translated. He had brought fifteen men with him, he said, to trade and he had three captains—Etseh, Tedeheza'édelt'ogh, and Matonabbee—and they would name those whom they had brought with them.

—We have twenty men and twenty men again, all come with fine furs and in expectation of good trading. You have always treated us well. And you have promised to treat us well always. We ask only that you give us good measure and nothing short. We ask that you give us no guns that can do harm to their hunter. And give us no brandy mixed with water. You are fair and just men and we know you will treat us fairly and justly—as you would wish to be treated by us if you came to trade at our houses.

Each in turn spoke. Matonabbee was the last. He kept his voice low. It was necessary to stay very quiet to hear every word. But he sat very upright and held his head straight, and unlike the old man he looked every person present clear in the eye. He said simply that he had brought with him ten good men who had fine furs and expected good trade. Then he said he would bear no grudge if the trader found his furs less than satisfactory. The servants of the king were free men, he said, and if their trader or their governor did not like his furs he asked only that they handle them with care and return them to him after inspection with no damage. Jacobs said afterwards he had never heard anything like it. At the time he only raised his eyebrows in a conspicuous way and got up the moment Matonabbee had finished speaking, perhaps in an attempt to retrieve the initiative.

—Good then, he said. We'll have Mr. Denman exhibit the wares for trade—if you please, Mr. Denman—and we invite you to examine them, as well as the measures we shall use to apportion them. There is no hurry. You are at liberty to examine the goods for as long as you please. We shall ring the bell for the trading window to be opened for those that want rum or tobacco, and then tomorrow morning we shall open for those who have furs.

The captains waited while Denman laid out the powder and shot and tobacco and samples of the liquor. He brought down several bolts of cloth from the shelves for inspection.

—And just before you go to the wares, we should be obliged if you would accept from us now some small tokens of our pleasure.

Matonabbee was smiling now. In anticipation, Moses thought, of the box of bread and the prunes that Mr. Denman was carrying in from the back, the rundlet of brandy that stood ready. But Matonabbee was smiling directly at him. He was across the room in two strides. He took hold of him by the shoulders, pulling him out of the chair. Moses tried to position himself to shake hands, but Matonabbee's arms were round him, holding him close.

—My brother! My friend! he said in English. And then he said, Moses Norton! Making his name forever strange to Moses' ears.

The solemnity of the occasion was all in shreds now, fowling pieces and beads competing with prunes and brandy and old memories for attention. Matonabbee had Moses by the hand and was pulling him towards Wâpos.

He said something to him that Moses didn't understand, though he caught his name again as if hearing word of a traveller come from a great distance. Wâpos smiled—the first time Moses had seen him do so—and said, Moses Norton, yes. Richard Norton, yes. He seemed happy enough with the information and Moses smiled back but there was no likelihood of a further exchange since neither had enough knowledge of the other's language. He spoke instead to Matonabbee. Matonabbee laughed and replied, then translated for Moses.

—He said you are my younger brother. Perhaps because you are not tall like me. I told him you are my big brother though you are smaller in every respect. He laughed hoarsely and Moses did indeed feel smaller, lesser, altogether inadequate.

He was out of place once more, had slipped his moorings yet again. He was the superior here—if not in charge, then at least attached to the very highest officer, the chief factor. He was the superior, Matonabbee the petitioner, the supplicant, come to barter his furs. Yet with his ink-stained fingers he felt like a poverty-stricken clerk being introduced to royalty. How did this reversal occur? Matonabbee still had hold of his hand. It upset every convention Moses had ever learned. Only last year he had imagined securing some kind of work for Matonabbee at the fort, had imagined Matonabbee, this captain of men, would be grateful to him.

—I'll open the window for trade, then, said Jacobs, if everybody has had their say.

Denman asked Moses to ring the bell to announce it.

In another moment the captains had left the trading room. Matonabbee had disappeared through the gates and gone to report to his comrades.

Moses was kept busy. He would have liked to have gone up on the ramparts to observe. He knew Matonabbee's women too would be waiting on his return.

He took a rule and drew a line across the page of his book and set down the date.

Sixteen years since they had seen each other. Matonabbee, a captain of his people now, would have been three.

Over the next four days of trading, Moses was fully occupied from dawn, when the window was opened for trade, until dusk, when the iron bars were once again drawn across behind the shutters. He did not see Matonabbee again until the third night, when he walked out to the Northerners' camp to find him. He had expected Matonabbee to come to look for him, he did not know why.

The camp thrummed with life. A tent that had been half-demolished in, Moses assumed, some kind of revelry leaned beside a tent where a family all unconcerned were sharing their meal for the night. A great crowd of people had built a communal fire, the flames feeble in the light of the low sun. A young fellow there was attracting their attention with his clowning. At Matonabbee's tent, everything was quiet. The door was drawn down. Moses called out and after only a second's pause Matonabbee's voice answered with his name. He lifted the flap and ducked inside.

Matonabbee smiled broadly. He was lying on his side, half-reclining. One of his wives lay beside him, his thigh a pillow for her head. Another was kneeling, picking through the first wife's hair. The regimental coat was flung against the side of the tent.

—Welcome to my house. Matonabbee smiled even more broadly. Sit down.

The kneeling woman made a place for Moses on the furs. The other sat up and went on with her hair herself. Matonabbee told her to stop and to get meat for them all and tea.

—To think we ran together, wrestled.

—Do you remember it?

—I remember everything. I remember when you tried to open the brick stove.

—I burned my hands.

Matonabbee laughed.

—Why did you leave the fort?

—The next governor would not have me. He sent me into the country. Where I belong.

—I'm sure he didn't mean it like that.

—No. It is what I mean. Where I belong.

—You didn't miss the fort?

—Did you? The fort is work.

The woman poured smoky tea from the kettle that hung over the fire and they passed the bowl between them.

—Well, said Moses. So many years. And so much distance between us.

Matonabbee said nothing but he continued to smile.

—You a captain, Moses went on.

—And you a servant of the Company.

—But been to England and back since last we were together. Many times.

—And I have walked as far all over my own land on my own feet.

Was this a comparison now?

—Where did you travel in the winter?

—Far. Farther than you could walk.

—With your wives?

—Of course with my wives. Who would carry the meat? Who would put up the tent?

—The hunting was good, then? Moses felt a need to get away from that particular topic.

—Everything was good.

And if this *was* a comparison, Moses knew he could not say the same.

—You men without wives here. You must borrow one of mine. Matonabbee gestured towards the women. They looked up sharply but without fear or apprehension of any kind. Indeed it looked to Moses, once Matonabbee made her intentions clear, like some kind of mischievous delight.

—I could not . . .

—Why? Are you lacking?

He repeated his joke for his wives, and they joined his laughter.

Moses knew he had to quickly retrieve what was left of the situation.

—Matonabbee, I thank you, thank you heartily for your hospitality, but I could not take one of your wives . . .

—Not take. Borrow. Look, she is already thinking about it. The kneeling woman was smiling, but shyly now, making a display of bowing her head and tilting it, looking aslant at Moses.

—Her name is Marten Tail.

All rational thought was deserting him, obliterated by

the single phrase *O God* repeated in his head without pause. He thought later he might have lied so easily. He thought of a hundred lies that would have served. He could have said he had a woman coming to him that night already.

—The governor keeps a strict curfew . . .

But Matonabbee was getting up, taking his second wife by the hand to the door.

—I did not say you have to stay with her. And I did not say she has to enter the factory with you. He was pushing his wife from the tent, backing out after her. He had his hand raised to draw the door down after him.

—Matonabbee?

Matonabbee cocked his head in question.

—Thank you.

It was not what he intended. Not at all. To be sitting in the middle of a camp of these Northern men, whose language he did not speak, in the house of his brother, who was in fact a stranger yet who spoke his own language so proficiently, with Marten Tail, a great strapping girl, fifteen perhaps, strong, sitting opposite him. But dear God, beautiful—that tilt of the head, those eyes. God. Matonabbee's wife. It was not what he had intended.

The girl came over and knelt down in front of him. She waited.

Moses was stricken with the imagined figure of Matonabbee tall outside the tent. Within earshot. What he would not do— God help him—for a mouthful of rum. Right now.

Marten Tail got up and lay down instead on the skins. In the broad day! Moses' heart was beating in his chest like a loose tent flap in a gale but his blood refused to do its work where it should and he was as limp as an expired bird.

The girl did not offer much in the way of help. He tried to help himself but she laughed. If Matonabbee were outside. O God.

And then, in that little circle of silence within the softly roaring camp, Moses felt the dangerous burn of tears. He closed his eyes tight and kissed the girl hard, doing his best to bruise her lip. Then he got up and quickly ducked outside.

He thanked God, on whom he had called so fervently, that Matonabbee was nowhere to be seen.

Later that day, on his way to the latrine, Isaac Conachie, making his way back, stepped into his path. He asked if he was going outside the walls after dark.

—You know, he said. See if there's a lass on the loose. He waggled his tongue obscenely.

Moses, whom no man could bribe at that moment to re-enter Matonabbee's camp, replied that he had no intention of doing any such thing. But before his answer could mark him yet again as a failure, he added, suddenly inspired, And if it comes to the governor's attention that you have, I'll ask him if I can deliver your punishment personally.

Sitting in the stinking hut, he liked the way the words on his tongue took away the taste of humiliation—masked it, at least.

THE NORTHERN INDIANS never stayed long at the fort when trading was done. After the fourth day they began packing up their wares and dismantling the tents. Moses was relieved to see it. He busied himself with the books and hoped the fort would soon be quiet again. He had seen Governor Jacobs walking outside the ramparts with Matonabbee. He would join them when he heard the signal for departure. He could say his farewell in a dignified manner. But only minutes later a man came in and said the governor was asking for him in his quarters.

Moses went along to the room that served as both the governor's office and his dining room. Governor Jacobs seemed particularly genial.

—Well, Moses. How do you like your man?

It was hard to know how to respond.

—He is a fine fellow. The voice he used noncommittal, wary.

Jacobs, on the other hand, threw his full weight behind his own endorsement.

—That's exactly it. A fine fellow. One of the finest Northern men I've seen. And not a day over . . . How old are you, Norton?

—Twenty-two, sir.

—There you are. Nineteen that would make him, eh? He could be twenty-six. But the thing that impresses me most is his command of the language. You can converse with the fellow . . . well, more intelligently than with any Orkneyman.

—He speaks very well.

—And think how useful that could be to us, Norton. Do you know he speaks the Southern tongue too?

—I didn't, sir.

—Yes. Like a Native.

Jacobs in as fine a humour as Moses had seen roared at his own joke.

—He could be very valuable to us indeed.

And there were his cards on the table, laid out so plain. Jacobs seemed to remember his point.

—So I've been thinking, Norton, about your father's wishes. Clearly he intended to do something to help the fellow along, and I should like to honour that worthy intention. I've invited Matonabbee to reside the year here at the factory. What do you think?

—My father would have been very pleased.

Governor Jacobs looked hard at Moses. His face was impassive. His eyes gave nothing away. For the first time in Jacobs' presence Moses was aware of his own skin.

—Exactly my thought. Now, since you have established some connection already with the fellow, perhaps you'll go to the trading room and pick up a few small gifts for him—some tobacco, the usual. You know, encourage him to accept the offer.

—Yes, sir.

Without further discussion Moses went along to the trading room. He could hear the commotion building outside as the Indians assembled for their journey. Miserably he cut a length of tobacco, picked out a japanned box, then hooked a jug of rum with his finger and went out to the gate.

Matonabbee was waiting in his tent. He showed no signs of having begun preparations for a journey. Marten Tail was tending a kettle over a small fire. Moses could smell the oats of the fort's kitchen. He was made again to look a fool, hopping to Matonabbee's tune. Matonabbee had no need of gifts, though his eyes were on them anyway.

—Come and sit, he said.

—The governor sends you these things with his compliments.

Matonabbee reached for the jug and sniffed.

—The governor is a man of good faith, Moses said.

—The governor had better send port wine next time, like he gave to Wâpos when he asked him to feast.

Always this man took Moses' breath.

—The governor says he would be happy if you lived here at the fort.

—What does he offer me?

—He has told you already, I believe. If you stay here and teach your language to the officers and to some of the Homeguard, the governor will provide for you and your family. You will not have to give any furs in return.

Matonabbee laughed and said he would have none to give. There were no furs to be had in these parts.

—He said you are the man to talk reason with your people and with the Kisiskâciwanak in times of trouble.

—That is a job for a fool.

—On the contrary, the governor deems it a great honour to the man he chooses.

—The governor deems. The governor chooses.

Moses decided it was time to return to the material goods.

—That is why he has sent me to bring you these gifts. He hopes you will stay here and be an agent for peace.

—Ask the governor to give a gun powerful enough to reason with troublesome people. That is what your father had when he was sent to make the people think of peace. The port wine he can send now and I will send him my answer in return.

On his way back to the fort Moses could not shake the renewed sense of humiliation. The world out of kilter. He was a go-between. Nothing more. Matonabbee was the man who wagers at dice and knows already how they will fall.

He made his report to Jacobs. Jacobs showed no surprise and readily agreed. He ordered Moses to carry over one of the small rundlets of wine.

—And invite the fellow to breakfast with me at midday tomorrow. When it's too late to change his mind. You come too, Norton. And Denman. He's done well.

For the rest of the day, all night, and all of the following morning, Moses felt as if his whole being was crawling with discomfort. Every task he undertook was pointless, every action of his clumsy. His words fell like stones when he spoke. He could hear his own voice, and it was the voice of a dolt. When Jacobs asked him to alert the watch that Matonabbee was to be admitted freely, he thought about going out to tell Matonabbee. Make his point. *I have alerted the watch and on my orders they are to admit you.* But Matonabbee might well know a hundred ways to reverse the tables.

The breakfast as it turned out was an amicable affair. How could it not be? Matonabbee brought his wives, which altered everything.

He came through the gates beaming and looking at his women to see if they were suitably awed. Moses walked outside to meet them. His stomach lurched when he saw Marten Tail but she regarded him as if he had never existed—for which he was truly grateful. Matonabbee clasped him like a brother, owning him for the benefit of his wives. So he did after all have some worth. Matonabbee was talking volubly to the women.

—What are you saying?

—I am saying you are my good friend, the son of Richard Norton who built this house of stone.

Moses thought ruefully that it was a little late for introductions.

The women nodded and said *Richard Norton* and smiled. The name was not new to them.

—They know, said Matonabbee. Your father and mine too when I lived in this place.

Moses could feel the pride radiating from Matonabbee. He saw it reflected back in the eyes of his women, who were proud of their husband. Proprietorial now, Matonabbee stretched his arm wide and embraced the whole fort in the gesture, explaining in his own language and in English the lien the stone had on his heart, claiming it in a way that had eluded Moses.

As they made their way to the governor's quarters he spoke to Moses in English, glancing at his wives once or twice to make sure they noted it. The women became very quiet. The oak door to the governor's rooms would have silenced the most talkative. Inside, even Matonabbee was stilled. Governor Jacobs had dressed in his European clothes for the occasion and was standing in the centre of the carpet that had come over on last year's ship. Careful not to show his surprise at the arrival of the women, he asked Conachie to draw up two more chairs and tell the cookhouse. Moses watched while Matonabbee took it all in. The carpet, the brick stove, the table and chairs, the shining silver, the china plates. He wondered aloud if they would bring in the cups for the port wine.

—Man after my own heart, said Conachie, returning with extra settings. What do you say, Governor? Bay rules in effect today?

They ate hot burgoo prepared with currants and raisins and there were salted herrings and lemons to follow, which the women did not appreciate. Matonabbee called out for water. But the governor's reputation was safe. He had ordered fresh soda bread from the cookhouse, knowing it always impressed his visitors and cost next to nothing. They drank tea and chocolate. Matonabbee and Denman drank port from pewter cups. Moses saw how Matonabbee glanced at Denman and adjusted his hold on the cup.

Jacobs was courteous, genial. Matonabbee was in his element answering questions about the abundance of beaver, the presence of the Canadians inland, the troubles with the Kisis-kâciwanak, the possibility of large deposits of copper in the north. There was no question that he could not answer with authority. His women said nothing and no one spoke to them. Denman was interested in Matonabbee's earliest years at the fort and Moses dredged memories and dreams for his benefit.

—There were women at the fort in those days, he said. We lived like brothers.

Though at once he was annoyed with himself, speaking as if it were the greatest achievement to be raised alongside Matonabbee, who was—what?—an uncouth Northern hunter.

—Strange how life takes turns and twists, he said. Now in the months to come . . .

He didn't know where his words were leading. He wanted to say that he could teach Matonabbee European manners, customs. He wanted to shine a light on his ignorance, say he could teach him to read. It all sounded foolish. He hesitated too long.

—In the months to come Matonabbee could teach you some of his hunting tricks, eh, Mr. Norton?

—Until the sloop demands my attention, perhaps. He remembered Matonabbee's dismissive attitude and tried it for himself. —Though there is not much hereabout in the way of game for that.

—Yes. Yes. There is much to hunt. Not deer, not wolf close by, or even marten. But many animals, many birds. There is good hunting. Matonabbee tipped back his cup and held it out to be refilled. —I'll show you.

Conceding defeat, perhaps for as long as his old companion remained at the fort, Moses said quietly, Then I'll be pleased to learn.

THE WINTER WAS everything Moses Norton had feared it would be. The months of numbing cold as he sat for hours over Jacobs' paperwork—the fingers of his right hand had developed a pronounced kink at the first joint—were now punctuated by bursts of the most extreme discomfort.

—Come with me.

He had begun to dread the words he heard each Sunday when Matonabbee arrived at the door of the mess in all his winter furs, his hunting gun in its tasselled bag at his back. It was useless to protest or to make excuses. Matonabbee would become grave.

—I made a promise. No man will ever live to say I did not keep my promise.

The jeering of the men was no help at all.

—Afraid of the cold, Norty?

—Or the big boy?

—Look out for the big boy. You might never come back.

Moses always rose from his breakfast and went to put on his toggie.

The man at the gates, stiff-legged from the cold of the last watch, always said, Good hunting to the both of you. Bring us back a fine one.

Moses rarely enjoyed the day. His poor eyesight made his aim less than perfect. Perhaps it was a hindrance too in spotting the signs that Matonabbee said were so abundant. In any event he missed half of what he was supposed to have seen and he allowed his mind to wander into an uncomfortable track: It's cold. It's far too cold. With every step he wished himself back at the fort.

Often when they were out together, Matonabbee asked about Moses' women. Moses took to lying extravagantly. Matonabbee in response maintained a gallant silence and Moses knew he guessed the truth.

Once after a particularly thin day Matonabbee said the

country hereabout was inferior. He said Moses should see his own country to the northwest. There is abundance, he said. There is plenty. The deer, he said, would come and kneel when they saw the gun. And because they were on their way back and there was no longer any need for silence, he roared his great laugh. Moses should obtain leave from the fort, he said, and travel with him next year to see for himself. At that moment, unable to draw the frigid air past a rotting tooth or to walk without pain on a foot that had likely frozen, Moses could think of nothing he would like to do less. He was only glad they were not sleeping on the land that night. But later, when he heard Matonabbee regaling the men in the mess with an account of how he had mistaken the dung of two muskox for the droppings of a hare, Moses wished they had been.

—You need to use your nose, man.

And there in response was the wretched youth Isaac, dropped from his chair onto all fours to sniff at the floor. Another man joined him and the performance quickly turned obscene.

Yet in the course of that winter Moses did learn. He learned he did not love the land. He did not love to hunt. He did not love the weather. He did not love his would-be brother. He resisted every attempt on the part of the men to yoke the two of them. He was not Indian. He was as English as any of them. He learned that his own opinion counted for nothing. The others seemed determined to use him for their amusement. In his father's house. He was becoming an object of derision in his father's own house. By the time the river was breaking up he had made himself a promise: He would make himself if not loved, then respected. If not respected, then feared. He would carve a place for himself in this fort, his only home, his true and rightful home. He would begin by making himself indispensable. He would insinuate himself so deeply in the affairs of the post, would prove so conscientious in his work, that Governor Jacobs would come to rely on him. And he made other resolutions. No one would stand in his way. He would overtake Denman in the command. He would insist that the Company letter of introduction be adhered to—to the letter. He would advance through the ranks and there would be no stopping him. One day he would assume the office of commander-in-chief. And then the men would have no reason to laugh. He would be governor of his own house. Head of his own family. And master of as many women as cared to come to him.

IT WAS A WHITE BEAR that delivered Moses Norton's first real wife to his hands. With one blow from its forepaw, it felled Nêwositêkâpaw's Mashkêgow hunter before it staggered and reeled sideways, the ball lodged near the base of its skull having shifted with the force of the blow to bring a curtain of darkness down on its world too forever. When Moses heard about it he wished he could congratulate the bear for its happy sense of occasion, for his star was in the ascendant. Governor Jacobs was on furlough, and after four years of steady application to his work Moses had stepped up to temporary command of Prince of Wales Fort.

The week after her husband's death Nêwositêkâpaw,

with her daughter Wâpiskasiniy on her back, went to the trading room herself to collect what was owing to him. There she found Mr. Norton—she called him governor now—eager as always to help her.

Moses offered his condolences again. He had read a prayer at the husband's burial in honour of services rendered. He had not then been able to catch his sewing woman's eye. He looked directly at her now across the table.

—You have no one to provide for you and your daughter, Nêwositêkâpaw. But your husband served us well. We can provide you both with everything you need. It is our duty.

Her look told him she understood him completely. She was not a callous woman. She had loved her husband. But she was practical. He knew the goods so closely guarded at the fort and so scrupulously apportioned for services rendered were in her eyes a cache of the finest meat and fish, the warmest clothing. And he could add toys and tools and trinkets beyond her dreaming. Within a month she was beside him in his bed with her daughter, whom Moses insisted should be called Jane, curled like a small dog among furs at their feet. She did not understand him so well when, on the governor's return, he told her she had to move back to her people. It had been less than a year.

—And this child? She put her hand on her belly. To run fatherless like your other children?

Moses said no. He said one day he himself would be the true governor. He said on that day they would all three of them return to live at the fort. And he kept his word. He said they would know excess of every kind. And that too proved true.

PART TWO

Molly Norton's Dream

THE LONG JOURNEY NEVER LEAVES ME. Every storm we weathered more fierce than the one before. Or our failing strength made it seem so. On some days we did not walk at all but sheltered together under the skins on into the night— our breathing all the sound we made against the wind's high moan. We did not freeze and were thankful when we woke. But still we knew starvation had crept closer in the night and we had no choice but to walk again.

We followed the river away to the northwest. There were seven of us and our progress was slow. We walked at child's pace for the sake of Athîkis's short legs and for my small cousin. For my grand-mother too. She was glad of the many stops I had to make for my daughter for then she could rest. And then we saw the smoke in thin drifts like the combings of an old woman's hair across the sky to the west. We thought at first it must be our hunters but when we walked there we saw only some tents of the Wêcîpwayânak. An old man came out to meet us. His legs were bent like a grasshopper's and his head shook violently. We did not know what misfortune would send an ailing man to greet strangers. We cared only to know if he had food to share.

We asked him in his own language. He made as if he did not understand. He made many gestures of enquiry. We spoke my father's name and the name of my home but he shook even more telling us something of terrible import but we could not understand everything he said. He took us to the largest house. The people within lay on their sleeping skins. Someone on the far side moaned and a child cried. A woman who lay near the door had skin like purple berries. She pulled her sleeping robe over her face to cover it. A man lay without covers or clothing and his body glistened like fat melting in the fire. The old man spoke to the woman who attended him and she came to us and spoke our own language. She asked why we had come for they had no food but were themselves starving. She said they had been on their way to the fort when the sickness struck. Four of their men had died. Only one was out hunting for them. He had met with two men from the fort who told him what had happened there but he had not believed them. He said he thought it was a lie put about by the Pedlars so that all should turn away from the fort and carry their furs to the Pedlar houses instead. Now she said she knew the impossible thing was true. But it made no difference true or false for all were too weak to travel. We should not stay she said but should go away from their houses and from the sickness. She said we should try instead to meet our hunters and she told us how to find the way to Deer Swim Lake. She said there were sometimes fish and they would go there themselves but now it was too late. She said she had heard Matonabbee my uncle was also out on the land on his way to the fort. She fetched water for us from the fire and she said if Matonabbee passed by on his way back to his people perhaps he would bring them meat and she would tell him of our plight.

We walked for two more days sucking on the bones of the ptarmigan my aunt had caught. On the third day we saw more tents. We stopped as soon as we saw them for there was no smoke in the sky—only buzzards floating. We walked closer and saw dogs outside but no people. We stopped again. My aunt and I thought it best to pass by these tents and keep a wide distance from them. My grandmother and my mother thought we should go to them for we were in such need of all that could help us live. We walked closer. I stopped with my cousin and held on to Athîkis. I did not want to see. The others went forward. The dogs came running at them but they kept walking. They stopped at the largest tent and none came out to greet them. My mother went inside. She came out almost at once then together with the others entered the next tent. A dog followed them out with something in its mouth then another dog came out and tried to tear it away. I watched while they went to the last two tents. When they came out their faces were straight. Stricken. My grandmother brought away a hatchet and an ice chisel. No one else carried anything away. My mother said there were good skins there but none wanted to touch them. The dogs she said had been feasting on the people. She said the people and their children lay everywhere as if the dying had come so fast that none could be buried. She said some of them were without clothes and it must have been the burning fever that had come upon them. She said they were Wêcîpwayânak and we felt strangely glad as if this meant we could ourselves be safe—though the truth is that our greatest need was of others who might see our need and help us.

To keep walking was hard. It was harder than anything I had ever done or anything I would do. Dying was easier. I walked for my daughter and most of all for Athîkis. The next day as we approached a dip in the land the air was raucous with crows. We saw many of them flapping up from the ground only to drop and settle again. When we found the carcass they had led us to none of us knew what animal it had been. The shreds that remained were very bitter.

My snowshoes had long since come apart and the walking was slow. Even before the camp of affliction we had walked through one whole waning of the moon and almost another. After the camp the days and nights were not to be counted for all congealed in a dark hunger. We walked in silence brimming with the things we had seen quiet with the things we feared. The days were nothing but the wide expanse we had to cross before starvation drew level. Nor was our trail marked by any animal come to save us but only by our own feet scuffing the snow until at last we walked through pain and exhaustion into a place of no feeling and our bodies became like those whose souls are stolen away. We walked in the direction the woman had told us and we trusted her lake was the same our hunters had named.

When the light went out of the day we dug a hollow in the snow and lay down on skins and covered ourselves over with the remnants of the tent skins for we had no strength to cut poles. When we lay down we fell at once asleep. Our feet still treading the snow of our dreams behind our eyes. The ground still rocking beneath us from the motion of our long walking. Sometimes we woke under the flaring green fires of the sky fanned by the flickering winds. I held Athîkis close for warmth with my daughter between us. My grandmother lay at Athîkis's back to keep the cold from him and my mother and my aunt kept my small cousin between them.

We did not meet our hunters again. I have looked on this in all the long days and I have seen how the people were like seeds adrift across the land and blown by their hunger. And some of them were lucky blowing as they did ahead of the fire of the sickness and turning north away from its path. But some knew only ill luck turning unwittingly directly into its path as it drove up in two great arcs from the southwest and the southeast and engulfed them like birds in a net.

My grandmother said it is enough. We did not at first understand her meaning. She gave the ice chisel and the hatchet to my mother. She said go and provide for your daughter and your granddaughter. She said her feet had numbed for walking and pain was feasting on her belly. She held her robes close even though sweat had begun on her brow. And then she grew fierce when we did not walk on. Her old mouth working at the words like a deer's jaw. Her words contained no promises only the command to walk and to reach the lake and the shelter of the thicker woods ahead.

We left my grandmother sitting with her arms round her knees and her bones would lie there still were it not for the wolverine and after that the foxes that carried them and left them strewn across the snow so that in summer she brightens the moss on the way to the lake.

I can see now from this great distance the pattern of our dying from this fiery affliction for that was what it was. First the pains like a steel thrust into the gut and the next day a violent purging with the poison burning as it leaves the body. And the day ending with a smouldering fever that cannot be extinguished though the sweat runs like rain on the skin. And the last of it comes with the skin of the face bubbling like a caribou stomach held over the fire. Burning craters breaking out on every part of the body both inside and out leaving it blackened as a spent coal. I can see York Factory in flames with it.

Men walking out of the fire with sparks eating into their backs. Not the Englishmen. Only the men of the country. Men all unawares carrying the invisible sparks in their hair in the furs over their shoulders. Carrying them in their mouths to the camps of their friends and their families. Men arriving already sick shaking out their furs and sending the sparks flying to fall on the furs of their friends and all all in this way slowly coming into flame. For there was no putting out the sparks only the sparks' dying of themselves on those who went about untouched.

And I can see more. How it was the very blood of those of us who escaped that kept us safe with some protection. We had the taint of the white blood already in our veins our mothers having lain down for the Englishmen. The affliction did not touch us but raced thirstily after those whose blood was rich still and untainted. And perhaps my mother knew it too.

She knew our own dying had already begun. It had been coming on us slowly since before the camp of the affliction. It began when we walked away from the fort without dogs without enough guns with so little to sustain us. It began when the days of winter arrived too soon. It began when the animals turned their heads from our path and did not show themselves. We had already walked into the jaws of starvation and of sickness. There was nothing now to be done. Only lie down or walk. Try to walk away. There was no cache of meat at any place and we began to know another truth. That our hunters too had fallen to the sickness and were folded somewhere into the land in their private agonies. We did not know what we should do when we arrived at the lake. We did not know if we would arrive. We knew only to walk on taking what nourishment we could from small pieces of hide that we cut from our

blankets. It was necessary not to question that we could walk ourselves out of starvation and back into life. We had been blinded by
the endless land reaching north. We had slept through fierce storms
but we had woken to walk again. We had walked away from the
camp of the dying. We had found it and we had walked away. Then
surely not to fall on the trail.

My aunt walked ahead. My mother Nêwositêkâpaw behind her.
Sometimes the snow closed them off from my sight. Athîkis walked
beside me. He said nothing though his hand holding fast to my clothes
pulled me back as if to make us stop. I knew I would have to make a
sled for him from the moosehide for soon he would not be able to walk
any farther. I carried my daughter—my daughter!—on my back feeling her small body's agony through the blades of my shoulders. When
she cried out she had the voice of a dying animal an ancient crone but
it did not issue from her throat no. It lay deep in her hollow body and
dragged itself up on the sticks of her ribs so that I felt it bone through
bone until it escaped into air then curled and entered me again through
the dark passage of my ears. I wanted to call for my mother but she was
far ahead. The wind at my back was my daughter's breath both quiet
and hard. It was the sound of a small twig blown across ice. Scraping. I
listened to it scrape slowly more slowly. Behind my eyes I watched the
twig scrape one way and stick and my feet took six steps seven eight
before it twitched and was dragged back. And what I have to say is that
I longed for it to jam fast and not to move again ever. And at last it did.
It ceased. I fell forward to my knees and called for my mother. She did
not hear me. I watched her figure bent under the weight of our shelter
grow fainter and vanish in the blowing snow. I could not hear my own
voice when it called so soon was it swept away by the wind. I pulled at
my daughter's shoulder and she dropped from my back like a skinny

calf from its dam at birth no more than a loose gathering of bones in a skin. I dug in the snow for stones to cover her and found none so I covered her with my words—colder than stones heavier than my heart. Little daughter. Little girl with no name. Stay quiet. Stay warm. The summer river will run. I called in my heart to my grandmother to come to find her great-granddaughter in her new country of the dead. To keep her close. And I covered her with a blanket of snow.

Everything exists forever behind my eyelids. My daughter's small body. The dark shape of my mother vanishing in the storm. It was a hard thing. To see them walk away. To see my mother leaning deaf and half blind into the stinging snow. To feel the cold body of my daughter. To know myself alone in the world with none to help me keep Athîkis alive. I know why they walked away. It was to carry away the sickness for they fell each one.

But though I was saved from the affliction I knew my own dying was approaching. Returning for me. It was as if the great wind from the north that passed over us low and fast and close enough to snatch away my daughter was even now wheeling and turning to pass over us again grasping the life in my body and dragging it drawing it off away over the frozen rock and the snow. Still I held fast to what was left, feeling my life as it was sucked away stretch thinner and thinner.

There was much I saw in those days that did not belong to the world of the living. Sometimes I was caught in terrible dreams like a partridge in a net. Sometimes I dreamed I was awake and did not know I was dreaming. Sometimes again I fell into a pit of darkness and could hear only distant voices from the lips of those who stood at the edge of the pit. It was in my dreaming that the Dog Rib woman told me what I must do for my boy.

I told Athîkis we would walk out on the lake and fish. And

perhaps we did. I see the sliver of my own flesh cut from my thigh. Small and slick I dream it like a live red fish. And in no time it is frozen. I have a piece of bone still in my bundle. I break it and pierce through the sliver of flesh twice so that it stays. I split the thong that wrapped my bundle and tie the flesh on to the new length. Out on the ice of the lake the wind torments us. It takes a long time to chisel a hole. The first day we catch nothing. I walk out in the night under the light of the stars and reopen the hole. At the first pull on the line I draw up a frantic flopping fish and I laugh out loud. My voice is as hoarse as a raven's. And wakes me. And a vision comes to me. I see Matonabbee and he is wandering like a blind animal. His arms hang slack at his sides and in one hand he holds a bloody knife. I know the stories of extremity. The things a man—or woman—can be driven to perform. I do not want my body to lie in his path so I push myself to standing but I cannot walk. Instead I let myself fall again to my knees and crawl away like a beast. In the morning I give Athîkis a sliver of frozen meat and he is happy.

I no longer know how many days we lived there in this way. I knew this stretched and thinned life of mine would give very soon like a thong of deerskin stretched to the breaking point. The pain of holding on was very great. The roots of my life were deep in my gut. I could feel the slow tearing. One day I did not rise at all. Athîkis held his face over mine and let the snow he had melted for me run into my mouth. My throat contracted and swallowed only the smallest sips. The sips passed into me like small stones and a little while after the pains came as if my insides were being removed from my belly—and I still alive. So severe were the pains that when they came my legs too were drawn and weighted with them. I could stand only with the greatest effort and then the world tipped and reeled before my eyes. I heard the small sound of a wave lapping soft at the shore in summer and when I opened my eyes I saw Athîkis's face close to mine. His eyes peered into mine searching for me. I smiled for I remembered my knife and I knew what I had to do. I gave it to Athîkis and turned away my face. Then I closed my eyes and was grateful.

1772

I T WAS THE MIDDLE OF JUNE WHEN TWO young Wêcîpwayânak came to the trading room with news of Samuel Hearne's approach. They said he was with a large party of Matonabbee's people eight days off. They had a letter.

Governor Norton read in silence. He thrust out his lower jaw and breathed heavily.

Still more than a week away and he was making demands.

—Soap! Gone nineteen months in the God-forsaken wilds of the north, up the goddamn Copper River, and suddenly the conceited English upstart needs soap! Though that was not the cause of his irritation. What rankled more was this business of homecoming. If anyone could ever be said to have truly come home to Churchill, it was he, Moses Norton. He'd done it—twice—without fanfare, without palaver. And quietly, without histrionics of any kind, he'd risen to his present position. He'd savoured that particular return privately, thinking it sweet enough. And he'd led expeditions too. He'd sailed up the coast and back. No one had ever fired a salute on his return, nor did he expect it—or so he told himself. Yet as governor he'd had to tolerate Matonabbee's antics every few years or so, put on a show for his arrival. And now it seemed the precious Mr. Hearne was expecting the same— even though the last time he'd come back from this expedition his tail was between his legs.

—I have more. The older boy pulled a damp and thickened piece of paper from his pouch and repeated its message, which he had by rote, as he handed it over: *a short length of black buckram.*

As if it were a matter of life and death. Norton imagined Hearne calling the runners back with his afterthought. He threw the scrap on his chief trader's table and gathered up his books.

—See to it, will you, Mr. Leask? I don't have time for that.

But at the door he turned. Tobacco too, if you will. Mark it all down.

Mr. Leask pursed his thin lips and stared hard at Norton's back as he left, but he made no comment. Such a grudging manner. He did not understand it. Always did have a mean streak, the governor. His way of keeping the whip hand. But he was vexed almost all the time now, usually over nothing at all. That was the governor these days. Mr. Purvis, the new surgeon, said—privately—it was his constricted digestion.

He gave the boys some oatmeal cakes and a drink of rum that set them to grinning while he packed up the articles. He wrote a note, just in case.

All here sent as per your request, viz., shirt, razor, soap, scissors, comb, and ribbon. In addition please find one (1) small box of goose livers from the ones we've just done up, tobacco one (1) foot, and brandy two (2) quarts. Make sure you ask for it if you don't see it. God speed your way home.

For himself, he was nothing but happy to hear Sam Hearne was so close. He'd known too many servants over the years who'd met their deaths. Left the fort sometimes only to go wooding and met with some accident. Usually the weather. The lad deserved to succeed just for trying something so ambitious.

Samuel Hearne's last two attempts at what Leask considered this mad idea of the governor's had ended in failure. Each time, he'd been forced home again almost before he got started. He'd been gone this time well over a year. And no word from him since the middle of this last winter. The men had begun to talk. Third time unlucky was the none-too-clever phrase they used. There were even a few wagers. Leask didn't like to see that. Taking a man's life— or death—so lightly. He was glad the men who'd backed failure would be out of pocket. He'd placed no bets, though he could have. Sam Hearne was in good hands, he knew that. If anyone could bring him back safe it was Matonabbee. Although you didn't want to say that too loud around here.

LESS THAN A DAY away from the fort, after crossing the Pocothîkiskêw, Sam Hearne tucked into cooked goose livers packed in their grease. The flies were biting unmercifully but they had endured worse. They had walked sometimes for days without food and the spectre of starvation had never been far. He knew some of the women had died on the journey back. They had been left behind. There was no help for it. And those who were sick always knew. They had a way of falling back. Only one refused abandonment. When she came up to them again as they slept he had been glad for her. Her family embraced her, thinking her recovered. But in the morning she fell back a second time and her husband wept as they walked on. He was close to tears himself when she reappeared that night, dragging herself to them like a creature with a broken limb. He could not watch. The next morning her family wrapped her in a mooseskin and left her with an oiled pouch of water while they moved on. Once he looked back and saw her at a great distance seeming to follow. And then she wasn't there any more. There was no hunting to keep others alive. He'd kept his ammunition for his own use. Game so scarce. How rapidly the body creates its own imperative, revises it when the danger passes. How dirty its tracks on the field of conscience.

—Ambrosia.

—What is that?

—You tell me.

He handed the livers to Matonabbee. Matonabbee bit off a piece and chewed thoughtfully, his eyes reading the high pink clouds.

—Not as good as prunes.

Sam clapped him on the shoulder and stood up.

—Sit. You won't get back tonight.

—I know. But I shall be closer.

Matonabbee stood up. He had led this Englishman to the Northern Sea and back. He would not let it be said he had walked any part alone. He gathered his wives, secured their loads, helped those with the small canoes. The grumbling and the sighing were perfunctory. The rain had abated. The bronze of evening glowed on the new grasses and sedges ahead of them. A few of the others followed. Matonabbee would wait for the rest in the morning. They knew that. He would arrive at the fort with the greatest possible number. They walked on, splashing through gilded pools. They, like all the world, turned russet and gold. Their eyes glittered when they turned their heads. Their long shadows lay purple and aslant before them. An hour or so before midnight they stopped to rest. They did not put up the tents. The sun had not yet reached the horizon and they were asleep.

Three hours later, as soon as the sun reappeared, Sam was down at the edge of a shallow runnel with his soap and his razor. In the first glow he stripped off and washed himself down, leaving off the deerskin breeches while the early sun dried his skin. When he had combed out his hair he cut off a couple of inches and squatted to shave off his beard, feeling his face return under his fingers. He splashed away the soap, then stood up and put the breeches back on. He picked up the shirt and pulled it over his head, tucking it in at the waist. He combed his hair again and tied it back with the black buckram.

Back at the camp the women giggled at his approach. Marten Tail laughed out loud.

—You are half-blood like the governor!

—What do you mean?

—Your father. Your mother. She gestured up and down to the white linen shirt, the deerskin trousers in turn.

Sam laughed with her, but he still did not know the figure he cut.

THEY WALKED ACROSS the marshland behind the river. Hawks accompanied them, skimming the ground for the young of the plover they scared up. When they had walked for two hours, Sam saw the first glint of the river ahead of them, the familiar gulls. At the river they could make out the bold geometry of the stone flanks of the fort farther down. While they were getting the canoes in the water, Sam took his gun and punctured the wide morning with three evenly spaced shots. In only minutes a cannon replied with a single retort. The reverberations thundered round the dome of the sky. They could see the smoke.

—They must have been waiting.

The idea pleased him.

When all the canoes were in the water they started downstream past the stony flats.

GOVERNOR MOSES NORTON put on his jacket and buttoned it. There was something unsavoury smeared and dried across the cuff. It had been an excellent meal last night. He did remember that. Moses these days had an inordinate interest in his meals. He went to the washstand. The pitcher was empty and no one had replenished it. There was bile in the basin. If only the women kept house as well as they disordered the bed. He found his wig and put it on in front of his looking glass. Disorder. His room really was not fit for his station. His children out there somewhere, running barefoot. Shot out of their beds by the goddamn cannon. He had a headache.

He would turn over a new leaf. Make some changes, some improvements. He pulled the drape from the parrot's cage. It screamed at him and he swore. The parrot swore back and then it said good morning.

—*Governor*. The parrot, like some of the men, seemed to forget his title on purpose.

It was ten years since the Honourable Company had kept its word and appointed him chief factor of Prince of Wales Fort. Though it was no kind of favour. He knew he had earned it. But still, the satisfaction was huge. He remembers how when he returned from furlough to take up the post, even the gravel under his boot—his governor's boot—felt different. But he, Moses Norton, Richard's son, was careful to disguise his grin as a grimace as he brought his other foot out of the longboat and stepped ashore. Just another of the myriad tricks the English had taught him: you don't always have to show your hand as soon as you come to the table. James Dupeer, with his bland, innocuous face, had taught him that. He remembers his return to the bay as clearly as if it were today. Inhaling the complex vegetal taint of the Churchill River, pretending to snuff the air, but no. He was breathing satisfaction. Chief Factor Moses Norton—Governor Norton—was arriving. Done with small cruelties and privations, done with harsh apprenticeships. He had paid his dues and he was arriving. The very air he snuffed was full of promise. His boxes, which had been set down earlier in the morning on the small shingle of the landing stage, had already been carried up. The bigger items, bought on furlough to mark his new position—a pedal organ, a cherry-wood desk, three Turkey carpets, and a chaise—had been taken off the night before. Standing there for the first time as governor he had felt the shadow of his younger self at his side. The boy who had carried his own box on his shoulder while Governor Jacobs walked on down to the longboat to meet with Captain Spurrell. The boy who had burned to see Matonabbee stride through the fort his own father had built, lording it over him as if he were nothing but a Hospital boy. At least he had known patience then. And to keep his resentment close to his heart inside his jacket, that too a trick he had learned from those who would keep him down. All things come home.

Governor Norton, having spent the best part of an hour at stool—another legacy of Mother Dupeer's—went outside to find that Leask had taken the liberty of organizing a guard of honour. Everyone more than ready to leave his duties and stand like a numbskull in dumb formation at the gates. Leask himself was already down at the beach with Purvis and some others. Moses saw Nêwositêkâpaw and her sisters starting down with their children, Molly among them, a fox cub with a wobbling gait close on her heels.

—Bring those children back here.

The women turned, hesitating. Molly bent and scooped up the cub.

—Now! Get them up here now or by God I'll come down.

Without complaint or question they returned. Moses pushed them aside.

—Only Molly, he said, taking hold of her elbow. In the absence of a son—one he could be sure of—Molly, twelve years old and beginning to look interesting, was his blood's best hope of continuity in the world. Her young cousins were no more than brats. Her elder sister, Jane, had already been swallowed by the place, disappeared now for over a year and said to be on the land with a Wêcîpwayân man. And as for the children he'd fathered, God only knew. One of the women outside had just had a child, but what use was that? No. He was grooming Molly, his apple dumpling Molly, for a Company man with a future.

—I want to go down there.

—He comes to us, Molly. He comes to us. He sniffed surreptitiously. The sun on his sleeve was bringing out a decidedly unpleasant aroma. The fox in Molly's arms had caught it too. Moses elbowed it away.

SAMUEL HEARNE FELT his legs strangely unsteady beneath him as he climbed out of Matonabbee's canoe. Legs that had carried him three thousand miles—more! Feet that had foundered almost to rags and healed again. And here came the dogs sniffing, eager. He kicked them away. Matonabbee was making a show of playing the great captain, directing

the activities of the rest of the canoes coming ashore and
beginning to unload.

—Mr. Hearne! Well met! Well met!

Grey, wispy Mr. Leask, who himself was clearly far
from well, held out both his trembling hands. And Matonabbee! Welcome, man!

Mr. Purvis was actually blinking.

—Mr. Hearne. Sam. The surgeon shook his hand,
shook Matonabbee's. Matonabbee read these men easily. He
beamed pride.

Sam let himself be embraced again by Leask. His legs
did feel very strange. Several people seemed to want to support him but he shook them away. He restored his hair to its
freshly groomed state and pulled the ribbon tight.

—Matonabbee.

Matonabbee shook his head.

Sam waited. His debt to this man so irredeemable.

—You go, Matonabbee said. We are not ready.

Sam and the officers started up the beach. Six shots from
the twelve-pounders shook the air in salute. The children
screamed and ran about laughing, falling. No one now from
the fort who had not left what he was doing to come and watch.

For a moment, glancing at the two ranks of sweaty,
grubby individuals making up his guard of honour, two or
three with jackets over bare chests, Sam hesitated and looked
back. Down at the beach more canoes were arriving. Matonabbee was making a great show of directing the unloading. Sam
took a deep breath and strode forward. Several men reached
out to pat him on the back.

Governor Norton stood at the far end dead centre of the gate, his hand tucked in the opening of his coat. Beside him stood one of his daughters in European dress. His wife Nêwositêkâpaw and one or two other women and younger children a little distance behind him.

—Welcome back, Mr. Hearne.

—Thank you, sir. Sam shook hands and waved to some children who had climbed up on the ramparts.

—Nineteen months, eh?

—One year, six months, and twenty-three days by my reckoning, sir.

It was innocent enough, this admission of his day-by-day existence, but its precision, or perhaps the cultured tone of Hearne's delivery, rubbed some sore place in Norton.

—Either way you seem not to have hurried.

Whether it was a joke or no, Sam laughed. He could not seem to stop. Moses Norton looked faintly irritated, even affronted. He would have liked to issue a reprimand. There was something about such uncontained laughter that called for one. And now they were all at it, though what was amusing Norton would never know.

Joseph Hansom, the governor's own servant, broke rank and stepped forward.

—Welcome home, sir.

—Thank you, Joseph. Thank you.

Sam smiled at the governor's daughter, unsure which it was.

—Miss Norton. And towards the women standing farther off, Nêwositêkâpaw. Miss Molly.

Nêwositêkâpaw nodded. She was clearly amused. She folded her arms across her comfortable belly and waited to see what was next.

Moses Norton raised his arm and put it on his daughter's shoulder.

—This is Molly here. My Molly.

—Of course. Sam inclined his head to the girl a second time. A stupid mistake. Of course this was the younger daughter beside her father. Grown he saw now, though she cradled a small fox cub, its face painted an astonishing red. And that in all likelihood was a cousin over there with the mother. And the eldest girl wasn't with them at all. A pity. He'd had not a few thoughts about Jane as they drew nearer home.

—You'll have a great deal to report, I'm sure, Mr. Hearne, but we'll hear it in due course. Meanwhile get yourself looking like a respectable Company servant again, man.

—Do I lodge with the tradesmen still, sir?

—Officers' quarters. Hansom will see what you need. You can take Mr. Hearne along now. He might lose his way without his famous leader, what do you say?

Hansom wondered why the governor thought a man so emaciated, so worn and with his face bitten half to pieces by the black fly was a suitable target for his sour humour.

—Officers' mess, this evening, said Norton. My quarters in two hours.

A GUARD OF HONOUR. The last time he had seen two such lines formed had been nine hundred miles away. A gauntlet. Some of the Wêcîpwayânak had been out on mischief and returned with prisoners. Every member of the camp drawn up in two close lines to receive the captives, the future slaves. To make them pay for the privilege of their lives. Three women, three children, and two young men. Taking the gauntlet at a run, their backs bowed, their heads protected with their tied hands while blows from enemy hands and from sticks and clubs rained on them without restraint. One of the children, a boy, stumbling, losing momentum. The whirling sticks merciless. And Matonabbee stepping forward out of the beating line, grabbing the boy by one hand and lifting him, taking giant strides between the batting, thwacking walls. The boy had clung on with both hands, his feet swinging clear of the ground. It had made Sam laugh aloud with jubilation, his voice lost among the wild yells. Matonabbee a redeeming angel. As he had first appeared to him. Matonabbee who could be the very devil.

He closed his eyes. The land they had crossed loomed again behind his eyelids. He saw it as clearly as if it were etched on them. Step after step after step without end. Three thousand miles, he'd calculated. To the Northern Sea and back. The ground under his feet never still, unrolling like a patterned carpet before his eyes. Every kind of terrain, every season in succession, as if he stood still and the world turned under his feet. Rubbled boulder, frost-heaved talus, ice ridged hard as rock, drifted snow, old ice under water ankle deep, treacherous marl and water-logged sedge. He walked over low stone outcrops tapestried with silver and olive lichen, now with magenta and yellow. Under his feet now spongy thick green moss, now tough springy willow to snare them.

Now his eyes blinded by snow in every direction, the tug of snowshoes at every step, the contours of land vanished in a trick of light.

He woke to a face he did not recognize telling him the governor was waiting. He had not meant to sleep at all, only to sit momentarily on the edge of his bed while he looked over the equipment and belongings that Hansom had carried in. His gun and ammunition pouch, the quadrant, the sextant. His fire tackle and his hooks and line. His game bag like a rag picker's sack full of the empty skins of small birds and mammals. His satchel containing his journal wrapped in oilskin, and the survey book and the maps he had made, the small book of drawings, his pencils, the Company's timekeeper and compass, the thermometer, his three knives in the moosehide sheaths his first woman had made. The heavy moose bedskin he had longed to discard on the return leg and had been grateful of only two weeks ago, when a sudden flight of snow turned the country back to winter. The razor and soap and comb he had requested. The bag of rock samples that had caused such conflict he had had to carry it himself. All had tilted as he gazed until the softness of his mattress, the goose feather pillow for his head had claimed him. And then he was back out there. Carried off on the feathers of a goose. The way to travel.

—ALTOGETHER A SORRY disappointment, I have to say.

Norton blew his pipe smoke into the parrot's cage to watch the bird blink. It obligingly called *Fire!*

—With all due—

—No passage and no copper.

—But respectfully, sir, no failure. He left it at that, preferring to savour the governor's French brandy, but Norton picked it up at once.

—How so, Hearne?

So. He swallowed. The brandy warm, fortifying. But he must after all think abstractions. Ideas unrelated to the body's dictates. Englishmen's ideas. He had almost forgotten how.

Norton settled himself at the table and leaned back in his chair.

—What the journey accomplished, Governor, is confirmation. Affirmation. I have travelled the entire length of the Coppermine River. It is unnavigable. I have traversed all the country to the east and discovered no connection with the bay. There is no navigable passage to the northwest from Hudson Bay. The results of my exploration are beyond dispute. The question can now be laid to rest.

—As may be. But nineteen salaried months, nevertheless . . .

—And I can give equal assurance that no copper of any quantity is to be found in that direction. In ascertaining this fact beyond any doubt, I have saved the Company inestimable time and expenditure. It was an argument Sam had rehearsed more than once when only curlew and plover were within earshot.

—Pure conjecture. We have no way of knowing what the committee has in mind for future explorations. What we do know is that after nineteen—

—Almost nineteen.

—Mr. Hearne, if you're after precision perhaps you'd care to include the two previous expeditions—salaried expeditions—those you cut short prematurely. Or perhaps you would not. I repeat, after nineteen salaried months we still have nothing to show them as financed your enterprise.

An end then to *due respect* and *by your leave*. This seemed to be a squabble.

—But it was not I who promised we would.

Without speaking, Norton hooked the brandy bottle to himself and filled his cup.

—And it was, Governor, their enterprise, not mine. He did not go so far as to say *your*. I challenge any man to accomplish the same in the same short time.

Norton swigged at his cup and refilled it. Brandy dripped from his chin. Nêwositêkâpaw got up from where she had been sitting on the floor watching them and went to his side. He shoved her away with his elbow, spilling more.

—The fact remains, I sent you on a mission and you have precious little to show for it.

—That is your opinion, sir. May I?

Sam held out his cup. He was in danger of having the brandy delivered to his face. Norton's wife came to his rescue, reaching the bottle first and carrying it round to Sam. She filled his glass, clearly used to performing the service. Norton seemed to observe and to thwart convention as it suited him. Sam looked up.

—Thank you.

Nêwositêkâpaw acknowledged him with a quick glance. He found her face hard to read, expected to see there the traces of her life with this difficult man. But the lines at the corners of her mouth were imprinted by laughter, not tribulation.

—You had another daughter, Nêwositêkâpaw. Where is she?

—She is older now. Her eyes flicked a glance towards Norton.

He folded his arms across his chest and cocked his head.

—Of course, said Sam.

—By one year, six months, and twenty-three days, said Norton.

OUTSIDE THE WALLS that night, Matonabbee's companions celebrated their arrival by consuming every last morsel of food in their possession, every last drop of rum that had been sent out to them. Matonabbee was careful to keep his wits about him. Though tonight was Sam's affair, he intended to enter the fort in style and reap his own share of credit the next day.

Inside, in the officers' mess, the atmosphere was congenial, the conversation affable and still coherent. So much tobacco smoke hung in the air that the door could be left open without fear of mosquitos coming to feast on the feasters. Who also would be neither hungry nor thirsty. Leask had seen that full rundlets of brandy and rum and port stood ready for refilling the decanters.

At the prospect of five courses ending with a glass of Madeira to accompany Jimmy Frost's special custard, Norton was in better humour. He was prepared to listen agreeably to Hearne's tales, prompt him to enlarge on them. Above everything else he seemed to want news of Matonabbee: the number of women he travelled with, the provisions he supplied, his exactitude in navigation, his skill in managing his followers.

—And in general he cared for you well?

—In general, yes.

—Was he lacking?

—No, indeed not. Only . . .

—Yes?

—I don't quite know how to begin.

—Come on, man.

—We encountered some Esquimaux, sir, when we were quite near the mouth of the Coppermine.

—Ah. No love lost there.

—Indeed not.

—So what did he do?

—He attacked them.

—He would. What then?

Every face was turned in his direction, heads tilted, eyebrows lifted. All of them—Norton, Purvis, Johnston, Leask—like men enchanted. Leask had his fork halfway to his mouth. Only Johnston, the sloopmaster, broke the spell and went on with his meal. He kept his eyes down. He was eating unnaturally, as if it was particularly important that he deliver the food to his stomach before the details of the story reach his ears. But Sam was not about to give the details.

—Many were killed. I have no wish to dwell on it. It was an unfortunate incident, an unhappy time.

—How many?

—I have no idea.

—Were you there?

—Yes, sir.

—Did you have your eyes closed?

Purvis shot a glance at Norton and back at Hearne. Leask scratched the back of his head as if he had a sudden attack of lice. He gave it all his concentration.

—As I said, I have no wish to dwell on that unhappy time.

—Well, but what can you say about it? In truth? Matonabbee is a savage, will never be more. And as for the Esquimaux, they bring it on themselves, poor blighters.

—Those I meet are peaceful enough, said the captain. You have these two boys here without any trouble.

—They're children, said Purvis. Brought down from Marble Island while you were gone, Mr. Hearne.

Sam too had brought boys down in the sloop, the year after he arrived at the fort. Only one survived. He did not want to think about any of this. His first sight of the people had taken him by surprise that year. The tales he had heard back at the factory had led him to believe them fierce beyond imagining. He was more nervous as they sailed north than when he was a lad sailing to meet the French. He had not imagined the Esquimaux so soft in manner, had never pictured them smiling.

—Get one of them in here. Norton jerked his head in the direction of the Company servant attending them.

And what an easy thing it had been to procure the boys. Some bartering on Captain Johnston's part, the gift of a gun, some ironwork. The boys had remained smiling until the *Churchill* cast off, and then they had wept freely. A place was made for them to sleep on deck. They sat all night back to back, their eyes open.

—Which one, sir?

—The young one. He's quick as a fish.

His heart lurched. He put down his knife.

—The rockfish is extraordinary.

—It is. And a rarity. You can thank the good doctor here. Mr. Purvis. He's the man for delicacies.

They raised their glasses.

—The doctor!

—The fisherman!

The heavy platter was pushed across to Sam.

—But no, thank you. I've had quite my fill.

In fact the rockfish seemed to him to be flopping at the back of his throat. He pushed his chair back.

—If you'll excuse me. Governor. Gentlemen.

—No, wait, Hearne. You've not seen this lad.

The serving man came back with a small lad following. He was about the age of the boy who had sickened and died. Sam did not want this memory to compound the other. Did not want any of this. Children killed alongside the women and the men in Matonabbee's raid. Mercy nowhere to be seen. The boy had a face round as the sun and did not stop smiling.

—Come here, boy.

The child went to stand at Governor Norton's side. Norton put his arm round his waist. He pointed to items on the table and said their names. The boy, who was being trained as an interpreter, repeated them. Norton pointed again, but this time without speaking, and the boy, without hesitating, again said their names, missing none.

—Any object you like, said Norton. He'll not only say it, he'll never forget it.

When they had run out of examples Norton started on his face, pointing to his nose and ears, moving on to his body parts. The laughter was loud. The boy laughed along.

SAMUEL HEARNE HAD eaten too much and drunk more than enough but he lay without sleeping, his waking mind supplying the details he feared from his dreams. The boy, small like the one at Norton's side, running unnoticed, almost away until he was struck down with a spear. Getting up and running on, the spear waving from his back until he fell and disappeared under the frenzied stabbing of his assailants. The woman clinging to Matonabbee's arm even as his men thrust spears into her and thrust them again. Matonabbee's face turning to seek more victims. And himself. Crouched like a coward behind a rock, unable to move, though inside, he, Samuel, convulsed in denial and scrambled to escape his very skin, frantic to not be there, to not be in that place, to see nothing more. Only he crouched there still and he watched. He saw everything. The old man stabbed in the face. The infant dashed against a rock. And his eyes had not the power to close but devoured all. And now all was inside him forever.

THE FOLLOWING DAY, Norton invited Matonabbee to dine. Matonabbee sent a youth to ask for his coat and hat and sash from the trading room.

Molly was in the compound with her cousins when he arrived that evening dressed in regimental finery, yellow and red goose feathers in his hat and a silver gorget gleaming on his breast. The children ran to him and he lifted them in turn and swung them round, making them squeal in delight.

Samuel Hearne watched. When it was Molly's turn she smiled and let herself be lifted, but she turned in silence, her long legs swinging out from Matonabbee's body, catching the evening light.

He walked over and the children went back to their game of corralling a flurry of goslings with their legs. Molly followed them. Matonabbee clapped him on the shoulder.

—Full bellies tonight.

—For you, said Sam. My belly was filled last night. I shall not eat much.

—A jest?

—No. True.

—Did you feast with a woman?

Sam laughed.

—I finished with a good night's sleep. And no dreams.

—You will starve and wither with no dreams. The same as with no women.

—Not for a while yet, I hope.

They went in to the mess together. Matonabbee as at ease as if he were at home. Which in a manner of speaking he was. He greeted the officers with an easy dignity and they responded as if he were an old friend. A glass of shrub was placed in his hand but he drank very little, knowing there was better liquor to come.

When the governor came in Matonabbee put down his glass and embraced him theatrically. Norton looked like a man trying to keep his head above water.

—On my right, he said. Place of honour. Hearne, you can take the end.

Matonabbee, unable to fathom the complicated politics between the two men, waited for laughter. Instead Sam went meekly to his allotted place.

—And in your honour, sir. Norton turned to Matonabbee again. We have . . .

He paused.

—Haggis!

Haggis was Norton's choice. It was the closest equivalent to a dish prepared by the Northern women and he was sure it would please. And ten years in the trading room had taught him that nothing established superiority more effectively than a gift well chosen.

The officers raised their glasses to toast the haggis as they—for there were several—were carried in. Matonabbee said he considered this manner of acknowledging the caribou, who had reliably and obediently surrendered their stomachs, to be much better than the usual custom of addressing the ever-capricious One Above.

When the haggis was served, Sam noted that Matonabbee watched for the merest fraction of a second to see how it was attacked before he followed suit. Biting in, even Sam knew it would not equal the fragrant delights of the authentic dish, cooked by hanging all day over a fire carefully tended by a wife, seasoned with smoke and love. Matonabbee gallantly declared it the best he had ever tasted. The men raised their glasses again.

Throughout the meal Matonabbee answered the officers' questions, obligingly giving his opinion on everything from the severity of the past winter to the productivity of the beaver, the quality of the Pedlars' goods, the navigability of the Coppermine, and the severity of the winter to come.

—And the Esquimaux? It was Matonabbee himself who asked the question. You do not want to know why I walked so far to kill them?

His words resounded in the silence like the booming of distant ice.

—I have my people to care for. When my people fall sick and die for no reason at all, it is the work of our enemies to the north. In the winter before the last just gone, six of my own family died, falling to their knees from where they stood and dead within two days. My own aunt who raised me and loved me and five of her family. There is no sickness in the world that does this thing. It was the work of our enemies and they could strike again with their conjuring. That was why I walked to seek them out. No leader would do less.

—Or no savage. Norton's laugh was solitary.

Dr. Purvis coughed. If your people fall sick another time, sir, could you bring them to the fort? We have medicines that can help.

—We are too far.

—Perhaps . . .

—A Wêcîpwayân man—a brother-in-law of mine—
traded for a bag of medicine. It contained the dried fruits and
pieces of bark that you stir in to your porridge.

—Then he must have been a scoundrel, said Norton.

Matonabbee withheld his opinion.

—There is much more that we have, said Purvis.

—And we too. But against conjuring there is no medicine.

—Tell them, said Sam, hoping to break the atmosphere,
how you healed your wife's foot.

—It was swollen. Huge. I made a small cut in the skin.
Here. He took off his moccasin to demonstrate. The width of
my thumb. And I lifted the vein and drew the knife along it
gently. So.

And though Norton had suddenly acquired a thunderous scowl, Purvis and Matonabbee engaged happily in a comparison of the techniques of venous scarification.

By the time the pudding arrived—plum pudding, again
for its certainty to please—Matonabbee had had the opportunity to ask some questions of his own, the real advantage of
dining with the English. But tonight, whether the liquor had
a soporific effect or the men were being evasive, the answers
to his questions—In what ways does your Supreme Being
intervene to help you? How do you know? How can he help
your families in England so far away and help you at the same
time? Is the king a good man? How do you know?—provided little enlightenment.

When the port arrived, Moses Norton rose from his
chair saying he would have it served in his quarters.

—You and I together, he said to Matonabbee. Good night, gentlemen.

Matonabbee rose to follow but went first to each man to bid good night before he left.

—And you also, he said to Sam.

—No. I have told my stories. Now the governor will hear yours.

—But I shall ask him. You are like my nephew. My son.

—I think it's better if you don't ask him. Better for me.

—The governor is going to ask me to speak about you.

The man's astuteness never ceased to amaze. Sam had the feeling that he was in a hopeless situation regarding the governor's opinion. Whether Matonabbee's reports were good or bad, Norton would continue to nurse his hostility. Such a man always begrudged another's praise.

He listened warily the next day when Matonabbee recounted the number of glasses of port that had been consumed. He said he had spoken highly of his skills to his brother the governor. He said he had told him that Samuel Hearne was not the helpless child he, Matonabbee, had rescued two years ago. He said he had told him that Samuel Hearne was now a man. That he could take care of himself. And of a family too. That he would provide well for any wife. That it was time he had his own wife. That the governor should consider giving him his young daughter. My own niece Molly, said Matonabbee. The one Moses calls his apple dumpling.

Sam smiled and thanked him, now quite certain that the governor would do no such thing. He said he would not take a girl so young yet.

—Then you'll have to go on borrowing the wives of others. Like my brother. And he laughed his stupendous, rolling laugh.

I HAVE TRIED to understand how our lives that seem so brief that end so soon can linger. Are they as dreams that in the telling snake out and extend? So that of our lives even the smallest segment takes yet another lifetime to relive to remember? Sometimes the moment is so small it barely exists yet while seasons roll away from me I can breathe again its whole length. I can stand again in the light of his fleeting glance the year he returned from his journey. A glance so fleeting it fell on me like spring snow through sunlight mysterious and weightless. And I not knowing whether it touched me but feeling changed—never to return to the body I stood in a moment before.

No one saw the change. All about me were as before. My father my mother Mr. Purvis and Mr. Hansom all of them. And Samuel too with his face still bony from hunger his eyes ringed with travelling and red. Only I knew and the moment of my knowing was as a life in its entirety complete in itself.

In the days that followed I watched for Mr. Hearne wanting the light of the soft snow to fall on me again. Not knowing how to call it down. Sometimes the snow-light fell whether I willed it or no. It melted on my skin and I inside melted even after he had walked away.

Seeing once the heat of my skin my aunt laughed and said a Company man for you too then?

I hear the words again and what has been is one with what is and what is to come. Moments return to hang like stars in the sky forever. Like promises they shine there. I see his face when he brought me two fox kits. He gave them to me when I was alone. Two fox kits plump and heavy after my own ran away. He unrolled them from his jacket. Their fur was pale yellow. Paler than his hair. It was like the time of the Frost Moon—*ihkopiwi-pîsim*—when the sun is veiled by cloud. And they were warm. Their tongues warm and quick. They curled themselves into a ball together and rolled on the ground as one. I had not heard a man laugh as softly.

These are the moments I summon when the pull of the long journey abates.

Often I summon his voice. Kind as a woman's. Quiet. A voice to enrage my father.

—Molly? My name on his tongue like cool water over warmed stone. Molly?

My father's voice like hard rain hissing.

—Mr. Hearne. If you have time for idle gossip I suggest you send yourself to the wood and help them there before we all starve for want of fuel for the cook's fires.

I summon his face his eyes. He showed me small creatures he had captured. Dead things he had found. Feathers. Snakeskins. Eggs. Nests. And he showed me how he laid their likeness on the pages of his books each small book its own world with its creatures walking through it or lying on the ground gazing back at me as I gazed at them. Samuel's own eyes watching all of it. Smiling.

And he made promises. He promised to take me on the sloop. I mistook his meaning being not yet grown. I thought that he would take me voyaging across the sea. He said perhaps that too. Perhaps in time that too. Eyes as constant as stars.

—

IT DID NOT take long for Samuel Hearne to see that life at the fort was increasingly disjointed under Norton's double standard. The governor was more unpredictable and choleric than ever. He could spend the night sequestered in his apartments with up to five or six of the women and in the morning, bleary eyed and foul of mouth, flog a man for scaling the walls to find himself a companion. He favoured birch rods for the men who contravened Company rules. Six for visiting outside the walls at night. A dozen for bringing a woman within. He was threatening to hang poor Thomas Kelsey for the theft of a goose and he had three men on the list for return to England, two for habitual inebriation interfering with their duties and one for theft. The thief would be saying goodbye to the wife and child he happily provided for from his small allowance. Two weeks before the ship was due Norton had the entire fort searched for hidden furs, his own quarters suddenly beyond bounds to every man.

Sam had written to London the year he embarked on his journey and was hopeful of receiving news of a change of posting when the ship came in. It could not come soon enough. Meanwhile, there was the sloop to make ready for her summer run. Though Norton had ordered him to get a full report ready in time to send back to London, he did not seem inclined to free him from regular duty. Sam was forced to snatch spare moments at the end of the day to do a little more work on the log he had kept of his journey. Seated at one of the long tables in the mess, with a new leatherbound book that would go to London along with his maps, he carefully transcribed the pencil notes from his log, entering them word for word in ink. The books he had taken with him were soiled and worn. In some places the pencil had rubbed almost away and the words were faint as ghosts. But he could remember. He had a fair copy completed in time for the ship though there was not time to attempt drawings from the rough sketches he had made in the field. It was a bald account of his movements, a rough survey of the land they had traversed from the coast to the mouth of the Coppermine River. In the winter when he had more time he would make another copy, one that might interest the general reader and tell more about this country so remote and interesting.

When ship time arrived, the discipline Norton imposed on the men was suddenly tighter than ever, the governor more despotic. He made it known that any man late to his duty when the bell was rung would forfeit his next meal. His family mysteriously dwindled to one respectable wife and daughter—Nêwositêkâpaw and her daughter Molly. The rest were somehow spirited away, perhaps back to former husbands. With the other women and children absent, Molly—Norton's darling—was now conspicuous about the fort. Sam seemed to meet her at every turn—and wished he didn't. She drew his gaze with her ungainly body reaching for womanhood. Inevitably the governor would round a corner, tell him to get his loitering body back to work. And his eyes.

The correspondence from London was a disappointment. Captain Richards brought no answer for him. Norton informed him he would be appointed to the new brig, the *Charlotte II*, under Captain Johnston for the remainder of the summer. They were to go after black whale. He knew well enough it was not what he wanted for himself. It was almost, Sam thought, as if Norton relished thwarting a man's ambition. Since he had returned with Matonabbee, his very presence seemed to provoke the governor to a tooth-grinding irritation. He began to think he was safer expressing no opinion at all. He did not want to find himself consigned to the fishery for life. When he was a lad the lure of the sea had been its promise of freedom. Experience had taught him better. A man aboard ship could glimpse freedom but never taste it. The captain held every man in fief, and the vessel held dominion over all. It was not unlike life at Norton's fort.

The work aboard the *Charlotte II* was unproductive. The whales they encountered were plentiful enough but chasing them down was another matter altogether, and the harpooners returned again and again without success. The captain's log was a veritable litany of loss. The *Charlotte II* was already bound for home when finally a harpoon drove into the streaming side of a black whale. They towed it back to the river, its blood marbling their wake, the gulls screaming overhead. Sam knew that the life of the sea was no longer his life. It was days spent in backbreaking work, nights exhausted in a drifting, tossing coffin. And for what? A few tuns of oil to light the nights of the very men paid to obtain it. In some way that he had not yet fathomed, he sensed some paradoxical link between purpose and freedom. On his journey he had lain on the land like any other of its creatures and now, short of breathing the stars at night, nothing could match it. Still he carried out his duties, resigned to waiting another year for change.

When the brig, returning, came in sight of the fort, Sam could see from her decks that Matonabbee had already left for the winter. The absence of his tent left Sam ridiculously, absurdly stricken. He had imagined Matonabbee would be glad to see the *Charlotte II* coming in. He had imagined a long smoke and tales of the hunt. He had imagined above all that when Matonabbee was ready to leave, they would bid each other a warm and heartfelt farewell. Until next year. Wish each other good fortune. Good hunting. Three and half thousand miles together. That was not nothing. And everything they had been through. And the long talks they had had. He was more than a paid guide, surely. He was his travelling companion, his comrade. Sam had a powerful longing to be once more stepping out in his track into the coming winter. Instead he gave Johnston's command to heave to. His voice was unsteady.

Over several weeks the heap of chores diminished. They butchered the whale and rendered the oil on the beach. They floated the *Charlotte* on a returning tide to her winter haven in the cove and set about putting her up. The weather was coming on fast with every day some new foretaste of winter thrown their way—freezing fog, frost, ice, snow—or suddenly revoked for sun again. The waters of the bay began to lose their lustre as the surface assumed the blear and smear of new ice. Sam and Captain Johnston carried their bedding back from the cove. Sam walked out each day to check on the men who had work still to finish. And walking was good. No one could have told him this when, foot foundered, he struggled to move his body in the tracks of Matonabbee.

Now it was almost nourishment. He walked the three miles slowly and came to know each rock and tussock along the trail. Every day different from the last. Every evening different from the morning. The light a blessing every time. It was on the land, away from the ship, away from the fort, that Sam felt most himself. Life his own, not subject to the whim of any master. No Norton, no Johnston. Nature the only potentate. The support of life the only duty. Whaling. He did not remember ever having contracted to serve as a fisherman.

By Christmas he was wondering how he would get through the winter. The long hours of darkness were more oppressive within the fort than out in open country. There the black sky was netted by glittering stars and their light fell on the brilliant snow and all was resplendent. The lovely moon. The splendid glowing curtain of the aurora rippling with its winds of light. In the depths of the country the night was not dark at all. Inside the fort the dark prevailed, candles and lamps—unless you were the governor and lived like King Louis—a poor assault on its smoky density, its suffocating gloom.

As the days shortened to mere hours Governor Norton spent more and more time in seclusion. No one knew quite how many were living in his apartments. They had their infants with them, their young girls. They had their work in there too. They would go back and forth for skins or for new birch wood for the snowshoes. If by chance the door was left ajar, a man passing by might see a woman sitting on the floor, quietly sewing. And he might see others slumped, sleeping, the smell of brandy and malt as strong as that from any inn.

The governor himself sometimes did not appear until past noon and regularly retired early. Leask did his best to establish order, but he lacked the governor's ferocious temper. The rowdiness from the servants' mess increased. Sam paid the carpenter two pounds of tobacco to make him a chair and a small desk so that he could continue work on his notebooks and his drawings in the evenings. There was barely space for them in his small room. Working there was almost as cold as outside and certainly darker.

ON THE LAST NIGHT of the year Sam sits at his new writing desk staring at the account of his journey with Matonabbee. Though he can hear the fiddle and the pipes he has no particular wish to go down to the servants' mess where the men's revelries will be marred ultimately by their excesses, and though he likes his fellow officers he certainly does not want to spend the evening in company with Norton and his particular brand of excess. But he cannot settle to his journey tonight. He has worked hard at it, carefully transcribing his hastily pencilled field notes into the new book obtained on account from the stores. He writes in ink, his pen drawing long elegantly sloping letters, artful curls for the capitals. He has been writing more and more slowly. He is not in a hurry. He knows what is coming. When he gets to the place where the Esquimaux were encamped on the river, he stops. He can neither skip over the incident as he did in the brief record he sent back with the ship, nor write it out. He hesitates, blots the dry page for the tenth time. However many times he reaches for his ink he stops. He cannot get past it. On his map he has named the place Bloody Fall.

Perhaps for no other reason than to keep from going there again, he gets up and reaches for a leather wallet on a shelf over his bed. He keeps a few papers in it and a small notebook covered in moleskin cloth. The last night of the year is a good time for reminiscence. He brought the book out with him from England and began it when he first arrived at the factory as mate of the *Churchill*. The ink has bled slightly into the flock of the cover where he made the careful inscription "Prince of Wales's Fort 1766." The first two pages are missing. They were written in the shadow of the dismay he felt at meeting his new employer and he tore them out soon after and fed them to the stove. He can remember the sense of scandal induced in him by the governor's lifestyle—*the lap of luxury*—his shock at seeing costly indulgences shipped to this remote outpost. *His apartments in the factory display more elegance than any man in these parts could reasonably expect.* Turkey carpets, looking glasses, twenty-four-candle lamps, and silver and porcelain dishes for his table. A parrot, no less! And Norton himself playing the prince. How the man swaggered about the place *like a lord—a drunken lord—as the hour advances.*

But the whole place had presented a conundrum. The building had every appearance of a military stronghold, the massive walls and the wide ramparts, the parapets pierced all along with gun embrasures. A ravelin like a stone shield protected the gates, yet there was not a redcoat to be seen behind them. The men, he noticed straight away, the officers included, went about in moccasins and they rarely wore stockings with their English breeches. Some wore linen shirts; others went shirtless or sported soft leather waistcoats, long and laced together at the front. As the weather deteriorated they turned more and more to their deerskin breeches and jerkins, moose-hide coats and great beaver toggies with long sleeves and hoods that the women had made for them—women who put on woollen blankets from Scotland as the winds increased. Governor Norton was the exception. Though all the world knew that Indian blood fed his dark complexion, Norton stub-bornly persevered in his English coat and breeches, never appearing without a respectable if somewhat soiled suit of clothes beneath his beaver coat, or without his wide-brimmed hat jammed on top of a yellowed wig at least twenty years out of style. So here then were the Company servants dressed like Southern Indians—excepting the governor, who was one—while a good number of the Southern men, at least until the weather defeated them, persisted in their serge jackets and fancy hats and gold braid, deerskin stockings on their legs and moccasins on their feet, looking for all the world like play-ers in a pantomime. But there was more. The governor in his shiny boots, his yellow waistcoat, and his long narrow coat surrounded himself night and day with women of the coun-try, dressed beneath their blankets, as they might be for their own men, in beaded buckskin gowns. Yet he decked his eldest daughter, Jane—though she was as like a Southern Indian as any Sam had seen, with hair like a black serpent at rest on her shoulder—in all the finery of England. *This young woman swims about all day in a voluminous dress of green silk amply buoyed with petticoats that fall from a hoop fixed just below her waist and that hamper her wherever she goes.* She wore a jacket, he remembers, of green satin and over it a folded square of printed cambric—which, Sam could not help thinking, must do little to keep out the cold—crossed and tied at the waist. True to the topsy-turvy nature of the place, this fancied European was barefoot the first time he saw her. He noted her often. Three months later she was in moccasins and leggings and half-hidden in a beaver cloak against the cold.

His observations if he remembers them rightly could have issued from the lips of a governess. *Norton seems ready to prove every scurrilous rumour and every scrap of wretched gossip true.* Surrounded by women, the governor lived a life contrary to everything Sam had been led to believe was permitted by the Company. And only Norton. They had walked out that first fall to see the hunters try for bears that were about on the other side of the river. Norton with a spyglass, his family behind him. He can remember saying to him, You have a fine entourage. Norton drawing a deep breath and pushing his finger ends in behind his belt.

—That I do, he said. That I do.

And when he asked if they accompanied him wherever he went, Aye. Me and no man else. How he broke into a laugh and clapped him on the back. It was the menace of that laugh that had sent Sam back to tear out the damning pages. Norton and his family never appear again.

The eleventh day of August. More geese together in one flock than ever I have seen. They turned the sky dark and we had to shout to make ourselves heard. The nineteenth day of October. Took a turn in new snowshoes and find them easier than first thought. The sixth day of December. Cold so severe that breath crackles in front of the face. He volunteered for hunting or wooding parties as often as he could. He had never experienced anything as exhilarating as the open country of this place and the wealth of natural life within it, above it. His first purchase was a serviceable gun, and on Sundays he would go out hunting for himself, bribing one of the hunters out of his snug home, away from the warm bodies of his wives and children, taking him along to learn from him the secret paths of this wilderness. Walking against the knife edge of the wind, Sam would barely notice the hunter ahead of him, the hunter grumpy because didn't this English boy understand—he said it in his own language—the ptarmigan would not be feeding today, the hares would be under the snow? But hunting was not the point. The point was observation. Every feature of this limitless expanse, every wrinkle of this new world. Stopping to dig under the snow to discover the nature of some twisted twigs poking through, he would hear his companion sigh and repeat—not having said it for quite a while—that the hares would all be under the snow.

Sam learned in that first winter that time never passed more pleasantly for him than when he felt himself alone on the turning surface of the world. He asked a Homeguard woman, dead now, to teach him how to set snares, and this he liked even better than shooting. As if the land itself silently presented him with a gift. Yielded it of its own volition. Time expanded in walking, in observing. He was bearing witness to the vast strangeness of the land and its minute and wonderful details, the rime furring every blade of sedge beside the river, thickening every twig until a scrub willow became a bush of crystal thorns. *The fourteenth day of December. Passed a frozen pond today, its sheet of ice broken into the hundred diamonds of a snake's skin.* Sometimes he forgot to hunt at all. His day's production was often dismally scant but he learned too that if he stopped to converse with the Homeguard, especially if his pouch contained a few desirable items—a pair of scissors, a few needles—he could easily supplement what he brought back to the fort and make his time seem well employed.

In the evenings he would sit at one of the tables in the servants' mess and record what he had seen, an otter with a silver back, the nest of a hair-tailed mouse, keenly aware that only his eyes—or at best his mother's or his uncle's—might ever read the entries. Sometimes to try to fix the details of the beast in memory he would make small drawings at the edges of the page. There was something not quite moral in such waste of knowledge. All through the fort men would be drinking, a few playing at cards, most of them sleeping. All these men labouring day after day, sleeping night after night, for what? To keep this great edifice of the factory standing—strengthen its roofs, clear its yards, repair its beds, its stoves. To keep its heart pumping—feed it, warm it. All these men. Sam saw it all with the naive clarity of the newcomer. The paradox was that without the fort they could be of direct service to the Company. They too could be out on the land, sustaining themselves as the Indians did while at the same time amassing returns for the ship in August. They could be learning from the Southern Indians where to find the best furs. Mapping the inland expanses as they went, the most useful rivers. They could be classifying the flora along the way, experimenting with its various uses and applications. They could be undertaking investigations on different materials, subjecting them to the lowest temperatures. There were no limits to his youthful ambition. Who knew what benefits might accrue to the Company over time, given the right men put to work in this way? Instead the men here spent the better part of their time in a round of self-perpetuating tasks in support of their own lives. It seemed to Sam a strange manner of furthering the interests of a company.

He remembers saying as much one day to Governor Norton. With all the lack of circumspection of his years, he shared his insight. He told the governor that the man will be remembered who adds to the collective storehouse of knowledge, not the man who advertises the greatest profit.

Governor Norton had never really forgiven him. He could see that now. It had put their transactions on a shaky footing from the beginning. Telling him that the discoveries of science would outlast the endeavours of commerce. The upstart, the newcomer telling the old hand, the native of the place, that the fruits of his labours were as sand to be washed away by time. The fort was Norton's principality. Trading was his life. He might as well have told a ruler not to believe in his realm, a priest not to believe in God. Perhaps Norton had sent him into the country three times in the hope that he wouldn't return. The illogical thought contains a crumb of credibility. How much more acceptable to the committee for a man to die in the line of duty than to fail. But now he is letting Norton's antipathy to him cloud his judgment.

He turns the page. *Anno Domini 1767.* He had been not

quite five months at the fort. *The first day of January. A match of ball was played on the plantation at midday, the governor having declared a holiday.* It tells nothing. The snowy playing field, the expanse of ground outside the gates—optimistically called *the plantation* by the Europeans and *home* by the Indians who erected their tents there—had been littered with bodies, many of them in women's dress. The surgeon not knowing who was most in need. The master of the *Churchill,* his makeshift bonnet under his chin like a bib, was on the ground clutching his eye; two of the labourers, though one was simply tangled in his skirts, declared they could not stand; the cooper's apprentice had a broken finger, and the carpenter's mate has been knocked senseless. And those were only the Europeans. Several good goose hunters and two of the best trappers were also down and moaning loudly. Governor Norton, furious at the incursions on the trade goods, was not in evidence. He had seen early in the proceedings how the rum had taken hold. Any order from him would have been roundly ignored even by his officers. Nor was there a way to countenance the foolery without participating—and he had not the confidence or the largeness of heart to willingly make himself a laughingstock. He had retired to his quarters, no doubt to drink his own rum.

Though he had wrenched his knee, Sam was conscious only of his ribs, sore with laughing. He had heard a great deal about this annual match but nothing about the attendant buffooning. The morning he remembers was fine with a hazy sun, perfect for sport once the customary rum rations had been distributed. Sam's team, led by Purvis, had been prompt to assemble, first to take possession of the leather ball and begin warming up among themselves. The opposing team, headed by Captain Robinson, was slow. No one knew what was taking them so long until a motley parade began to filter through the gates. From a distance they might, from their silhouettes in the watery sun, have been mistaken for women. Closer they were ghouls with rough stubble breaking out under bonnets and muscled shoulders straining beneath lace. It was the tailor, someone said, who had managed access to the trading goods, though later he denied it. One way or another whole lengths of red flannel had spirited themselves from the bales for trade and onto the paunches of the Orkneymen, where they were tied in place with lengths of gartering. Some of the flannel had been cut, and some worsted too, to make shawls to cover their shirts, and then it seems one thing had led to another and every man had a bountiful bosom. There was no stopping the flights of the imagination or the havoc wreaked in the stores. Laced hats intended for the Northern captains were bent into bonnets and tied under the chin with ribbons meant for the captains' wives. Special supplies of orris, the rich gold lace so loved by the Northerners, were now doing duty to ornament the shawls, and everywhere there were flounces and frills improvised from the sashes meant for the men who came to trade.

Norton had stared in disbelief at this assault on the Company's goods and properties. Sam could see his face working as he composed in his head the opening lines of his fulmination. And then he had turned on his heel.

The Homeguard too had stared incredulously and then had fallen to yelling with laughter and eventually to giving chase, their children running out to join them. Sam had noted with satisfaction that the opposing team was thoroughly winded before the game began. But all rules now were scrambled. It was a free-for-all, the outcome of nearly every manoeuvre determined by the exigencies of the dress. Casualties had never been so numerous, the surgeon said.

Sam can see now what he was too close to see that New Year's Day, lying on the snow in the aftermath of the battle, in the thick of the fallen field. How the game was a splendid illustration of all the routine vagaries of Rupert's Land. How, whatever is communicated in letters to London, the fort would always exist beyond the reach of any society save that which it created for itself.

After the January entry, he had barely kept up the journal. He flicks the pages over. The entries are sporadic, a line here or there. *The seventh day of February. Fourteen of us at wooding. The twelfth day of February. Currie's fingers amputated today.* Two pages all it takes to contain the passage of the year. Tucked in them, easy to miss, are the Esquimaux boys. It is as if his fingers delayed leading him to this page—where he knew all along he was heading. *Twenty-eighth day of July. Arrived safe at Ch. River at 9 o'clock this night with a good haul of skins and some oil and two Esquimaux boys to remain with us until next year.* And there, the following year, 1768, tucked in just as unobtrusively, the record of their fates. *Heard the geese return in the night. To Brigs Cove to free the shallop. The surviving Esquimaux boy put on board the* Charlotte *for return to Marble Island. Messrs. Wales and Dymond arrived on the* King George. *The Governor to England.* Nothing about the dead gaze in the surviving boy's eyes.

Nothing about how hard it was to learn the language from one who did not want to speak. His thoughts are dangerously close to the falls again and he has even less inclination to go down and join in the carousing.

The new year is marked clearly in his book. *Anno Domini 1769. The first day of January*. It begins with a list—a strange thirsty mix of ambition and impossible optimism, inspired by the presence of the two Royal Society men.

> 1. *Make full use of Messrs. Wales and Dymond.*
>   *Improve accuracy of navigational readings.*
> 2. *Learn the language of the Northern Indians.*
> 3. *Make a detailed map of the country N. S. and W.*
>   *of the fort.*
> 4. *Draw up a list of birds with their habits and*
>   *descriptions. Make drawings of the same.*
> 5. *List likewise all non-fur-bearing creatures.*
> 6. *Fish.*
> 7. *Study habits of the Northern Indians, their food,*
>   *their implements, their religion, if any.*

He was hoping at the time that the governor, on furlough in England, would obtain the committee's permission for an overland expedition—and that he would be selected to lead it. The two astronomers out from Edinburgh and waiting to observe a transit not due until June were generous with their time. The pages now are crammed with notes so tightly packed Sam can barely read them. He gets up and lights a third candle. The pages seem to vibrate with an energy of their own in the extra light. All winter there had been observations to make, new knowledge to acquire. Inside the circular observatory that housed Wales's refracting telescope, he had crouched for hours at the tiny shelf of a desk with permission to practise taking readings and making drawings. At night by candlelight he worked beside Mr. Wales and Mr. Dymond in the officers' mess. He learned from them how to achieve greater accuracy and make precise diagrams of the heavens. How to measure distances with greater accuracy. He copied their calculations. No one would be able to say he did not possess the skills for an overland journey.

Walking out on the still-frozen lakes and marshes, under starry skies that shone down on the sparest of features, he had tested his skill with the instruments and his memory of the tables, taming what other Englishmen saw as a wild expanse of snow where a man could lose himself, his life, perhaps obliterate his very soul, and making of it instead an accurate map of precise locations between which a civilized man could travel with ease. In the absence of any memory of the land, navigation was a fine way to assert mastery over it. Or so he believed, seeing the scientist as so much more subtle and sophisticated than the trader.

The third day of June. The Transit of Venus! He sees he has marked it an exclamation. He remembers clearly the excitement of that dawn. He followed Wales and Dymond out to the southeast bastion. The carpenter and the smith both arrived to check the bolts on the quadrant, the telescope, the drafting tables, and the great clock. Mr. Leask was out soon after to see that all was in order. He watched Leask pick out one of the smoked glasses from the box and ascertain that yes, indeed, there was nothing yet. It was a harsh wind and breakfast was a warming thought but he offered to stay on watch though Venus would not appear for hours. Wales's drawing paper, marked ready with a grid on which to plot the journey of the planet, was pinned firmly to the drafting table. The reflecting telescope was set so that the image of the sun at the appointed hour would be cast full on the grid. The door of the observatory would be closed and Wales would trace the trajectory of the planet across the image, timing its passage. From his work he would learn the exact distance of the sun from the point at which he made his drawing. With that reckoning in hand, a man could locate himself in all time, in all space. He could map the heavens. To work under the auspices of the Royal Society, with the full support of the king, the parliament! The work these men did would endure far longer than a beaver hat. A cold wind was nothing.

Alone in the observatory while the astronomers took their breakfast, he felt himself at one that day with a fraternity of scientists across the world, men engaged in pursuits altogether more worthy than those of a Company servant, a common merchant man. When the astronomers finished their breakfast and returned, his fantasy was at an end. He stood on the rampart in the afternoon with the rest of the men, each with his piece of smoked glass, gazing at the sun. A shout went up and then a cheer as a black dot appeared in the southwest quadrant. He imagined Wales and Dymond inside their observatory, concentrating on their drawings, though their hearts must have been pounding.

The journal entry, after recording that the observation was a success, goes on to note that Second Factor Leask distributed an extra ration of rum for every man in the factory. *The twenty-ninth day of July. The Governor returned from England. He has obtained permission for an overland journey to the North and brings me a letter from the Board of Governors. They have fixed upon me to conduct the journey and raise my wages to sixty pounds per annum for two years. I am in addition placed in Council at this Fort. Messrs. Wales and Dymond leaving on the* Prince Rupert *when she sails.*

Sam smiles to read words so cool and detached. The news when it came had ignited a fire in him and he could not wait to be gone. He felt then as he feels this year: he did not want to live another day under the same roof as Norton. The journal ends with his entry dated the fifth of November, 1769: *Preparations for my journey now complete. Wm. Isbester and Thos. Merriman to accompany me. We depart tomorrow in good hopes of success.*

There is no entry for the day he returned—to everyone's surprise—just five weeks later. Sam closes the journal—and on a second thought, opens it again. There are a few blank pages left. He turns to the first one and dips his pen. He considers. They must be close to midnight. The noise from the mess is very loud. The singing can barely be heard for the laughter and the shouting. There is a rhythmic thundering beneath it all and he guesses they must be dancing. He blots where the pen has dripped.

Anno Domini, he writes, *1773. The first day of January.*

1. Obtain another inland posting.

There is nothing more he wishes to write. He will tell the story of the intervening years in another book. All three journeys in one volume. With a survey of the land and its people. Its flora and fauna. It will be grand and it will be an honest, an enlightened account without judgment of any kind. It will include all that happened at the falls. It will begin with his first two journeys, his failed attempts. They will help his reader understand the measure of his final achievement. He knows now what he must do. Before he puts the leather wallet back above his bed he takes out a small slip of paper.

He will begin with that first ill-fated attempt in November 1769, when he, Samuel Hearne, unlearned everything he knew about navigation and woke up to his fellow man. He smooths out Norton's written instructions from three years ago. Tucked away in the wallet for the memory of the pride he felt at the time, they beckon now as if signalling him to begin. *To trace the Far-Off-Metal-River to its mouth, to determine there the latitude and longitude, to observe what mines are near the river, what water there is, the nature of the soil. To establish a friendship with the far-off natives, dissuade them from going to war with each other, encourage them to procure furs.* It all sounded so orderly, so easy, on paper. But words were not hostage to fortune in the way of deeds. It was a shambles. There was no other word for it. All his life he had taken orders and thought himself more than able, more than competent, yet when he found himself at the head of an expedition of His Majesty's Company of Adventurers events conspired to prove him otherwise and he found himself instead at the mercy of every misfortune. The sleds broke, the deer vanished, his ironwork and his ammunition were pilfered, and his guide, Chawchinahaw, appeared to have not the slightest intention or ability to take him to the Coppermine River. Navigation skills alone would not get him there. He knew that. Navigation could tell him in which direction he was walking. It could not tell him what obstacles lay in his path. Experience and memory were the only reliable guides, and the man who was leading him had neither. Two hundred miles from the fort he made the decision to turn back. Thomas Merriman could not have been happier. Merriman complained that his head ached blindingly. He had an ugly cold. The skin of his face was cracked, and his snot froze to his face.

Both Isbester and Merriman said, without conviction, that they would accompany him on a second attempt, but Sam could not believe that their hearts were in the enterprise. He would do better without them. He wondered too what rumours they had put about, for not another servant in the fort would contract to go. But he was not discouraged. He remembers how confident he was when Connêkwêse came forward. Connêkwêse had seemed like the man he needed. He was a Northern Indian. He knew the land. He promised he had been to the copper mines at the head of the river. He promised he could take him there. He and two of his companions knew the way. Sam agreed. He took on two Southern men as well. In the third week of February he was ready to leave. But when on the snowy morning of his departure he tried to share out the equipment, they laughed in his face. Women bore their burdens for them. Mr. Hearne should get himself some women.

He tried. He had almost settled a last-minute price with two sisters, handsome women he would have been glad of, when the governor put a stop to it. Norton sent the Indians out of hearing while he hissed and frothed.

—You have stepped beyond the bounds of your contract. There is no allowance for bearers. You will not—do you hear?—not under any circumstance remove a woman from this post where she is needed for other duties. Do you hear?

Sam could not fail to. The governor had him by the elbow and his yellow teeth, almost brown against the falling snow, were an inch from his ear.

Norton turned to Leask.

—Get those men down from there. He gestured to the men furiously digging to clear the guns.

He declared the cannon too deep in snow for a salute. The twenty or so Company men who had gathered to bid farewell were deprived of a show. They lifted their voices instead for three encouraging cheers as Samuel Hearne and his party passed through the gate. Outside, the Homeguard contributed their own shouts. The customary echo from the walls was deadened by the thickness of the snow.

THE EXPEDITION ITSELF lasted longer than the first, but it was not successful. Looking back on it, Sam can see that it was even more of a fiasco than before. He wonders if his guide knew all along that time was too short to reach their northern goal that summer. They wandered after deer for many months, wandered right into summer. All those aimless months they wandered the barren land after deer. No, Connêkwêse never meant to undertake the journey that year. His promise had not specified a time for completion of his part of the bargain. Still, they were a good way on and Sam was prepared to winter with them and make the journey when Connêkwêse thought fit. But the elements were not so accommodating. It was as if the wind had eyes and sought him out. Out of nowhere it sallied and toppled his quadrant, knocking it to the ground and breaking the glass and rendering it—and the whole expedition—useless. He could make no useful reports without the quadrant. If he believed in portents and omens . . . And yet how hard not to. From that moment the whole undertaking had unravelled. With some difficulty he had persuaded Connêkwêse to take him back. Not two hundred miles now but five hundred from the fort. Worse. He was robbed again. A small Northern party they met with connived and threatened until he and his two Southern companions were without proper clothing or tent or bedding or snowshoes. And nothing to trade for necessities. What good science and learning now? What good the highest fruits of civilization? There were others they met, many, with wives who might have helped him and his two companions. They had women with them. They could have sewn their winter clothing, offered their tent skins. But being plundered he had nothing to give in exchange and all had turned their backs, kicked up miniature storms as they tracked away on their snowshoes until there was no woman left at all in their party save the wife of Connêkwêse and she was resolute in her refusal. She had dressed her husband's furs and her own, her brother's too, sewn them into warm winter suits, but for him and his companions, without the wherewithal to work, she could do nothing. She wore snowshoes when Sam and his men had none, and she walked with her husband and his brother always ahead. They strode over the new snow as if it were a fine firm strand, pitched their small tent and slept soundly at night. Sam and his companions were without shelter in this land scraped bare by wind. They floundered on, many miles behind their guides. When they came up with the others each night, the family would already be asleep under their furs, snug in their tent. Sam shivered in the worn-out garments of summer. Not all the calculations and readings and tables in the starry heavens could ever transform his sleeping skins into a suit of clothes. He undid the bundle and tied the skins stinking and awkwardly slipping around his shoulders. With every step his thoughts lurched between the self-interest of his fellow man and his own lack of foresight. The only thing of which he was certain was that if—*if*—he got back, he would set out on a third attempt. He would not be written into the Company's records as a man who failed.

They were many weeks still from the fort when Matonabbee appeared, and if Sam had been at all religious he might have said like an archangel, out of the north. He came with his family and a great band of followers making their way to the fort with furs. Strange that it should have been at that very moment, the very nadir of his journey, that Matonabbee should enter his life, stepping into the desolate country of his doubt like a visitant from a world of ease beyond. Matonabbee greeted him—in English—with every courtesy, even as his eyes were registering that here was a man at the end of his road, still two months from the fort, clad in the raiments of summer—the rags of the raiments of summer—and with the harshest weather approaching like death itself from the dark of the year. With the utmost politeness he asked if it were their preference to dress in this fashion. And when Sam laughed—though he almost cried, sensing relief so close at hand—and said it was not, Matonabbee said simply, Come with me. Bring your furs.

Working together, Matonabbee's wives had already cleared the ground of snow where they would pitch his tent. They watched the approach of Sam and the two Southern men, sensed at once extra labour walking their way on six legs. These men need winter suits, said Matonabbee. He dropped the furs in the centre of the cleared circle, stopped Sam as he was taking his skins from his shoulders, said, Keep those. One of the wives came forward and lined up the three men by size. She took a length of hide from her waist and held it against Sam's outstretched arm, made a knot at the tips of his fingers. She looked at them all again, then went back to work on the tent.

—You have snowshoes? said Matonabbee. Sam felt like a schoolboy who has lost his pencil. Matonabbee said it was a difficulty. There were no suitable trees on the way to the fort or he would have his women make some. When they had their clothing they would have to make a detour, he said, and go to meet the trees. He walked them over to a rise and pointed out the direction to take once they were properly fitted out. He said a small stand of trees grew beside a river there. He said they could find there all the materials they needed for frames and they should make sleds too to ease their journey. When he found they had only one awl between them he lowered his eyes, perhaps so they would not see his poor opinion of them. He said he would bring two more and he would give them parchment skins sufficient for the netting when the clothing was ready.

—You are going to have a cold night again tonight, but you will not freeze, he said. When you have the right clothing you will see. The world is not a foreign place in a warm suit of clothes. It is your home.

They ate that night at the tent of one of Matonabbee's cousins. His own tent, he said, was flooded with a sea of furs and they would have to swim in the door. There was no space to sit except upon a new suit.

Like figures from an ancient tale, two women came at noon the next day carrying the clothes. For Sam, Matonabbee had provided a suit of otterskins, thick and soft. Sam guessed he had been taking them to the fort for trade. It must have contained at least two score of pelts. Before they left for the woods Matonabbee checked to see they had understood his directions. He made Sam a promise that he and his party would not press forward too fast, so that Sam and his companions would have ample time to catch up with them again. It was no grain of salt, his promise. Sam knew it instinctively. Though he and his men were incompetent and slow and clumsy, though it took them four whole days to make their snowshoes, still they were able to come up again with Matonabbee. They walked and they talked and they feasted together. As the weeks went on they walked into weather so ferocious it killed his dog where it lay sleeping, freezing it forever in a sad semblance of comfort. But they survived. He owes his life to the man. He has never lost sight of that.

And it was in his company, walking in snowshoes beside him, that Sam's true education began, with Matonabbee supplying him with knowledge and skills undreamed of and without name. He learned about the land and the weather and the animals, but he learned too about how a man must manage himself in the world and how a man must live to win the respect of others. He would trust this man with his life— and for that Matonabbee would protect him as a child.

When they got back to the fort and Governor Norton asked, not without a taint of a jeer, if he thought he could be third time lucky on this bedevilled undertaking, he knew his terms.

—Certainly, he said. If I can name my guide.

Norton interrupted.

—Sâsâpokîsik and his brother. They know what they're about.

—They're Southern men. I wouldn't even leave this yard again with those two. Two of the most unreliable men on the plantation.

He realized only after he had spoken and caught Norton's look that the men were his relatives. It was too late to redeem himself.

—I'd rather not, sir. I'll take Matonabbee for my guide. He can choose who accompanies us.

Norton's skin seemed suddenly too tight for his face, which was slowly darkening with the flood of his anger.

—If Matonabbee agrees to burden himself with *you*, he said. And you might remember, Mr. Hearne, that it's for me to draw up the terms. Matonabbee holds no sway in this fort. He chooses nothing. I'll have your orders sent to you.

OUTSIDE HIS DOOR Sam's name is being called to come down and raise a glass. He calls back to say he will come. He is no further advanced on his journey. The memories are distractions. They have taken him neither nearer to the place nor through it. It is Matonabbee himself who blocks the way. How to get past him? He was an incomparable guide. A man could not wish for better. He was fine company, amiable, good-humoured, thoughtful, and he knew his country. More than that. He was one with his country, attuned to the least discrepancy in the weather, privy to the closest secrets of the animals. No one would starve or go naked in Matonabbee's company. A man follows such a leader with a peaceful heart, knowing his life is secure. But Matonabbee was to lead him to a place he had not asked to see, though it lay at the very destination of his journey. He had coolly, with careful premeditation, led all of them to a place where no devils are required to stoke the pain of the world. Man's own delight in the suffering of others was enough to keep the fires burning. Is enough.

Sam closes his book at the retort of the first gun. A cheer drowns the reverberations. The pipes are bidding the old year farewell. Someone at the watch bell is ringing in the new. He will go back to it. It will be a grand book—if only he can get past this place for which he has no heart, this place that stops him every time. But he knows no science on earth can help him make sense of that night at Bloody Fall or forget what he had seen. Nor is there any map that can lead him out of the stony fields of the human heart—away from all that he has learned about the heart's capacity to hide even from itself.

IT BEGINS WITH his own heart beating in the darkness like an accompaniment to the mutterings of his companions as they tie back their hair and his too. He can feel Matonabbee's hands like the sucking mouths of two great fish draw back the skin of his scalp so tight across his skull that he thinks it will split. Matonabbee wraps a thong expertly, so that Sam has a strange bunched brush sticking out at the nape of his neck. He thinks his eyes will start out from the front of his head.

And now they are urinating to make their paints—a sooty black mixed from the spent coals of their last fire, carried here for the purpose, and a deep blood red compounded from the clay they carried in a pouch. They concentrate on their work yet they are relaxed. They joke with one another in lowered tones.

Sam feels a rising panic and cannot be still. He helps them, finding new twigs for their paint, even urinating for them. They sit in pairs opposite each other. Like women in their boudoirs who paint and pretty their own and each other's faces. Someone comes to paint his. He refuses. The man raises his voice. Matonabbee hisses at him to be quiet. They start now painting on the shields. Sam observes the figures appearing on the rough boards. Some he cannot make out. Others are clear—the round red face of the sun, sparks flying from its mouth, the moon. Sam finds it calming to wander among them like a buyer at an auction, a patron looking for an engraving in a print shop. Here a monster rising from the waves, there a deer walking like a man on two legs. Matonabbee comes over and offers Sam one of the shields they have made. Sam refuses it too. The illusion he had created is broken. His heart begins beating fast again, wishing that time would hurry forward, praying that it would not. That the night would never unfold.

They are walking again. The ground beneath his feet has changed. They are deep in waterlogged white clay, treading a stiff, difficult marl that sticks to their shins and hangs on their feet and drags at them. It makes a soft sucking noise at every step. He is praying that they will turn back, knowing that they will not. Behind them the trodden clay shows whorls of white in the night's low sun.

Matonabbee is solicitous of every man, reaching out a hand, pointing the easiest way. No one is speaking now above a whisper, the soft hiss of wind through marsh grass.

Matonabbee's hand is on his arm. He motions with his chin towards the lip of rock where the river falls. And there below are the five tents at the foot of the falls. Sam lies face down at Matonabbee's order. He is trying to pray for it all not to be but it is and there is no going back. No rearranging. No not happening. Only happening. One dread moment following inexorably on the last.

While they wait, lying in the cover of the land's own lumpy terrain, the movements of the Esquimaux at the tents detach from the soft roar of the falls. And their voices. Like birds flying above the water in the last of the sun. They are putting their camp in order before the night's rest. At ease.

Someone is singing. The same two phrases over and over. The sun is now a small eyelid on the horizon, only half asleep. The sounds thin and fall away, then gather again suddenly like snowflakes caught in a sudden gust of wind. There is a flurry of activity and then it subsides. A space of silence. A curlew calls. From farther off another. The plash and ruffle of ducks landing in the thin, the scarcely dark. There is no more movement in the camp. Sam's blood pounds through his dream. He can scarcely draw his breath, cannot breathe quickly or deeply enough to satisfy his blood's raging.

One of Matonabbee's men makes water, then another. No one else stirs. Matonabbee's breathing becomes heavy, rhythmic, beside Sam. He stares hard. Matonabbee's eyes are closed. Should he wish for the man to sleep until the opportunity has passed? Or should he hope for him to wake, for he is the only man Sam feels safe with? Matonabbee who saved him from freezing. Matonabbee whom every man heeds. Sam takes out his watch. He guesses eleven o'clock. Only two more hours of this twilight. He listens. Others too are asleep. If he could sleep. If he could sleep and wake a whole day and night later. If it could all be done and over. The river makes a steady lap and gurgles past the rocks. Its waters make a soft commotion at the foot of the falls. If the sun would only rise to show an empty bank below, all of them fled in the half light while it rested on the horizon. If he could make perhaps as if by accident some great noise, alert them. Matonabbee would be enraged. Perhaps Matonabbee has walked fifteen hundred miles just for this. He has seen Matonabbee in a rage. Matonabbee murderous. The tents have been quiet now for at least an hour. Matonabbee gets up and goes quietly among the men. An owl flies up with a harsh urgent cry, and then another and another. There must be a dozen beating their wings against the lightening sky. Turning their faces from side to side they beat away over the tents and come back as if they are flat-faced angels sent from heaven to alarm the sleepers—or devils from hell to mark them out. Sam opens his palm. He can read the time quite clearly. Ten minutes before one o'clock. The men are picking up their weapons. Matonabbee is already cutting in back from the bank so that they can descend and come out downriver behind the tents, blocking escape. They make the descent low, crouched. The owls continue to fly back and forth overhead, their urgent barking alarm lost to the depths of the sleepers' dreams. Matonabbee pauses only moments for those in the rear to come down. And then it begins. In Sam's mind it will always begin and there is no way of stopping it. A flock of geese rise with a clatter of wings, filling the air with their rusty clamour. The first shriek tears apart the stillness of the pre-dawn. It is a cry bearing all the grief of the world and it comes not from any in the camp but from Matonabbee himself as the five tents, like pods bursting, empty their wretched sleepers to the only moments of the new day they will ever know. They come naked with their arms flung wide as if to gather all they love before the blow.

Away up the river the geese are still crying murder as Matonabbee's nephew bears down on a young boy trying to reach the river. The boy looks back and stumbles. The nephew plunges his spear at an angle between the boy's shoulder blades. In an instant he has withdrawn his spear and rolled the boy over. He makes a feint towards the boy's chest and then plunges the spear a second time, transfixing the boy through his open mouth. Sam closes his eyes. When he opens them again there is no bird in the sky and the uproar in the air has given way to the shrieking below.

No one escapes. An Esquimau runs towards Sam as if he, the only still figure in this storm of killing, offers the possibility of reprieve. The Esquimau is a sturdy man, solid, tight with muscle. The pursuing Indians shout out to him. He knows what they want him to do. He holds the spear Matonabbee gave him for his defence. He steps aside. The man hesitates, his refuge lost. Three of the Indians fall upon the Esquimau and strike repeatedly with their spears. They are out of breath with the effort of draining this man's life but though he is clearly dying they do not leave him but strike again and again until he lies still.

Sam looks for a way to remove himself. Everywhere he turns death is. The Esquimaux have scattered in every direction and Matonabbee's men have followed. He sees a dip behind an outcrop of rock and makes his way there to wait out the slaughter. But this is to be a nightmare conjured for his own personal horror. A young girl is running to the very spot. She throws herself at his feet and the wailing that issues from her throat is like nothing he has ever heard before. It is the very shape and colour of pity. He hears his own voice breaking in strange agony, and his lips and tongue plead the same word over and over. No. Afterwards he will tell himself that the word was his repeated revolt against all that was happening. He will have to explain the meaning to himself many times throughout his life.

—

WHEN I LIVED I too dreamed. I dreamed that I had embarked upon a journey of my own. It was after the summer of my first blood when my mother and my grandmother built my lodge of seclusion. In my dream I had been for years a grown woman. I had embarked on a journey and was walking upside down upon the sky. And the sky was as a great rolling path across a marsh of light where geese swam away from my feet. Above my head was the dark land and it was scattered all about with what I thought white flowers until I saw that they were stars. And then I looked again and saw they were not stars but the people themselves frozen in winter and lying still and shining like shards of ice.

My mother said this was not a dream to speak of. I had wanted her to laugh at it for it chilled me and I did not understand. But she did not smile. She said I must return to the lodge and stay apart from all the people for three days and nights more. At this my father said he would lock me up. My mother replied he would then have to lock up every woman for every woman would depart from his house and none would return. He cursed her and kicked over his chair as he left the room. My mother said she would watch over me day and night. She said I must neither eat nor drink but only moisten my mouth with the berry called *sikâkomin* and at other times sleep. She took me a little way off to a rock that stands above the marsh. She said I was to lie there at night and to remain in the shelter of the lodge when the sun was in the sky. When I came back I was to speak to no one about my dream or any dream that the rock brought forth.

On the fourth morning my mother came to me. She carried a

kettle and a bundle of twigs and moss and she made a fire to brew tea for me to drink. I did not tell her when we walked back that in the night the same dream had come to me again and this time was filled with a soft hushing. When I opened my eyes the dream had continued for the hushing was all around. And there was no way to tell if it was the voices of the ice people or of the spears of grass that whispered so. And so I kept the dream tight closed within my heart and even later when it seemed a small thing and unable to cause pain I did not tell it. Even when a woman I lay with Samuel and he comforted me for the dream of all the people I did not tell it. Would it have changed the path he took—the path he sent us on? If I had told it would the dream have dared to come even a third time as it did visiting us all? Would we have made our journey still?

1773

THE BOOK OF JOURNEYS LAY UNTOUCHED. He had wished only to write a sentence or two to tell the events of that night. But there was not one that did not constitute a treachery of some kind. He could not write without betraying the slain, or the slaughterers, or himself. Samuel Hearne worked on his maps and he began to draw in earnest. On Sundays he walked out to forage for samples of moss and lichen to examine under the Company's microscope. He had no way to interpret what he saw, but the arcane calligraphy of the living tissue was its own reward. He made his observations. The date of the first appearance of the white bear, the number of eggs in an owl's nest, the forms of the aurora. And he made drawings. He was never satisfied with the birds, the feathers, the rabbits' heads. He could see that they had a stiff wooden quality about them and seldom looked convincing—

only exceedingly, excessively dead. The distance between the
drawings and the life that stirred his blood out on the land
was too vast. A drawing became a disappointment. He had
greater success with the inanimate objects, the snowshoes
and the pipes. He thought how they might enliven his journal if it were ever published at home. If it were ever written.
Moccasins were harder and the dresses of deerskin. Those
things in life retained a quality of the flesh. They seemed to
have a breath and it could not be captured. A fowling piece on
the other hand was satisfactory—though all the world knew
what a fowling piece looked like so what purpose was there
in its rendition?—and then too a hatchet bound with thongs
and trimmed with . . . He'd have to lie if it were for a reader
at home, and say trimmed with fur. Still he had no reader at
home, and of this he was keenly aware. He completed a careful drawing of an Esquimau canoe and it pleased him. He
made another on a separate sheet and showed it to the round-
faced boy and the boy's eyes brimmed with his delight. Sam
gave it to him and turned away quickly.

As the year progressed, Norton's excesses perversely
offered respite. Because he remained so often in his quarters,
routine wooding and watering and hunting could be pursued
at leisure. The daily round acquired a certain harmonious flow,
a sense of give and take. Whether there were oats to grind or
ice to be cut from the provisioning hole in the river, the duties
were performed efficiently, for once they were completed no
one burst upon the scene to make extra work where none was
necessary. Sam spent more time with his books and papers,
making new notes. When he tired of writing he worked at

his collection, sorting, stretching, repairing. He had brought a number of specimens back with him from his journey. He was learning how to stuff these small birds and mammals from Maskwa, an old Homeguard man who had learned it from Mr. Isham at York Factory when he was a boy. He could get lost in the work, creating the illusion of life—or so he believed, his imagination was so strong. To others the small creatures were as lifeless as stone. To Sam they were objects of tenderness or perhaps pity with their strange bead eyes. He had found a willing helper in one of Norton's women, who had returned to her own family outside. Her name was Mithkwacahkwan and she sewed so finely that the stitches were undetectable.

She had two small girls constantly with her. They had a lighter look about them. One of them had the grey eyes of the Norton girls. He risked a question.

—Governor Norton's older child. Where is she now?

—Molly?

—No, the older one.

Mithkwacahkwan raised her arm and pointed far behind her.

—She's gone. A Wêcîpwayân man took her.

—She doesn't live here any more?

Mithkwacahkwan shook her head.

—But Mr. Norton's other daughter?

—His other daughters.

Sam hesitated. He could be wading into the governor's murk.

—Nêwositêkâpaw's daughter. She still lives here?

—Nêwositêkâpaw's daughter, yes.

—Molly.

She nodded.

—She's here still? I never see her.

—She's here. The governor keeps her close.

Sam wondered exactly how many women and children were living now behind the closed doors. He did not ask.

HE DID NOT GIVE Molly Norton much more thought until the beginning of summer. The river had forced itself to life and brought the wreckage of winter rumbling and groaning down past the fort. The days warmed quickly and on an afternoon in early June when he was on his way out to the cove, Sam saw that their own plantation—though it would never match even the poorest farm at home—had come on apace. Here were rows of dandelion and patches of cress racing upward to drink the sunlight before they could be deprived of it. Two young girls were working there. Their smiles irresistible. He stopped to talk to them, said things he knew would make them laugh. Those are fine stones you have there. Pull up those weeds so they have room to grow. He wondered— not altogether idly—if he might risk bringing one of them inside the fort. Be like the governor and have them both. Norton these days was more irascible but less in evidence, rising late and retiring early and showing all the signs of suffering from chronic overindulgence. His frequent absences from the day-to-day affairs of the factory were a blessing to everyone except Leask, who shouldered his responsibility.

—When your green leaves grow you must bring me some. In my room.

His eyes, caressing them head to toe, lingering, made his meaning clear. They laughed and looked away.

—What else are you planting?

But they would not be drawn.

—Where are your husbands? Your families?

Nothing would make them lift their faces again. He tried a different tack.

—Tell me, he said, what is that place?

They looked up at his change of tone. He pointed to the edge of the encampment, where a tent stood apart from the rest. A smaller shelter about the height of a man's shoulders stood beside it, a structure like a box or a cubicle covered with hide like a blind for hunting.

Now they shook their heads and became serious, went on with their work.

It was clear he was not going to make any more progress. But his own curiosity was aroused by the idle question and, thinking the structure might be a conjuring tent, he walked over. As he drew near, an old woman came out of the last tent, shouting and waving him away. There was no arguing with a woman like that. He meekly turned away and made a loop back. Two Orkneymen at work on a drainage channel had enjoyed the comedy.

—Got yourself in trouble there all right.

—She wasn't about to ask me in.

—Nor any of us. That's a woman's hut. Jimmy tried to see in and the old witch broke a stick across his back.

Jimmy protested but the Orkneyman only laughed and showed his scrawny neck.

That night Sam told the story at dinner. It met with thundering silence and Purvis changed the subject. Sam did not have an opportunity to ask him the reason.

The next morning he rose before dawn and took his gun and ammunition, his game bag, and his spyglass. He had to wake the watchman to have the gates opened. He walked along the riverbank a way and then cut back in where some new willows had sprung up. He stopped there, settling low where he would be able to train the spyglass on the shelter.

One by one the stars over the bay went out and the sky paled to a delicate duck-egg blue. The first rays of sun slid to the fort, the tents. They struck full on the door of the hide shelter. Sam watched as it lifted. A thin figure came out. A girl. He could not see if it was Molly Norton, for her face was covered with a beaded fringe. She began to walk in his direction. He took up his bag and gun, tucked his spyglass in the bag, and continued on up the river, unwilling perhaps to have his purpose discovered just yet.

His suspicions were confirmed a few days later when he witnessed a straggly procession of women approach the gates through a thick summer fog that had come in from the sea. The fog had leached all colour from the world, every man and woman a ghost in their own lifetime. The women shuffled forward with deliberate slowness and swayed as they went. Nêwositêkâpaw was among them and the old woman who was at the tent. A slight figure trailed some way behind them. She was still wearing the fringe of beads and she walked with her head down, with the air of one who is greatly dejected.

At the gates they stopped. They seemed to confer among themselves. Sam could not tell if the discussion was amicable or not. Then the girl was pushed towards the gates.

—Molly Norton. Joseph Hansom, on his way down to the landing stage, stopped to watch. That's her. Her mother sent her away. You know. Getting her reds. If you'll excuse me, sir.

Sam turned to him.

—That would explain her absence.

—Yes, the governor don't like it but the women, you know. They get their way. Every time.

Sam was intrigued. Governor Norton with all his English accoutrements—his wig, his carpets, his silver coffee pot, his prints and books, his organ—and now his daughter bedecked as a country girl.

Norton evidently had word of what was occurring at the gates. He came striding out of the trading room and with three words forced things along.

—Get her inside!

Molly quickened her pace, keeping her gaze to the ground, Nêwositêkâpaw on one side, the old woman on the other.

Norton reached out and snatched at the old woman's elbow. He spun her round and shoved her back towards the entrance.

—Gaggle of bitches! Close the damn gates.

—I'd better go.

—Yes, sir. I'll be up shortly.

Sam was curious to see what next, but the two women

were spirited into Moses' quarters. Moses apparently found it necessary to berate a few men for their existence before he went inside. Sam was not quick enough to see it coming.

—And if you've thoughts of loitering, Mr. Hearne, think again.

He closed the door behind him.

THE NEXT EVENING Governor Norton invited all members of the council to his own dining room. He had had another table brought in and arranged at a right angle. The tables covered with long white linen. Every candle in the place burning though the world outside was bathed in light. A cushioned chair in place on the right of his own. A man employed to serve. A glass of malt whiskey handed to every man as he arrived. The attendant rang the bell. The officers drained their glasses and found their places. A slim dark figure stood in the doorway. The yellow satin of her dress caught a sheen from the candles. Her hair the same. It was fastened up at the back of her head. Round her neck a glitter of crystal teardrops. Conversation tailed away into silence. Every man eyeing every other with surprise and pleased expectation.

—Gentlemen! My daughter, Miss Molly Norton.

Molly raised her eyes momentarily, taking in perhaps only one-quarter of the room, and then lowered her eyes and went without hesitation to the cushioned chair. They had rehearsed.

There was a murmur. Miss Norton. Good evening. There was coughing. Silence. The men took their seats and suddenly the topic of conversation was the weather, while the attendant reached around them to pour their wine.

—And welcome to you, Miss Norton. Sam down at the end of the table raised his glass.

—Miss Norton lives here, Mr. Hearne. She is not on contract.

Molly, seated between her father and Mr. Leask, said not a single word, nor did any of the other men care to try their luck.

The attendant brought in the soup tureen. White peas in lemon juice. The men ladled second helpings. The glass teardrops shimmered. Molly's hair gleamed. Not a man at the table could ignore her new status among them. Every one of them betrayed into silence by his sharp awareness of her sex, her youth.

The soup plates were removed. The attendant returned with a dish of partridge eggs and cress. Mr. Leask, immune to the pangs of desire, held forth on the prospect for a hay harvest that year and the hard life of the horse the year before. He had moved on to the life of the cow when the attendant came again to take their plates.

Norton leaned to his daughter and said something without smiling. Without collecting her skirts, Molly made to get up. Norton with great ostentation put his hand on her arm. She stopped. When every man had risen Norton let her go.

—Well, he said to the table of men who had once again fallen silent. Well then, let us resume.

There were many more courses to come. Norton had arranged for a full English dinner for that night. It took several glasses of wine before the subject of his daughter was openly broached.

It was Mr. Jefferson, the chief trader, who took the plunge and braved a compliment.

—Your daughter, Governor, has grown into a fine young woman, sir.

—My daughter, began Norton and every man knew by the tone of these two words to brace for a caution.

—My daughter is the apple of my eye. The apple. No one will ever know what she means to me. She is my pet, my lamb. My cherub. She is my treasure, and I do treasure her above any of my women. She it is who carries my blood. My rich brew.

The men looked at the crumbs of their treacle pudding. Captain Johnston chased a few with his finger. They knew Norton hadn't finished with them and when he spoke again his voice had swelled considerably.

—And I shall not, shall not, let it be adulterated with that of any common damn bloody sailor or filthy servant. And if any officer is to win her favour, it shall be the man of my choosing. Because if any of you in this factory so much as—

Leask said quietly, Sir. There is really no need, sir.

—look at her or shake a leg—

—Sir. The man is waiting for his orders.

The interruption was enough to break Norton's train of thought and every man was grateful when he transferred his bluster.

—Because he can't think for himself, that's why. Get the

damn chocolate and the coffee, or have you no brains to work with of your own?

—And the port. We'll have the port now. Beautiful, she is. A beautiful young woman. Unsullied. Pure. A pure, beautiful young woman.

The only thing to do was to drink until he was done.

Several men that night went outside the gates. The man on watch found himself with an embarrassment of rum and tobacco. Sam lying in the arms of the youngest girl he could acquire imagined she had a European dress in heaps on the ground beside them.

THE SAME YEAR his daughter became a woman, Moses Norton, his track greased with gluttony, slid into degeneration and disease. His mind swung helplessly between rage and delusion and found no resting place. There were days when he banged about the factory like bad weather in a barn. He roared and bellowed, slamming and crashing into every flat surface, wheeling and driving the force of his anger into the men's faces, sometimes his fist. On other days he was quieter, intent on gratifying his insatiable appetite for brandy and prunes and Gloucestershire cheese, the choicest of the provisions.

He exiled all of Molly's pets from his quarters, keeping only a cat now to deal with the rats that came after his food. His belly was swollen, the girth of his neck huge, and his face above his soiled cravat congested. When he could no longer keep his breeches up he went without and wore instead a great coat that reached to his unlaced boots. On most days he dispensed with his wig, which was now so stiff with grease that it would no longer sit snugly on his marbled scalp.

The best days, for the men, were those when he did not appear at all. Purvis, a paragon of discretion, would report that the governor was indisposed and unable to leave his bed. Increasingly it became true.

JULY WAS HOT. The *Charlotte II* lay careened at the cove until the shipwright and the carpenter had devised a way to mend her keel. Sam sat at the end of the day in his room under a tent of muslin and resumed his journal. The muslin was ineffectual. Sooner or later the mosquitos would find their way in—first one, then a score, a gross, and in no time a cloud. Then he would have to stand up, fling the muslin back over his head, and flap with a tablecloth like a demented housemaid. Settling back, he would work carefully, trying to remain true, stopping often, the memories sometimes so close, so clamorous, he needed to live them again.

Once he heard laughter at the door and turned to see Molly, her hair in braids, grease shining on her face and throat, no shawl to cover the gaping neckline of her dress.

—You are like a man whose soul is stolen. She struck a pose, setting her mouth and widening her eyes to stare fixedly into empty air. Sam smiled.

—I'm just remembering.

—You look like a stone carving from the Esquimaux.

—I have one. He got up and pushed the muslin back so he wore it on his head like a woman. He went to his box and fished.

It was of light grey stone, a small round bird with a fine short beak, plump. Perhaps a plover. It was smoother than any river stone. He held it out in his palm.

Molly took it and turned it over. She smiled and held it out to him.

—I'm giving it to you.

—Where did you get it?

—You don't have to ask that.

—I want to know.

—You do know.

—Did you kill a child for it?

—I killed no one.

—It's pretty.

—Have it. Take it.

—To keep?

—Certainly to keep. Keep it safe.

Molly smiled. Her eyes narrowed with her pleasure.

—Thank you, she said. Goodbye.

And she pulled down the net like a curtain on his face.

—I shall bring you some grease, she said. And then you won't look so stupid.

SHE DID NOT COME BACK and Sam did not see her for days. The next time he saw her in the passage that led from the officers' quarters, she was laced tight into her dress, though the weather had not changed, and had a shawl crossed over her breast. Her hair was again wound up at the back of her head and she wore no grease. When Sam asked where she had been, she only smiled thinly and walked on towards her father's apartments. She closed the door behind her. Sam could hear laughter. It was not clear how many women Norton was currently keeping. Anyone passing his door could hear the muffled cries and the bursts of uncontrolled laughter, usually from Norton. The voices were loaded with rum. Sometimes the parrot screamed its own obscenities and on one particular night someone played upon the organ—it can only have been the governor—and did not stop until a loud crash put an end to it.

Come Sunday evening, however, when the officers gathered—those who had a mind—for the service the governor held in his own drawing room, all was in order. The room was swept and aired. The parrot's cage was blanketed and the governor sat at the little organ, his hands and feet as mechanical as its workings, squeezing and pumping out the relentless chords of "From Heaven's Throne." The women were banished, sent away with an armful of provisions, a jug of brandy, to their husbands, or in the case of the two youngest, to their mothers.

Molly Norton on the other hand, in her strange European dress and looking like part of the furnishing, stood at his side and turned the page when he nodded.

THE DAY BEFORE the *Charlotte II* sailed, Sam interrupted Moses as he was leaving the storehouse.

—Sir. A moment with you?

—Well? Norton kept walking.

—I'm thinking, sir, I have a duty to keep my word to young Molly. Which did stop the governor in his track.

—I promised her some time ago that I would show her

over the brig when she was a little older. I think she would enjoy a grand tour now.

Sam laughed self-consciously, for now Norton was staring straight at him showing not a trace of agreement.

—My daughter, Sam Hearne, is not at liberty to consort with the Company's servants.

—I didn't intend—

—I don't give a damn what you intend, young man. Your job is to take that brig up to Whale Cove and come back with . . . Hazard a guess, eh? Go on. And come back with?

—Whales, sir.

—Right, Hearne. Whales. So you damn well better be considering how it's fitted for that and not pondering designs on my daughter.

—Sir, I—

—And any further reply will begin to look like insubordination.

Moses' cheeks were beginning to flame with genuine indignation. A shred of dried meat hung in the corner of his bottom lip and waggled in confirmation of his sincerity.

—But she's just a child. I should never think to—

—There you are mistaken. You will treat her as a lady at all times.

THE *CHARLOTTE II* left for its summer voyage. Molly, laced and buttoned into womanhood, sweltered in her father's apartments, bent over the hieroglyphics of Mr. John Newbery's *Primer for the Young* or treading the pedals of the organ with her long brown feet, hoping for air enough to sustain a note.

Outside the walls the season for duck hunting began. Her younger cousins ran across the short springy cushions of tufted grass or lay on their backs on the moss after spinning and watched the streaks of high cloud whirl round the sky like water in a pail.

SOMETHING HAD CHANGED. Sam saw it at once on Leask's face when he came down again with the brig in August. Leask was on the landing stage to greet them as they rowed in with the jolly boat.

—Governor's indisposed.

—Oh, yes? It did not seem a surprise.

—Been that way for a few weeks now.

—Drink himself to an early grave, you ask me.

Sam ignored the sailor who had spoken, though there was no disputing the opinion. Leask came to his chief's defence.

—I don't think he feels too smartly.

They walked up together. Once they were through the gates Sam became aware of a sound that he took for the roaring of a bull—he did not recall a bull arriving—but as they entered the yard it was clear it was coming from the wing that housed the governor's apartments. It lacked anyway that quality of the bull's perfect obedience to perfect need, that patient desire, sure of fulfilment. This roaring rode on pain and pity.

—Maybe not feeling smartly but he's feeling something.

—He's having his legs blistered, poor bugger.

Norton's women sat cross-legged outside his room, rocking gently to his bellows and shrieks of protest. They were smoking one of his own pipes and a bluish haze hovered above them the way the mist hung low over the marshes in early summer.

Leask went into the bedroom and Sam followed.

—Come now, sir. If ye cannae stop kicking, I cannae start stopping.

Purvis was doing his best to keep matters from tipping into the tragic but the joke was lost on Norton, who lay on his bed with both legs elevated by ropes running from the beam above. He lay without breeches though his torso was fully clothed. Molly sat at the head of the bed, shielded from most of the grotesque by the bed curtain, which was partially closed on that side. A great bowl of thickened mustard paste stood on the low chest next to the bed, with bandages cut and ready for the plasters laid out beside it. A young lad with freckles assisted. He held a hot poker in the mustard and it was his job to return it to the fire to reheat when no more bubbles broke. Norton's left thigh and calf were draped in heavy blisters.

—We're almost finished . . .

—Who the devil is that? Those gawking sockers. Sons of bitches. Get them out—

His last word rose on the pain as Purvis struggled to hold the plaster in place on his thrashing leg. Moses' voice climbed higher still and came down in a torrent of filthy imprecations.

—All right. We're gone.

—Molly, you come with us.

Molly was trembling as if the bellowing voice itself were shaking her bones.

—Leave that girl. She stays with me.

He roared again. He might have been having his eyes put out.

—Spigot-sucking fuck-beggars.

But by then Leask and Sam had already ducked out and were on their way outside again.

—I thought your arrival might have distracted him somewhat.

—And so it did.

Leask looked askance at Sam. He smiled.

THERE WAS NO WORK that afternoon. Norton had sent word that not a skin, not a feather was to be taken off the *Charlotte II* until he was on his feet. That evening the brig still stood at anchor in the gilded river, all her cargo still on board, while the gulls fought and screamed in a white wing storm over the back of the whale she had towed. Sam sent a man out in the jolly boat to fend them off, there were so many.

At dinner in the officers' mess Sam agreed with Leask and Johnston. The governor's deterioration had reached the point where it was affecting the operation of the factory.

—I do my best, said Leask. God knows.

—We know.

—It's taking its toll. But he did not have to tell them. They could see from the way his hand wavered as he tried to bring his cup to his lips. Purvis knew Leask's own health was failing.

—The governor's condition takes its toll on us all. He doesn't give orders any more. He makes demands. I've seen boys and men run to his needs. I saw him summon a boy to fetch his match, which lay not five feet away. Then he clipped him for being slow.

—But that's a small thing. There was Thomas Kelsey. Poor bastard.

—No. Sam paused. His own lit match flaring an inch from the pipe he was about to light.

—While you were away.

—No?

—All the naes in the world won't bring the poor bugger back.

—For a goose?

—And buried on the goose ground, the one nearest. Norton said no marker, but he can't walk that far to see. We gave him a mark.

—It's the women I pity.

Purvis, who was facing the door, rose from his chair.

—Sir, he said loudly.

Moses Norton, leaning heavily on two sticks, Molly at his elbow, stood in the doorway. His long coat swung open to reveal his swathed and bandaged legs beneath his shirt-tails. He was breathing heavily.

They made a place for him at the table and called for the food to be brought in again. He had Molly seated at his side.

—You didn't eat it all, you gluttons, then?

The laughter was far from relaxed.

—We saved some for Miss Norton.

Always a risk, the mention of her name, but Purvis was temporarily safe. He filled a glass for Norton.

—So you, then, Mr. Hearne. Are you going to give us your report on the season? It might be your last.

For a moment Sam thought he had received a threat, but he saw Leask's eyebrows rise and he gave a slight nod of encouragement.

—I thought, Governor, you might be more comfortable to hear it tomorrow.

—When you've figured out what you want to tell and what you think you'll hide.

Sam let his arms fall to his lap. He looked down at his hands and took a deep breath while he decided whether to let the insult pass.

—I'll fetch the logbook.

—You'll tell me from memory.

—I'll try, then. If the other gentlemen will excuse me.

And Sam gave his report of the season's returns on a whaling voyage that as usual had hardly repaid the trouble of fitting out the ship.

—So then it's a good thing you'll be gone.

—Sir?

—Graham has sent word from York. You're to an inland house. You'll set it up yourself and you'll take your orders from him. Where's the goddamned food?

He made to get up and doubled over suddenly.

—Goddamn.

Molly stood to help him. Sam got up and went to help but Norton waved him away.

—Leask. I'll have Leask. And get my food sent along.

He did not look like a man who could tuck into a good

dinner. Purvis from his angle could see a dark stain spreading rapidly on his thigh and knew he would have to go too.

The trio made its ungainly passage to the door, Norton's sticks tangling in Molly's skirts. Leask on his side barely able to support the weight.

—Wouldn't want that girl's life right now. Purvis tossed back his wine, knowing he would be summoned at any moment.

Sam said nothing. His thoughts were fully occupied with his own life. The prospect of another inland journey was like sunshine breaking through storm clouds. He could not wait to get to York and receive his orders in full.

In two days he had hired his guide and was gone.

THE YEAR is almost done. Moses' bed in the centre of the room is its own house with walls and roof of thick drapery. Closing out light. Closing in secrets and pain. It exudes its own smell, a rancid stink like the great wheel of cheese he keeps underneath it next to the foul pots of waste. The smell of his breath is sour with the foods he reserves for himself and gorges upon all day. The acrid bite of it hangs like smoke from a fire but repellent. The window is shuttered and boarded all day against the cold. There is a hook in the beam above the window and a chain for the cannonball he has had heated in the stove and brought in on an iron shovel. The ball, set with a hook by the smith, hangs there like a fierce sun. Moses keeps candles burning night and day against all Company rules. Great branches of them like the fingers of strange trees clasped to the wall. They light the carpets and the cushions and where their light falls the colours glow like lichen in the late day. Nêwositêkâpaw and her sisters take turns to lie on the great soft bed and this pleases him. He does not give any mind to who it is. Warm bodies are all he ever seeks. The comfort of the breast. Molly's sister knew that long ago. It was why at trading time Jane spent all her days outside the walls. She was searching for a man who would take her for a wife. Someone who would take her far away. In his lucid moments Moses talks about his women. He says he has more women than the great Matonabbee and he sleeps with them all.

Sleeping is everyone's pleasure. When Moses sleeps, all can sleep. They lie in each other's arms on the soft skins and are grateful he does not wake.

Only the dead can see that all dreams are the same dream. Dreams of the blood and its delights. Dreams of comfort and satisfaction. Dreams of the warm body, the full belly. Dreams of losing what feeds the heart. Moses cannot retrieve the dreams that fly into daylight. He searches for them where they cannot be found and his pain is the pain of a small child torn from the breast. And the rage of a child dispossessed knows no bounds. If the child unassuaged become a man he is himself an affliction in the world, so great is his desire, so untenable his loss.

FROM THE TIME of his blistering, Moses has lived in the bed with the heavy drapery as if it were truly his house. There he has eaten and there evacuated all in the same place. And the more he put into his body the more disordered it became, until the pain of his bowels was more than he could endure without crying out. Every day worse than the day before until Mr. Purvis administered the calomel. No more linen sheets and woven blankets for Moses. He slept on hides as if he were in a tent so that the ones he had fouled could be discarded and replaced with fresh skins the women prepared for him. Nor would he let the women creep away as they wanted. He kept them at his side with promises of fine things to arrive on the next ship. Pretty things. Guns for their husbands. He promised them all new gowns like the yellow silk that Molly wore. They sewed skins for his blankets all day long. Sometimes he got up and took himself with sticks to the trading room but his body was so huge and his legs so weak that at last he had the account books and the writing tools brought to the bed. Mr. Jefferson was allowed to come and assist. Sitting as far as he could from the reeking mound of Moses' flesh.

And then came the day he sent for his writing implements and had Mr. Jefferson write down every article, stating beside it to whom it would belong after his death. Every article down to the last penknife, the last handkerchief, the exact quantities of brandy and rum and tobacco that he would give to each man. So that Jefferson, who was not a thinking man, had to wonder if his chief had after all a conscience for all the small and not so small irregularities that had helped him to his store of goods. Or was it a softness in the heart, a need perhaps to extend his hand towards his fellow man, a desire to do for him one last good thing? Perhaps he saw that at the end of his life all his goods were as nothing, that amassing such a store had not raised him up in the eyes of men. And Jefferson had the unkind thought that perhaps the governor hoped with his gifts to win esteem at the very last. Hoped thus to outfox death and have himself remembered fondly after all.

When the last item was entered, Moses closed his eyes and seemed to surrender to whatever was taking hold of his body. He turned and shifted in the bed. The women lit their pipes and smoked ceaselessly.

Molly knew he was dying, felt his fingers releasing their grasp little by little. Yet still he insisted on his women. He seemed to want their comfort. He disposed them in his room according to his orders, determining where each one should sit or lie. He had the furniture removed and pelts brought in and laid all around the walls of the room. He had them heaped in the corners and on these the women waited out his final hours. Mr. Jefferson, not wanting to disobey orders, kept them there with rum.

No one then could be sure what was in Moses' mind except pain. Only Molly when her life is over will see one day into his distant dreams and know how they tossed him from loss to attainment and back again. Will see how his grand bed became at last no more than a frail barque upon a raging river, her father no more than a small boy trapped in a dying body. How they, his daughter and his wives, became no less for him than his mother. To whom he would return.

MOSES NORTON DREAMS that it is March. The day is very bright. Wisps of white begin above the western horizon and streak the blue high over ahead with long fingers to finish in a whorled flourish above the bay. Two young men leave the fort and the tents behind and walk out over the blinding snow. They wear hoods and capes of beaverskin, double layers of deerskin for their jackets and stockings, linings of hare fur for their shoes and mittens. The hairs in their nostrils prickle with cold but the men will be warm before they have walked a mile.

The wind that blew last night rearranged the landscape, filling hollows and carving crescents of snow against the least obstruction. They walk in an easy rhythm, their snowshoes falling in step. Matonabbee says it is the perfect day to hunt, his words hanging in puffs of vapour on the crisp air. All the old tracks have been swept away. Only the fresh will show. Behind them follow their women, four of them, bent under the weight of the poles and the skins. Ahead the surface of the snow glistens. Its whiteness extends unbroken and featureless as far as the eye can see. They cross a lake and then another where the walking is easy and then they turn to the northwest, where the scented spruce woods will emerge as if rising from under the frozen marshes.

They will hunt all day while the women make camp in the shelter of the woods. Hare and fox will pause in their tracks and turn their faces towards the gun's retort. A single deer will wander into their range of fire, pause and present its breast to the musket ball. Matonabbee will draw his knife across the throat and they will drink in turn blood hot and ferrous on the tongue and seeming still to pulse and jet. Matonabbee will make a second pass with his knife, slicing the length of the belly. He will nod and Moses will reach into the steaming cavity until his fingers close around the hot smoothness of the liver. It is as slippery and elusive as a live fish and he will just manage to pull it far enough to cut it free. He will slice it in two and share it with his brother, no end to the reciprocity of their bond.

They will butcher the carcass and leave it in its red bloom for the women to haul and no ravens will appear to scavenge or maraud. They will walk back together tired and satisfied and no man feeling less than his companion in their day's labour.

The blue day is draining from the sky and the low sun is colouring all the world. They take off their snowshoes. They smoke their pipes by a fire whose flames leap orange against the mauve shadows and he tells Matonabbee of his travels. He tells him about his years in England before his days with Spurrell. The soft warm rain, the feathered bed (though it was straw), the dairy cows in the shining meadows. The milk! The cheese (and here the rancid spotted chip that skips from the knife balloons to a great wheel)! The high street where the sour night smells were sweetened with the warm aroma of baking bread and roasting meats. He tells him about the England he longs to know again (though never did) on furlough: the heady brew of hops and hot rum and tobacco emanating from the inns and taverns—on every corner! The laughter of friends, the rustle of silk. The dreamed crowd of rowdies, young bloods quaffing ale and squeezing thighs, are dreamed again for the benefit of the dreamed Matonabbee and in their second coming acquire vitality, more real to Moses than the very bed he lies in. The rain-lashed ports with their pugnacious drunkards, the lonely rolls on black-toothed, broken-toothed weary grateful women, are not admitted to his tale. They recede, become as distant and vague as his bewildered meanderings through sullen streets in search of the inn where he thought he had a bed. When the women return the first stars are appearing against the deepening blue. They leave a kettle of meat to simmer over the fire and the two of them lie under their robes, each hooking the compliant body of a woman to warm him while they talk. The women are yielding and warm and there is no hint of mockery in their laughter, which is all for pleasure.

In his heart he knows that he can never learn the land. But if he travels with his brother in this way he can pretend to knowledge. If he travels with his brother he will come to know pleasures and satisfactions in this very day, here, now, greater than a man can dream. He can dream himself that brother so great in stature, so skilled on the land, that men and women come to him to offer their services. Dream himself a captain with hunters and wives at his disposal and a great crowd to follow him. One who turns the heads of the Company men when he approaches and secures the respect of the chief factor himself, who though he affects amusement takes him in earnest and curries for his favour. A captain who both is and is seen as a great captain. Who when his day's work is done retires to his rest surrounded by his wives, whom no man dare contest.

But comes a man now who enters his room and lays a hand upon his daughter.

—Miss Molly. You've done enough. Come.

Moses Norton can hear the words but cannot place the

voice. He can see the man's hand but cannot turn his head to see his face. He wants to speak but his tongue has turned to stone in his mouth. He wants to tell the man, tell them all that they can't, they shan't have her. She is his own Molly, his alone.

He summons all his strength and rises up on his elbow. He points a finger at the thief who will steal his wives, his women, his daughter.

—Damn you for a cur! He gasps for air. Damn you! Lay a hand on the bitch and I'll knock out your brains!

He falls back heavily, his vision clouding again to smoky darkness. He feels the bolster adjusted under his head, a hand on his arm. He breathes heavily, concentrating on building the strength to speak again.

—Mr. Norton? Moses, sir?

He wants to tell them to get out. To get out of his room. Away from his bed. His women.

—Shall we read a service, sir? Shall we pray?

The very thought is a joke. He wants to tell them to pray that they will damn in flames if they touch one hair of one woman.

—He don't hear you.

But Moses Norton does hear. He hears whispers everywhere. He hears a roaring in his skull and he hears the crashing of waves of blood in his head. The room spins. His women fly, colliding. His bed tilts. And the pain in his bowels, in his heart, his lungs, is white hot, rigid, and reaches into his skull. He is impaled, begging, as the bones of his ears turn to smoking ash, to die.

MOLLY NORTON, strange to say, was bereft. She felt as if a gaping pit had opened at her feet. This monster gone to his heaven or his hell. Vanished. Only the ruin of his body left in the centre of the bed, the centre of the room. To be hauled outside on a moosehide.

Nêwositêkâpaw went to his box full of things and lifted the lid. She pushed away Mr. Purvis's hand. He watched her carefully to see she stole nothing. She picked out a long roll of tobacco like a rope and held it to the cannonball at the window until it smouldered and under her breath took fire. Then she made Mr. Purvis climb up and hang it from the rail of the bed for its smoke to sweeten the air. She laughed. She said laughter cleanses the air. Afterwards she told Molly she had heard Mr. Jefferson say, low in his throat, A waste of tobacco.

Nêwositêkâpaw and her sisters lost no time in petitioning Mr. Jefferson. He said they must return to their mother's tent or to the tents of the husbands who had previously provided for them. Nêwositêkâpaw explained what he well knew, that unless they brought with them a sign that the support of the fort—in return for services rendered—would be ongoing, their welcome would be cool. To that end she negotiated with him for a number of useful items that would ease their return to the lodges. Nêwositêkâpaw's mother received two of her daughters. Nâpeniska, brother of Nêwositêkâpaw's first husband, took her in and gave her the place of second wife. She told Molly to come too. Molly went out to the tents, covering over her foreign dress with winter skins. The other wife examined the dress and said she was like a mouse in the sea, a fish on land, a bird under the earth. Molly said she was like a deer newly born.

—Let her keep her English dress, said Nêwositêkâpaw. Who knows how useful when we ask for the good favour of the new governor?

Mr. Jefferson sent a man to ask for women to wash the body but none would come. Out in the tents they smoked their pipes all night to make sure the dead man's spirit stayed away. The next day Jefferson returned and asked for women to sew. Molly was about to offer her services but Nêwositêkâpaw stopped her. Jefferson went to women in every tent and none would accompany him back to the fort. On the third day, he sent a man out to them in the morning to say it was time. Six of the Company servants carried Moses Norton's body away from the fort. It was lying on a heavy board and they had hoisted it to their shoulders. He was sewn inside a closed sack. The women saw by the rough foreign stitches that it was the work of the Company tailor. They carried Moses' body out to the point and laid it on the ground next to the place where they had buried Mr. Leask in November. Molly stood beside her mother and the other women. The last time Molly had seen Mr. Leask he had not been able to stand erect but seemed to be searching for something at his feet. She was glad for him that he was relieved of the hard work of living. The men from the Homeguard stood watching and waiting for their orders. They had assembled a great pile of stones. Mr. Purvis read the prayers and Mr. Jefferson read a passage from the Bible. It seemed the book was too heavy for him to hold. The wind riffling its pages sounded like the wings of the small ducks as they skim the surface of the lake. When they had finished the Homeguard men carried stones one by one to lay on top of the body so no animals could partake of the flesh. They built the stones into a flat cairn the shape of an upturned boat. They had not finished before the women walked away. Mr. Purvis was still reading but his voice was sucked away by the wind.

Not long after she had returned to her mother's tent Molly saw that her legs had begun to freeze. They showed patches of deep blue and white like clouds reflected in a swampy lake. The two wives set about making long stockings of deerskin to tie at the waist. Nêwositêkâpaw returned to the fort and obtained enough skins—on credit—from the men's store to make a suitable winter dress, with sleeves and a hood and everything her daughter needed for warmth. Molly lay under skins next to the fire and wondered how she could ever go to England as her father had promised unless she put on again the English dress. Nêwositêkâpaw said she must keep it. She said it was her safe passage through the great gates of the stone fort and might be needed in times of famine. No one knew who the new governor would be.

That night Molly dreamt that Mr. Hearne came back from York Factory. He came into her tent and picked up the English dress. When she woke she believed it a vision of what was to come. She heard the next day that two men had been dispatched to York to report that the post was without governor or second. She began to think her vision true, and she began to wait. She spent her time in making snowshoes. Her fingers were unpractised. She did not leave the tent until the shoes were finished. She walked out. The shoes came apart before she had reached the last tent. Her third pair held together. She had no idea where she should walk to. There was only the fort. Nowhere else.

Sometimes, when it snowed or when the wind began to blow, she slept. Sometimes she slept for days, snug under a pile of skins but afraid to wake for the cold air outside. Jefferson gave out no labour to the families but opened the stores whenever they petitioned for food. He recorded in his book everything he gave to them.

PART THREE

Molly Norton's Dream

THOUGH I AM THIN AS WATER THINNER than water the body that carried me on my long journey still summons itself at will. It carries me back as it did today just as the sun was climbing and returns me to the place of my trials. Between where I lie and the sun's path across the sky is a short aspen like none that grows near to my home. It stands apart beside the lake and lifts its bent branches. In spring it is tufted with the fur of its flowers and in summer it flickers with green and yellow. When the frost comes it is furred with light. It holds its skinny fingers against the pink sky in winter bare except for the few rags of leaves that linger. I saw today a leaf like a black coal in the sun's red fire. I remembered then how my back seemed to hold just such a coal the day that we walked out from the fort and my journey began. My body that day alive and speaking to me advising me how to go about the world in best safety and preservation of its life. I was afraid but my body told me to keep walking with all the others for there was nothing now to keep us or save us at the fort.

There were more than thirty of us when we walked out that day. We carried sleeping skins and a few carried tools—fire tools knives awls. Much was left behind in the turmoil. But the days were warm and the land was full of berries the lakes full of fish. For twenty days we waited not far from the fort in hopes that the English ship would come and bring all that we needed to survive the winter for the French soldiers had taken our stores for themselves. But those we sent back returned each time with the same news which was no news at all. The river was empty. And soon it was too late for any ship to come. And so we walked.

I can see now how when we walked it was without foreknowledge without any sight of what was to come and it was good that it was so. Good that in my blindness I could look on Athîkis's sturdy body and dream a time when we would circle back and find our home again. That I could love him without pity for what was to come. That I could feel the live heaviness in my belly the fists and elbows of my unborn daughter pushing to test her strength for the journey. That I could see her born and at my breast while the flames of a bright fire warmed us. For in that time we were sure when we left the fort that the men would provide for us. After some weeks of walking small distances each day it was decided that we were too many and that we should separate ourselves into smaller parties. The main body of the people would travel fast after the deer. We—the women with children and the old people—would travel with two hunters and take a different route. The men marked out on the ground the places where they were going to try for meat. They showed us the direction we were to walk. First west along the river then turning north along the line of trees keeping close to the lake just beyond and when the cold arrived turning west again into the woods to make for Deer Swim Lake where we would winter and where we would meet with the rest of the people. They said by then the deer would be returning across our path and there would be meat and skins for all. They said whenever the kill was sufficient they would leave a cache within the woods.

It did not seem so terrible a thing to be walking with the people who remained. The farther we travelled from the fort the more they remembered. At all times they knew where to turn to find the ripest berries. They knew what part of the river to fish. They could make sinews for nets from the roots of the willows. Strip them finer still for thread. They knew how to make hooks from the jawbones of the fish they caught. There was nothing they did not know—only what was to come.

For many days while we followed the edge of the first lake my grandmother and two of the others fished. They caught pike. Some trout. Enough to dry. Our walking was slow with the small children and our old ones. The little food we had with us had been soon expended. We gathered berries wherever we found them and in this way the slowest among us could catch up to the others again. On the sixth day after we had left the lake and turned in to the woods we still had not found a cache. We ate all the berries we had gathered and lived only on small pieces of the fish we had dried. The days cooled too quickly towards winter. We could feel its presence just over the horizon. Soon a great layer of cloud dark as any gun barrel pushed over the edge of the land from the northeast dragging with it a grey curtain of sleet. We suffered greatly from the want of tent poles for though we had left the lakeside and were among a huddle of small spruce we had no hatchet between us to cut poles and our fires could not withstand the rain. In the night the wind that had brought the rain died down leaving the cloud directly above us where it rolled and thundered sometimes striking distant points and showing us in a flash of light our whole country. Showing us too our faces. Laying bare our hearts.

We knew as soon as we came in sight of the cache that all our hopes were ravaged for the stones were all overturned and the cache looted by beasts. The skins of the deer were torn and spoiled but some of the meat was still strewn around. There was a bundle of three fine deerskins for our use and rolled inside were the sinews still untouched. We gathered and saved what we could. My grandmother said that now we must every one of us set to trapping or fishing for we could not go much farther without a proper supply of meat. We turned our path then towards the little lake they called Jump Fish.

On the same day we met with a small party of our own people from the land making their way to the fort with furs. They did not at first believe what we said but then they understood our plight—which now they shared. And though they had pity they could not spare their furs for they intended to seek out instead the Pedlars to trade.

I had the knife Samuel gave me but I would not trade that. I thought of the sharp scissors at the fort and of the files to sharpen knives and all the useful things there. I thought of the guns for hunting and the awls, the fire steels and the scrapers, the kettles, the food that spilled from the warehouses, and I thought of clothing. My mother told me to unwrap my bundle. She shook out the skirts of my English dress. Someone named a price but my mother put her hand on my arm. We waited patiently while two of the strangers argued about who should have it. In this way I had four fine skins for Athîkis when we left them. I saw how the women of my own party looked at me askance and I knew from that time I would have to fish for myself.

Ten days we stayed there. We caught nothing in the nets the first night so we moved farther along the lake in the direction our path lay and set the nets again. This time the fish came to us. White fish enough for one and one-half for every person who shared then with the children. The nights now were brightened with frost as thick as snow that stayed all morning on the rocks. We cut our clothing for the winter from what skins we had and we wore our sleeping skins against the wind. We gathered great bundles of twigs for our fires in hope of drying a large catch of fish that could carry us several days. But every day was the same. Still none of us knew what lay ahead. We dreamed only a time when the fish and the birds would leap and fly to our aid.

It was hard then to believe all the world innocent of the great turmoil at the fort. That every bird and beast could go about its business as if nothing untoward had taken place. That none of them could interpret our great need.

We talked sometimes about the fort and what might have happened to the Englishmen there and we tried to dream the outcome. We asked ourselves if they would all be killed. Every one of them.

And then one of the children came running with news that her uncle could be seen in the distance walking in our direction and it looked as if he was carrying meat. She ran back again with two of the others to meet him and indeed he carried a deer across his shoulders. He stayed with us to share the meat and he told us where he and his companion had left another cache for us only two days' walking from our lake. He said that on the way we should watch for the Pedlars who would take pity on us if they heard what had happened. And even the smallest kindness from them—the use of a hatchet the gift of an old scraper—could be to us a great one. And then he left us to go again in search of deer. We followed his directions and in two days we saw the mound of stones. But when we came to it we saw that across the mound lay a broken gun its barrel burst asunder. And we knew now that our men though they had bags of shot had only one gun to hunt for all for us.

We stayed some days at that place to dry the meat and to dress the skins and then we walked on. We walked through the thin woods with ragged trees black and the sky glowing pink and green behind them. The wind began a high moan of complaint. Those who knew were in agreement that it was best to catch up with the two men for they would have to use spears when the deer in their great numbers arrived and they would be in need of us to assist in building traps and fences to catch them. But something was happening. Cramping pains came low in my back so that I had to stop often. My grandmother and my mother waited and with them my aunt and my cousin but the others drew away farther and farther into the trees. And then the pains increased and I understood that my child was trying to be born. The pink light had gone from the sky and a glowering grey dusk was filling the woods when the first flakes of snow came searching in from the northeast.

We cleared what ground we could and broke down spruce branches to lie on when night fell. And in the deepest part of the night my daughter was born. Bending my bones to escape my body and enter our hard travelling. Slipping from me like a live fish. Alive. I put her under my clothes and felt the long draw of pleasure as her mouth caught the teat. Yes pleasure even in the raw day of our need. We lay together for warmth and kept the children beneath us covering ourselves as best we could with the pelts we shared. I was sure we all would freeze like my poor sister at home but in the morning we were praising the snow that had blanketed us from the cold and the trees that had shielded us from the bitter wind of the bay. Even on the way to our deaths there are kindnesses to praise. And I can see how this is true for all men and women yes and every little child too for we are all all our lives from the moment we are born on the way to our deaths and a bitter journey it would be without thanks for the gifts that lie on the path.

1774

WHEN HE HAD BEEN GIVEN—IN SO OFF-
hand a manner last year—his orders to transfer to
York Factory, Samuel Hearne was pleased to have been
relieved of his duties on the *Churchill* sloop, and delighted
at the prospect of being out of reach of Governor Norton.
Late summer was pleasant for travel, and the journey would
take less than a month. He had set out with a small party: two
Homeguard men, Otôthapith and Namîpith; their wives; and
his second, Robert Longmoor. They paddled south until the
river turned, then they beached the canoes and left them in
thick sedge for the guides' homeward journey, striking out
southeast to cross the open country between the two rivers.
They left the fringe of trees and walked over marshes studded
with rock and woven with every shade of purple and white.
They walked to the accompaniment of bird calls and the soft

breathing wind and the small voice of water in the runnels. They skirted still pools that had swallowed the sky. For several days they lived off the provisions they carried, but when patchy stands of spruce began again and fires were possible they roasted the ducks they picked off from the larger pools or raked out of the sky with birdshot. It was for Sam like walking back into a world of harmony where man and nature walked hand in hand. He carried a notebook and made drawings whenever they stopped. His notebooks, back in England on some far distant winter evening, would be his living memories of this remote and beautiful land. These were the fine last days of summer, with the colour thinning and leaching from the upper air, the blue thinly veiled, ethereal. The nights were cool but not yet chill. The moon when it rose was huge and orange. He heard in the night one of the wives softly moan. He guessed it was Nipiy-nikamew, Otôthapith's young wife. She was not much older than Molly Norton. The sound she made was like breathing, rhythmical, but with voice. It spoke of melting pleasure against the forcing breath of her husband. He wondered how soon Norton would find a suitor suitable for Molly—or even willing. He was like a foam-mouthed bulldog in a gateway.

He would be some weeks at York while plans for the undertaking were formulated and agreed, and then they would be off again as soon as Governor Jacobs, who had made the coveted step from the Churchill command to the factory at York, had drawn up his orders. He could taste it already. The air like ice crystals on the tongue, the tiny hairs crisping and freezing inside his nose. And these things would come with a new sky—high and brilliant but able to change in an instant. A wind would arrive announced by forerunners of grey and livid purple rags, themselves announced by a long wedge of urgent geese. But he would be ready, would welcome the whole battery of nature's vagaries.

—MR. HEARNE, sir. Welcome! Ferdinand Jacobs strode out to meet them, his long jacket slapping at his thighs, his white shirt open at the neck. Sun-beaten and hale, his face beneath his cropped and grizzled hair looked younger than his years. He was smiling broadly.

No Moses Norton this, no overlord but an amiable superior officer with a manner on him more like that of a colleague, a partner in business.

—Your journey was a pleasant one? I hope your guides took you to their best duck hunting, picked the most succulent berries for you on the way?

—The guides were excellent men, sir.

And he could risk the truth, or near it. Governor Jacobs was never averse to life and its enjoyments.

—They proposed a rest whenever the prospect pleased them or the fancy took them to enjoy a pipe.

—Well earned, I'm sure, Mr. Hearne.

So amiable. So relaxed in this brief space before winter's exigencies. It was another world.

He ate each night at the governor's table and there, to the accompaniment of fresh goose and salted pork and the new cheese out from England, they worked out the best means of establishing an inland trading house. The plan was not com-

plicated: to take a number of boats—as many as needed—
loaded with supplies and provisions and an assortment of
trade goods, up the river; to select a suitable spot; and to
build. The post would be under his own command, at a place
of his choosing, at least four hundred miles from the coast. He
could not have wished for a more agreeable prospect.

The plans sounded good over a pipe and a glass of brandy
but their execution was fraught with difficulties. There were
setbacks, unforeseen problems with men and with supplies.
Guides they hired left without notice to catch the end of the
goose hunt. New guides had a falling-out. One of the boats
came afloat in the night and was carried out to sea. The man
who was to be house carpenter required new saw blades to be
made. And Robert Longmoor fell sick. In the end the weather
rose up and settled the matter. The river was locked and Sam
and his second had no choice but to overwinter at York and
wait for break-up in the spring.

Much as Sam wanted to be away, the delay was not dis-
agreeable. The fishery at York had closed for the winter and
when he had helped to put up the boats, Sam volunteered
regularly for hunting and wooding. It was still good to return
from the trails with the body pumped full of the astonishing
air, the sled creaking under the weight of a fresh haul. And
Sam would lend his hand to any duty. He was well liked,
and in the circular way of these things, because he was well
liked he was full of cheerful goodwill—and was better liked.
There was no duty Sam could not or would not assume and
when in the depths of winter a packet arrived bearing the bad
news from Churchill, he was the first to volunteer. The letter

announced the death not only of Moses Norton but also, two months prior, of Mr. Leask, his second. Governor Jacobs, whose job it was to oversee the Company's houses at the bay, was grateful to have an able, willing officer on hand to help with the crisis. It would be autumn before the London office heard the news, and the following summer before he could learn from them who was to succeed. He decided that Governor Graham at Severn, with his years of experience, was the man most fitted to take temporary command. But Governor Graham was old and ailing and would need help on the journey, would need help too establishing himself at Churchill. And here was Samuel Hearne, who knew the ropes and was young and fit and willing. He could be of the greatest advantage.

For Sam the long wait for break-up began to look most interesting.

—You'll not let the inland house be forgotten in all this, I hope, sir.

—I'll not, Mr. Hearne. I'm committed to the success of the undertaking—as Governor Graham will be. He'll not keep you long at Churchill.

ON THE DAY they came in, Molly was watching. Samuel Hearne was accompanying an Englishman older than her father, or anyway his hair was whiter. They walked slowly, the older man bent with pain and supporting himself with a stick at each step, though it was said afterwards that Sam had pulled him much of the way on his sled. They went straight into the fort without greeting. Nêwositêkâpaw's new husband said it was the governor. He meant it as a joke. When it proved true he laughed even harder and said that he would allow Nêwositêkâpaw to re-enter the fort if the old man asked for her. She kicked him hard at that and he kicked her back. He did not want his younger wife learning an old wife's unruliness.

Governor Graham's first duty was to read Moses Norton's will and see that all its stipulations had been met. Jefferson said, Good luck! He said it had taken twenty minutes to read aloud. Not all the wishes had yet been carried out.

—What do you make of this?

Graham handed the document to Sam. The original will was quite short, the codicil long, detailing every last suit of mourning, every ring. Sam's name did not appear—he had not expected it to—though every man on council was remembered as well as half the fort. He minded the omission not for itself but for what it signified. The absence of his name was a mark of the strength of Norton's animosity towards him, because the document, in his opinion, was clearly the work of a man in the grip of his conscience. What moment of lucid terror had prompted all these mentions, all these sudden remembrances? Ferdinand Jacobs' son? Thomas Hutchings? Joseph Hansom? Johnston and Wills and Jefferson again and again. Bequeathing sums of money, gallons of French brandy, his pictures, his books, sugar, tea? What lives might have been enhanced by a few sudden remembrances in life, a few quick kindnesses in place of the bellowing outbursts?

He tried, he really tried, to rise above the omission of his name. He concentrated on the flush of bequests, the anxious afterthoughts of the codicil. Did Norton see his actions and his words suddenly as if he watched an actor on the stage? Was he appalled at all he had been able to get away with in the trade? Or did it come to him that he lived among friends? Despite himself Sam began to feel a kind of pity for this man examining his life too late, finding too late the ones he loved. And he did love.

He reread the passage that referred to Nêwositêkâpaw and Molly. Norton had loved them both.

—I can inform his wife, if it's not been done.

—If you would, thank you. That would be a help. You know them, I take it?

—I do, sir. It will be easy enough to find them.

Jefferson said they were living outside the walls. Sam restrained himself from saying he would go right away.

NÊWOSITÊKÂPAW AND MOLLY Norton sat on chairs to listen, their hands folded in their laps. Andrew Graham sat on the other side of the trading-room table. Samuel Hearne stood beside him. He smiled at them. They seemed unsure what to expect, though Sam told them the news was pleasant. As he said it Molly lifted her eyes and looked straight at him. She held his gaze while Graham read:

In the Name of God Amen I Moses Norton Governor at Prince Wales's Fort North America having formerly made and published my last Will and Testament I the above named Moses Norton being minded to make some addition thereto or alteration thereof for that purpose make this as a Codicil to my said will and first not recollect-

ing what sum I left to my natural daughter Molly Norton hereby order in case it should not amount to thirty pounds per year that it be made up to that sum but if it should exceed the Sum of thirty pounds then to stand in full force according to my former will out of which Sum of thirty pounds or upwards I oblige my aforesaid natural daughter Molly Norton to pay her Aunt Neo-see-ta-ka-pow my Sister whose name is in my Will and has a Legacy left the Sum of five pounds a year but after the Decease of my said Sister the former Sum of five pound is to return to my natural Daughter Molly Norton.

—It means you are provided for, both of you, as long as you live in this place. We shall open a book for you and you may come to us for what you please up to the amount of thirty pounds per annum, which is to say in the course of one whole year's turning.

Such a gift. No. A payment. That was it. A payment for their years of servitude. Nêwositêkâpaw understood at once the implications, how at the whim of her tyrannical husband, with these pieces of paper lighter than the finest skin, she had been set free of dependence on men and become suddenly dependent on her daughter. Her support continued only for as long as Molly continued at the fort. And Molly, growing taller and more desirable each day, would not remain at the fort forever.

—I am not his sister.

—No. We know that, Nêwositêkâpaw. It is a manner of speaking. It does not change the intent. You are provided for. Mr. Norton has provided for you both. Graham smiled broadly and waited for the smile, like a yawn, to take hold.

The women stood up to leave. Nêwositêkâpaw went to the table and thanked the governor, then she stepped round to Sam and embraced him like a son.

—And there will be work too, Graham added. Whenever you are in need we can give you work. He got up to see them out.

—I never had to work.

It was the first time Molly had spoken and the men were not sure how to respond, the statement so undressed.

Nêwositêkâpaw answered in her own language.

—That is because you were never a wife. You will be.

Molly laughed.

—The wife of Mr. Hearne, she said in English.

The men shifted uneasily, the words like a sudden trap at their feet.

Graham did his best to treat them lightly.

—Well, Mr. Hearne! A proposal from a lady! You must be flattered. Perhaps you should speak to her privately while I walk Mrs. Norton to the gate.

No one else took it for a joke.

—Thank you, sir.

Sam nodded to Nêwositêkâpaw and took Molly's hand. He walked like a blind man from the trading room, thankful that they passed no one on the way. He all but pushed Molly into his room and closed the door behind him.

The world fell in upon them both. There was no act of kindness, no tenderness. There was only Sam's ferocious need and Molly's survival. Afterwards she laughed and he panicked.

—Don't you speak of this, he said, still out of breath.

—We always tell each other what we have done. We like it.

—It's better if you don't.

—Why?

He could not think of a reason. He relaxed.

—So then we can do it again.

Molly smiled.

—It is nothing to me.

Sam caught her by the shoulders. It was not what he wanted to hear.

—Molly.

He gave her back her name.

—Molly.

He closed his eyes and pressed his forehead to her smooth brow. But when she turned her face up to his, he did not find in her eyes what he was looking for and he let her go.

IN THE NEXT MONTHS Molly asked him several times when he was going to take her to live in the fort again. He said she knew only the governor could do such a thing. He said anyway he liked it when she came to his room in the afternoon. And even when she left. He said it made the next time all the sweeter.

All through March and April and most of May he made himself useful to Graham so that he could stay on. But by the end of May the rivers were clear and he could postpone his leaving no longer. He told Molly he was going overland to York Factory again. Governor Graham had asked him to deliver instructions for his young daughter to be sent to him from Severn. And it was true. He did not like to tell her goodbye, they had become so fond. And she was such a child still. He thought it best to let her assume he would be returning.

By the time Graham's wife and daughter and newborn son were escorted by a guide to Prince of Wales Fort at Churchill River, Sam had already reassembled everything he needed in the way of boats and supplies at York. The plans this time fell into place without obstruction. He gathered his men and embarked at last on his journey inland, elated at the prospect of a new kind of liberty.

MOLLY NORTON became something of an anomaly at the fort. Though there were Homeguard men enough who looked her way, there were few who desired her for their own. Molly Norton was notoriously unschooled in the many skills they looked for in a wife. Then too, Molly herself gave them none of the familiar signals that might tell them she was ready. She considered herself already taken by Samuel Hearne. Who would, she was certain, be back.

She took to visiting the fort almost daily, hoping for a chance to see Sarah, the governor's little girl, who lived there now in his quarters. The child had the soft-patting hands that Molly recalled of her own sister and cousins. She never laughed as much as when she played with this child. The child herself sometimes laughed so hysterically she toppled to the ground and rolled in ecstatic agony. Governor Graham's wife, who, he said, was to be called Jenni, was glad of

Molly's company. Jenni spent her days in Graham's rooms, swaddled in idleness and boredom, nursing her young son and sleeping. Governor Graham did not object to Molly's visits. He liked his family to be happy and enjoyed his children when they were smiling. Like Sam, he had made no mention to his wife of the fact that he would be leaving. Due to return to England, he was waiting only for his replacement to be named. Molly's continued connection to the fort was a comfort to Nêwositêkâpaw, who was content with her own situation. She had her allowance, she had a husband who had taken her in, and she was well respected for her knowledge of the workings of the fort. Above all she savoured the respect. For all concerned, save Graham, it felt like life as it would be forever.

In August everything changed. With the ship from England came the news that Graham had been waiting for. A permanent replacement for Norton had been appointed. Samuel Hearne had been named and a letter from York had been forwarded to him at his inland house, recalling him from his duties. Mr. Jefferson was to deputize and Graham was free to board the *Prince Rupert* for his return voyage to England. His boxes were already packed. On board were the English clothes he had ordered to be brought out for his daughter. He asked that the package be kept on board. The night before he was to sail, he sat Jenni down. His infant son would remain with her, that much was clear. He was far too young for the voyage. As for his little daughter, he had many points to make, foremost among them the well-being of the child. Sarah would be provided for. She would be educated.

She would learn to read and write. A thousand pounds would be settled on her for life. In England she would live a life of ease. Her house would be furnished with the finest fabrics and tapestries. She would never have to sew her own clothes. She would eat cherries and drink chocolate. If she fell sick the most prominent doctors would attend her. She would bathe in hot water perfumed with flowers. She would eat apples and plums. Custard would be her breakfast. She would live the life of a queen. How could a mother deny her child such riches? She would—though this he did not say—be the delightful ready-cut jewel in the Edinburgh establishment he would share with his wife, a wealthy widow, Patricia, who had not produced an heir for any of her three former husbands.

Jenni sat grim-faced as her heart was squeezed of its life's blood. She did not speak. She would not speak, though Graham pleaded with her to say she accorded with the plan. Instead she made her own plan. In the early hours of the morning she got up quietly and roused the little girl, took her to the door, thankful that both Graham in his bed and the baby at her back continued to sleep. But when she put her hand to the door she found it locked.

Graham woke to a hand moving, searching under his pillow. There was shouting and there were tears and in the end Jenni slept in the passage with the baby, her daughter, Sarah, in Graham's room the other side of the locked door. He did not like to do it but really it was for the best.

Molly Norton had not guessed what was occurring when she stood with the others the next morning down at the landing stage. She bent down beside the child.

—Say goodbye to your papa. She waved to show her how.

Governor Graham heard and turned from Jefferson, saying he had best get the child on board. He came over and uncurled his daughter's fingers from her mother's dress, then picked her up. Grimacing slightly as he always did when bearing a weight, he leaned towards his wife.

—Goodbye, Jenni dear. You'll be in my thoughts always. Farewell. And my little son.

He kissed the top of the child's head. Jenni leaned away so that their faces did not touch.

—God watch over you both and protect you always.

Jenni did not answer. Her gaze was on her daughter. She watched the longboat row away. Graham waved several times. The water carried the voices in the boat back to the shore. Her daughter was calling for her, her voice a small flame that flickered at the wound of her heart.

—They'll bring her back in the boat. They'll come back. They will come back.

But Molly's words were only remnants of the instant before, when she had not fully understood, and her face already streamed with tears. The child once she was in the boat had known. Molly had heard it in the thin voice carrying over the water. The child knew.

They watched until the shape of the longboat merged with the mass of the *Prince Rupert* as it drew alongside. They could see movement as the men climbed the ladder.

The landing stage had cleared now. Jefferson had gone up to the fort to give the orders for a salute as soon as the frigate set her sails.

Molly waited beside Jenni, whose eyes had not once left the ship. She watched the fort's longboat return, the two sailors pulling effortlessly now. Perhaps, just perhaps, the little girl would be asleep in the bottom of the boat. Two men were coming back down to the shore to help haul the boat onto the beach. The sound of the *Rupert*'s anchor chain carried clear across to them. Molly had to go to the longboat to see for herself the child not there. Jenni did not move. Behind her the sound of the fort's guns, firing almost in unison, broke the quiet of the river. They fired three times. The reverberations died away but still Jenni did not move, perhaps did not even blink until the speck that was the *Prince Rupert* disappeared from view. The baby at her back had cried himself to sleep.

William Jefferson was not unmoved by what he had witnessed. He saw the women coming back into the fort and was at a loss. Graham had left no instructions except to keep Jenni and his son, Joseph, at Churchill; he would send for his son as soon as the boy could leave his mother. There were two small houses, stone huts no more, that had been built for the astronomers some years back and never since put to proper use. Joseph Hansom was using one of them in his attempts to domesticate the deer. There were two sorry specimens in there right now. He would get them moved, the place cleaned up. Leave it for Sam Hearne to decide how things should proceed when he took command.

MOLLY NORTON helped Mr. Hansom take his deer to the cowshed, then came back to sweep out the hut. Jenni watched unmoved. Jefferson was not sure if she understood a word he said. He asked Molly to communicate with her. He wanted her to know that Mr. Graham had provided for her. She could come to the trading-room window when she was in need of victuals or clothing. Jenni looked him in the eye and then she went to the far corner of the hut, turned and looked him in the eye again, and urinated.

Graham's wife stayed at the fort. She did not know what else to do. In the night she had been prepared to walk into darkness, with not a thought for what might happen next. In daylight she saw more clearly. It was a long walk to her home at York Factory. She had made the journey only once and in the opposite direction, following a guide and paying little attention to the path. She had no meat prepared, no one to hunt for her along the way. She would wait and she would watch and listen for the means to make the journey when others were going with a packet. Meanwhile she would eat and drink at Andrew Graham's expense.

The next morning she was at the trading-room window asking for rum. At first it made her sick and then it made her cry with the pain of her world coming apart. After a while it brought a deep unconscious sleep. When Molly came to see her in the morning she did not wake. Molly stayed at the hut and gave the infant boy water to drink, warming it in her mouth and squirting it as gently as she could from her mouth to his. But still he spluttered. And still he was hungry. She knelt down and pushed at Jenni's shoulder. Jenni only moaned. Molly lay the baby down beside his mother and opened his mother's dress. The child found the breast at once. It was as hot and hard as a river rock in the sun. He took the nipple noisily and the milk ran from the sides of his mouth. He was happy. Molly sat and watched.

In the afternoon Jenni woke and was sick. She did not get up until the next day. There was rum still in the jug.

Molly came each day to see if Jenni would get up. She seemed to want only to lie with the baby at her breast. The baby slept, sometimes nursing in his sleep. When he woke up, he seemed unwell. His eyes wavered and his skin was hot. Molly brought Nêwositêkâpaw to see him, and Nêwositêkâpaw declared him badly sick. She said the sickness of the mother was making its way into the baby. She took him away to find a wet-nurse. Jenni lay and sobbed. She refused to eat the food that Molly brought, no matter how choice. Molly brought Mr. Purvis to attend her. Even as he walked over, Purvis suspected what he would find. One glance through the door of the hut confirmed it. The smell of rum was overpowering. He laughed dryly and said she would get better, then he went away to make a preparation that would help. He told Molly to return the infant to the mother as soon as she could get up and walk around.

SAMUEL HEARNE and his small contingent of men had no trouble establishing the new house inland. Their movement up the Nelson River did not go unnoticed. They told everyone they met about the planned house, urging them to look for it upriver in the winter, perhaps even past Basquiah. They travelled almost four hundred miles, then slowed their pace to search for a suitable location. They settled on a near-perfect site overlooking a lake with a small island in the middle and pine woods at their back. They called the lake Pine Island. It would supply them with all the water and fresh fish they required. Once the decision was made they hurled themselves into the work of clearing the land and squaring the timbers for a sizable log house. Word of their activity and of the goods they carried up spread quickly. It was not hard to find hunters to bring them a steady supply of fresh provisions, or women to make a start on their snowshoes and promise them clothing when the fresh furs were obtained in the winter. The weather was so fine and exceptionally clement that they had the roof on the new house by October. They called it Cumberland, as the committee had instructed, and celebrated with several times their ration of brandy.

By the time the first storm struck, Sam had found himself a young girl, a Pwâsimow who spoke no English, to keep his bed warm in winter. Small and slight, she would not be in demand as a wife. Nonetheless Sam found her beautiful. He liked the way her eyes narrowed when she laughed, disappearing until they reminded him of the gleam of distant water behind the high ridges of her cheekbones. She would not be a strong bearer for her husband, nor would she be a quiet helpmeet. She was fiery and truculent and not long out of childhood, quick to laugh and quick to learn. And he did with her whatever his heart desired in the deep of the winter nights, facing down the ribald remarks of his fellows in the morning.

He had not known such liberty. She was never serious, asked nothing of him as long as he pleased her. Sometimes she played with the trading goods—the beads, the gorgets, and the laces, adorning her hair, her body. And then she returned them.

She asked nothing but to be fed and entertained in return for a little sewing and her favours in the night. And then one day in spring Sam told her that soon she would have to do no work for him at all, for the young men who were planning a raid on their neighbours had promised to bring him back a slave. The day came when the young men prepared to leave for the long-planned attack. It was an old enmity. There was no fathoming its source, nor was there any end in sight. The girl came to Sam with her eyes shining. She had asked them, she said, to bring something back for her. She would not say what it was. That night in Sam's bed, she had to remind him that there was something he wanted to know. Her eyes were shining again.

—I have asked them, she said, to bring me back a boy.

Sam did not at first grasp her meaning. He joked and said in her own language, You have me.

—A little boy, she said. I cannot kill you. You are not a child.

He thought he had misunderstood and asked her to repeat it, and she did. He could not take his eyes from her face. So pretty. So young. Never asked for anything. It made his head spin. It flung his ideas like wet clouts at the walls of his mind. It rearranged his world.

He told her to get out of his bed, out of his house. She pouted at him and turned her back. The ferocity in his voice could not move her. Her stolid resistance set a match to his anger so that he had to push, shove, drag her to the door while she cried out that he was hurting her. Enraged that she should even think to protest he struck her on the back as hard as he could even as she left.

He might have fought a bear his chest heaved so tremendously. Back in his room he felt filthy, polluted with the shame of it all. Who thought he lived in peace. Who thought he was above such anger. He was no better than Norton.

FROM THAT TIME Sam slept alone. His rage at the girl was not to do with her, he knew that. Her request for the boy was a mere step removed from his request for a slave, and that a mere step from his request for her favours. His rage was at finding his conduct different only in degree from the abhorrent. In his ideal society, men and women favoured the rational, the human. They curbed their appetites and shunned violence. But he had seen his ideal trampled over and over. His rage was at the dark seed of violence hidden in every man. On his journey with Matonabbee his party had encountered a girl much like the Pwâsimow girl. Separated from her people she had wintered all alone in the deep of the country, cutting a hole in the ice of the lake to fish. She was both beautiful and brave. In no time, Matonabbee's men had her on her back. One after the other they took their pleasure. He witnessed it all. Though their depravity disgusted him, he had made no move to end it. How could he? But he did not have to watch.

Sometimes lost in depths of longing he dreamed of holding someone close, but it was never the Pwâsimow girl. It was as if he had denied her existence. Instead he dreamed of Molly Norton. In his dreams she always wore the English dress. It flowed around her like water and her black silk hair was a river.

Rarely did he remember the dreams. He would wake

aching for her, knowing only that he had seen her, held her, all the delight of their dreamed union lost on him. There was one dream that was different and would live deep and unseen inside him until he remembered it many years later. In this dream her father stood in his nightshirt on the riverbank. The tide was falling. The waters of the Churchill drained away, exposing a villainous grey marl. The people from both inside and outside the fort went down to walk upon it, pleased with this new phenomenon until it began to ooze around their feet and draw them down. Molly in her silken dress was among them. He woke holding only a few fragments in his sight. He knew he had been holding Molly and trying to save her. He did not know from what. He only knew he was not able.

—

ALIVE WE KNOW NOTHING of the dreams of the dead. If we knew we would see how the days we think so brief are forever. We would let no day pass in darkness without the fires of our hearts to light it to warm it. The dreams of the dead return and return like birds after winter to the places where love was. When the days of the long journey abate I seek out the days I want to live again. I summon my spirit again to my youth to the time that I knew Samuel would one day keep me as his woman. The year came when his eyes looked for mine mine his. The year after my father's death. Our meeting in the eyes a secret shared. I knew then that he would come and take me and he did. It was done quickly in a moment after we left the trading room.

He pulled me to him and pressed me close breathing hard in my ear. Don't make me wait he said. Don't make me wait. His hands clambering like creatures alive with legs. We fought and we bit clawed and pinched until we both were mad like martens closed in a sack together. He clamped his hand over my mouth and held it there though I had the cushion of his palm between my teeth. When he was done rutting and shoving the noise of our breath was like a waterfall rushing and then slowly slowly freezing. He pinched me hard as I pulled away. I showed my mother the mark. A love bruise she said. I said I would one day return it.

It is a time to live again—that time when nothing is known of what is to come a space where the spirit flies with no jess to restrain it. I guessed then nothing of his leaving. In my dreams he always stayed. He lived here with us always. In my dreams he was governor and kept me for a wife and lay with me at night. In the days—the days in my heart—I was going to be by his side forever in our house of plenty. In my heart I was with him always. Sewing his shoes for him like a real wife out on the land keeping his cup full.

And some of it was true and came to be. And though I was not the wife that I had dreamed and though I sewed no shoes for him sometimes we did travel. Not far. Not to hunt or fish like the other people for there was no need but only so that together we could eat the land with his eyes. Take its measure with his feet. And though we slept in a deep bed of feathers in my father's room in my heart I carried our bedding on my back as a real wife should. In my new young woman's dreams there was no end to the comforts I could provide or the pleasures I could taste. I imagined no end to my life in the stone house playing with the children and the animals in the day keeping him warm at night. There was no end to our days. We walked across the face of the yard at evening as if it were the face of the land itself. Under the shifting light we climbed the walls and watched the horizon deepen to black as the sun vanished. We closed our shutters for the night never doubting the next day would come. Never guessing he would sail back across the water and I would stand alone. And would the nights have been sweeter still if we had known?

Sometimes the remembering is so powerful I imagine I am in my body. Feel again that warmth that makes the soles of the feet burn and courses through the thighs. My inside opening. My belly drawing in drawing in. Who would have thought that these things we believed would never come again would be like this—without end? I return often to that place to that time and to others also. Now that I know that times are but places that can be entered at will existing forever I yearn less for them and am at peace. At peace waiting and watching the unending unfolding.

1775

SAMUEL HEARNE HAD BEEN INLAND AT Cumberland House for little over a year when the news of his advancement to the command of Prince of Wales Fort came to him from Governor Jacobs at York. Though he had written to the committee to express his interest in assuming command of the Churchill fort, the new trade at Cumberland House was occupying all his thoughts. Jacobs' letter took him by surprise. He had been down to York in the summer and had only just returned, ready for another year of trade. When the letter arrived, he left at once and made his way downriver to York again, leaving his second in charge of the post until a chief could be appointed. Once at York, he was delayed for several months until the ice was fit to travel on towards Churchill.

Despite the unpleasantness with the girl, he knew he had left behind a small Eden at Cumberland: a house newly built in a position of his choosing, as fair a prospect as any English manor, a handful of men who were not afraid to work and were content to live peacefully, and a corresponding number of women. There was nothing they wanted for—or if there was, they could barter with their Indian neighbours or send back down to York. At Cumberland, he had had a taste of the kind of peaceful coexistence he dreamed about: a company of men and women living in harmony, a self-regulating society where the purpose of duty was as clear as the consequences of neglecting it. If a hunter was not treated with courtesy, he would not return; if the wood was not felled, you would freeze. The woman he had expelled from that private garden was his sinful Eve. Sometimes with her in his arms he had begun to think that paradise was more than just a notion.

This promotion to Churchill, though he welcomed it, was his own expulsion from Eden. He would simply have to recreate it. This time he would be more careful whom he held in his arms. He had no wish to see the underside of another's soul again, or his own. He made himself a promise that his command at Churchill would not be as graceless as Norton's. Every man, he believed, had a right to enjoy his life on earth. An enlightened governor would see that every man could. There would be demands from London. There always were. But London was four thousand miles away and unless they cared to come out and try things for themselves they would have to settle for his manner of doing business. For business, he liked to think, could be conducted fairly without cheating and deception, and without breaking men's backs in the process.

He came to the Churchill River on a clear day at noon towards the end of January, a day when the subtle lengthening of the light was at last noticeable. He and his two guides had walked most of the last night in the flooding beauty of a full moon, the glittering land a mirror to the night's numberless burning stars. Though they were tired, the elation of nearing the end of their journey carried them forward. A group of Homeguard men out hunting after ptarmigan, Otôthapith among them, saw him approaching and walked to meet him, greeting him with grave faces. They said the cookhouse had burned to the ground and half the buildings with it. They said Mr. Jefferson had been asleep at the time with his new wife Molly Norton and did not want to be disturbed. Then they laughed uproariously and mimicked his expression. Sam had them all load their guns and fire a volley to alert the watch and then they walked on together, the Homeguard men escorting his small party to the gates. The bell began its tolling. The new governor arriving in style. He was surprised at how it felt more like coming home.

It was already growing dark as they crossed the yard amid shouts of greeting, the officers assembled in his honour. But he saw Molly at once. He had not expected to see her inside the fort. She was standing a little way off, at the door of William Wales's little stone house. She did not run to meet him.

He spent the next day in the trading room with Jefferson and Captain Robinson and Richard Wills, the new chief trader, reviewing the books and catching up on the London correspondence of the preceding summer. London was still placing a heavy emphasis on the whale fishery. Sam was glad his days in service to that industry were over. It was the very opposite of Eden, a hard and ungenerous existence. They closed the books and the boxes as soon as the light failed and retired to the mess, where they ate and drank as long as the stories lasted. It occurred to Sam that they lived like princes—princes of whales, as he, more than a little drunk, proposed as a toast.

All the news of the previous eighteen months was rehashed for his benefit. He had heard most of it from the Homeguard men on the day of his arrival and from Jefferson in the evening, but he enjoyed the extended accounts, which came with a good deal of licence. Matonabbee had come in the year he left. He was sorry he had missed him. Purvis said he had never seen so large a contingent. He said they were arriving for the best part of a day and their tents filled the plantation as far as the marsh. He thought they had at least three years' worth of furs and likely would not be back for another three. Wills said if they were princes, Matonabbee was an emperor. He had eleven wives. Jefferson corrected him and said seven. Sam said it was very pleasant to smoke a pipe and dream of seven wives. Wills said you would need an entire fort just to feed these seven. And servicing them all would kill you. They were burly as men and you wouldn't want to pick a fight with any of them. Purvis said not quite true, he'd seen a sweet young girl— But he didn't manage to finish his sentence for the ribbing he brought upon himself.

—And you've seen our whorehouse, I suppose. You'll be wanting to pay a visit there.

Wills, who had himself paid a visit to the unfortunate Jenni one dark afternoon, was pleased with his remark.

Jefferson, who as deputy had done his best to prohibit all advances in that direction, was not.

—You do yourself no honour there, Mr. Wills. He's not serious, sir. That's the brandy talking. Mrs. Graham is lodging with her child in the astronomers' house. At least for now.

—Jenni's as poor a lost soul as you've seen, said Purvis. She'd be better off away from here altogether.

—Can she be sent back to York?

—Not with the boy. And she won't be parted.

—Not that she couldn't get herself another at the drop of a hat, said Wills.

—And young Molly?

But Sam was being disingenuous. Even in the dusk he had seen that young Molly was a grown woman. He had fears for her now that had not occurred to him before Wills's remark.

But the shared opinion seemed to be that young Molly was a case all to herself. She'd wandered for a while like a ghost outside the walls, but since she'd come to spend so much time in the Wales house she looked happy enough, at least according to Purvis and Jefferson. She'd taken again to wearing the English clothes her father had bought her, but if you looked closely you could see she had her own clothes on underneath. She spent all her time with Jenni and the boy. The real puzzle was why she refused every offer, for she'd had plenty.

—Support. That's your answer, said Jefferson. The governor's provided for her. She don't have need of a man.

THE NEXT DAY Sam went to see Molly in the hut. He was at first surprised by what he found and then on reflection not surprised at all. It perfectly accorded with the nature of the place that had so struck him in his first year. For here he was, the governor, paying a call on two ladies of the estate. If he had been wearing a hat he would have removed it and kept it in his hand. And here *they* were in a little stone house as you might see on any dale, only inside was no stool or chair or table, no bed of any kind but skins, no boards underfoot but pine boughs brought from up the river and laid on the earth. A fire crackled in the centre of the hut, its smoke hanging thick under the timbers of the turf roof before it twisted away through a rough vent. Molly had the infant in her lap. She looked so easy it might have been hers. Jenni, who had been sleeping, sat up.

—It is the governor, said Molly, her voice flat, almost indifferent.

—Mrs. Graham. Molly. Sam bowed to each. May I?

He sat down opposite them. Jenni reached in silence for her baby.

—It is a fine-looking boy, Mrs. Graham.

But Mrs. Graham only nodded. Molly still had not smiled.

—You did not come back with Mrs. Graham, she said.

It was an accusation, not a statement—and Sam was glad for what it revealed.

—I did not. But I am back now.

—Governor Samuel Hearne. Now Molly smiled despite herself. I was afraid to greet you.

—I'm still Sam. Greet me now.

Jenni's sudden laughter broke the silence between them.

—She'll greet you later.

They drank tea together and talked about nothing at all. Before he left Sam asked Molly if this house was her home now. She said no.

—Then it is with Nêwositêkâpaw.

—Yes, she said. But it is not our home.

—Where can I find you again?

—I am always here, said Molly. I don't go away.

SAM SOON REALIZED that his promotion had brought him a new kind of freedom, as real as the freedom he experienced outside the walls. Granted, he had his duty to the board but the execution of it fell to the men and council. He had only to see that it was done. It was not arduous. Nor would he make it so for those under his command. What his position gave him was opportunity—and time. It was not long before he went again to visit Molly.

She sat wrapped in furs by the small fire in the centre of the room. As before she held Jenni's baby in lap. She smiled and asked Sam to sit down. Jenni was sleeping. She didn't rouse.

Sam sat for a while without speaking. Some current of vitality passed between the two of them. They sat breathing it in, passing it back to the other on their breath. For many minutes it was enough.

—You know why I've come, Molly Norton.

—I know.

—And you'll come?

She looked at him with a trace of uncertainty.

—You'll come to my quarters tonight?

—Yes. Her gravity, her lack of artifice or any show of modesty, was unsettling. And then she spoke again and this time there was amusement in her eyes.

—And now I know what you say next.

Sam looked at her with his head tilted in question.

—Don't make me wait.

Their widening smiles were mirror images, as gratifying and as unsatisfying as a kiss.

SHE DID NOT wait for evening but went across to find him that very afternoon as the sun was setting, carrying furs for them to lie on. She said there was something that must be done first. Sam had hoped to be more discreet, less proclamatory, but he agreed. He asked one of the men to carry his mattress out into the yard. He followed with a cask of train oil and drizzled it over until all parts were saturated. It ignited at once under the brand; several of the men came to see what he was about and stayed to watch. The scorched feathers stank and lifted as they caught, floating up in the smoke to splash the darkening sky with fire and disappear into the night, small brightly coloured birds from another country. It took a long time to burn. The next morning the sooty feathers lay everywhere on the white snow.

EVEN WITHOUT a mattress it was clear to Sam how his fortunes had risen. He did not mind making love to his country

wife on the floor. The pleasures of skins on skin were not to
be dismissed. And she had promised to make a feather bed in
spring. As soon as the geese were brought in. He considered
her skills and decided privately that he would farm out the
work, perhaps to Nêwositêkâpaw. It would be preferable to
sleeping in constant flurries of down. Molly. That was who she
was from now on. Fully her own woman, his own woman, no
longer her father's pet.

HE SPENT the ensuing months making many small changes
to improve the day-to-day affairs of the fort. He was determined that life here—for everyone—would be bearable. More,
would be enjoyable. He had the steward make an inventory of
all that needed repair and set the carpenter to work. He put up
a sheet of paper in the men's mess and devised a simple system
for them to order more mitts or shoes before their worn ones
put their extremities at risk. He even kept the welfare of the
horses in mind and had a new stable built for them on the north
side. Where before he had resisted the notion that so much
labour was required just to keep the factory in operation, now
he saw it as a wheel that properly oiled turned with little effort.
It was scarcely even necessary to give the orders. The tradesmen knew almost by instinct what was required. The tailor
saw when stocks of vests for trade were low and set to making more. The sawyer knew precisely where the next log tent
should be built for the men employed in wooding. Everything
ran on wheels that meshed as in a well-made clock and helped
each other turn.

On Saint George's Day Sam felt justified in calling a

holiday. The day was cold and cloudy with what might jus-
tifiably be called a gale. He sent Joseph Hansom round with
the rum rations in the morning while the carpenter and the
cooper constructed a new mask for the targeting match. It
was a rudimentary affair. No one would be standing inactive
for too long in such a bitter wind. He sent four men to haul
in more wood from the stacks. He had already checked to see
that there was a sufficient quantity of brew on hand. With the
fort full, the men having come in from the various log tents,
it was an easy crescendo towards the hilarity of the evening.
When the dinner in the servants' mess was over, the cook was
carried in at shoulder height on a chair, an apple in his mouth
like a roast pig. By this time Governor Hearne had retired
from the officers' mess, leaving the rest of the council to their
port. He knew they were restraining any ribald observations
until he was out of earshot.

He closed the door of his room, deadening the raucous
voices and the singing.

Molly was still awake. She said she had been waiting for
him since she left Jenni.

Sam was suddenly ashamed not to have thought of Jenni
alone in the stone hut. There was no question that others
would. He reached for his coat, telling Molly he would not
be long.

He could tell as he opened Jenni's door that there was
more than one man inside the hut. They were men who worked
on the sloop in summer. He knew them. Jenni was not visible although he could hear her beneath the heavy sailor. The
second sailor was thrusting at the buttocks of the first.

They did not hear him when he told them to get out. He had to reach for the second man and pull him off.

—You'll come to the trading room at eight o'clock tomorrow morning. Don't return to the mess tonight. His voice was shaking.

The men nodded and cringed and said *sir* and stumbled out into the night. Jenni got up and pulled her dress down over her deerskin stockings. She stared ahead, her mouth fixed.

—Are you hurt?

She shook her head.

—You'll come with me tonight, Jenni. Bring the child.

She looked him directly in the eye. He was ashamed for what she was thinking.

She had drunk so much that he had to help her across the yard. He knew how it would appear to an observer.

When he reached his quarters he let her in. Molly smiled to see her friend.

—Jenni is to sleep on the floor, said Sam. I'm going downstairs. She is not to sleep in the bed. Do you understand?

Molly nodded, though it was clear she could not see why.

Dinner in the officers' mess had developed into supper, with Wills and a servant he had seconded for the task serving salt fish and pickled lemons. Hearne's reappearance provoked a flurry of jibes. He weathered them as best he could, a half smile on his lips, and poured himself a large glass of brandy.

The next day he set the smith to fashion a lock for the door of the stone hut.

The two men appeared at the appointed hour in the trading room. They stood stinking and queasy, squinting against its dusty light. He wanted to flog them personally but Norton's shadow cooled the thought. He told them they would be returning on the next ship.

—Perhaps you'd like to tell me what, exactly, I should state as the offence?

The men shook their heads. Sam waited.

—You could say, sir, we was peace breakers.

—Thank you. You'll work all week at the lime quarry. Report to me at eight every night. Dismissed.

He heard laughter when they were a safe distance away. By evening the reason for it had circulated through the fort and come back to him. We should have told him, the sailor had said, sputtering, we should have told him: Buggered Mrs. Graham.

Though the affair was laid to rest, Sam remained troubled for several days. He sent Molly away, preferring to be alone with his doubts—and his conscience. "Peace breakers" was a description more apt than the man had known. Sometimes—when the conversation in the officers' mess turned to the migration of birds or to horticultural experiments—he could believe his cherished dream of a rational society. The men's bestiality not only robbed him of his dream but made him feel shamed, their depravity a reminder of the ugliness within.

SAM WOULD HAVE liked to send Jenni away, back to her own people, but there was always the question of the boy and so she stayed on, entirely dependent on the storehouses for all her needs. It was a cost to the Company but one easily absorbed, and so that the debt did not appear so high in the books, Sam sometimes took a portion of his own allowance and transferred it to Jenni. In any case she ate very little. Often, if she had been given rum or brandy, she slept for days. The child too slept. It was a listless little creature with dull eyes. Sam mentioned the fact to Purvis. Purvis asked that Jenni bring the child in. He saw at once.

—That is one very sick babby. He took it from her and went into the mess. He laid it down and unwrapped it. It was a skinny child but there was nothing obviously amiss. Except that it did not frown at the sudden exposure to the air—and then it did, but not until a full minute had elapsed. He scratched the baby's cheek lightly with his fingernail and watched. It was almost a minute again before the child raised its arm in response.

—He has a lethargy.

—Can you give him medicine?

Purvis had no preparations for lethargy. He shook his head.

—Please.

—We'll give him a dram. Just a wee one, mind, or we'll make matters worse. He took a flask from his pocket and unscrewed the cap, poured a little brandy in it, then set the flask down and dipped his little finger in. The baby sucked and pursed his lips. Purvis did it a few more times, the baby now squalling angrily, and then drank the rest himself.

—Something you can try from time to time when the need arises.

Nêwositêkâpaw too tried to help. Once she took it away and gave it to her husband's first wife to nurse for a while.

And then it howled angrily. She told Molly she should start some milk of her own and give her friend's child suck when it was hungry. Molly liked the idea. She spent night and day with Jenni, but she did not persevere. Instead she would offer to carry the child about with her until it fell asleep.

By summer it was at her back most of the time. Sometimes he slept with Molly in Sam's bed. Jenni didn't seem to mind. One of the labourers had taken her for a wife. Sam was unsure what to do. To have the man in Jenni's hut was like establishing married quarters within the fort against all regulations, and this for a man whose best skill was with a sledgehammer at the lime quarry and whose greatest achievement and delight was to have once hammered his friend with his fists until he lost his teeth. He asked Jenni to build herself a tent outside and she was happy to comply. Sam didn't mind where the man slept, as long as he reported for duty at the first bell.

The sight of Molly and the child became so familiar at the fort that it was easy to forget she was not the mother. Sometimes one of the men, speaking with the governor, would refer to "your boy." Sam would quickly set them right.

—Governor Graham's boy. She's raising it only.

If he had a child by Molly it would be one with bright eyes, looking all about the world, a curious boy. A boy he could teach. Hunting. Naval skills. Drawing. Letters and mathematics. Like the Hospital boy he had taught to draw. Like the Esquimau boy when his eyes had shone with pleasure. For Sam one life seemed hardly enough to accomplish all he wished. But for a boy like this babe of Graham's, one life might be altogether too much effort.

Still he grew accustomed to seeing the pair of them about the place. By the time the fort was ready for winter and he had leisure to draw a breath, he realized that the three of them made a kind of family. It would have to do for now. When he and Molly lay down together, they slept. What had begun as a lustful frenzy for her had twisted on itself to become a kind of shame. Sometimes the memory of her father strode into the room. And there were other spectres to impede him. The girl at the inland house had seemed to want him to be rough with her and it had excited him. In recall he knew why. She had brought to mind the Dog Rib woman so abused by his companions on the journey. It only added to his shame as he lay beside his wife.

During the winter, Sam took up his pen again. He did not want to return to his book, not yet, and so he drew. He began a large drawing of Lake Athabascow, where he had wintered with Matonabbee. It gave him great pleasure to live in two places at once. To be here within the massy walls of the fort, hearing the men arguing or laughing, hearing them sometimes sing, breathing the choky smoke of the too-green wood—to be here and at the same time to be out on the frozen lake, its level surface stretching away on both sides and ahead, behind, dotted with small islands, each with its own perfect composition of slender pines, its own offering. To hear again the owl's wingbeat, nothing more than a breath, a soft exhalation through a rounded mouth, passing close by his head as it floated down from the trees. To see the tracks of the fox and the faint fine line beside them where perhaps the claws of its kill trailed. It was a double life. A man who drew could live twice—without dying once. He promised himself that when he was more at ease with his duties and his men—for he spent far too much time checking up on them—he would make more drawings. He had sketches he had made on his journey. Perhaps he would teach Molly too. She was observant. Perhaps draw Molly. Molly among her pets, one of her mice in the palm of her hand. Or the otter draped like a scarf at her shoulder, Molly laughing. Or draw her as he had seen her today, dangling beads for Jenni's infant. Her expression so concentrated, willing the boy to reach.

1776

I T WAS MAY. IT SHOULD NOT HAVE HAPPENED. The winter was behind them. There had been a thaw. God, the days they'd spent hauling snow out of the yard. The horses willing, thinking perhaps of succulent new grass springing. If they were patient. The waters of the river and the bay were still locked up—the real thaw was a month away—but there had been a melting, a softening. Everywhere they walked they left tracks until the snow became a field of troughs to slow them down. And the softening had been in the air too. The sun rays suddenly strong enough to blunt the edge of the cold. The geese had arrived and Joseph Hansom had gone in good spirits with a hunting party to the North Point. He'd been up to Sloop's Cove a few days before, and the master and the men were working there without their coats. There were men up at the wooding camp too. It was only luck that had brought them in before it began, for the next day the weather had turned without warning. The day had dawned overcast with a grey light, hardly a line between land and sky. But though the thermometer had plunged, there was yet no sign of what was coming.

They had gone about their usual business at the fort. That business of keeping the fort itself alive and breathing. The business he had complained about to Norton when he was a wide-eyed youth. He was working in the storeroom with Jefferson and his assistant, sorting goods and determining what should go on the indent, discarding what was spoiled. His steward had taken a couple of men to help with brewing the beer for his own table. No one had taken much account of the sudden return of the cold.

And then one of the men from the North Point had come in with a note. It was from Joseph. He was sending some Northern Indians in with new provisions: one hundred and sixty geese, one swan, and several ducks. He hoped they would arrive safe.

Sam had looked up then like an animal from grazing, suddenly aware and remembering its position in the wide expanse of the world. The weather had closed in on them while they had been working. He realized that the storeroom, though the window was unshuttered, had gone uncommonly dark. He went to the door. The sky was darker now than the grey yard, heavy with a promise of harm. He thanked the man and went to fetch his coat.

Dressed now as for winter, he walked out to the ramparts and climbed the stair. The steps were glassy underfoot. A savage wind was slicing across from the northwest. He pulled his hat down and walked round to the northeast bastion. From there he could see clear across to the goose grounds. Except that it wasn't clear. Either it was snowing over there or the wind was lifting the drift. He was looking into a cloud of freezing whiteness.

An hour or so later he went back up with his spyglass. The weather had worsened, the sky massing low now, heavy with its ballast of snow, the wind howling at the walls. It was hard to see Button's Bay at all. Jefferson came up beside him.

—My eyes are watering. You try. He handed Jefferson the glass.

—It's like looking at a bedsheet.

—To the north another three degrees.

—There's something moving.

—What I thought.

—But they're far.

So far in fact that they were two small black dots appearing and disappearing in the whiteness.

Sam took back the glass and watched again.

—It has to be them. They're coming this way. It's them.

They climbed back down and hurried across the yard to the storeroom.

—I'd not want to be out there.

Like an incantation against the eventuality.

—They'll know what to do.

Like a prayer.

The work after that had a hollow quality to it. It was a way of filling the time. Sam ordered the watch, who had long since come inside, to return to his post at the gate in three hours' time in case the Indians continued walking and came across the ice. He guessed it would take them at least that long if they were heavy laden. The man set up a brazier there to fill with coals from one of the stoves. He left a supply of wood beside it, but when it was time for him to go out, there seemed no point, the weather was so bad. They dragged the gates open a little so that any who had persevered could enter. By the afternoon the blizzard struck in earnest. They rang the bell continuously until Sam had a report of every Company man accounted for.

Sam took some record books to his quarters. He was glad to find Molly there. Even wrapped in a blanket like an old woman she cheered him.

—Who is on the bay?

—Some hunters. He knew what she was thinking and did not tell her they were Wêcîpwayânak and were bringing in the geese. They would be the wives and the strongest daughters.

—Wêcîpwayânak? My sister's husband could be with them. Perhaps my sister.

He wondered why he had not rung the bell sooner.

The cold was extraordinary. No one even passed between buildings. Inside, every stove was roaring and pinging. The men in the servants' mess had started a game of cards. A storm in May was a fine thing without the prospect of another and another and the dark days of winter like a cold tunnel to be negotiated.

TOWARDS THE END of the afternoon a dark shape formed in the blowing snow and approached from the northeast. She came with a burden on her back, bent like an animal that must butt its way through a thicket. At times she seemed to be pushed sideways and staggered to correct her course. No one saw her come close to the wall and pause for an instant before she rounded the northeast bastion. She made her way to the gate on the south side. Here in the lee of the wind the snow eddied and swirled and flew up into her face. She was wrapped in the tattered moosehide she had been using to haul the geese. Forced to abandon them, she was bringing in just three tied together so that she could carry them over her shoulder. She wore no winter stockings, no cap. Her hands were bloodless.

Jonathan Hull, only two years on the bay, had been persuaded—bribed in fact with a promise of rum—to go to the woodpile. He saw her as she struggled through the gate. He shouted a greeting but she had not the breath to answer and when he went across to her she looked at him with eyes he would not soon forget. It was as if she were offering him some unknown flesh, laying it on his tongue for him to taste its bewildering mix of pain and exhaustion and relief.

He stacked the geese outside the trading-room door. They knocked like rocks against each other. She dropped to her knees and let her forehead fall against them. He managed to get her up again and into the trading room. Suddenly free of the load she staggered and he steadied her, but she could no longer stand without support. He left her slumped on the floor and went for the governor.

Sam helped him take her across to the servants' mess, where the stove was burning almost red hot and the men were pleased to have a diversion.

It seemed the woman was alone. She could do little but sign yes or no with her eyes. She did not know where the others were. A man came with a blanket from his bed and they covered the woman and left her to lie by the stove.

Sam ordered a watch to walk the ramparts every half hour and the bell to be rung at fifteen-minute intervals.

The man who walked the walls had little chance of seeing anything in the driving snow. Like the woman, he met the world at an angle, butting into the wind. It was all he could do to keep a straight line. Visibility was no more than thirty feet.

In the servants' mess, the men's sense of holiday was dampened by the two silent figures at the stove. The Northern woman was curled there like a dog, the governor's wife beside her staring mournfully with unfocused eyes. When darkness fell Sam came to take his wife away but she would not go. He asked her to be reasonable. Pointed out the unsuitability of staying. She calmly said no. She was staying. He knew it was useless to force the issue. He sighed and waited until the last man was gone and then he went to his bed.

In Sam's dreams that night black specks moved outside the perimeter walls. They gathered and bunched and broke apart again. He called to them but his voice ululated with the wind and he could not control it. The black specks rose, continuing their strange dance in the white air. And then they drifted high like a cloud and dispersed in the wind.

The cold woke him in the morning. The shutters of his room were glazed over. He could hear the wind outside. It had not abated.

In the servants' mess the two women were sleeping. His wife looked like a child beside the older woman. Sam woke them. He asked the Northern woman to hold out her hands. The blood had not returned to the tips of her fingers. She smiled at him and said, It will come. It will.

He said they should both go to the cookhouse.

There was no prospect of work of any kind outside the walls. He began a mental list of the duties he would assign indoors. They could not begin the brewing for the servants' tables. They would have to wait for that until the weather warmed again. They could begin packing some of the furs ready for shipment. Some unlucky souls could haul out whatever was rotten or spoiled from the root cellar. He had a couple of men in mind for that. He could set two or three others to repairing the floor of the guardroom where it had subsided. There was always work.

Outside, the storm was bent on obliterating the fort. The snow flew as fast as ever. He put on his winter toggie and mitts, found his otterskin cap, and went up on walls. The drift on the north side came almost to the top. There could be no one approaching in this.

He took his breakfast with Jefferson in the officers' mess. Purvis joined them. Purvis had been at the bay for longer than either of them. He could not remember a storm of such ferocity so late in the season. He hoped that what the woman had said about others coming in behind her was not true. But it was not a useful observation. They were all three uneasy at its emptiness, and even as they were rising to get to work, a man came from the gate saying several Northern Indians were coming in.

The meeting in the trading room was sombre. One man squatted on his haunches and tore slowly, evenly at his hair, rocking back and forth. Another stood swaying, his eyes hopelessly blank, registering nothing. Their spokesman said they had lost their wives. He said they had found two women frozen. He said everyone was in great distress. He hoped some of the women had arrived.

—One.

—One?

—One. Fetch her here, will you, Wills? She's in the cookhouse.

The swaying man had come to his senses. He said the women were not prepared for winter. They hunted geese every year. Every year the same. There was never any difficulty.

Every man now had something to add. Out there, they said repeatedly. Out there. They said the snow was so thick it had been impossible to tell if they were walking in the right direction. They had begun with the wind at the right shoulder, but the storm had been turning and had swung them in a great curve. It was only chance that brought them in. They had hoped the rest of the women were here before them.

Every man turned as the door opened. The man who had been tearing his hair got up and went forward to clasp his wife. They rocked to and fro in the middle of the room. Sam wondered if she would suffer for the handfuls of hair he'd left on the floor.

—Come. We'll find you all something to eat.

But three of the men said no.

—Give us coats. Give us pemmican to take with us.

One of them said what no one else would voice.

—Give us sleds.

At that his friend came close to tears, contorting his face in the effort to stem them.

Sam tried to dissuade them from going out again but they would not listen. Molly came in and saw them putting on their coats. She saw her brother-in-law among the men.

—My sister?

—Out there. We'll find her.

WHEN THEY HAD been gone a little while, Molly took the moosehide robe from behind the door, wrapped herself well, and battled her way down to the gate. She stood outside, not sure at first what she was seeing. Unfamiliar shapes loomed in the whiteness. The tents were covered with snow on the windward side so that only a sliver of each was visible. She thought of finding Nêwositêkâpaw's tent and ducking inside. She thought of telling her mother about Jane's plight. She thought of Nêwositêkâpaw's reply. There is nothing to be done. Nêwositêkâpaw could not help. She would be warm under her sleeping skin. She turned and made her way back, half running, lurching, keeping her head down.

Before nightfall the Wêcîpwayân men returned. Two of

them could barely walk. They had searched through the day, working carefully so that they did not get themselves lost. Out there, they said, you could not hear the bell.

—Was the bell rung?

Purvis asked it under breath.

Sam shook his head.

—I think what the man said is true. There would have been no point.

—Let's take a look at your feet, said Purvis. Then we'll get you some warm food. You'll be fine.

But one of them clearly was not. He began swaying, repeating a phrase over and over.

—He is grieving for his wife.

Sam nodded, said he understood. He was always embarrassed by such displays. He felt he was in the presence of something more sacred than an altar, and he did not know where to look.

THE TALK THAT NIGHT was all of the poor buggers who got caught. They told stories of other such storms, none of them in May. It was the lack of winter clothing that would get them. They wouldn't stand a chance. The consensus was that none would survive. Joseph Hansom and his companions would be all right. They would be at the log tent on the goose grounds. Built five years ago, it was kept stacked with wood for fires. It was those who had had to cross who would be in difficulty. Who would, to say it plain, surely perish.

In the morning, the trading room was crammed with

volunteers. The day had dawned brighter and though it was snowing lightly visibility was greatly improved. Sam fitted out a dozen men with snowshoes and beaver coats and sleds. He walked out to watch them disperse in a fan towards Button's Bay.

Jane Norton, Wâpiskasiniy, was one of the last to be found. She had lain down or fallen a little distance from the truss of geese she had been hauling. The blowing snow had almost covered her from sight and it was Robert Coults's dog that found her, barking and diving repeatedly at the mound of her body, crashing its front paws into the snow. He called it off. She lay with her knees drawn up and her bent arms covering her face. Coults thought at first she was alive, whimpering, and then he saw a movement at her breast. The dog had woken a child somewhere deep in her clothes.

Coults took off his mitten and reached to feel the woman's neck. It was cold and hard. It was at least two hours back to the fort. He did not know how much longer the infant would last without her warmth.

Big, bear-like Coults had never held an infant in his life and was unsure. But he did not want to take a chance. He bent and lifted the woman onto the sled first. She was as compact, as solid, as furs bundled for shipment. He could hear the mewling of the child. He squatted down and lifted up his beaver toggie, opened his coat inside, his shirt, then gingerly reached inside the woman's clothes. Tits like blocks of ice, he would say whenever afterwards he told the story. Talk about a cold woman. Trying to save his virility from the advance of sentiment. The child's body came alive under his hands, the arms and legs squirming. He picked it up like a pup or a cat, its head dangling, and crammed it into his shirt. He shuddered.

—Don't shit on me, now.

The little thing's body pushed and riled at the stinking hairy expanse of him. He felt the head turning, searching. He buttoned his clothes not quite to the top and pulled the toggie down in front. Then he pushed himself to standing and tied the woman's corpse securely. Halfway back to the fort the baby fell asleep and he was thankful. He was almost there when he was joined by a Wêcîpwayân man. The man's face had a ravaged look. He shouted as he approached. Coults stopped and the man bent to look at the woman's face. He stood up and jerked his chin towards the harness of the sled, reached out his hand. Coults passed it to him. He thought to encourage him.

—Listen. He shifted the child, who had just begun to stir. He shifted it again and the child obliged with a cry.

Coults smiled broadly. The Wêcîpwayân man looked him once in the eye with an expression Coults described afterwards as like a dead man but angry and walked on towards the fort.

THE BODIES were laid in the yard outside the guardroom. There were ten in all, seven women and three children. Of six families, only two women and two children had survived. The husbands wept openly, sobbing and wailing in their grief. The Hudson's Bay men were not sure what to do in the face of so much pain. They coughed and shuffled their feet and hoped the storm would soon subside. Purvis tended to those who had been crippled by the cold. Several men, including those who had gone back out on the first day, were unable to walk, their feet blistering now.

Molly waited. As soon as she saw the two men coming in her tears began. As long as they were still out there she had been able to dream her sister found alive, walking back. Her sister's husband went to the back of the room and sat down on his haunches, breathing heavily. He pushed his friends away. But Coults was smiling.

He pulled the baby from his clothes. It screamed with hunger and with rage at the affront. He pushed through with it to the father but he would not take it. Molly picked up one of the blankets and wrapped the child and without a word carried it away.

Sam found her later in the afternoon where he knew she would be, at Jenni's tent. She said she was staying. He said Jenni could nurse the child without her. She said no, she would come back in the morning. He wondered how, living as she had a cosseted pampered life with her father, she had ever learned such independence. But it was no bad thing for a woman in this place.

When dusk came, some of the Company men helped the more able erect a large tent outside the gate where they and the two women could spend the night. Two of the men refused to go. Though it scared them half to death to stay in the yard, they would not leave the bodies of the women in the hands of the Europeans. Against all regulations Sam agreed but said he could not give them shelter. They said they wanted only some skins to cover themselves. The storm was over. Sam put two men on the watch that night. He knew it was not necessary.

Alone in his bed it crossed his mind that the fort under his command was as out of joint as ever, with the goose hunters curled in the yard and his own wife—the governor's wife—out on the plantation. No one slept much that night, for the Homeguard men began firing their guns to keep away the spirits of the dead. They did not stop until dawn.

THE NEXT MORNING a crew walked out with crowbars and pickaxes to the burial ground on the loose, rocky hinterland between the shore and the marsh. Under bright sunshine they worked at the place called Whistling Hill—no more than a low ridge—to quarry enough rocks for seven graves.

The Wêcîpwayân men who were able loaded the bodies onto sleds to haul them to the site. The two surviving women carried the skins and the tobacco Sam had given them for the graves. Molly walked a little apart with her sister's child on her back. Sam and Purvis followed. One man carried his wife the whole distance. He would not be helped.

—Did you ever see a sight more pitiful?

—Will you read?

Sam shook his head and thought about the passage he usually read, the words full of false promises. It was no better than the rigmarole of their conjuring tents.

—No, he said. It would be like the bell in the wind.

At the gravesite, though they still cried unashamedly, the men worked quickly to cover their wives. As soon as it was done they returned without ceremony. At the fort they began to collect themselves for departure.

—Those men shouldn't be walking, said Purvis.

But their companions were insistent. They helped the injured men onto sleds.

—And that's our sleds, sir, they're planning on taking.

Sam put his hand on Wills's arm.

—We can replace sleds.

Molly went to her brother-in-law, who was helping one of his friends. She slipped the carrier off her back and stood it down between her feet. The man shook his head.

—You raise your sister's child. I don't want it. He snorted back tears. It's spoiled.

He repeated the words he had said the previous day when Coults had tried to hand it to him. He had looked at the big man with disgust. He had shaken his head.

—Give it to my wife's sister, he had said. She can raise it. It's spoiled now. I have no wife. I have no child.

—

WHAT I COME TO SEE is that there is never a time of sadness or of joy for both are mixed as waters mingling and are one. I leave this journey and go back often to the time I first put Athîkis to my breast. He had no name then. He was only my sister's boy new in the world and motherless. And now too without a father. I took him to Sam's room and wrapped him close against me using the shawl I wore with the English dress. Then I covered us both with winter robes and went down. I carried him outside. Single snowflakes floated in the blue air lost. Though they had put my sister under rocks I would see her always as she returned to the home of her childhood curled on the sled. Like an infant herself. Or a stone. Her teeth were jammed fast together giving her face the look of a stranger. She was someone I did not know locked there in her last resistance to the cold. No tears could melt her or warm her to life again.

I passed the place where her body had lain and I took her child to Jenni's tent. Jenni smiled when she saw. Just like my boy was she said. Like Joseph. I gave him to her to hold. Joseph was under the sleeping skins but he got up to see this new infant. He reached to touch its face. My sister's baby blinked and looked at him and Jenni's boy laughed. No one had known he was able.

How strange the bleeding of joy into a wounded heart. As if a river runs suddenly with water as warm as the sun.

I told Jenni I wanted to make milk for my sister's boy.

Jenni said we would need more patience than for fishing. She sent me back up to the fort for a bag of pemmican. When I returned I gave the bag to Jenni and settled myself to watch. Jenni opened the bag. She squeezed some of the meat between her fingers to take the grease and then she took her own nipple and rubbed it with the grease.

—Give me. Her hand inviting.

When I placed the child in her lap she put him to her breast.

—Now you do the same. Only a little. Do both.

The baby suckled while I prepared myself. Then Jenni sharply took him off and handed him back.

—Now.

I put him to my breast and he at once found the nipple. His mouth closed round it and he pulled. He sucked mightily and worked his jaw and his gums in the effort to find milk. When he began to cry I put him to the other breast. At first he was pleased and made a noise of satisfaction and then again he began to cry.

—Now me Jenni said. But just a little. Then we do it all again.

Then you will walk with him until he falls asleep. When he wakes we'll start again.

My mother came to see her grandchild and she was glad even in her grief. She said good. She said you will sing to him too.

Jenni's sailor husband came next. He raised his eyebrows to see the three of us and said what's this?

Jenni said this is women's work. Go away and don't come back.

He said for how long?

She said until athîki-pîsim the frog moon is big. And we laughed at his dismay though our hearts were squeezed with pain.

Nêwositêkâpaw said athîki-pîsim that's his name. Athîkis.

I return often to the five days I spent with Jenni. Softening the pemmican. Applying just enough to scent the flesh and wiping away the excess. Pulling the nipples to make them hard. Putting the small face back and back again to her breast. Saying drink. For your dead mother drink. My nipples sore with his fierce pulling. Jenni saying never cry. It won't help. My mother bringing me a tea of pale twigs and bitter bark. And then on the sixth day a sweet new sensation like the tip of a hot hard tongue sliding down inside my breast and the child motionless suddenly and swallowing and then pulling again but different now. Happy now. Drinking.

I carried Athîkis to Sam where he was talking to the armourer in the forge. I told him I had something to show him.

—By all means.

The armourer looked at me from under bushy grey-and-white eyebrows. I was suddenly shy and drew Sam away. It was an easy thing to place the child there at the opening of the English dress.

Sam frowned and did not understand what he was seeing.

—He's drinking.

Still he did not understand.

—He's drinking my milk.

And now Sam was shy. The look on his face confused like that on a man who no longer believes in the world before his eyes.

And that is why I choose to go back often. To feel again the child's limbs soften hear his throat drowning in its joy. His small nose sucking air. To see his eyelids flutter in unbelief at such bounty. To feel his warmth one with mine. And the days that followed with the river releasing its flood. The broken ice pans like a herd of swimming animals jostling in their rush to reach the bay. We stood together all of us to watch the ice spin and tilt and ride up floe upon floe in the current. And I see in time that the people ride on the current of their lives like the ice only to fall upon one another and become all one thing like the waters of the bay. And strange to say the river was a comfort to me when I thought of my sister lying on the ground. Melting into the land the way ice melts into water.

—

RUMOUR RAN AHEAD of Matonabbee wherever he went and the news of his approach to the fort was announced with the usual sense of moment—as if the stores should be checked, the gates flung open, the ears of everyone straining to catch from upriver the first shot of greeting. His party swept to the fort like a river in flood, lifting all into motion. Flotilla after flotilla of canoes rounded the flats. They were still being beached when already there were two boys running up to the gates asking for the governor. With hardly a glance about them the women from the first canoes were carrying tent skins and brush to mark out their pitches. They came like familiars, sure and at ease, every action coloured by custom and by right, as if it were a matter not of years but of only weeks since they last performed it.

Matonabbee had heard who had succeeded as chief factor of Prince of Wales Fort. He could show Sam Hearne how to arrive. Not emaciated and drawn from travel. No. Like a king.

The boys met Sam at the gates, where on his way down to the shore he had stopped to speak to the watch. He had never seen such a large number of canoes at one time.

The two boys were intent on gaining access to speak to the governor. When they learned they were speaking to him they became suddenly self-conscious. They seemed unable to repeat the message without turning their eyes elsewhere. Matonabbee it seemed had one or two requests. The boys were expert at signing each item: his regimental coat and hat; his calumet; breeches and shirt and waistcoat; stockings and garters and shoes; two coats for his lieutenants; hats for them too. And six hats for his wives.

Sam was mildly disappointed. He did not want this facade of ceremony, this pantomime of formality. He wanted friendship. He would give his life for Matonabbee, who had saved his own.

He told the boys it would be taken care of and called a man to take them to the trading room.

—Matonabbee and two lieutenants to be fitted out for trade. Hats for the wives. All of it. He knew the boys would make themselves understood.

There must have been at least twenty tents going up. The air was humming with voices, the whole outskirts alive with movement. He found Matonabbee's tent easily. Two of the wives were busy laying brush they'd collected upriver. Matonabbee was outside directing the women carrying the furs up from the canoes.

He too was disappointed at the turn of events. He had wanted to meet like leaders, not common servants. He smiled nevertheless. There was no chance now to rescue any sense of occasion. He abandoned the etiquette of silence and polite civilities.

—Where's your hat, Sam? The governor must wear a hat.

—I'll wear mine when you wear yours. Tomorrow morning.

Their grins slow as garter snakes sliding.

Matonabbee was pleased enough to take Sam by the shoulders.

—Well. The boy now a man. How many wives?

—One wife, Matonabbee. One only. Only ever one.

—It is not enough for a governor.

—How many would you suggest? Six?

—It would be a beginning.

—When I'm your age, perhaps. Your honourable age.

—You might die first. You die easy, remember? Remember when I found you?

—I remember, Matonabbee. I don't forget easy. But now you want to know who my wife is, surely?

—I know. It's my own niece, Molly. Past Sam's shoulder he could see her hurrying down, the faded English dress visible beneath the robe she wore against the cold. Sam turned.

—You are too quick, Mr. Matonabbee.

—And you are not slow. She has a baby on her back.

Sam, experiencing vicariously a father's pride, had no wish to spoil his friend's delight. Molly came to greet Matonabbee. The two of them embraced like father and daughter.

Sam, in demand again back at the gates, left them to each other's company. Molly walked beside the man she called her uncle, Athîkis asleep deep inside his cradle, only his feathery black hair visible at the opening.

That night with Sam she took great delight in recounting her visit. She had gone, she said, to sit in Matonabbee's tent a while. His youngest wife had given her tea to drink. When Matonabbee had asked if "this child of the governor's" was a son or a daughter, she had not corrected him but had answered only "It is a boy." She told Sam she did not see why it should not be his child. She wished it were. Athîkis should have both a mother and a father.

There was only one thing, she said. Matonabbee had gestured to what he could see of Athîkis in the cradle.

—It does not look like Sam's son, he had said. You are lucky. You would not want a child with hair that looks like the underside of a sick dog's tail.

She said the joke had amused the whole tent.

IN THE MORNING, Sam was ready to receive Matonabbee formally. He combed and tied his hair. He brushed his coat and wore his tricorne hat. When he heard that Matonabbee was assembling his wives he called for Molly and gave her a chair behind the table. Jefferson had set out his samples. The brandy had been duly cut with water and the glasses stood ready by the cask. The piper was in position at the gates. They heard the drone begin and then the first skirl. Sam could not think why he felt nervous.

When Matonabbee's party arrived it filled the trading room. Matonabbee, resplendent in his red coat, looked taller than ever. Sam sent a man for extra chairs, though the women preferred to settle on the floor behind their husband.

Sam saw there was to be no escape from protocol.

—Was the winter a good one?

—The winter was not a good one. The beaver were scarce and the fox too. The deer were not numerous. The hunting was poor. Scarcely enough to keep us alive . . .

Sam was patient, ready with his response when the time came.

—The ships were not heavy laden this year. We may not have everything you require. But the quality of the goods far exceeds any other year.

He really did not like this work. Would rather be out hunting with the man than stuck in this dark room bartering. An exercise in fakery. Like a game of cards.

Matonabbee got up and spread a glossy beaverskin on the desk.

—And our quality too is good. We have not a skin worth less than this. He brushed his hand down the fur. Feel it. Tell me this is not the best you have seen at this post.

Sam obliged. Acknowledged that it was good. It merited a pipe.

He reached for the calumet. Matonabbee laid his own pipe on the beaverskin. The women shifted, anticipating the pleasures of the smoke as the trader laid out a clay pipe for each of them.

Little by little the smoke began to pervade the room. It smothered the irritating empty phrases most satisfactorily. Now Sam was in no hurry to curtail the interlude, all activities, all demands, suspended in favour of an idleness. He knew the value of time passed without activity. It produced its own peace. His days with Matonabbee had taught him that. In times of plenty, when they had eaten their fill, he used to wonder why they were in no hurry to move forward. He was about one day to ask one of the old men in their party. The man was sitting aside from the others. Sam hunkered down beside him. But the man did not turn or acknowledge him and it seemed rude to interrupt his reverie. Sam raised his eyes and followed the man's gaze. The barren land rolled away under the late sun. It was October. The carpet laid before their eyes was richer, subtler than any woven by man.

Matonabbee filled his pipe again. Though he looked relaxed, he was thoroughly engaged. The unseen presence of more than one hundred of his followers sharpened his mind. It was to them he would answer for any bargains struck within the trading room. He launched into a long account of the trials and troubles they had endured to make the journey down to Churchill. He larded it liberally with accounts of meetings they had had with the Pedlars, of how they had resisted selling far back up the river, though the Pedlars' goods were very fine. And he had a string of requests to make before they even opened the trade. No less than five more lieutenants' coats, fifteen common coats, and eighteen shirts and hats. And guns—eight guns, to be precise—with one hundred and forty pounds of gunpowder and the shot, ball, and flints to go with it. And there was more. Hatchets, ice chisels, bayonets, knives. And tobacco.

Mr. Jefferson developed a severe cough as the list continued. Matonabbee, astute as ever, leapt to his feet, rummaged in his skippertogan, and pulled out a small box.

—Here. Chew it. Don't swallow. He had the lid off and was shaking some of the dried leaf into Jefferson's obedient palm.

He resumed his seat and continued. He wanted cloth and blankets, combs and looking glasses, stockings, handkerchiefs, sashes and lace. And even then he was not done. He would have needles, paint, awls, and files—Sam got up to help fetch the articles—hawks bells and buttons. He asked Mr. Jefferson to note it all down.

You had to admire the man. On the land, in the trading room. He knew what he was about. By the time Matonabbee had stopped speaking the desk was piled high with all he had asked for.

—It gives me pleasure to bestow these fine gifts on you and your friends. Tell them when you give them that we wish you all to come every year for more. It is an honour to trade with your people.

—You are an honourable man. Your Company is an honourable company. We shall not desert you for the Canadians.

Amazing how the man had finagled those goods onto

the table. Again Sam thought how much more honest and forthright their dealings were out in the country, where every action sprang from need, immediate and valid.

—Then it will be my pleasure to accompany you with our gifts to your friends.

Sam stood up and waited while the procession formed. He and Matonabbee to be followed by the other captains, then the wives, then the Company servants bearing the gifts. They waited again in the yard for the piper to resume and then they walked, as slowly as possible without appearing unnatural, out of the gates and down to Matonabbee's tent. Once there they settled themselves for another round of the calumet. A crowd had gathered outside in the expectation of their gifts. Sam was glad to leave Matonabbee to the task of distribution. It would be necessary to remember every promise he'd made before the trip began. He hoped Matonabbee's memory was as prodigious as his strength.

Back at the fort, Sam asked Mr. Wills to ring the bell for trade. There really was no need. The first of Matonabbee's men were already crowding with their furs for a place at the window. Sam braced himself for a long day. The first request of every man was rum.

MATONABBEE that night was in fine form. At the fort he never indulged in spirits to fire his own. He did not need them. He enjoyed instead good wine and port with his supper. Sam had requested the pleasure of his company, and the expression was no idle formula but a sincere invitation. Tonight they dined in the officers' mess. Tomorrow he would have

Matonabbee to his own apartments. There was no discourse more interesting to Sam than a conversation with Matonabbee on any of the great questions of life. The man was an original thinker, his views bound not by any institution or convention, only by good sense and experience. Molly too enjoyed listening to Matonabbee. He did not jabber as some of the men did, hardly drawing breath, making themselves difficult to understand. Nor did he ever answer a man straight away. Instead he paused and considered carefully, composed his speech, and then delivered it. Sometimes one or other of the men would have already raced on to a new topic. But Sam would always wait. And Matonabbee, sometimes with a simple observation—something you had always known to be true but never voiced—sometimes with a joke or a story, rarely disappointed. He never asked her opinion as some of the officers sometimes did—but they never listened to what she had to say anyway.

At Sam's table the following night he was more talkative than usual. They spoke about Molly's family. He asked where Moses had died and nodded when Sam told him.

—And you took him out by the door.

Molly said that they burnt the mattress. She said Nêwositêkâpaw sweetened the air.

—But still you took him out by the door.

—We had no choice. This is not a tent.

—You have a window.

—You're not a superstitious man. You don't believe in things that are not true. Like God.

—This is not a belief. It is a way to live your life. You must have regard for this place. For your home.

Sam was going to say that it was not his home, it was a factory for the furs. But he could not say it. He had sat up all night when Coults, stricken with a fever, had begun to suffer delusions. He had taught old Chisolm to read using one of Molly's primers. Besides, there was Molly seated now on the floor and nursing the boy—their boy, as he had begun to call Athîkis. And the damn otter was curled in his own lap like some odorous kind of cat.

—I'll come tomorrow and do it for you. Molly can find me something sweet to burn, jackashipuk or some birch rind. Moses was a great man. Not a man who could enter the country like you, but a great leader for the Company, for the trade. He set men to build even more houses here where his father, our mothers' husband built.

Again Sam said nothing. He thought it best to allow Matonabbee time to pay due homage to the man he called his brother.

—This house, Sam Hearne, your son's grandfather's house, is greater than any man could dream. Our tents serve us and fall to decay and we make others. No one can make another house like this. A house made over two lifetimes.

Sam was wondering if he should raise the subject of Molly's sister.

Matonabbee poured another glass of port and laughed.

—But I will tell you one thing, I would not live in a house of stone if you gave me all the treasures it contained. If I lived in a house of stone it would be as if I had been captured by a great enemy—and buried under a pile of rocks.

—I'm sure. But I'm sure you'll never have to. You belong in the country, Matonabbee.

Matonabbee laughed hugely.

—Yes. Making trade for you Europeans. You are still a boy, Sam Hearne, and I can see to the bottom of you. You are a clear lake.

Sam glanced at Molly but she would not look up.

—Don't worry. I like to work for you, even though the world is upside down.

—Meaning?

—An uncle working for his nephew. You married my niece, Samuel. You're the father of my great-nephew.

Sam grinned.

—Uncle Matonabbee.

The idea, the ridiculous idea, pleased him, but he could not let the game go on.

—Matonabbee, I have to tell you about your other niece. Jane.

—I've heard about Jane. All of them. It is sad beyond tears. But they cannot come back to us. I heard too about how the child's father walked away.

Molly looked up sharply.

—You are his father now. And Molly is his good mother.

She turned her face, suddenly shy.

IT WAS A SWEET family he had, Molly and Athîkis—his Athîkis—and Jenni's young Joseph. He could not wish for more. He reminded himself of that if ever he caught himself wishing for a son of his own blood. With time he had learned to suppress the memories that had threatened to destroy his union with Molly. The falls were a nightmare from another life. The Dog Rib woman rarely disturbed his nights. He could not wish for a gentler, more sympathetic companion than Molly. She could read a little, thanks to her father, and under his own instruction had learned to draw. She shared his curiosity about the natural world and loved the animals that together they tried to domesticate. It occurred to him that the governor's quarters were once more a capital of copulation, but the couples this time were furred or feathered.

Sometimes he worried that she had not acquired all the skills she would need when he returned to England. For he knew he would return. He would grow old, but he would not grow old like Norton or Graham. Life on the bay offered little to a man who could not be out on the land. He would return to England, where he could immerse himself in books and learning, enjoy the company of educated men. It would not be a place for Molly. Occasionally, when he saw Molly reading or heard her playing a hymn on the organ, his conscience would speak to him, telling him he was merely perpetuating what Norton had begun when he purchased the English dress. Sometimes he made an effort to remedy matters.

He dropped a toggie and a pair of snowshoes at Molly's side. It was February and a fine day. She was sitting on the floor playing with Joseph. They had trapped a mouse inside a glass decanter and were watching its efforts to reach the top.

She looked up, reluctant to have her concentration broken.

—For mending? Making it clear she would rather not.

—No. We're going out to the beaver ponds.

—No. You go. She bent again to the mouse.

Sam dropped to his haunches and reached to lift her chin. He smiled.

—You'll like it. We'll come back with something for you. For you and Athîkis. And Joseph.

—You bring it. Again she bent her head.

—No. You come.

—It's cold.

—And it's not cold in here?

—Yes. I'm being frozen. Like an old dead piece of deer.

—Then bring Athîkis and come with me. We'll walk fast. There are seven others. There is a boy too.

—And Joseph?

—Joseph must stay with Jenni. He'll not keep up.

In the yard they loaded tent skins and poles onto travois that themselves would double as poles when they stopped to make their shelter for the night. They walked through a shining day solid with cold and still, as if the air itself had congealed. The frozen snow made for easy hauling. Then, because the moon was almost full and the walking good, they walked farther still. Molly trailed slowly behind the two other women in the party though she carried only Athîkis. Sam circled back often to encourage her. He could not tell if it was the snow's glitter that filled her eyes.

When a decision was made to stop for the night, Molly stood apart. The other women erected the tent.

Sam held her that night as a mother holds a damaged child.

—You must work for your prize tomorrow.

She said she would, her speech already slurred with sleep.

In the morning they left the tent standing and walked again, passing a clutch of small poplars. They cut the stakes they would need and went on. Kiyâsk, the man who had located the beaver house, walked ahead. The two other women walked apart from Molly. Molly had cut no stakes. Ahead they could see the fringes of stiff dun sedge that poked out from the snow and marked the borders of a creek. Dark spruce curved towards them, obscuring its further course.

Sam dropped back to walk beside her. He gave her his hatchet.

—You will have to work when we get there.

—I know.

And yet she did not know. She was a stranger in her own country. Sam squeezed her hand and quickened his pace to catch up with the men ahead. Several pines leaned in drunken betrayal of the beaver. The lodge came into view as they followed the creek round the shoulder of the stand. There was no missing it. It stood chest high and was almost the length of two men across at its base. While the women were cutting more stakes the men set to work breaking the ice across the creek so that a fence could be driven through downstream and another on the far side of the lodge. Kiyâsk, meanwhile, broke away the ice in places at the sides of the creek and probed underneath for escape holes. When he found one he marked it with a stake for barricading. Almost before his work was finished the women arrived and began at once to demolish the house, smashing at its roof and walls with their hatchets to break the frozen mud that held the whole together.

Sam watched Molly's ineffectual battering. The women were climbing on parts of the lodge to pull it down. Molly kept her feet firmly on the ground. It would take days to dismantle the house in her fashion.

Those who were watching at the holes saw the water begin to agitate. A shout went up and then another and the stakes were driven down to trap the animals. Sam joined the women who had broken through to the centre of the lodge. They knew what he wanted and they knew exactly where to look, in the furthest reach of the house. The woman who found the young ones grunted in triumph, then she turned, grinning, and dropped a live kit into Sam's open game bag. It scrabbled furiously at the bottom of the bag as he closed the neck.

Now Molly was interested. She could not wait to get back with her prize. It lay still as a rock in the darkness.

Sam waited. Two would be a fine entertainment.

That night at the tent, Molly shed tears of exhaustion. She said she could not walk farther, would never get home. He held her again and tried to quiet her. She did not belong out on the land.

1778

Sometimes Samuel Hearne thinks he
would do anything for this wife of his. He sits down
and pens a letter to the board.

Honourable Sirs,

*As I have already sealed my annual letter to you for return
on the* Sea Horse *with Mr. Christopher, I am sending you by
the same means this additional correspondence. I received by
Mr. Christopher your instructions to embark Mr. Graham's boy
for England on the said* Sea Horse. *It is my sad duty to inform
you that the boy is unwell and I find myself unable to comply
with your request. On the advice of our surgeon, Mr. Purvis, I am
compelled to keep the boy at Churchill, Mr. P. being of the opinion that the boy is too sickly to endure a voyage of such a demand-*

ing nature. We shall do all in our power to continue to care for the
lad and bring him to health.

 I remain, Honourable Sirs,
 Your most obedient and humble servant,
 Etc.

—Tell me what you said.

—You have learned to read, Molly.

—I cannot read your writing. It looks like a spider's
web.

—I said my wife is not to be denied. I said I do whatever she tells me to do, and in return— He makes to grab
hold of her but she is too quick. He hears her laughing as
she goes out. Sometimes Sam thinks a man could not be happier. He loves this time when the stores and the goods are all
ashore, the last of the furs are loaded; when all the news has
been exchanged, the gifts given and received and the trade
discussed down to the last button; when the ship is riding at
anchor, ready for the morning tide. He loves it best when he
sees her sails diminish as she crosses the bay and makes for
home. He feels a lightness as she vanishes—the weight of
duty, responsibility, commerce sailing away.

He has come to love his life as commander of the post.
His journey to the northern ocean now seems like a dream.
His yearning to be out in the country, to survey remote
reaches no white man ever glimpsed, has melted away. It
is no more than a faint remembrance of something that
once belonged to him. The memory of the journey itself
is as vivid as ever. It is one of the reasons this time of year

excites him, because winter is not far off and in winter he can settle with his book, which is slowly taking shape and always growing.

No, he is a different man now. He loves the rhythm of the days at the factory, the self-sustaining round of duties—against which he no longer bucks—and the peaceful presence of his wife. He is not the same young blood who pressed against Molly in the stone passage. And she is not the same child-woman. She is complete now, as whole and as near perfection as a human creature could ever be. Her fall of hair. The gleam of it. Her eyes alive with light like the surface of the sea. Every part of her body smooth and warm and strong and humbling. He is besotted with her and would not think now of a journey. When the wind is in the right direction he walks out still, taking his notebook always with him. Yet he always on his return he begins to savour in advance the comfort of his quarters, his soft wife and the sound of her laughter. Perhaps because he knows he will not have them forever, his family pleases him the way Molly's pets please her. And Jenni's boy is perhaps one of Molly's pets. She loves him as her own. She will set him down beside Athîkis and the two will find amusement for hours. Yes, Molly when she made herself a mother made him a father. Though he has not given his wife a child he has a family.

When Molly had heard about the letter asking for Joseph's return, she had gone straight away to see Sam. There were many arguments to be made. The boy was sickly. He should stay with his mother. He should stay in her care. He might not survive. He was like a brother to Athîkis. Sam listened to them all.

Sickly. As an accurate description the word was misleading. Joseph was simply dull, not boisterous like other children of his age. Content to spend all his days with the toddling infant. Content to loll like an infant himself and stare at the clouds for an hour at a time.

But Sam knows there is yet another argument. Once Joseph is gone, Jenni will be destitute, her allowance from Mr. Graham cut off—along with the interest of her English sailor—and Jenni has no hunter. Sam seals the letter. He knows he is doing the right thing.

THE YEARS THAT FOLLOW are the years Sam will wish to dream again when he has lost them. But they will return to him only once and will be ever after irrevocable. He will remember the bliss just touched. He will not be able to see it. It will be like being blind. In these years the children flourish, the menagerie increases, and Sam manages repeatedly to resist the annual pressure from London to expand operations of the factory. The one thing he never writes to the board is that he is far too busy living to make room for cutthroat commerce.

But when a letter arrives with a second request to have the boy Joseph embarked for England, Sam sees he has no option. He cannot put it off another year. It is Graham's son, after all. And it will not be a loss. The two children spend little time together now that the younger outruns, outtalks, outsmarts the older.

He refolds the letter. He is determined not to make the same mistake as Graham. He has heard from Molly how the daughter was wrenched from Jenni at the landing stage. He decides it best to give Jenni time to accommodate the idea and as soon as he has a moment he goes himself to tell her. She will have at the very least six days to grow accustomed to the inevitable.

He did not dream she would be so attached to the lad. The next day neither Jenni nor the boy is anywhere to be found. An old Kisiskâciwan man who has come from up the river says he passed a woman and a boy. Not far, he says.

Sam sends two of the Southern men whom he knows to be fast runners. He tells them not to harm her. They come back with Joseph. Jenni, they say, would not come. They say she was looking for a place to cross. Sam surmises she is going to double back on the other side and swing towards York. He surmises there will be enough small game and fish for her journey, berries in plenty. Both assumptions make it easy for him to let her walk away.

The boy stays in Sam's own quarters. Molly will not speak to either of them until she sees Joseph struggling with the suit of clothes sent out by his father. She shows him how to put it on. Every time she puts the shoes on him he takes them off again. She lets him be. He stands in front of the looking glass and stares blankly at the strange boy looking back at him. He asks for his mother. Whenever he walks, wherever he walks, he looks behind as if expecting to see her catch up with him. By the fifth day he has stopped asking. He is wearing the shoes.

On the day of sailing, Sam tells Molly to take Joseph down to the longboat. He is just finishing up with Captain Fowler. Molly looks him in the eye and says no.

—You do it.

She puts her arms round Joseph and quickly lets him go.

—Go with the governor now.

She keeps her hand on Athîkis's wrist to stop him from following.

All the way to the gate Joseph, hand in hand with Sam, looks back over his shoulder. Molly does not come out.

OHPAHOWI-PÎSIM. AUGUST. WHEN the young birds fly. A moon promising days of warmth and plenty even when the cold already advances like the Wêcîpwayânak out of the north country.

When Molly was a child, the flying moon was the time she loved best. She loved it for its wealth of warm dark meat and soft new skins. For its heaps of feathered flesh. Abundance everywhere. Scarcely time for the first berries to be stripped from the bushes, all the greedy birds—the partridges and the *wishepithêsis*—working among them. The last canoes coming down with their furs. The trading house filled with the business of men. The unlikely claims and extravagant promises and anxious laughter of the late bartering. The songs and the carousing before the men turned again with their families for the winter grounds. Every day shimmering with anticipation of the ship. The bales stacked ready in the yard. Then the day of arrival lifting and whirling everything familiar and strange like a wind over summer dust. Her father in his must-smelling wig, his best coat, his hat. She and her sister in their English dresses. Hard leather shoes making the backs of their heels bleed, but they loved to wear them. Forbidden to play outside the walls. Only to walk out in greeting.

—My daughter Miss Jane Norton. And Miss Molly.

Learning how to incline her head extend her hand, the gestures stirring a dream of something more to come.

—How do you do, sir?

Hearing the Englishmen laugh, say *little English lady*, adding substance to the dream.

And ohpahowi-pîsim when her Samuel first arrived. His soft voice she will never forget. Words spoken in kindness.

—A beautiful child, sir. She must be your delight.

—Aye. I s'll have one at least fit to return to the country of her birthright.

And later in her father's rooms, her barely formed dream confirmed in its shape.

—You are an Englishwoman, Molly. Never forget that.

And Molly did not forget her father's words. Each year the ship's arrival reminded her. It foretold its own departure. She too would leave one day, would sail one day without fear to the country of her birthright and all its delights. She longed for departure, never guessing then the cold shadow departure trails in its wake.

She understands it now. She has seen Joseph's sister taken. And now Joseph. Joseph who needed her. For whom she could not stop crying.

MOLLY'S TEARS were no help.

When Sam returned to his room he tried to console her. He said it was his duty to the Company. He had orders and it was his duty to obey. A thin trickle of fear cooled Molly's hot grief. She began to know the gulf that stood between her and her husband.

She dried her eyes. Athîkis, relieved, asked if he too could go now on board the ship. Molly looked at him. One thing she knew then. One thing more certain than any other. She waited until the ship had sailed, for she did not want to see it. The next morning she rose early while Sam slept and signalled to Athîkis to dress himself. Then she went down to the gates and asked for them to be opened. Hand in hand with Athîkis she walked out to the burial ridge. A pink sun was floating up into a sky of delicate duck egg blue. An old moon hung behind them in the darker sky, as if reluctant to leave. There had been a thin frost touching all the rocks and the moss, and it was melting fast away, rising in white trails of mist. It vanished quickly in the sun's warmth except above the stream bed and the small pools of water, where it hung like the ghosts of clouds.

As the sun rose higher a wind sprang up from the shore. It was like the wind of life carrying with it all the scents of the new day, all the memories of the old. She caught the dark green tang of the sea-wrack on the beach. The sweet pale grasses of the ridge, the burning tar from yesterday's work on one of the boats.

There were many burial mounds but Molly knew where her sister lay. She touched the stones that covered her and she spoke in her heart. *This day I make a promise to you my sister to your shrivelled flesh that lies beneath these stones to your bones and to your spirit which has left your bones to melt into the land.*

Here is your boy. His name in this place is Athîkis. With the love of your own heart I love him. She went in turn to the stones of each woman buried on the ridge, taking Athîkis with her. *May you bear witness to my words as I make my promise this day. Sister of mine I promise with the love of my heart as long as your boy has need of me I shall be by his side. No one shall have the power to take him from me nor shall I abandon him as long as I live and breathe the day.*

When she looked up it seemed to her that she saw burial mounds stretching far back into the land, and on away to the horizon. She spoke aloud to Athîkis and said the frogs are still calling and they went together in search of one that he could hold in his hand.

1782

O<small>UT ON THE LAND</small> M<small>ATONABBEE IN HIS</small>
moon-washed tent lies back to back with his favourite wife. He has been travelling intermittently for almost
two years—in these last months seeking out and gathering to
him the hunters who have the finest harvest of pelts, persuading them to join him for the long journey down to Prince of
Wales Fort. His reputation among them is solid. He promises them the very best terms for their wares and they do not
doubt him. Even those who have made the trip before and
are familiar with the route are content to join with him. The
gifts he has obtained in the past—tobacco boxes and looking
glasses, coats with gold braid—are beyond what they could
expect to obtain for themselves.

They have settled on the north side of the lake called
Little Fish Hill, setting their tents in a great semicircle with

their backs to the wind to wait out the weather. Spring is not a good time for travel. Those who attempt it can find themselves up to their knees in water or wet snow. Then too fine skies can slam closed in a moment, hurl sleet as hard as birdshot into the face of the traveller, turn wet snow to ice, turn spring back to winter, and catch the cavalier and the unwary in the trap of a full-blown blinding snowstorm. Matonabbee has been content to rest here before they move out onto the barren grounds where they will assemble, before starting down to the fort in the fall. There is wood here for all their uses and deer in plenty moving north now in scattered herds. Most of all there is the warmth of family. No one sleeps with his own cold shadow. Tonight there was singing. The wind earlier in the day had veered and swept the sky clean. It was good to sit in starlight again, good after the last preparations for the night were made, the last kisses and pinches exchanged, the last child softly consoled, to settle under the skins and mingle breath with breath until each turned as one to warm the back against the other.

Now the night is so bright it barely holds the sleeper. Matonabbee opens his eyes. The moonlight, entering from the peak above, leans in a long pole against the opposite wall. But it is not the light that has woken him. It is a sound. He thinks at first his wife is humming, for his body seems to thrum with it, every bone in his back answering. But his wife is sleeping soundly, her breath as gentle as a child's, scarcely there at all. He is not a man who knows fear. But perhaps this is what it feels like. He gets up quietly. He waits until his daughter draws herself back down into the warmth of the bed skins and then he goes outside and stands looking towards the lake. The surface is polished with light. The sound he hears is distant yet it is distinct. It is the sound of grief. He turns to look towards the tents and he feels the small hairs at the nape of his neck prickle and stir. The tents are quiet as grave mounds. He looks back to the lake, so quiet, so smooth. He does not want this. He will not listen. He turns and kicks aside a dog that has come to sit with its head cocked as if it too can hear. He ducks inside his tent and yanks away the sleeping skin. His breath is thunderous. He throws himself against his wife's back and grabs her behind the knee, taking her violently, noisily, making her call out, drown out the voices he never wants to hear again.

—

IT WAS AS IF the blood inside my head was singing. I wondered if I was about to die. I opened my eyes. The sound inside my head stopped yet I could hear it still. It was the same sound though distant.

I pushed at Samuel to wake him but he lay as a dead person broken by his labours. I got up and went outside. Light from the moon was poured over the ground and on the walls but the moon itself was not to be seen. The sky all around was filled with lumpy clouds like sacks stuffed full of the moon's light and spread on a great plain. Now the sound was more distinct. It began low but huge like the murmur of thunder far away yet it was coming from the river. The man at the gate said no sleeping tonight. I looked at his face. He had not heard. I said I wanted to go outside and though he did not want to he opened the gate for me. Now the sound arrived in waves like the moving ocean and each wave rose a little and separated itself from the murmur. And I saw that others too had heard it for some stood outside their tents in silence listening. It was the sound of many voices raised in woe. And they were human voices. There was no mistaking it. Men and women and children were crying in the river. A man walked away to see what he could discover there.

My skin came alive with crawling. I went to my mother's tent. She too was outside. We listened together and then she went to wake Nâpeniska. He came out bleary and stumbling and stood scratching his head. More of the people now ducked outside their tents to listen.

—It is the wind.

Nêwositêkâpaw did not answer him and I knew why. The wind had a voice but it was one voice. It could screech like a *pâkahkos* and it could whisper like a woman. No wind had the sound of men and women and children young and old together. The river had filled with a great sorrowing of all the people lifting their voices in unison each one in his own pain joining with the next.

Nâpeniska was going to speak again but the sound of lamentation rose higher in a ragged chorus and stopped all speech. It entered our skulls and locked words up between our deafened ears before it sank again. Now it seemed to us like the sound of a great crowd of people wandering away. We listened. Our ears ached with the silence that followed.

—Or ice. Ice away up the river.

I walked back to be with the silence and to understand.

Samuel held me close. I said for certain it was my mother's people out on the land. But how could that be? There was no sign of travellers in any direction even though the crying was as close as the river and the night was lighted nearly as bright as day.

In the morning Nêwositêkâpaw and some of the people came to the gates and Samuel invited them inside to the trading room. Every man had his own opinion. Someone said it had been a pack of wolves. Those who had heard wolves sing and call to one another agreed. But everyone knew wolves did not frequent the factory and anyway there had been words. Words that could not perfectly be caught but words nevertheless and everyone had heard them. And even though wolves shared the heartsickness of men and women they had no words to speak it that the people could understand.

Mr. Purvis listened carefully to all accounts. He knew he was expected to speak. He was regarded as a clever man. The one who bled his friends when they were sick and cut off their fingers and toes when they were frozen. Their ears and noses too sometimes. People listened to everything he said.

He considered. He said it was a picture of voices in the same way that *ohpinahtêw*—when mountains or islands rise from the sea and float in the sky—is a picture of far-away things that can be seen only at one time and no other. A picture of things that vanish in the air. You have all seen these things he said when the rime frost is thick and covers every least thing. Perhaps you have been travelling across a wide expanse. In front of you is only the blinding ice of the bay or of a lake. And then it comes. It is at first small on the horizon but it rises up and rises up and is not to be stopped or challenged or denied. It rises up. A band of tree and rock and now mountain. An island pushing skyward until it is afloat unassisted and hangs wavering in the blue sky. This he said was the same thing. In a distant place over the horizon a people were grieving and mourning and the sound of it had risen up whole and complete and been carried by the water to this place for our ears to hear as if it were present in the very river. You say he said that it was faint at first then rose and rose until your heads were filled with it. Well then it was fully present in the river in the way the island that does not exist there is fully present in the sky. And you say too that it sank and receded. Well that is the manner of the vision of the island or the mountain that recedes when you approach. And so you can understand how it is a mirage—a mirage of sound coming to us from a great distance on the back of the water.

Samuel agreed and the others too. And Mr. Purvis was almost right. For the voices were far away. They did indeed come from a distance. Though what he did not say—what he did not know—is that it was a distance neither man nor woman could close by walking. The voices came across the distance that stood between the people and the time that was to come.

PART FOUR

1782

A MILE ACROSS THE RIVER FROM THE FORT, on the highest rocks on the point, lies the battery of Cape Merry with its lodge house and its cannons. Sam has not had enough men to station there for the past three summers. The lodge house is serviceable. It is not such a long paddle or row to reach it. The men take a boat sometimes and cross to the cape to hunt for foxes or ptarmigan, but now at the approach to shiptime every man is needed at the fort.

Sam puts it to Molly that it would be a good place for her to take the boy. They would be out of reach. The isolation of the place would be perfect. It would not be forever. Sam is making all kinds of unusual decisions. He has closed the gates and kept them closed. He has detailed men to direct any who come in to trade to set up their tents well away from the Homeguard. He has heard too many reports in recent weeks.

It is almost certainly the smallpox. Every group that comes in has a story to tell—of others who could not come in from the west, of whole families who have been stricken. Two Wêcîpwayân men themselves bear the marks of the sickness upon their faces. Sam begins to wonder about Matonabbee. He has expected him all year but still he hasn't arrived. No one seems to know his whereabouts. Sam bars the visiting captains from entering the fort in the usual way and instead meets with them outside, sending word among the Home-guard to avoid all contact. When the ship arrives it will be harder to keep track of movements in this way but for now he feels he has done all he can.

When a packet comes from York telling of three women and two children who came in, all that remained of six families, he is adamant. He insists Molly and Athîkis cross the river out of harm's way. Molly sees no good reason to leave the fort just before shiptime. She does not want to go over to the battery. The Company servants take women over there. Everyone knows it. But they do not keep them. They send them back. It is a place built for English guns. No women's fires have warmed it, nor any laughter. No children have run in its spaces. But Samuel is adamant. He says the sickness is coming down the river. He tells her to stay until he sends word.

—You'll be safe and you'll not be in need. I'll send provisions. I might come across myself if the factory is quiet.

—And if it is not?

—If there is trading I'll send a man.

—Send John Mortimer.

She laughs at his sudden attention. The young apprentice is barely seventeen, strong, healthy, and with eyes that glint behind long lashes.

Sam walks away to find Wills. He tells Wills to find Chisolm. Chisolm is in his last year of service and spits through his missing teeth when he talks.

Chisolm and four of the Homeguard load one of the jolly boats. Sam meanwhile negotiates with Nêwositêkâpaw and her sister Wâpisiw. He has wondered about sending two men over but has decided against it, preferring to keep Molly from another kind of harm. Down at the beach the men take on board a canoe for the women's use. Wâpisiw brings tent skins. Sam has arranged for a supply of moosehide so that they can be usefully employed cutting thongs for snowshoes.

—I cannot knit snowshoes.

—You can learn. It is time you learned.

—I should learn to be an English lady. You cannot take an old snowshoe-knitter back to England.

—Why not? I could take you to all the great houses. You could demonstrate your many country skills—once you learn them—to ladies who knit only lace caps.

It is not often Sam indulges in fancy. Molly likes him when he does. She nudges her mother.

—I could teach them the country skill I taught you. "In the manner of the porcupine."

The women chortle with delight and begin to develop the vision. But it is enough for Sam, and he removes Molly's hands from his shoulders and turns back to the business of loading their supplies.

—And our beds, Samuel. Am I to take our feather mattress?

—You must find your bedding. It's time, Molly. Nêwositêkâpaw will help you. You may need all these skills one day.

And there it is again, separation's dark shadow. Molly tries to forget the words as soon as she has heard them.

The two older women continue loading. Wâpisiw puts down a hatchet in plain view. Pointedly. They will paddle upriver until they find spruce trees and they will cut boughs for their beds. Cover them with skins. Molly has slept in such a bed in Jenni's hut, on the trail with Sam. It will not be the bed of her choosing.

She suspects she is being schooled as much as protected. Sam is sending her over to school her in the ways of her mother's people—ways she has always chosen to ignore.

Athîkis is already sitting in the prow, hugely pleased and waving though they have not cast off. Sam kisses Molly lightly before she gets in. With his own hands he undoes the rope. She sees him starting back up the beach and then turns to watch the bright skeins of waterdrops falling from the oars. All the way across she listens to the small waves slapping. Like bare feet running on rock.

It is like a beginning. The beginning of a dream she cannot undo.

When she steps ashore on the other side a sudden nausea arrives like a wash from a distant wave to lap at her belly. It continues as they go about unloading, even though she is on solid ground. It reminds her of the secret she is carrying and why her body, so thick, so full, thrums with life. It reminds her she does not need to make snowshoes. She needs to make a rabbitskin blanket for the child who will be brother or sister to Athîkis.

She asks Chisolm to come with rabbitskins next time, addressing his bent back as he helps the men push the boat out.

Nêwositêkâpaw says she should be ashamed. She says this side of the river is crawling with rabbits. Anyone would know that.

Molly's dream that night is filled with soft white skins, the fur delicate as floss from the willows, so fine it is impossible to tell when it touches the back of the hand. Only the throat can detect it, or the eyelid. Fur that lies flat under the weight of a word. Fur to match the down under a swan's wing. She is making a blanket. Beside her the soft heap of skins. In her hand no knife but the scissors Sam has given her, the blades flying like birds' wings through the fur. He does not know why she needs to make this blanket and she will not tell him. Not yet. She has seen him once put a governor's boy on the ship. Why not his own? No, she will go away to have this child. She will send Samuel mad with loss. He will have only the otter and the squirrels. And then she will return with it wrapped in its new blanket, so beautiful, so needful that Samuel will make her a promise. Her whole night's dreaming she works, taking the cut strips and braiding them, and her fingers do not tire. She is braiding warmth. She is braiding love, ensuring the future. A new needle from the Company lies close by, but morning comes before she can learn the stitches fine enough for the work.

The dream will return to her in the months to come and she will wake and remember the small heap of skins that had only just begun to accumulate beside her at the cape, when she believed all days were numberless.

SAMUEL HEARNE was outside with Purvis at the tent of a Wêcîpwayân man when word was brought to him of a sail on the horizon. He had gone to the tent after supper, on hearing that the man's wife was sick. It did not sound like the small-pox but he wanted to be sure. Purvis took some persuading to leave the walls at so late an hour. They had gone together to the tent and found the woman, who had given birth two days before, sick with a fever. Purvis said it was almost certain to be the childbed and not a threat to others. He would send a little verjuice to bathe her limbs and calm the fever. Or she could drink it. It made no odds. They were just taking their leave when John Mortimer came across to them, his eyes bright with the news of the ship.

Sam smiled.

—God be praised for bringing her safe, he said.

He told the Wêcîpwayân man that he was lucky. He would be able to see the ship come in in the morning, if not that night. Then he and Purvis walked back to the fort. Mortimer, in his excitement, had already run back to climb up on the wall again for another glimpse.

Sam thought he might thank Purvis with a glass of brandy—and celebrate the ship's arrival with another. They could even take their brandy up onto the wall.

—Join me for a glass, will you, Purvis, when you've

mixed your magic brew? I'll get Jefferson to join us.

Inside the fort, word had run like quicksilver and every man was into his ration of rum—or another's on credit. Some were already deep into plans for breaking curfew later and celebrating outside. Sam asked Joseph to set out the glasses in his quarters and then climbed up to the east rampart. Jefferson was there with his spyglass to his eye.

—Always a pretty sight, isn't she?

Jefferson did not reply. He was concentrating on the horizon. He handed the glass to Sam. Sam too fell quiet as he tried to get a clearer view.

—What do you think?

As he watched, the image seemed to split in two. A second ship was following.

It seemed unlikely that the ship for York would be accompanying the Churchill ship so far. And anyway the first did not look like the Churchill ship at all but a vessel at least three times her size. Or it might have been a trick of the light.

—Let's not assume the worst. Come. We can't tell anything at this distance.

They walked together as far as the northwest bastion. Tried to saunter. The country in that direction was saturated with the richness of the late sunshine. Swallows so numerous they seemed a strange trembling veil working the air above the marshland. How hard to force oneself to look in that direction, away from the water, and yet once seen, the sight burned the eyes as if it were the last a man should ever see. They walked the circuit round and stopped at the southeast. A third sail had joined the other two.

Sam handed the spyglass back to Jefferson. Jefferson held it to his eye for a full minute. When he lowered it, he had to moisten his lips before he spoke.

—French.

—That's my opinion.

The two men looked at each other in silence.

It was as if the air between them were thick with strange birds come to roost, and all of them with the same cry: What now? What now?

—Mr. Jefferson, have the bell rung for muster. And find Mr. Wills. Have him detail some good men and look to the guns.

The words hardly seemed to belong to him. They had a foreign sound in his mouth, a foreign taste.

—Mr. Purvis will be waiting downstairs. We'll hold council in my quarters, Mr. Jefferson.

And the iron tongue of the bell when it begin to toll—as it did for a death or a killing storm—it too sounded foreign, laid out on the cooling air of this August evening.

SAM POURED BRANDY for Purvis and Jefferson. While they drank he replenished the otter's pan with water from the pitcher. Jefferson broke the silence between them.

—Out of the blue, eh, sir?

Sam shook his head in disbelief. Purvis was silent. His thoughts had raced ahead to frigates swivelling their guns on the fort, to French soldiers swarming the beach.

—Certainly puts a different complexion on the day, though, don't it? Jefferson wanted only some human voice to sound in the sudden void he seemed to have slipped into.

But Purvis was occupied with his visions of the battle-field and Sam was on his haunches watching the otter observing them from behind the chewed curtain ends. All he could think was, What next? What next? He did not know the steps, the stages of this game. It was business for a military man. And Molly at the cape. What about Molly? They must light no fires there. Nothing to announce their presence. Better, they should remove themselves. Get themselves out of reach. Wait to see how things turn out. The French could be approaching for a dozen different reasons. It might not be an attack. It could be a false alarm. He forced himself to reply, and it was quite another man who stood up and spoke with his voice.

—It does, Mr. Jefferson. But we have to deal with what's on our plates. When the men are assembled you will draw off the requisite number to prepare the guns. Let's say one dozen.

—For forty-two cannon?

—We can't spare more. And they'll have to work like devils against the light.

—We'll not have the men for a quarter of them when they're ready. Our complement stands at thirty-nine.

—Mitchell cannot walk without his sticks. We're at thirty-eight. I've made the calculation, Mr. Purvis. We cannot mount a proper defence. But we can act as if we're three hundred and eight. You'll take a man and set up surgery in the mess. Send him to me as soon as you're finished. I'll detail the remainder.

—There's all the Homeguard to think about.

Sam knew the particular Homeguard Jefferson had in

mind—a soft-spoken woman and two sturdy young boys out there on the plantation.

—And there's all the goods out there ready for loading. That's our priority. The Company stands to lose a year's trading if we don't get them inside.

—You'll have to work the bollocks off those men.

—I think they'll see the need.

—Let's hear, Sam. What do you think we're up against?

—In my opinion the man-of-war is not going to be showing less than seventy-four guns. Probably more. The two frigates maybe twenty-eight. We'll see soon enough.

—And the Homeguard, sir?

—What about them? Though he understood well enough.

—Well, just that. What about the Homeguard, sir? Do we bring them inside?

Purvis drew in his breath sharply. He said the Indians could look after themselves. If the French did indeed launch an attack, he said, it would be against them, the English. They would not be wasting ammunition on the Indians, who anyway would soon enough see the intent and take to their heels.

Jefferson was of the opinion—with more than enough grounds—that they needed every man who could lift a gun. He proposed that the Homeguard be allowed into the fort to assist in the defence. Their women and children, he said, should be told to remove themselves to a place of safety— except those who had special ties within. They should be brought inside.

And who, thought Sam, would make the selection? He

was not fit for such decisions. Nor did he like the reference to "a place of safety." There must be no sign of life on the cape. But Purvis had his own response.

—So armed Indians? Inside the walls for a defence that could take days? Weeks, even? Just how long do you think it would take them Southern men to see how they could make it all come out? You'd be putting us all in peril, Mr. Jefferson. Open the door to treachery and betrayal in no time. Talk some sense into him, will you, Governor?

Purvis was winding himself to a pitch of distrust and anxiety that took Sam by surprise. He disliked finding himself in alliance.

—I think, Mr. Jefferson, the important point to make here is that we don't yet know the intentions of the French. If, as I sincerely hope is not the case, they do indeed mean to attack, then "inside" is no guarantee of safety. The Homeguard would do well to make themselves scarce. And if the worst comes to the worst we shall have that put about. An affair with the French is not a matter that should pertain to our friends outside in any way.

—And that includes your own family? *Governor*.

—My own family, if an attack does indeed seem imminent, will be advised to go upriver at once, and I'd be obliged—*sir*—if you'd offer the same advice to your own. Tell them to go upriver. Tell them not to make their way down, not on any account, until they hear word.

It seemed a sorry kind of protection—no protection at all, in fact. He would not have listened to such words from any man, yet they were issuing from his own mouth and even as he spoke he was beginning to understand they were the best that he could offer. Thirty-eight men. The only certainty was blood.

—Now let us go out.

The yard was in shadow. The men mustered at the flag-pole fell silent when Sam came out. He tried to begin, then faltered at the sight of open, honest expectation on every face turned towards him. No one doubted he would know what to do. One thing at a time, he told himself. He began again.

He said there was work to do. Everyone had seen the ships. They did not have to wait to see the flags to know that they were French. There was little doubt. But as long as the fort was secure and all the goods inside, they had nothing to fear. Their sole duty was to follow orders. To the letter.

One of the Orkneymen shouted, Blow their sodding heads off. How does that spell?

Sam heard his own voice speaking to Jefferson, as if someone else were working his tongue.

—Lay hands on that man.

—Or get our'n blowed off, cried another.

—And the next man, Mr. Jefferson. I'll see them both after.

The muttering of the men—like geese feeding, thought Sam—did not subside. He raised his voice again.

—Before another man makes an insolent fool of himself, let me remind him that we cannot afford today the luxury of having any man in irons. The penalty will be flogging with a birch. Any further insubordination will be met with the whip. Now we have work to do.

While Purvis told off the men into parties of six, Sam

gave silent thanks to his predecessor, for the ghost of Moses
Norton seemed to have come from nowhere to prompt his
speech.

When he had given each work party its orders, he went
to the gates. Most of the Homeguard families were there,
waiting for whatever news the tolling bell had announced.
They too had seen the ships and expected only goodness and
plenty. Sam told them that the ships belonged to enemies of
the king, but that they should not be alarmed. Those who
manned them, he said, would have no cause to harm men such
as themselves, living peaceably outside the fort. He urged
them to move their camp upriver to the site of the old wooden
fort. An old man who had been born and raised at Prince of
Wales Fort asked on behalf of them all for entry to the fort
instead. Sam showed no hesitation. The greatest danger, he
said, awaited those inside: bloodshed or capture. There it was
again. Set free on the air. Thought about to become fact. As if
he himself were bringing destruction into the world. He told
the families again that they should make ready to move off
if he gave the order. It occurred to him that the Homeguard
were in a better position than his own men. If, as seemed
likely, the French gained control of the fort, they would need
these people. There was no surviving without them. The
French would know that. They would not shoot their provid-
ers. He repeated that they were in no immediate danger. But
as he turned to go back in he wondered if it were true.

The families who dispersed had the same thought. The
governor's words contradicted themselves. He was no leader:
that was the only message he left. The old man said he could

see the way things would turn out. The French—with three ships full of goods and guns—the French were the keepers of their well-being. They should begin, he said, to assemble their gifts of meat and furs in readiness. The French would be in need after so long a journey. You know how the English look, he said, when they come off the ship. That starved look of deer in spring. That will be these French—and the gates of the fort will be shut against them.

TWO HOURS LATER the three foreign vessels stood at anchor within a league and a half. The year's trade, the bales of furs and the tuns of whale oil that had been stacked on the beach near the landing stage, had vanished. Every man had worked at a run. Only two of the Homeguard families had taken the advice to leave. Those who remained had worked alongside the Company men. A burly crew had rowed all the small craft upriver, mooring them out of sight. They had drawn almost a week's supply of water from the cove, transporting it down on the raft and using the horses to bring it off the beach. When the last of the barrels had been hauled off, even the raft was dragged inside. One of the men lay on his back now on the floor of the cookhouse, too exhausted even to wipe away the sweat that trickled into his ears.

There was an hour still before sunset, an hour still of good light after that. The armourer and the smith had finished conducting Sam on a tour of the guns. Seven of the cannon were out of commission, their carriages rotted from disuse. Two others had trunnions missing. The smith said he could fit them with new in a matter of hours. He had the forge fired ready. He wondered privately at Sam's silence but he pressed on. Almost every man now had a firearm of some kind. Thomas had seen to that. Checked and primed and a supply of powder and shot. The governor could call the men to present arms whenever he liked. The armourer too was waiting for acknowledgment.

—Good, said Sam. You've done well. Exceedingly well. Though he wanted only to sit on the ground with his back to the parapet, put his head in his hands, and weep. There were two longboats in the estuary right now, the men on board sounding the river, their foreign voices carrying over the water. All this willing—this willed—advance to destruction. The frenzy of preparation he himself had ordered. Leaving himself no option but to mount a defence. To ask these good men, these tradesmen and labourers, these anything-but-soldiers, to lay down their lives for commerce. He had had a great quantity of the most valuable goods removed from the storeroom and locked in the cellar under the northeast bastion. When they were finally overrun, would he have a man stand with a weapon there and defend them to the death? Would he?

—Thank you, Smithy. Thomas. He nodded to the armourer. Never a man more meek. I'll have Mr. Jefferson give the order.

He was halfway down the stairs to the yard when he was called back up. Out by Hare Point the longboats were pulling for the shore. One of lads on watch was raising his gun to sound the alarm. Sam called to him to stop. He told him to send word along the wall to hold the alarm. Two dozen men did not constitute an attack. He watched through his glass. They were indeed disembarking. Their movements made little sense. Other members of the watch left their posts to come and see for themselves. Sam kept the glass to his eye, watching as the Frenchmen dispersed. They seemed to be moving not towards the fort but northward.

—What do you think, sir? The man spoke almost in a whisper, though the men were mere specks.

Sam shook his head and laughed. He thanked the stars for the little extra time he had been granted. A distant but unmistakable sound confirmed his suspicion.

—They're duck hunting.

SAM THOUGHT he had never known a night so dark. And Molly out there somewhere; Athîkis too. What imbecility had overtaken him? He would never forgive himself if they came to harm. Yet he had acted in good faith. When the air was filled with conjecture, with projections of firepower and estimates of militiamen, with musketry and cannon and calculations of range, it had seemed right to have them as safely distant as possible. His orders were explicit. And she had promised. Mitchell had at least come back with that. But now, in the dark, he wanted her within the walls to lie with him a last time—for he had begun to know the unfolding of the unseen day. Stretched out on the great feather mattress now, in this uneasy lull, he wanted her.

There were hours still before the tide would be right for the French to approach.

The labour of the day had taken its toll. Those who

had worked hardest in the heat slept for an hour or two after they had been fed. The majority of the men had sat drinking or stretched on tables in the mess hall until Sam insisted on extinguishing the lamps so those who were not on watch could rest. They had retired to their bunks but by midnight there was barely a man sleeping. The laughter was frequent and nervous.

Trying to comply with his own orders, Sam got up and extinguished his lamp. He lay back down, but his eyes refused to close on the familiar contours of his room. He listened to the two beavers resettling in the house Molly had made for them. He could smell the brackish water of their pool. Athîkis would have had the otter in here too if he had let him have his way.

—And what about the Indians? Jefferson had asked it a second time when the two of them and Purvis again conferred briefly in his quarters. Jefferson was right to ask his question. Nearly all of the families had worked alongside the men. Sam insisted the Homeguard were safest as free agents, unattached to the English cause. It was a nice version of the bald truth: that they—they themselves—might all be blown to pieces. Jefferson must surely have figured that much on his own.

But Jefferson brought their attention back to where the discussion had been left earlier in the day: the vastly uneven odds against them.

Sam had tried to make a second, more accurate estimate of their potential firepower while the ships were illuminated by the low sun. The two frigates accompanying the man-of-war carried more than he had thought. With thirty-six guns apiece, they came close to doubling her number. On a rising tide all three ships could easily come within firing distance. The fort was a target none of them could miss.

—Well? Purvis liked a commander to command.

—We still have no evidence that this is in fact an attack. It may be no more than a show of force.

The doctor shook his head but Sam pressed on.

—Or an honest need to come ashore for provisions. They may move on. We shall wait. We shall see in the morning how matters proceed.

—Or tonight, said Jefferson.

—They won't come tonight. The tide is not with them.

But Purvis was still looking for action.

—Tonight would be a good time to send a contingent over to the Cape, he said.

—No.

As soon as he spoke Sam was aware of the two men waiting to hear his rationale but he offered none. Purvis would not drop the matter.

—We could get some good men over there under cover of dark. Have the guns ready to turn on the French if they decide to come upriver. It makes sense.

—What are you suggesting? A dozen men? Leaving us with twenty-four? Six guns firing on boats that, being busy with us, will be lying just out of range. Or, once the presence of the battery is made known, might decide to turn and cut across, silence it with a direct hit? Send longboats over out of range, then approach by the shelter of the high land, launch an all-out assault with—what?—fifty men? A hundred? It's out of the question.

Sam remembered Purvis's sceptical eye, his scornful lip. Well, but the man could think what he pleased. All Sam knew was that the command was his, and at the end of the day, no matter the outcome, it was to himself and his own conscience that he must answer. Purvis should be thankful that responsibility for the factory lay in hands other than his.

AT MIDNIGHT Sam relit his lamp. Joseph Hansom must have heard his movement, seen the light under the door. He knocked and, when Sam answered, leaned in to ask if everything was all right.

—As it can be.

—Them creatures'll have to wait for fresh water this time.

—You're a good man, said Sam. Come in. Close the door. What would you do to defend these walls? Would you lay down your life?

—That would depend, sir.

—On what?

—I suppose on how much I valued them, the walls, sir.

—I think that's what I'm asking you, Hansom.

—Well, that would be telling.

—Then tell me.

—No stones is worth the same weight as a life. Not if you ask me.

The light flickered over their faces, found out their eyes.

Sam wished he had the ability to pray. He had never felt so alone.

Joseph would take a French ball in the neck, even to

defend stones, despite what he said. The man would do his duty. And some commanders would ask it of him.

It was as if a chasm had opened at his feet and on the other side stood his men.

—Now if you asked me what would I do to save another soul, now. Now that's different. Even one of them Southerns out there. Only thinking about it, perhaps not that goddamn bastard McIlroy in here. He's only out to break heads.

Sam smiled. McIlroy. A great destructive child of a man who picked a fight whenever he could. And now here was a fight he could throw himself into.

—Well, he might prove useful. I think I'll read a while. Good night, Joseph.

—Good night, sir. Don't punish your eyes there when they want to be sleeping.

SAM COULD NOT CONCENTRATE. But he knew anyway what the pages had to offer. He thought about the chain of fate, about the chain of cause and effect and how that chain stretches back unbroken to the beginning of time. And he thought about how a chain of events need not stretch forward to the end of time but could be broken by any man along the way. About how, in Voltaire's words, every being has a father, but every being has not children. What would come to pass tomorrow would be the child of his deliberations tonight. But tomorrow's child need not—need never—become a father. Like a rock in a stream tomorrow's child might turn events aside. Tomorrow's child need never produce offspring of its own.

As his mind tracked over and over itself, his imagination began to people the room and before long all rational thought was scuffed out of existence, leaving only misgivings and doubts. Molly of course was there, with Athîkis, with Nêwositêkâpaw. He saw them watching from the cape, saw them pack their things and make their way out of danger until the affair was over. And then again he saw them overrun because they chose to stay. A longboat thrusting onto the beach, coarse and drunken French soldiers scrambling and clambering up to their lodge. Men brandishing knives and taking the women, Molly first, by force. The potential—no, the certain—violence of the coming day was a bloody dawn about to break. Men changed into brutes mad for destruction. Unspeakable acts. He had seen it before, and not only at Bloody Fall. When he was still in his youth, serving in the Bay of Biscay, he had seen men wild, seen them fire, with eyes glittering, on boats disabled and burning. Direct hits. He had cheered along with the others. But his notions of honour and glory had been suddenly overturned when the *Vestal* came about and a young officer, detailed to pick up prisoners, instead made sport of drowning men, taking aim at them from the gunwale as they struggled for their lives.

The upturned faces of his men earlier in the day mingled with the upturned faces in the water. His men but his friends too. Men he laboured alongside here in the common home. Men he hunted with, broke bread with. He celebrated St. George's Day with them, caught the ague with them. And he was to see them blown apart by a French ball or transformed to cornered beasts when, as most certainly would happen, they were finally overrun? For what? Shed blood for what? The contents of a Company warehouse? He did not have to answer.

Only the question of Molly and Athîkis remained. Only his whole life.

And Sam, who had never valued the trade for itself, saw it suddenly now with the eyes of a broker. The trade was come by barter. It could as easily be bartered away for something more valuable.

He did not know at what hour he finally fell asleep, or for how long. It may have been mere minutes, for the sun was still below the horizon when he woke.

—

I DREAMED SAMUEL handing me into the boat just as he had done when we crossed over the river. He handed in Athîkis and then he stepped in himself. I dreamed us all watching the fort grow small and smaller still while the men rowed us to the great ship. But the dream was not to be trusted for that day Samuel was to turn away from us and step into the boat alone.

We had seen the ships the night before though we did not know that they were strangers. We laughed to think of defying Sam and returning to view the arrival of the stores. We had decided to cross when the work got under way and when Sam would be too busy to pay us any heed. But just before the night closed in we saw a canoe approaching and in it two of the goose hunters and the Company man Mitchell who walks now with sticks. We went down to the water thinking they had come to ferry us across but we knew at once by their faces that it was not so. While Mahkesîs and Kâkwa were getting out James Mitchell spoke to us. He said he had an order from the governor for our safety. We were not to cross to the fort on any account but to watch carefully. If we saw the ships making farther into the river we were to leave at once and make our way upstream crossing when we were past the site of the old wooden fort and waiting there for news that all was safe before we came down again to the fort. I went down over the rocks to the water but he had already pushed away and turned the prow into the gathering dark. When I tried to reach our canoe Mahkesîs jumped down and took up the paddle. He was grinning when he climbed back up. He was grinning while my mother cursed him and struck him on the chest. He said that they were under orders to stay with us through the night and that we were to light no fires. I began to think that this was a trick of Sam's. That perhaps the ships belonged to the Company after all and the flags to a new governor. That perhaps Sam was planning to leave in the great ship without having to bid us farewell. I did not understand why he sent no message by his hand. Was it for nothing that I had learned to read?

Athîkis was the only one of us glad to see new company. Mahkesîs sat on the paddle until dark. Athîkis sat beside him. My mother said my father would have had us inside the house. She did not understand Samuel Hearne and his safety. Safety was inside the fort where a governor could fire on all who approached. My aunt said governors did not ask to be understood. She said a new governor was certain. She said she had dreamed it but I did not believe her.

There was no moon at all that night. I shed tears into the dark for all that I was losing and for all that I did not yet know. No one heard. My mother and my aunt were sleeping, Athîkis too. Mahkesîs and Kâkwa paid me no heed. They were sitting at the edge of the water drinking the rum they had been given for their trouble.

I heard the great chains dragging. The sound of timbers creaking. It was still dark. I stepped around Mahkesîs and Kâkwa asleep on the path and went down to the rocks to listen. Nêwositêkâpaw came down with Athîkis to sit with me. The ships had come in. We waited for the light. The surface of the river began to shine showing us the colour of early morning sky though the sky overhead was still soaked in dark. We began to see many small boats passing from the great ship to the shore and in the boats what seemed like many men. In my breast I felt the whirring of the wings of birds when they scare up from the marsh grass. Nêwositêkâpaw said if we were to go we needed to go at once. I took the paddle from where it lay close to Mahkesîs's side. Athîkis and I walked down to the canoe. A long time I looked across the river wishing for a spyglass to show me what was happening there expecting every moment to hear the sound of the fort's great guns. But we heard none. Nêwositêkâpaw too came down. She said nothing was certain. If they were enemies we would have heard the sound of firing. She said my father would have fired the guns. I told Athîkis to get in the boat. Three ships in the river. Men arriving. And surely then men leaving. And Samuel? Three ships and one of them so great and room enough surely to take his family with him?

Nêwositêkâpaw said if I was going across we were all to go for no one could be certain now what was happening. She went back to our lodge to wake my aunt who came to us grumbling for the disturbance and saying we would have to wait for now she had to attend her own needs and she walked away out of sight.

By the time we had launched the canoe and climbed in the sun had drawn a white mist from the woods up the river. It hung low over the water and seemed to drift towards us with the current. And still there was no sound of any gun. My arms were aching from the paddling before we had reached the middle of the river. The current was strong and tried to carry us seaward so that we had always to point the canoe into the mist. And then we were like birds caught in cambric and the fog was all around us and we had no sight of either shore. After more paddling we heard voices louder and always louder until we were surprised to see the beach loom empty out of the mist. Up at the fort there was a great movement of men to and from the gates and all about the plantation and every man in sight was dressed in white or in blue.

We walked up from the beach. We could see now that all was in turmoil in every part. The men in foreign dress were all about the plantation and some were carrying away the fish and the meat from the drying racks. A man came and took hold of me. He spoke a foreign tongue and did not understand when I said I was the governor's wife. But my words meant something to him for he shouted out and called to others to witness my speech. I knew that to get through the sea of men to Sam I must be like one wading against a strong tide. Again and again I told them I was the chief factor's wife. The wife of Governor Samuel Hearne.

The men made my mother and my aunt speak to them but my mother said in her own tongue I have nothing to say to you who do not belong here. One man spat at her and the brown juice ran on her leg. They prodded my aunt and she said in her own tongue and for our own ears leave a great distance around these men. They wanted Athîkis too to speak to them but I put my hand over his mouth and pulled him to my side.

I made them understand that I wished to go in the direction of the fort.

Two men in blue jackets saw us walking towards the gate. They came and took hold of us and pushed us back in the direction of the tents. My aunt said to keep walking. She said we would be safer with our own people than with the foreign soldiers. But I no longer knew who were my own people.

When all the food had been carried away the men too disappeared. I waited a little while at Nêwositêkâpaw's tent and then I took Athîkis's hand and made my way back again to the fort.

A great crowd of Englishmen stood together outside the walls. Though all of them knew us none came forward and then I saw that they were bound together at the ankles with chains. Joseph Hansom and John Mortimer called to me to go back and to stay away but while the guards were busy with a cart coming through the gate I slipped inside. In the yard men were everywhere scurrying like weasels about the place—to the workshops and the stores to the cellars and the cookhouse and the men's house—up and down forward and back. A man with the face of a moose stopped us. I told him repeatedly Governor Hearne Governor Hearne and nodded my head towards our apartments. He looked doubtful but he took my elbow and held on to me all the way into the house and up the stairs.

Sam was seated on a chair and behind his great writing desk sat the foreign captain or so I thought it must be for he was well dressed and clean and on the desk in front of him was a great hat. He was not writing. A soldier beside him scribbled on a piece of paper.

Sam rose when we came into the room and I saw quite clearly that his eyes filled at once like a woman's but he did not open his arms to us.

You should not have come he said. He said it twice all the time shaking his head. He was breathing very hard like one who has run a great race.

Athîkis held my hand tightly and pulled me down close. In a whisper he asked me if Sam was sick. He said he was afraid.

You promised Sam said. James Mitchell said you promised.

I said the only promise I ever made was to my sister.

The foreign captain asked who I was and Sam said she is my servant.

The foreign captain smiled and said and the boy?

Sam did not answer. The foreign captain asked again and the boy? Who is the boy?

Sam tried to speak and could not. He tried a second time and at last he said it is her son.

The captain smiled again and said and no boy of your own? And Sam glanced so quickly at me it was no more than the flash of a dragonfly. He said no.

The captain said you know you cannot take your servant with you. You could have taken a boy. If you had had one.

Sam said he is not my son and again the captain smiled as if he knew a great secret though the only secret to be known was deep within my belly.

I understood nothing now for these men were not as enemies but almost as friends—except that Sam's face was drawn tight together parcelling up his thoughts. He spoke again to the captain saying the captain's name—Sieur de La Pérouse—and speaking of terms and conditions and trust. He spoke of honour and of gentlemen and of favours. Of promises kept. And then he begged safe passage—for this servant of mine—and I thought I was to go to England and it was as if the sun shone inside the room but he continued—back to her people outside.

The captain said something in his own language and the man who had been writing got up and went out.

Sam said thank you. He said I'd like to give my servant a memento.

The captain said please.

There were two items on the floor beside his chair. He bent down and picked one up and I saw that it was a hunting bag for small game. He held it out to me and his hands were shaking.

Athîkis said and something for me? He was looking at the packet on the floor.

Sam shook his head. It is not for you he said and he pushed the bag towards me.

Take it he said. I have nothing else to give you. I pulled open the neck of the bag and saw inside the blue silk of my English dress the one that he gave me from the ship. He said I was keeping it safe for you. And then he said in my mother's language they are taking even the shirts from the backs of the men.

But my thoughts were not with dresses or shirts. I had no mind for any of it. I wished only to know what these foreign men planned to do with Samuel and with all the Englishmen and when and where they were going to kill them and if they would just disappear the way all the living creatures that had run in these apartments had disappeared without a trace. But I could speak no words of any kind.

The man who had been writing came back with one of the foreign soldiers and the captain said say goodbye to your family Mr. Hearne.

And now my eyes began to burn with tears but Sam said it is not the time. It is time to go. He said very quietly go now and go as quickly as you can. Tell everyone. I did not move. He turned away and picked up the packet by the chair. Some more soldiers entered the room and spoke to the captain and he said in English to Sam that we would all go down to the gate together. A soldier walked on one side of Sam and I on the other with Athîkis and the soldier who was to accompany us beside us. I did not touch Sam nor he me though our wrists brushed once close. There were men everywhere about the yard. Some were shouting at each other some calling. Some were shouting into the air at no one. But there was no fighting for the Englishmen were all outside. Other men were intent on carrying away items. It was not the same as when men begin to strike or break a camp. There was no knowing to what end they worked. All of them together were more Europeans than I had seen even at shiptime. Some of the new men seemed sick and had dragged themselves in discomfort to lie where they could. The new captain stopped to speak to two of them and gestured to the men's house but they shook their heads and I guessed that the Englishmen's beds were already full. Yet others staggered from the kitchen stores their arms full of food. A great crowd of them had gathered round some kegs of brandy and they poured it into their faces like water.

At the gate Sam spoke to me fast and low in my mother's language. He told me to keep Athîkis close. He told me to take up what pelts I could find. He told us to be quick before the Frenchman changed his mind. At the gates he pushed me. He said for your life Molly. For your life. I wanted to look a last time into his eyes but he had already turned to go with the new captain—the new governor—down to the water.

If is a difficult word. It denies the world. If the husbands and the fathers were with us. If the Englishmen had fired their guns. If my father had been in charge. If Matonabbee had returned and seen what was to be done.

If is better unspoken.

If I had tears they could lie in their twin pools until the time came for crying. The time now was all for doing, for making away. Something had changed in the time we had been inside our house. The men moved like waves under a rising wind. Some of the soldiers were busy at the cannons on the foreshore. They were turning them to point back towards the walls of the fort. Then Sam's words became clear to me. The soldier ordered to accompany us walked only a short distance from the gate and turned back. I held tight to Athîkis's hand and we ran to my mother's tent. The people too had seen the change blowing through the men. They were gathering all that they could carry on their backs for foreign soldiers had dragged away the dogs to tie up shooting the ones that were troublesome. Some of the people tried to take down their tents but the soldiers shouted at them to stop all the time making signs for us to leave. There was no food to carry. The soldiers had taken all the fish and the meat and the racks stood empty or lay overturned. The bones of the winter to come. We gathered what knives and tools we could and some snatched up kettles and blankets medicine bags and whatever else in their reach. Some of the people had bundled skins and furs but when the soldiers saw any of the people with pelts they grabbed them. They tore them from their arms tore them even from the children. Some of the people hid what they had under their clothing and walked like old crippled things. Athîkis said not a word. When I looked at him I saw that his face was as the face of the other children his eyes wide his mouth turned down hard like the mouth of the jackfish.

The crowd of Company men had moved now from where they had been held outside the gates. The women who had taken Englishmen for husbands wanted to wait for it seemed then that all might be set free but it was not so. The chains were taken from the legs of the men so that they could get into the boat but their hands were bound still and the foreign soldiers had fixed their guns with bayonets and held them ready.

The Englishmen called to their wives and children and there was much shouting on all sides. The soldiers began to fire their guns over our heads to see us run until their captain appeared at the gate and fired his own gun high in the air to make them stop. Some of the people dropped the things they carried. They did not turn back but kept on walking. The older children kept on running. They vanished like deer. We were no more than fifty paces from the gates when a loud explosion shook the air so that all the ground beneath us jumped. When we turned we saw smoke bellying up from a place in the walls. The younger children remained holding fast in their fright. Athîkis was one of them. I feel his hand clinging on to mine his other hand clutching my sleeve even now I feel it.

One old man my mother's uncle still had not left the fort. Two others were with him. The confusion and fear were very great. Some of the belongings of the people were still in their tents. We walked farther until we were sure we were out of range of the guns. It was not hard to imagine the sound of firing beginning all over again and this time aimed at our backs. And that is when I felt the black hole burned in my back like a leaf against the sun. I felt it even though no shot had reached us. The hole was the not-knowing. The hole was the black mistrust of the world that had come into being and replaced the world of my youth. The hole was the place where the life that I knew vanished. We waited. When the three men caught up with us they came with six horns of powder and nine bags of shot the French commander had supplied. The French commander was not after all a bad man. Perhaps he did not know that some of the hunters had been robbed of their guns.

339

Would it have been better to have been hunted down—then there—to have fallen there? Heaped together? Was it better to walk away unharmed when in front lay the long journey of pain and sorrow? One walker falling then another. Days only between them even into the Frost Moon? But none of these questions were known to us.

None of us spoke. And then the convulsions began. Bursts of rolling thunder like boulders hurtling across the land making the air tremble and the earth shudder under our feet. Turning we saw the smoke clouds in the clear sky. We walked until the sounds of the fort began to be swallowed by the land. The explosions diminished and merged until they became no more than the distant voice of the sea unseen or far-off ice in the coldest moon. We walked until we could not hear the faintest sound behind us not even the barking of the dogs. The wind rushed to fill the empty places bringing with it the cries of the birds. When we looked back again the fort was out of sight even the flagpole. The white smoke in the sky had turned to black billows and we knew our home was burning. We walked so far that the last time we looked back we saw no sign at all. We walked on hearing the distant birds. The hushing of our feet over the dry sedge. All around us the hither and thither of the insects. And we could each one hear the breathing of every other. The sound of our own breathing filling our heads with the idea of life.

When it was late in the day some of the children had begun to whimper with a sound of injured dogs. These had been all their lives at the fort and used to lying down when they tired resting when they had no breath. I too was unused to journeying but I tried to find words to encourage Athîkis. There was no mark of a camp in any part of the land that we travelled no trace of smoke on the sky in any direction. When the sun was no more than two fingers from the land we stopped beside a narrow lake and drew together. My mother's cousin carried a bag of pemmican and her daughter two birds she called *aukuskow* caught with her flying net. Kôhkôhkahôw who would die before any of us though she did not know it made a sharp hook from one of the bones and bound it to a small piece of gut. She walked out into the water and began to fish. Though she stayed until half the night was gone she caught nothing and came back to our fire. We slept.

That all this can return with the quivering of a leaf.

Some days pass with no memory at all only the day itself and its soft unfolding. When I watch it is as if a day is nothing but the drawing of one breath. It is as if the light is like a breath filling filling the sky and then slowly leaving it the way the breath leaves our bodies almost unnoticed. Each day one whole breath drawing in expanding lifting filling growing lighter brightening. Then sinking shrinking down again dimmer until the almost black when all begins anew to draw in and slowly rise. And I can watch many days in this manner. Rarely do men and women pass this way and disturb the unfolding of the days. When they come they come on foot and in canoes. Sometimes in the long years I have thought that I glimpsed Samuel in his strange English clothes striding across the fall of the land at the edge of vision. Others limn the edges of my sight in loud wagons and I know I am sure of it their souls pass in the sky in growling specks. They do not pause in their journeys not even to see where they are. Perhaps it is the pain of the dying that can still be felt that keeps them from this place. Sometimes the animals pass across the breath though less often now. Sometimes—often—the birds. First they romance the ear. Then the eye. But they vanish as quickly as they appear. It makes no difference to me whether anything be seen or not. Nothing disturbs my own dissolution into the heart of the country.

—

MATONABBEE had a promise to keep. Eighteen men and their families were assembled, waiting on him, with their furs loaded on sleds and on dogs and on wives, to lead them down to Prince of Wales Fort to trade. He had worked hard finding these men and making promises. If they left off their trade with the Pedlars and brought their furs instead to the great stone fort they would be well rewarded with superior goods in plenty. As always Matonabbee guaranteed an exceptional standard of trade. And Matonabbee always kept his word. He knew the route well and before he left he instructed his family. He would head directly south, reaching the caribou crossing at roughly the same time as the deer. There they would kill all they could and dry a quantity of meat for travelling, leaving behind a large cache before going on to the fort.

He took Marten Tail's face in his hands. He knew every line, every track of the years, and she was lovely to him still. He told her to keep the others in order, to allow them no bad habits while he was away. She did not have to endure the journey. Nor did the others. His youngest wife would be enough. Marten Tail smiled. If you don't wear her out, she said. He pinched both her ears hard with his thumbs and kissed her long and warmly on the mouth.

In a few weeks, when they had finished at the lake, his son would go with the wives and the children down to the caribou crossing. All was as it should be and Matonabbee set out knowing his house was in order, his wives and children at their various tasks, the young ones warm and with food in their bellies. By the end of one week he was uneasy.

From the day they set out the hunting was poor. And there were so many mouths to feed. Each week was the same. One day from the river crossing, shielded from the view of an approaching herd by a long spur of land to the north, they made camp. The men left their families and walked on another day, settling in to wait down near the shoals of the river crossing. They dispersed and made themselves low shelters of brush covered over with snow, nothing that might alarm a herd as it approached. With no fresh meat they lived only on pemmican. When twelve days had passed they knew the caribou were not coming. The animals had used some other route to travel down into the trees to the south. Matonabbee sent a runner back to the women to let them know they were moving on. The hunters struck out towards the fort, taking the chance that the caribou might yet be coming down in the more open country farther east. There was no sign of deer in any direction. Reluctantly, Matonabbee sent another runner, this one all the way back to his own lodge, to tell them not to come down for the meat, for there was none. He gave the man powder and shot and he shared out his load, promising to obtain on his behalf all that he wished for his furs if by chance he did not meet with them again.

They walked on slowly so that the families could come up with them. On the way they stopped to break open a beaver lodge. They waited for the women to arrive. The meat was a welcome change though there was not nearly enough for all.

Four days later they had the good fortune to run down two large muskox. Matonabbee had never relished this pungent flesh but now it tasted sweet and seemed to signal that their journey would be successful after all. The meat was still in his mouth when two of their countrymen appeared, drawn by the smoke of their fires. The elder of the two asked for provisions, for shot and powder if they had any to spare. The other was strangely silent. Matonabbee told his wife to put two palms of shot into the man's bag and give him a twist of powder. He offered him scraps from the fire. There was something untold behind the old man's eyes. Matonabbee waited. When the old man had finished chewing he said they must all turn back. He said the fort was destroyed. He said the stones all lay on the ground. No one knew what to make of his account. The stones of the fort would not dislodge themselves so easily. Matonabbee knew it was impossible. He was certain the man was lying but he could not assign a motive. Perhaps the man wished to harm the fort by turning away its trade. Perhaps he was in the pay of the Pedlars, who had their eye on all the furs in movement over the country. Here was a man he could not read.

But what if he spoke the truth? He walked a distance off from his companions and sat in silence.

More than a month still to travel. And if the man's impossible words were true? If there were no fort? If they began the long journey home with no supplies for their families, no powder, no shot for their guns?

Matonabbee went back to the fire to put his case to the other men. It was time, he said, to turn towards home. One or two of the young men without families could go on and bring back a report.

But the men were impatient. They had already been

talking. They said the two strangers had spoken like fools or liars, and that they wished to go on. They said Matonabbee had his word to keep, and if he did not they would take all their trade to the Pedlars and never follow him more. The oldest of the hunters said that if Matonabbee broke his promise every misfortune that came to pass would be laid at the door of his tent. Matonabbee knew it was no threat, only a simple truth.

AFTER A WEEK, the men complained that Matonabbee and his young woman pushed forward too fast for their families, but he had no care for them. His only care was to get to the fort and return as quickly as possible. So long had they been hunting, so little had they left on their way for their return. And now to return empty-handed? The unease had come upon him when the caribou failed to cross their path. It would not leave. Dreams of his wives and children at home began to walk beside him on the trail, their bodies thin as sticks. The farther they walked, the more his unease began to congeal into fear. The dream figures did not dissolve but remained with him on the path, walking beside him, their bodies starved, their mouths devoid of speech. He made himself promises. If the fort still stood he promised himself he would wait only a day before he started back. He would leave the men to trade as best they could. For himself, he and his wife would return with all speed. Sam Hearne would give him whatever he asked. Sam, his friend who was in his debt for his whole life to come for the day he, Matonabbee, saved him from the jaws of winter. Governor Samuel Hearne, who depended on him for

345

all the trade he brought. Sam Hearne would deny him nothing. He told himself lies he wished were true. Governor Samuel Hearne, whom he, Matonabbee, had raised from boy to man, who loved him like his own blood and whom he loved the same, Governor Samuel Hearne would supply him with powder and shot for the whole winter, with provisions for meantime. And he, Matonabbee, would return with his wife, covering thirty days' walking in ten.

Matonabbee knew before they arrived that what they had heard was true. There was no trace of smoke in the sky, none. The fort cringed against the land. A white flag flew in place of the familiar colours. They came closer and saw the walls too changed—some standing solid, some with great entrances inviting them in. Here was no Governor Samuel Hearne. Here was nothing. Here was a barren waste of snow-covered rock. They walked over the yard and it seemed full of boulders. Only low, broken walls remained where the houses had stood.

One man cleared the snow from a fallen stone. It was blackened and left soot on his fingers. He cleared another. It was streaked with green and gold. And another. But no dead lay upon the ground, nor was there any trace of bones or any clothing. They walked beyond the walls to where the Englishmen buried their dead. The grave mounds seemed no more and no less than were there before, and they walked back to the ruins.

The wind blew over the empty spaces. Matonabbee walked without speaking. He walked in rooms that once were filled with goods from the Englishmen's country and were filled now with stones and blackened timbers. The men were chattering, saying all manner of things that they could not know and that could not be true. Things about great grief and mourning. About the English destroying their home and their chattels. Matonabbee told them to be quiet and set his heart to seeing what was no longer there, staring at the broken stones and willing them to reveal their story. No matter what grief befell the English they did not destroy the things they owned. This was not the work of the English. Nor of the spirits who wreak havoc. Still staring at the inexplicable stones, Matonabbee began to see. Enemies of the English: a ship looming into the mouth of the river at night; men breaking out from its belly under cover of darkness like maggots from a carcass, wriggling fast into the small boats and coming ashore in stealth; great guns in the flank of the ship turning on the fort; the hand of the enemy captain raised and the fort cracking apart like stones on a fire; the people in their homes outside the fort running swiftly away up the river, vanishing into the dark; the foreign men, each one with a weapon raised, swarming through the great holes in the walls; and inside, the English blasted awake, running in confusion, grasping at muskets and fowling pieces, bayonets, running to the broken walls, firing, firing though their eyes are still blinkered by sleep. And the enemy pouring into the place like an unstoppable herd.

Matonabbee lost in his dream ignored the rising anger in the voices of his companions. He saw his English friends fighting for their lives against the force of a river broken in spring. They could not possibly stop the flood. He saw every man, many wounded, taken prisoner and bound, and the dead too taken up and dragged away. And all, all carried away to the waiting ships.

Matonabbee knew then for certain that they would find no provisions, no powder or shot. He could hear his name being called but he would not turn round. He wanted to see the end of this dream, this story told by the stones. The ship's boats low in the water and in them the bodies of the Englishmen piled like sacks of oats. The rowers straining and gasping. Many hands using ropes to haul the prisoners and the dead by their ankles up the side of the great ship, strange fish drawn from the sea.

And now Matonabbee at last sees what he has been waiting for. He sees Sam Hearne. Sam is still alive. No warrior, Sam. His hands are bound, and the rope from the ship is round his feet; he is hauled up like a dead animal; his head hits the edge of the longboat. On the deck his wife Molly, now the woman of the foreign captain, watches everything.

When all the captured and the slain are bound securely on the ship, many of the Frenchmen return to the fort. They run about, taking everything for themselves—the furs first, every last one, and all the food and the many treasures, the silver knives and the carpets from the governor's house, and the blankets, and the glass drinking vessels and the great platters.

Matonabbee sees the Frenchmen run about all day like ants carrying off the litter of the soil. He sees his English friends bound on the ship, helpless as birds in a net.

Someone was shoving now at his back, wanting an answer, but Matonabbee wanted to dream to the end. The

English fort lies open to the foreigners, undefended. It is as if, as his companion said, there has been a time of great mourning, except that now the strangers are not grieving but celebrating. Matonabbee sees the enemies of the English are drinking and dancing in the smoking ruins; they feed the fires. And they have taken all the Southern women and they are everywhere coupling.

At last they finish. They fall down where they stand and sleep among the fires. The flames show where everything that once stood firm lies broken.

If these things were here before him now, if it were night, if the fires burned low, if the men slept on, Matonabbee would fall upon them with his knife. He would slit every throat that breathed, as he had done before and would do again. But it was not night and there was no ship on the water and the stones that were blackened with fire were cold. And he knew in his heart what had befallen his friends. Samuel and Mr. Jefferson and Mr. Purvis, all of them, thrown into the sea over the horizon where the water goes down forever.

He turned round to face his companions. They all spoke at once now, each man with his own grievance. They saw his face wet with tears and they spat on the ground. The man who wanted his wife took her wrist and started to walk away. Others went to the sled she had pulled for him and tore it apart. They took his furs in payment for their misfortune. They took all the powder and shot he carried, his hatchet, and two of his knives. They wanted his snowshoes but he would not give them up. In a rage one of the young men smashed the stock of his gun. When he made to attack Matonabbee another held him back. Matonabbee left them to their work and walked away, thankful he still had the clothes on his back, the knife in his belt.

HE STRIKES OUT across the frozen marsh and is soon lost to sight in the white air. The weather has to hold for him or he will lose precious time. When he comes to the trees, he stops only long enough to make himself a crude bow. He substitutes a lace from his tunic for the sinew, cutting lengths from the fringes to replace it. He winds his long hair round and round his palm and pulls it from its roots to fashion snares fine and strong. He walks on into the darkness each day, stopping only rarely to set his snares, after which he retires a distance, hollows out a shelter from the wind, and rests for a short while. For six days he eats nothing but a little rabbit meat. Once he sees the tracks of deer but he does not turn from his path to follow them. On the seventh day he comes upon a flock of ptarmigan busy among the willow scrub fringing a lake. At his approach they fly off heavily, only to settle a short distance away, reluctant to leave the sudden bounty they have found. He sets his snares and has scarcely removed himself when the birds return in a flock and settle again. By dark he has twelve birds tied at his belt. If he had his women with him they would have netted them all. But he can live, just, on one bird a day. He quickens his pace.

WHEN HE FIRST sees the lone tent his heart is lifted. He has lost, he knows, all bargaining power, can make no promises, incur no debts. But he can beg, and he will do that for his family.

The old couple in the tent bring him inside to their thin fire. He can see at once they have nothing to share. He fights down the thought of walking away with the old man's gun. The old man says this year has brought the greatest hardship he has ever known. He talks for a long time about the poor hunting. He talks about other years, before Matonabbee's time, when the caribou did not come. He talks about famine. He talks about the sickness that almost cost them their lives and that has stolen his wife's sight. They are making their way to the stone fort, he says, to ask for help for the winter.

Matonabbee tells them the fort is destroyed but they shake their heads in disbelief. He tells them it is true. They should travel with him towards the northwest, where the hunting will be better. He will hunt for them. There are people along the way who will be glad to be given a little meat and may have ammunition to replenish his stock. There will be women who will be able to sew for them, refit their snow-shoes. He can leave them there before he turns north to his home. The old man shakes his head. To the west, he says, is the sickness. He says they heard of a camp there where every person had fallen to it. Only dogs roamed. No, he says. They will wait at the empty fort. The foreigners will not give up such a place so easily. They will return.

While Matonabbee is tying on his snowshoes he hears the woman speak his name. No, the old man says. That wasn't him. He had not even a gun to carry on his shoulder.

TO THE WEST is sickness. Matonabbee is a deer running now, the words mad, flailing arms and halloos at his back, his family a sad enclosure before him where only death is. His legs eat up the land with the appetite of a young man for his woman but collapse and morbidity plague his dreams. He is four days from his home when he is saved the sight of his wives and his children, in his waking life at least. Following the course of the river that will take him to them he meets a young man travelling towards him. The young man is pulling a sled with a few furs. Matonabbee asks him where are his companions, where is his family. The young man says he is all alone. He is going to find the Pedlars. He has heard they are now in the Athabascow country. Matonabbee looks towards the furs and a chill steals over his heart.

—Yes, the young man says. I took them from one of the tents where the people lay. There is a great camp over to the northwest of the river. No one there can make use of them.

And then the young man too comes to know what is happening and he knows who this is before him.

—Take what is yours, he says.

Matonabbee shakes his head. He will not look at the furs.

The young man is nervous, not yet for himself but for Matonabbee.

—Then come with me to the Pedlars. They will have guns, shot.

Matonabbee understands then that there is no one left alive. The knowledge rushes in on him as if an ice dam has broken. He is drowning in it.

He takes a deep breath. It seems his chest will never stop filling.

—If I had a gun, I would dash it to pieces. A kettle, I

would pound it on a rock; a tent, I would tear it down. If I had furs, I would burn them. Then he turns to look the young man in the eye.

—Yes. Give me the furs. Give me fire.

The young man obliges. What else would he do alone with this man on the edge of his wits?

Matonabbee scavenges for moss and a few dead twigs to build a fire, kindles it with the young man's flint and tinder. He cuts pieces of beaverskin and feeds the fire. And now the flames are hungry for all he can provide. The furs are blazing. A pall of acrid smoke envelops him.

He pulls at the neck of his tunic, taking another deep breath as if he is about to tear at his clothes and strip them from his body, and then he stops. His arms go slack and fall to his sides. The young man will say afterwards that as he watched he saw Matonabbee's spirit leave, saw it flow from his nose and mouth, from his ears and from his eyes. It drained away, he will say, exactly like water leaving a lake, and his face that was once alive became the face of a corpse as he turned it on him.

—Now I will walk with you a little way, he said.

—GIVE ME the sled.

The young man is taken aback. They have walked for five days together, shared fire against the cold, matched each other step for step. The older man has spoken hardly at all but his silence has been comfortable. They have come to the heart of the wooded country, where the trees grow more profusely and the ground offers all manner of tracks to be followed. They have feasted on ptarmigan and hare. With no furs to trade, the young man is resigned to putting himself in the Pedlars' debt. Already they have a taken a large deer with a maimed leg and loaded it onto the sled. The older man's company has been solid, dependable, a steadiness against the random retorts of the trees exploding in the cold and the restless booming of the distant lake. The young man has lost his fear. Another day following the river and they will surely find the Pedlars, who keep a house farther on for trading. But Matonabbee repeats his command. He hands Matonabbee the sled and turns to walk on.

—Wait.

Matonabbee takes off his mittens and bends to untie the lashing.

—Here.

He hands back the sled, the carcass still on it. He doubles, triples the hide thong over on itself and ties it round his waist. He pats it.

—There. A sash now. Like a true captain.

The young man knows his face is all bewilderment. Matonabbee claps him hard on the back, then laughs and walks on, his smile vanishing as quickly as a whisky jack disappearing into the trees, his eyes as impassive as if they have never seen a human face. The young man follows cautiously.

That night he builds a fire bright as day. It crackles and spits. The shadows flicker and play all around the two of them. Matonabbee seems to be sleeping. The young man tries hard to stay awake. He knows a man near starvation may become a danger to his fellow. But it is not that. Though the hunting has not been the best, they have not fallen into starvation. So it is not that. But he knows the tales of men delusional with grief. He has heard the history of Matonabbee's exploits in the north and the terrible payment he exacted there. He has heard it was for the death of a favourite uncle. He tries hard to smother panic, to think clearly. Matonabbee has had more than enough opportunity to use his knife. He surely would have by now. But then there is the great length of hide. Who knows what Matonabbee has in mind as retribution for the deaths of his nearest kin?

1783

INDESCRIBABLE. SAMUEL HEARNE, WHO HAD heard himself praised—by his enemy yet!—as an *écrivain extraordinaire, un peintre de l'histoire naturelle sans pareil*, was stricken dumb in the face of it. They had been approaching the berg all day in a strange calm. It seemed not to be drifting at all. Against the evening sun it rose tall as a cathedral—a vast floating castle whose walls of glass assumed the colours of the sea it shadowed and gave them back, sea and ice taking one from the other and giving back again and again until its purple glowed deeper than the sea itself.

The men on the deck of the *Prince Rupert*, Captain Tunstall, his mate, and almost every hand, had debated its size and wagered while Sam took a reading to determine its distance from the ship and calculate its height. It surpassed all estimates. The carpenter at three hundred feet gained the prize but came a hundred feet short. As they drew closer, the men fell silent. The shadow it cast was so long that they sailed through its darkness before they swung round to the southwest.

Some drew in their breath and swore. Nearly all shifted for a better view, for as the ship came about the berg seemed to spin for them, turned like a rare jewel on the fingertips of a giant until it displayed the splendours of its farther side. The sun's rays struck aslant. Every plane and angle of the sculpted ice and snow, every crest and hollow, every gulley, every fissure presented itself to them with stark clarity.

Its topmost peak towered above them tinged with pink like the rarest bloom. Its height crushed the men who looked on it, listening to the intermittent roar and boom it made, like the sea entering a cave. They did not speak. The sculpting winds had rendered the thing fantastic, a gleaming castle of ice with tilted walkways spiralling up to its turrets and pinnacles, with cavernous entrances below and a high turret above. It was not of this world.

Even as they drew level and passed, Sam could feel it slipping from the grasp of his sight. He wanted to hold it steady, fix every detail, but the wind picked up and filled their sails and already behind them it looked smaller.

He scrambled down the ladder. On the way to his cabin he saw Jefferson and the new surgeon sitting at cards, a bottle of brandy between them.

—Get up on deck in a hurry, there. It'll pop your eyeballs. Though what he meant was *there is a chunk of heaven floating by*. He went straight to his satchel hanging on the back of this cabin door and tipped the contents onto his bunk. There was the notebook he had purchased in order to begin a new journal—untouched. He found his black-lead pencil, dull but it would have to do, and pulled himself back up the ladder.

Already the miraculous sight had diminished. Sam drew it rapidly, sketching in the contours, indicating the dark places, the light, writing in the colours. It was not a good drawing but it was not for the viewer. The lines were merely indicators, reminders of what was there, not meant to represent the thing at all. It was for him, to hold it in his mind, to remember it for Molly. He went down to his cabin.

CLOSER TO THE STRAIT, the weather soured. They had had a fine run from England. Fair and steady for weeks on end and little time lost to the few storms they ran through. Sam knew he was lucky. To be sailing this sea again. Stranger than any dream these two undreamed voyages in the space of a single year: to England in disgrace, beholden to La Pérouse for his freedom, and now returning. Governor Samuel Hearne. He wondered sometimes if his renewed appointment was intended by the London office as some kind of elaborate punishment. Pushing the dog's face in its mess. If so, it was lost on him. London would have been the punishment.

The *Prince Rupert* yawed heavily. Sleeping was out of the question. Sam closed his eyes to see the berg again. Four hundred feet. It was a castle, a floating castle. There were tunnels through its lower third—two green tunnels, one slightly above the other, an oblique plane of glistening white spiralling up between them until it broadened to a horizontal ledge, all above it elegantly sculpted and carved by wind and sun. Sam realized he was addressing Molly. He was rehearsing the words he would need to tell her about this marvel and allow her to see it too. Not at once, of course. He would save it for a tale to tell in the winter. He'd want to hear first how they had fared out on the land, if she had finally learned how to be a true countrywoman. She'd want to know what had happened on board the *Sceptre,* how he'd won his freedom. And she would ask him about England. An easy source of astonishment, England. But not so easy to tell. She was too avid for it. He did not like to feed her appetite. And yet he had never dismantled her dream. She hoped to see it one day, he knew that. She expected him to take her back when he left the bay for good. How then, ever, to explain the Company's resistance? His own—if only he were honest? But that was all far in the future and he had no present plans to return. Unless of course she bore him a child of his own. Then he would feel compelled to give the lad—a lad, certainly—all the benefit of an English education. He had thought briefly last summer that she might indeed be carrying a child. But then when she had stood before La Pérouse, with Athîkis at her side, the two of them as lost and alone as if they stood in a foreign country, he had stifled the thought. How otherwise could a man live with his conscience?

But it was all conjecture. Who was to say what the future held? One thing was certain: when the new house was established he would see to it that they had comfortable quarters, a bed built for Athîkis. He would take Athîkis out on the land every day, school him in its ways. Perhaps he would find a likely Indian lad to tutor him in all he needed to know. Or Matonabbee. Like a venerable grandfather. And he'd teach him English skills too. He'd teach him to read. He had no less than a dozen new books stowed in his box. Two were for him, and the rest were for the library he would build in the coming years in the new house. They included two primers in case there were men who had mind to learn. He'd had more than forty books at the fort. Half of them had been used to feed the flames until La Pérouse put a stop to it. He had shown him the ones he'd saved, but they stayed in his cabin and never were returned to Sam. The man loved books. He'd almost kept Sam's own account of his journey for himself. Sam had had to swallow his pride and beg for it. It was the drawings that had intrigued the French commander. Well, Sam would teach drawing to Athîkis too. A man who could draw was a man who could see the intricate wonders of the world. And he would teach him to take their measure. He would teach him the art of navigation, show him—quite soon he could do this—how to use the microscope that Mr. Wales had promised to send out. Athîkis would grow to be a man of exceptional understanding, skilled in the arts of both worlds. Like his mother—though Sam knew that was not quite true. He thought of Molly's long brown feet pedalling laboriously through the hymns she had taught herself when Moses confined her to the house—and he thought of her sewing, which always seemed to come apart where the other women's stitching could hold houses together in winter gales. But she would have been looked after through the winter. The women would have taken care of her. And Athîkis too. Athîkis would not have gone without. Poor Molly. With all her clumsiness she still charmed him beyond imagining. She would have been broken-hearted at the loss of her menagerie, sickened to know that all of it ended on the plates of the ravenous French. He would tell her the beaver pair ran off in the confusion. And the otter. He would make it up to her. Once they were established he would help her recreate her own small Eden.

When they were out of the swell, Sam got up and settled himself at his little table under the lamp while the sailors above prepared the ship for her passage through the drift ice in the strait. He opened the journal and tore out the sketch he had made, then he carefully set the date at the top of the clean page. He drew quickly, lost in a labyrinth of ice.

He had been drawing for some time when the unmistakable jolt and grinding of ice against the sides of the ship broke his concentration and he knew they were entering the strait. He put on his jacket and hauled himself up the companionway to the deck, was almost propelled out of the hatch as the bow of the ship rode up over a floe. All around, the field of broken ice reflected the sun's endless light on the uneven surfaces. The ridges and crests on the pieces of what was frozen sea were painted now in rose and lilac, purpled reds and deepest blues. There was no end to it.

The ship was well fortified, with the yards and the anchor stocks protected, but none of it would prevail against the shock of two floes jamming together. Such potential havoc lurking in such flagrant beauty. Nature utterly indifferent to the affairs of men. It was how Sam best enjoyed her.

Jefferson was up on deck too. He had wrapped himself in a blanket.

—Astonishing fine night.

—It is. Indeed it is.

—Shall we be looking out for the Marble Islanders when we get into the bay?

—I think yes. We've a deal of goods below and they'll not have seen trade since . . . Sam's voice tailed away, the unspoken words too disgraceful for the purity of the scene: *since the French attack, since my surrender, since we were taken prisoner.*

And how unlike was all this beauty before him. How unlike his passage a year ago with La Pérouse, when the fog hung like ice in the air and obscured everything. They had felt then the change of temperature as soon as they passed Frey's Island, and they knew what was coming. Not all of last year's ice had been driven out of the bay. In places it had jammed together and piled on itself to form dangerous drifts, islands where none should be. Ahead the new ice had already started forming under low swathes of fog. It had not been hard to persuade La Pérouse that he needed a pilot—and there was the Company sloop, the *Severn,* under uncertain French command, trailing in their wake.

It had been a gentlemanly arrangement. Mr. Turner, master of the *Severn,* would transfer to the sloop, taking with him the officers and a small crew, and would pilot the three French ships safely through the hazards of the strait. La Pérouse, once all the ships were safely through, would recompense him with an appropriate sum and furthermore would permit him and as many English from York and Churchill as the sloop could carry to sail in her to England.

Sam and Turner and Marten from York transferred to the sloop with a hastily chosen crew. Within hours they were under way at the head of the convoy. The irony of their situation did not escape Sam, though he wondered, as they entered the straits, if the lateness of the year would capture them all, French and English alike. The ever-changing sea was a maze of new-forming ice, a crazed paving constantly shifting. In places the ice dragged on the planking like a saw blade. As if the fog itself manufactured the ice—or the ice the fog. But Turner was well seasoned and they met with no mishap. The only men lost to the deep were those who had already succumbed to the ruinous conditions of their weeks of captivity in the bay.

Just off Cape Resolution, they hove to and waited for the *Sceptre*. When she rounded the headland and came alongside, the atmosphere was cordial, everyone, French and English, glad to be out of the fog and out of danger. A cheer was raised when the last of twenty-two more men were transferred to the ramshackle sloop for the voyage back to Scotland. Sam watched carefully as they came aboard. Joseph Hansom was not among them. Sam counted only seven from Churchill. The remainder—from both Churchill and York—were on the *Astree*, bound for France. It was hard to say at that moment which men were most fortunate—or least.

The passage in the frigate tonight was a far cry from that run a year ago in the *Severn*. Sam thought sometimes about the men who never had the chance to take the risk and transfer. But he had done his best for as many as he could. He had always to remind himself of that.

The two men shifted their footing as the swell increased.

—Chill.

—It is, sir.

His second extended a corner of the blanket. Sam declined such a womanish move.

—We'll get ourselves fitted out with some proper clothes, Mr. Jefferson, as soon as we get there. We'll make that a priority.

—When we find our women, sir. There may be no one about.

But Sam preferred his vision of a welcome party waiting. The Homeguard families would not have gone far. They would have wintered in the woods upriver, surely. They would have had the powder and shot La Pérouse had promised. La Pérouse was a man of his word. And after all, it was scarcely a year.

—Or we might find ourselves forced to re-establish our proprietorship. The place may be overrun.

—Matonabbee as chief factor?

Sam enjoyed the vision.

—Connêkwêse as second. Sâsâpokîsik as chief trader?

—Nabyah, surgeon.

—What a command. Still it won't hurt to be back. Too many boot-licks and duds this winter for me.

The two men watched the drifting ice for a while longer, until Jefferson announced he was going below.

—Shall I leave this?

—Thank you, no.

The wind now cut sharply. He would have a warm toggie made when he arrived, mittens and moccasins. A man's feet never froze in a proper pair of moccasins. Jefferson was probably thinking the same. But it wouldn't be Molly Sam would ask. Molly would have had enough of sewing. Molly could keep him warm in other ways. Just thinking about it. He'd had only one woman in all the months in London. A young whore with clammy limbs and a cracked front tooth, but one who knew her business. He'd been back several times.

The sudden unease took Sam by surprise, it was so keen. He needed to know that Molly and Athîkis had come to no harm. The need came from the deepest chamber of his heart. It was as sharp as this sudden wind from the north.

The prospect of sleep was remote. Sam took a walk around the timbers the Company had provided for him. Lashed under canvas on the deck. Carefully measured and marked in frame, there lay all the parts sufficient for their temporary home while they felled fresh timber for the new fort.

He gave the cords a tug, tightened two that had slacked off, and went below.

AT THE MOUTH of the Churchill River they fired a salute and listened intently. There was no answering musket shot. They listened until the gun's smoke had disappeared completely.

—They know what time of year we come. They would be here.

—Or on their way still. We don't know.

But their voices were useless against the great silence that rolled in after the detonation.

Every man in the longboat was quiet for the approach. The remains of the fort stood against the summer sky. A jaw of black teeth that had received an axe head to the centre. Of the forty-two cannon, almost a dozen lay at angles outside the walls. The Frenchmen at the fort that day had seemed to Sam like ants struggling with bits of debris, tottering, wavering, working with an intent frenzy as if trying to get the labour accomplished before a thunderclap let loose a downpour. And his men had watched. He could not make them close their eyes. He was at a loss. If he had been able give them orders, keep them busy, he would have, but he was powerless. They were prisoners without rights and without duties, with only a perverted liberty. And they would watch until their captors told them otherwise.

The flagpole was still there but the white flag of France, thank God, was gone. Not a flag at all but the linen cloth from his own table. That had been almost immediate after surrender. The French soldiers had poured through the place like water. An officer had emerged straight away with the cloth, had evidently had orders to find something that could be raised. A couple of soldiers had hauled down the Company colours and raised the white cloth. It could not have been anything more regrettably appropriate. Jimmy Frost had run at the soldiers and began to lay about them. The Company men, standing where Sam had marshalled them, began to cheer. Some tried to break away but the soldiers containing them had fixed bayonets. An officer knocked Frost to the ground. Another man beat him about the head with the stock of his gun. Sam tried to talk the men through the shame of their predicament. They were not soldiers. They were outmatched in every way. A peaceable capitulation was a worthy achievement. Calmness and reason. Lives saved, not squandered. Think of their families.

But the memories of the sack of his post came to Sam now in a relentless bombardment: La Pérouse refusing to accept that the walls would not come down, firing shot after shot from the *Sceptre,* anchored right off the point in open range of his own—unmanned—battery. He had never related these moments to the London Committee. Tell them he was on board the *Sceptre*—under guard—while she was taking aim? As if he himself were firing the charge? He had been taken to the captain's mess, the French corporal not even bothering to turn the key. The man had pulled a wig out of his coat and put it on. Sat sprawled in a chair across from him, his legs splayed, his head at an angle, declaring the lack of threat posed by Samuel Hearne, Chief Factor in command of Prince of Wales Fort. He had begun to hum. The melody impossibly at odds with the deafening detonations from the guns, the shuddering reverberations. Sam's nerves could not endure it.

—I have a mind to view the operations.

The corporal stared at him as if he had coughed or broken wind.

He tried it again in French.

The man feigned incomprehension. Sam was driven to fall back on pantomime, pointing and gesturing as if he were a dolt.

It pleased the Frenchman. He shrugged with amusement and complied, reaffirming his position that Sam could not possibly, on any account, present anything resembling a menace.

He slipped, he remembered, as a violent blast rocked the ship and he lost his footing on the companionway. The air above was thick with the guns' sulphurous smoke, catching at the back of the throat, making the eyes burn. The Frenchman took him to the stern. He felt a surge of elation to see the walls still standing. A cloud of dust and smoke hung above. He smiled, could not hide it, not repress it, and then with a speed that could not be foreseen and to his eternal shame, the tears were streaming down his face. Something else he did not include in his report.

From the longboat Samuel could see no sign of life, no one moving about outside the walls nor the smoke of any fire, only a crowd of herring gulls making raucous searches over the beach in front. The flat land to the west and to the north stretched away unmarked by any sign of human habitation. He had never seen the land like this. Surely, even before the fort was built, there would have been camps, the river so rich.

It was like arriving at the end of the world, the fort, symbol now of its own of destruction, presiding over the abandoned grounds. Sam had never seen the place without its usual village of tents out on the western approach, without the constant pluming of smoke from their fires, without men and women moving to and fro, fences of drying racks for their meat, clutches of children running, their voices ringing, dogs, dogs everywhere. Not one to be seen. It was a country where even the ghosts had vanished.

Jefferson continued to sweep the shore with the spyglass.

—No one waited.

—They are inland. Maybe down towards Basquiah.

—Why wouldn't they come up to see?

—It's a long way just to see.

—But a runner at least. Someone sent to watch for us.

Sam had no answer.

The landing stage was destroyed. The hoist miraculously still stood but the decking around it had been torn away. La Pérouse in a last act of insolence had fired a shot dead centre. The rest no doubt had been carried off by the spring ice. Not that it mattered. They were to build the new house upriver, beyond the cove. But still the landing stage represented something more, a bridge perhaps to home.

He and Jefferson would go ashore briefly, take a quick survey of the devastation and see what might remain to be salvaged in due course. A boat was lowered.

From the boat Sam scanned the banks again, and then he saw her.

He tapped Jefferson's arm.

—Someone.

The woman was blind, old. He knew by her walk: each foot risking air and balancing for less than the blink of an eye, ready to fall back if it met with an obstacle; the hands out low, palms forward, pushing mountains of air before her.

—No. No one.

But she was there; he saw her. Sam could not wait now to get ashore, though it was not how he had envisaged his return. In his mind's eye the people too had returned. They had waited faithfully for shiptime, their tents clustered in front of the ruins, the smoke, the children, always the dogs. His mind's eye had seen a village. He, the governor, returning, stepping ashore, perhaps a cry of jubilation from the men. For the winter would have been hard, no doubt about it. A long hard winter without trade, unprepared for what they had to endure—no dried meat, no snowshoes ready for travel, living for a while on the geese in the fall, then going inland for deer. It would have been hard on them all, living in the old way. They would be glad to return to the fort in the hope of a ship. He had seen a great crowd of them in the comfortable country of his mind, eager for the boat's return, its supply of comfort and plenty. Molly would be there, half proud, half shy. Her Samuel Hearne returning. As she knew he would.

—Perform your duty, Samuel Hearne. Her eyes mocking. Laughing.

He spoke to the rowers.

—Take us in as close as you can. There's no level place to pull her ashore with the tide as she hangs.

—We can delay, come back.

—Or we can get our feet wet. He was already removing his stockings and shoes.

THE BLIND WOMAN walked down to the edge of the bank and sat with her face turned to the sea. She turned her face to him as he made his way hobbling over the shingles of the beach.

—There are a great many of you.

He recognized her as the sister of the woman who had

taught him so long ago to set snares. He answered in her own
language.

—Sailors, Mother. But they will be leaving. The rest of
us are not so many as before.

—Samuel Hearne.

—Yes. I have come to build a new house.

—Not killed, then, by the soldiers.

Sam laughed but the old woman looked grave.

—They set you free?

—As I stand before you.

Still she did not smile.

—And the price?

—Of my freedom?

She turned her blind face full towards him. The emptiness had him swimming, he had lost all solid ground. He
reached for truth the way a man who has lost his balance
reaches for support. The price was his dishonour. But to
answer to this hag, this shoeless crone with holes in her deerskin dress, tears in the ragged Orkney shawl, burrs and gouts
of what might once have been food caught in the fringes, dirt
all over her hands and face . . .

She held him fixed, her mouth as expressionless as her
eyes, waiting for his answer.

—There was none, Mother. Trying to make his voice
soft, feeling truly like a son appeasing. None. I promise.

—Yes. A bargain struck, a promise made, a pact. What
did you promise?

Sam sighed, wishing to end this enquiry and turn back to
the question of this great emptiness.

—I promised, Mother, not to resist their entry to the
stone house.

—For your life?

—And for the lives of all my men. And for the lives of
your people, Mother, too. The soldiers harmed none, not a
soul.

—But they have gone and you have returned here. Have
my people returned? Tell me, can you see them?

She was angry now, turning her head this way and that,
mocking her own blindness, his sight.

Sam's voice was little more than a whisper.

—Tell me where they are.

—I don't know where they are. Tell me where you think
they are. They went deep into the country, and the deer—the
deer who come to us, who sustain us—the deer stayed away
from them. Tell me where you think they are. There was a
sickness. It found every person. There was a great cold. It
broke the trees apart and killed the fish even in the depths of
the lake waters. Tell me where you think they are.

His voice was shaking when he asked how she had survived.

—It matters to you?

—Yes. It matters.

At last she released him from her blind gaze. She angled
her face away and spat. Her mouth then was set tighter than
ever, the sides drawn down, the lips in a grim arc. She got up
in silence, balanced herself.

—But tell me how you have lived here.

—I came with some Wêcîpwayânak. They've gone

now. They waited nineteen days for the ship and would not wait longer.

—They left you with meat?

—It's gone now too. You are just in time. She gave a hollow laugh and walked away.

The emptiness of the landscape pressed in on Sam. This old woman, this crone, the only living soul. No one. No one.

He pushed himself to standing and saw that Jefferson was making his way over.

Terns wheeled overhead, calling. Sam could see clear down to the point.

—Did she go, sir? Did she tell you anything?

—Nothing. She was not right in the head.

The terns continued calling. Hundreds of them.

—Captain said he wants us back within the quarter hour, sir.

—Quite right. He's got his work cut out for him.

THE EMPTINESS had weight. As a winter night approaching, it had weight. It had certainty. He could almost see the bodies black upon the land.

There had been rumours all that year. He had known the sickness was on its way. All the talk of a burning fever. And he'd done everything in his power, taken every measure, to lessen the risk for all of them. But especially for Molly, though she'd resisted going over to the cape. She had not seen the need. He had told her the need to stay away was serious. He had told her to stay there until they heard no more of dying, but she had not replied. Give me your word, he had said. Promise me. He had thought her reply when it came was simple stubbornness. A land without dying, she had said, is not possible.

Yet in her eyes no fear. No distrust. Her eyes laughing at him.

FIVE MILES UPRIVER from the ruins of Prince of Wales Fort, Samuel Hearne lies in the very spot where Richard Norton once lay with his young wife. The bright boards of the new Company house shine in the moonlight against the surrounding darkness. The lead has been carried up to the roof and is stacked ready for laying down tomorrow. Though not finished, the house is tolerably comfortable and Sam has allowed the men to move in. The boards for the officers' own house were missing from the indent and will have to be sawn for the purpose. Samuel Hearne, William Jefferson, and the new surgeon, Thomas Seacol—Purvis declined to renew his contract—sleep in a tent hastily constructed from boards and canvas. Sam thought it was the least they could do for men who had worked with such a will to get the *Rupert*'s cargo ashore before the ice bound her in the bay for the winter. Goods for trade and supplies and provisions for one whole year. And all accomplished in ten days despite the severity of the weather. There had been ice already forming in the river and the sloop had run aground and the men had been sometimes up to their necks in the freezing water, the bales and sacks and boxes raised overhead. And then there was the ballast for her homeward voyage. They had moved what was surely a quarry of rock through one of the worst September storms Sam had seen. But the *Rupert* got away safely and the house for the men was finally fit to receive them by the last day of that same month. He would not begrudge them their comfort. He retired to his cot—it could not be called a bed—with a sense that now finally the worst was over and tomorrow perhaps they could start sawing the boards for the officers' accommodation.

Sam falls asleep wondering just how the boards were going to be obtained without the use of a pit saw—also missing from the indent. And his night begins.

WELL INTO THE NIGHT the carriages creak and rumble past the railings of the shining white church across the sea. And deep in the earth the grey dreamers dream. Under his mean headstone—the thinnest and the shortest in his row in Christ Church, where he has lain for more than forty years— Richard Norton dreams long and hard, day and night. The dreams of Richard Norton fly always to Rupert's Land, where the great stones of the fort—not smooth like the church above but rough-hewn and undressed—rise up block upon block in a geometry of power and strength. Again he dreams of the fort rising stark against the sky to defy all comers, to withstand both wind and time, a symbol of permanence rising from the frost-riven rock. His feet tread the unfinished walls, measuring the men's labour under his boot soles. The men are there too sometimes, with their bent backs and the patient horses, and sometimes they undo his work while he is up at the old wooden fort. They take their orders from the insufferable Robson, and when he comes down again to view the progress he sees his beloved project razed to the foundations and all must begin again. Sometimes he dreams a contest with the meddling Robson and grapples with him and once, as he did in his waking life, he strikes him on the side of the head with his doubled whip. Clouds of dusty lime envelop them both and the fort is lost to view.

The dreams he loves best bring him the luxury of flesh and fire, the taste of caribou and women on the tongue. Best of all, Moses' mother comes to him as he first encountered her, before he named her Abigail, before he gave her cause to stand in the river water and rend her clothes. A gift from a Mashkêgow man, she comes to him warm and compliant, smiling. The laughter of women. And his boy, flying like a plump bird between the outstretched arms of his aunts, their smiles bright in the sun. He tries to dream Moses' return to the bay. Moses a fine youth reunited with his mother, but it will not crystallize and all he is left with is the sense of Elizabeth's mean headstone at his brow. So he returns again and again to his first woman, who laughed with him in his bed of spruce and moosehide and made him weep and forget the shocking cold and dark and all the fears of his first winter in the heart of the strange country.

And comes another, his second wife, also from the Mashkêgow man, a Wêcîpwayân woman they have captured. Bought this time and paid for and kept briefly until she proved too much for him. If he is lucky he dreams his first union with her. He and the other officers have moved out of the old log house up the river and are installed in the new stone house behind the bright—still unfinished—walls of the new fort. Many of the people who live in this part of the country want to settle in the camp outside the walls. Such promise of plenty. More than the land can offer. No one knows the extent of goods and provisions the storehouses under the bastions will hold. Everyone is eager to please these prospective partners in trade. Richard has his own quarters—also unfinished—with, at least, a door. The woman lies down without a word on the floor of his room with her mouth set, her eyes blank. She raises the skirt of her deerskin dress and pushes the heavy leggings out of the way, parts her own flesh with her fingers, and jerks her chin to say, Come! He knows she wants it to be over. But all this new privacy. He wants it to last. He takes his time unfastening his clothes. He is nearly beside himself but he knows it will be over almost as soon as he touches her—she is so remote. And so he removes his own clothes item by item, starting with his moccasins and the deerskin gaiters, his two pairs of socks, and his worsted leggings beneath the deerskin breeches. He is shaking by the time he reaches all the British buttons beneath his deerskin jacket, but he persists until he is standing naked as Adam and cold as an icicle broken from the eaves. When he slips inside her he is on fire.

As soon as he is finished she pushes him off. Her face is still set firm. She will not look him in the eye. Richard Norton tries not to care. When next he has her in his bed she does not remain impassive but takes her pleasure on him violently, massively, though still she does not look him in the eye. And each time they lie together it is the same. He is almost overpowered by the surging storm of her. In the dreams that follow, her passion turns to attack, his to terror. Two weeks later when one of the hunters comes in to the trading room and comments on her size and strength, Richard on an impulse names a price, and that night she is gone to the man's tent, disappeared without a word. In the trading room the next morning, Richard glances often at the door. But she does not return. He writes the man's name in his account book and beside it his debt: fourteen made beaver. In the column headed "For What Gave" he writes, "For sundry goods and gifts sent Inland."

Norton does not expect to see her again and will not miss her. In her arms he entered a stranger's world he did not understand. He is happy to return to the compliant embrace of Abigail, who will not only look him in the eye but is rapidly learning English. From time to time he sees the woman when he passes through the camp outside. She does not acknowledge him and takes care to look away if he comes near. Once when he goes by, he sees she has an infant at her back. He has a mind to approach her then but thinks better of it. Only a few months later, after a party of Northern men come in to trade, she is gone and the hunter is there standing in front of him at the trading desk, demanding a gun for the fourteen made beaver he paid for his wife. He no longer has a wife, he says, only a son, in the hands now of his sister. Richard Norton gives the man a gun, one that has been repaired several times, and hopes it is the last he hears of the family. A year later, when he sees the man's sister waiting in the same place at the trading table, his heart sinks. A small boy, barely able to stand, is beside her, clutching her dress. He has heard about the man, her brother, who was killed when he was out hunting, his gun exploding in his hands and a fragment severing his neck. His sister says she has come to him, the governor, so that he can care for the boy. The child now has no one to provide for him. Afterwards, Richard will think about this moment often and about how perhaps the heavens contrive to order our affairs, for it is at that very moment that his own young son Moses runs into the room, stops in the centre, and beams with delight. He rushes to the younger boy and embraces him with the fervour of a bear hugging its victim. The smaller boy can scarcely breathe. Moses kisses his face and pats his head as if he is a small dog.

—Yes, says Richard. I shall take him. I shall care for him as my own. He sees with some relief that the boy's eyes are black as pitch. But he will never be sure.

WHEN RICHARD NORTON dreams of Moses, whether it is at his mother's breast or running full tilt with Matonabbee behind him, the dreams end always with the same bleak vision. He sees the boy standing in the centre of the carpet in the drawing room of the school where he left him. The carpet spreads and extends on every side until it is as wide as the great barren land to the northwest of the fort. The words he has whispered in the boy's ear—You shall inherit a fortress—are sucked away on the wind until they are thinned to the distant cry of a curlew. When this happens Richard Norton dreams a future that will never be. It begins always with a high blue sky, wisps of cirrus marking the dizzying height of air. He dreams Moses a young man, grown tall and straight like himself, setting his boot down on the shore of the bay, looking up at the flag flying from the centre of the fort, the August sun glancing off the bright new stone, the walls finished now with handsome parapets. There is handshaking, there is laughter. Some few mistake Moses for Richard, forgetting the lapse of time. He watches his son stride forward, recognizing his mother in the assembled crowd. She is old now, a little bent, but her eyes shine with fond recognition. The fort is magnificent—the fort that he, Richard, built from the very stones of the land. A governor there might think himself a king, the walls of his castle thirty feet wide and built to withstand all and any who might be foolish enough to assail them, though none would dare. Yes, built to withstand even the ravages of time itself. Richard Norton watches as the fort displays itself like a child's toy set upon a carpet, the men inside the walls moving to and from the various buildings. The roofs vanish and he sees the rows of tables in the mess, the rows of bunks in the men's quarters. He sees his own quarters not as they were when he left but as he would have liked them to be, and he sees his young son taking his seat at his own table, his mother dozing in a chair by the wood stove, a smile on her lips. There is an empty chair opposite Moses. One day a wife of his own will take her place there. But now it is meant for the tall youth his son has invited to the table. The youth is well built and strong but he is shy and does not have the bearing of his son. Moses greets him as a brother. The youth has waited long years at the fort for Moses' return, speaks perfect English, and has acquired all the manners of an English gentleman. He has learned all he needs to know for the smooth running of the factory. Moses pours French wine for him and announces that he will write to the Company to request that Matonabbee—he calls him Matthew Norton—be appointed second-in-command. The two young men raise their glasses across the table and drink to their own success.

SAMUEL HEARNE WAKES sweating in the night with ice an inch thick on the makeshift wall behind his head and a mouth as dry as oat bran, foul as rotting meat. Richard Norton's vision has dissolved into darkness under pressure of Samuel's own dream. He has been standing before the London Committee, as he did in November 1782 and again the following January, explaining his actions—justifying his decision. What came from his mouth is the reason for its taint. He tries to reconstruct his argument.

—Sir Bibye, Doctor Wegg, honourable gentlemen of the Company, in answer to your request to hear the justification for my decision to eschew the use of fire in the defence of Prince of Wales Fort, I can only answer at length, begging your indulgence.

Those among you—Mr. Browne, for instance—who are familiar with life at the factories on the bay will readily understand that while we organize ourselves, under your command, in accordance with strict military principles, we operate as a large family of many members, embracing every generation—and I stress every—and overseeing a considerable number of servants, many of whom we come to know over the years—just as any English head of household with his domestics—as our familiar charges. We live surrounded by dependents and feel towards them a sense of profound responsibility, mixed sometimes—yes, I shall say it—with a seasoning of affection. Only when this arrangement is taken into account can my actions on the eighth of August be fully understood.

Imagine, sirs, if you will, your own households: your sons within doors, your domestics at their duties on your behalf, your wife perhaps sleeping. And imagine, if you will, an assembly of armed robbers at your door. Your house is isolated. No help is at hand. And then let this assembly of plunderers be tenfold the number of able-bodied men within doors to defend your hearth. Shall you in defence of your good name, your family's honour, fire upon them from your windows? Shall you be proud to reduce their number by perhaps one-fifth, even as the other four-fifths, as they assuredly will, batter down your doors and enter freely—only to slaughter your loyal and courageous dependents, rape your women?

—A fort, Mr. Hearne. You were commander-in-chief of a *fort*.

He can hear the rebuttal exactly as it was spoken that day, the word heavy with scorn, like a bladder of grease about to burst. He ignored it then, intent on justifying himself, explaining again his rationale—the lives saved, the expenses spared—all of it, with what he knows now, rotten in his mouth.

And he had had his doubts. This is the thing, the thing he never revealed because how could he? Through all his talk of dependents and a family of loyal servants, even as he was addressing the Honourable Company, he saw Molly's face again. His intention to abandon her had bloomed in the depths of her eyes. His heart had been as tight as a fist in his chest. Yet still he had believed it was for the best. He remembers how, on the way out to the *Sceptre,* he sat in the longboat with his head in his hands, afraid that if he looked up he might see her with some of the other wives returned to the shore. Purvis, glad to be escaping with his life, had put a discreet consoling hand briefly on his shoulder, thinking he bowed his head in shame—and Purvis was almost right. Only not shame for yielding. Not that. Like everyone else, Purvis mistook the cause.

He had continued his testimony that day in Fenchurch Street with Molly's stricken face lodged in his memory. But he had answered every question, every thinly veiled accusation concerning the hour of the first sighting, the state of the powder stores, the roll at the time of attack, the time spent in parley—everything, even the questions concerning Cape Merry.

—No, Your Honours, there were no men stationed over at Cape Merry at the time of the attack.

You could almost hear the passage of air as it was sucked from the room and down their fat throats into their shirt fronts. The pantomime of responses—Sir Bibye elevating his eyebrows into his wig; Wegg wiping his face and turning his head slowly from side to side; James McIlvennie looking demurely down at his papers, as if politely choosing not to witness the embarrassment. None of it genuine. All of it performed for his personal disparagement. Sir Bibye pushed his chair back abruptly and got up. Flinging his coattails back—a fine touch that; you could almost hear him note it—he strode . . . no, he banged about the room, making sure he, Samuel, read the full extent of his outrage.

And so he, Samuel, stood his ground, daring to impute certain omissions, implicating the committee itself in the events that unfolded that day.

—Thirty-nine men!

He could not say it often enough.

—Have you any idea—deference deserted him—any idea at all how many men are required for the simple day-to-day operations of the factory, leave aside the question of an attack? Let us be conservative in our assessment. Let us say four men to complete the watches, one man at the gate. Then let us say four men out provisioning and four at wooding; let us put only one man on the surgeon's list with an injury, assign two men to the duties of the latrines and the cookhouse, one only to assist the trader. Ah, but we must include the trader in our tally. I believe we have arrived at eighteen. Twenty-one men, then, at our disposal. Whom should we send over to Cape Merry? Not myself, surely, nor any of the council. Nor the sloopmaster, nor his mate, nor any of the three men assisting them in offloading the fruits of the very endeavours allied to the fisheries that Your Honours yourselves desire pursued. Then the cook? The armourer? The smith? The house carpenter or the cooper? Perhaps we should send the tailor. Let him learn a new skill to crown his fifty-eight years. Plenty of men left, you say. But one is a mere boy sent out to write; one a tippler and not to be trusted with so much as a cup of custard, one is confined to the men's hall, awaiting transportation back to

England on the *Rupert,* and one has the use of only one hand, though he is no longer on the surgeon's list. The last two men, then? Of course. Let's send them over and reduce our complement at the fort to thirty-seven. There'll be no one to relieve them but they'll not mind, loyal servants that they are.

Sam pulls his damp shirt away from his chest and shivers, draws the blankets higher over his head. He remembers the way the sweat had started to run inside his shirt as he spoke that day. There was no way to convey to the committee the messy complexities of their lives at the fort. No way to make them understand that each and every man in this motley roll of misfits and heroes was like family to him—even poor sodding Blake, who had made sure to commit enough infractions to get himself sent home; that though they might fight and brawl, lie and steal, he would do anything to avert violence and save them from injury. If he'd had ninety-nine men he would not have manned the guns. And if he could not make himself understood with respect to the men in their employ, how was he to begin to explain his actions on behalf of his own family, his family who in the wilfully blinkered vision of the Company did not exist?

And now perhaps do not exist—except in his own pain, a low, barely audible echo behind, beneath every waking thought he has.

AT THE END of September two Homeguard men come down the river in small canoes. They carry no furs, have come only to see if any ship arrived from England. They ask for guns and ammunition and receive them in return for a promise to spread the word of the Company's return. They say they cannot tell the governor all he wishes to know. The people are scattered all across the land, each family following its own path in an attempt to survive the hunger. They themselves do not know who lives and who does not.

In the next months, few families come to trade. Only three of the original Homeguard families who lived at the fort have reappeared. They have lost between them seven members and have come to ask for supplies. They beg a little oatmeal, a little ammunition. Sam questions them all for news of Molly and Athîkis. No one has news. They talk of the devastation out on the land, the great number of sick and dying, the difficulty of finding enough food to keep the body alive. They say it is worse this year, so many of their hunters being carried off by the sickness last winter. They are only just now beginning to think of hunting for furs. But the weather is so harsh and the deer so scarce that Sam finds he is asking them to bring in deer meat rather than pelts. He needs food for his men, and four of those are in their beds with an ague affecting every limb. It is a sorry Eden he has built this time.

It takes a December storm, with all work stopped, for Sam to accept that there never will be news. The men, lacking the good winter suits they had hoped for, go about wrapped in blankets even within the house, even with the stove chimney beginning to glow and putting them all in danger. He sits on the edge of his bed and opens the notebook he began on the *Prince Rupert*. He tears out the sketch of the iceberg and then the finished drawing. He had started another of a crouching girl reaching to take hold of a fox cub. He tears it

out also and makes a twist of the three leaves of the book. He
has to turn and turn it in the candle flame to keep it burning.
It burns down to the small yellow triangle between his finger
and thumb before he drops it to the floor. The charred twist,
intricately cut and curled by the flame, writhes with exquisite
slowness like an animal drawing in its limbs in its last agony.
When he gets into bed he sees before he blows out the candle
how the smoke still hangs in a layer about a foot below the
ceiling. He watches it undulate slowly like the surface of the
sea as it thins and drifts towards the gap above the door.

BY SPRING his sorrow has doubled. Two Northern men
have come in with news of Matonabbee. They have told
him everything they have heard. It does not seem possible.
Matonabbee who could overcome any obstacle, endure any
hardship. He refuses the image that hovers at the edge of knowing. It is too terrible. It does not become the man. He does not
want it ever to enter his dreams, infect his memories. The land
outside seems suddenly empty. How can it be that emptiness
can fill a space? It has filled the land; it is filling him. All day he
is at a loss, at odds with himself, with the men. When, the next
day, some Southern men from York arrive, Sam sits down to
write to Humphrey Marten. The men can take the letter for
him when they return. He has really nothing to say, has no
requests to make, though if he cares to think about it there are
several necessary tools and supplies that are wanting and that
Marten might be able to provide. Instead he writes about the
weather—the coldest, windiest, and most unsettled weather
he can remember. He writes about the goose hunt—one

thousand seven hundred and ten killed. He comes closer. He writes about the Northern Indians who have been in—all of them in great distress and poorly gooded. They have brought only one hundred made beaver in all. He writes until there is only one thing left to write. He writes it: *When the famous leader Matonabbee heard that Prince of Wales's Fort was taken and destroyed by the French, he hanged himself.* There, he has written it. He will not write all that the hunter told him. How Matonabbee's grief, like a ravenous beast, sought to assuage its hunger but found nothing to consume, for Matonabbee possessed nothing to destroy. Nothing in all the world. How the beast then turned upon Matonabbee himself. They found his body hanging from a tree by a lanyard of hide. Torn apart, the man had said, by the winds. Sam writes instead about the other leaders also dead, others gone over to the Canadians. He does not mention the loss of his family. He does not ask Marten about his woman. Marten's letters too have been quiet on the subject. Some things are deeply, deeply private. Buried. He seals the letter. He does not want to sleep yet. He takes a book and stares at the open pages. He can neither read nor think. His thoughts have nothing to turn to. He will send the packet back when the men have had a chance to rest. His loneliness is unimaginably vast, like the land without his friend. He hopes the image that he glimpsed is sealed safe. He does not want it loose again.

WHEN THE SNOW has gone, the amount of work left still to be completed at the new fort seems overwhelming, an impossible endeavour as long as there is the constant need to hunt for themselves. Not enough families are approaching. Those who have camped outside need their help. The gap between Sam's vision and the raw facts of their lives in this place has widened like the dark water of a lead in spring. There had been times when there were forty families, more, living at peace outside the walls of the old fort, working to keep those inside clothed and fed. The men had wanted for nothing. As governor, he lived a sweet dream with Molly. He would always know where she was in the yards.

Now he lives alone in the midst of the men. Outside a dozen women make their camp, a couple of boys too young to hunt, an old man. He, who abhorred Governor Norton for surrounding himself with women, is now himself surrounded. Old women, young girls, grieving widows. The disease that raged through the country was a hunter, seeking out hunters. Those who are left without support come to him. He has not the heart to take a woman into his bed. His dreams are crowded enough. Sometimes he dreams he sees Molly. He dreamt once she came walking towards him with a soft, rolling walk, her belly heavy with his child. He woke before he knew if she gave him a son or a daughter.

He will be returning to England, he knows, without a child of his own. No son or daughter who will have known with him the growling break-up of the river, the ruddy light of afternoon, the sweet taste of caribou or the warmth of its fur against the skin in winter. In offices and coffee houses he will talk of his journeys and his listeners will see him tramping across ice and snow but none will understand how he traversed a different world. He will talk of his friends among the Wêcîpwayânak and the Mashkêgowak and no one will believe they were not savages. All the adventures he has had and the wonders he has seen here across the sea will be to them as stories in a book.

His nights now are never easy. He is waiting for the dream that will show him Molly lifeless. It is his dread. In his heart he knows it is true. He does not have to hear it. His heart knows many secret things, but not all. It knows that her fate was sealed when he opened the gates to La Pérouse. And yet his only thought was to save lives. He had made it clear. It was a condition of his surrender. La Pérouse when they sat down together had said he need have no apprehension on that score. His men, he said, were under strict orders. When they had carried off the provisions and the furs they were to burn everything. There would be no attacks launched on the camps of the savages. What was supposed to be reassurance was a terrible awakening, for Sam saw in that moment how the people, bereft of all they relied on for their support, would be destitute. Abandoning all pretensions to military protocol, he had begged. He had laid out in explicit detail the degree to which the people, in the absence of the fort, would have to rely on hunting for their livelihood. La Pérouse had seemed to listen. He was an intelligent man. He grasped at once the precariousness of people's situation. He promised he would distribute guns and ammunition, everything they needed for the winter. Sam will never know what they received, or how long it lasted. So much that he can never know. So many secret, hidden things. Secret, yet they have the power to haunt equal to any vivid, known thing. How will he ever know whether she would be living still if he had resisted? Often in the night the thought comes to him that it might have been otherwise, that though his men were sorely outnumbered, they did not have to hold the fort forever. Not forever. Only until La Pérouse became alarmed at the days' ineluctable progression towards winter and the freezing of the bay. The weather in all this, the changeable, capricious, mischief-making weather, his very constant foe, was the one factor he could have relied upon. He will always wonder if a show of resistance might have been enough. If the French, seeing that their operation might take some time, might have turned tail for an easier target across the bay. If he might have turned to Mr. Jefferson and seen him too grinning in near disbelief as the French soldiers flowed back like an ebbing tide. If he might be holding Molly now beside him in his bed, telling her again, because she loved to hear it, how the wind had snatched his hat away that day just as the last of the French sails had disappeared over the horizon.

—

AND IS TO LIE under this wide high sky a hard thing? Not now the flesh is gone. It is where I am at home. And I see all the world of people for what it is. A long ceremony to feed the earth. We dance upon it feed on it walk and hunt and shit and love on it. And then we die upon it letting our flesh add to its crust so that new things can crawl there and dig and nest. It is not a hard thing. The lovely sky is a changing vision that is unchanging. It unfolds itself at every moment and yet is never emptied. Always there is shining light or flying cold or the beautiful heavy dark. All want is foreign. Memory returns yes but without pain. With only curiosity and interest and wonder that it could have once been so. I can watch even Samuel as he turns his back on me.

Our lives are many lives lived as one. I see this now. I see Matonabbee and he is two men. I see him walking alone and naked with a hide lashing trailing from his hand. His face too is naked to the sky revealing his great despair and the pain of his love for all those who walked in his life. And then again I see Matonabbee walking with a great crowd of men and women and children. His mouth is stretched wide in a smile he cannot control. He is greeting my Samuel his friend. He is embracing him and they are laughing like boys. I see my father and he is a man bellowing at us in words all bleared with wine and he is my teacher showing me the magic of the letters that can speak the names of things. I can see Nêwositêkâpaw walking away from me with her back bent against the wind but I see her also smoking my father's pipe. Her mouth half-smiling her eyes closing with the pleasure of the smoke. And I see her too when she cupped her hand on Athîkis's skull before even he had a name and her eyes were glistening to see the sweetness of his face. I see Athîkis's tears but I hear his laughter see his small belly shake with it all the world funny and wonderful. I see him running with arms outstretched a bird his feet flying over the land as in his waking dream he flies above it a seagull calling laughing at the poor heavy men and women down below. And my sister Jane yes as she lay curled and frozen like a stone but I see her also in the half dark of my father's room her face close to mine when she whispered and told me about her Wêcîpwayân man. I see her eyes gleaming and her teeth. Her breath is fast and I know she feels him already pressing against her. And Samuel. I can watch even Samuel as he turns away from me. It is a dream that returns less and less often. Instead I see his face above me as it floods with release his face beside me on the feather bolster. His mouth quiet but his eyes speaking to me. I see him bending down out on the point where we have walked. His face turning up to Athîkis. His small hands with long fingers like a woman's lifting the rock to show the nest of mice below pink and blind and twining together for warmth.

The life of the world rolls with the seasons moves over the earth seeing all touching nothing. It watches the light flickering over the surface of the land as the sun passes and cloud and moon and sun again. It watches the face of the earth smile or sleep or close white eyes fast under the scraping wind. It watches the river flowing never ending and is itself borne by the same force. So I watch and so I live. And yes—though my voice is joined to the roar of all others—always alone.

Often I return to the young man waking in the woods. I watch him. He wakes with a start. He does not know how it happened. He slept. A watery light is filling the woods. He looks at once to where Matonabbee made his sleeping hollow. He can smell the spruce where the man slept. He can see the outline of his back impressed in the snowbank. The thought of the older man at large in the woods unnerves him. He is certain Matonabbee has run mad with grief and lost all reason. He sees himself as prey. He is to be stalked and Matonabbee is the hunter.

He examines the ground. The tracks of Matonabbee's snowshoes lead on in the direction they have been travelling towards the Athabascow country. He goes to the place where Matonabbee slept. Kneeling he bends and presses his face to the spruce boughs. Crystals of ice cut into his cheek. The boughs can tell him nothing. In this cold the warmth of a man would be turned to ice before he was a hundred paces off.

He straightens up and feels a softer touch on his cheek. It has begun to snow with flakes so light so small so dry they are barely there at all. It is as if the air is filling with tiny frozen specks. He begins to walk in circles from his sleeping place widening the circle each time then turning and circling in the opposite direction. In his heart he talks to the snow. Faster fall faster. Faster still. He walks directly out from the mess of tracks makes a long turn and walks back. He does it several times. At last he backs away noticing with relief that the sled where it lies beside the remains of the fire has already begun to whiten.

When his heart has calmed sufficiently he allows himself to turn in his tracks and walk forward. He is walking not west—the last direction he would choose—not towards the river and the Pedlars. Not into Matonabbee's trap or up in the direction of the terrible camps. He is walking south towards Deer Swim Lake.

The woods are quiet here. There is an empty feel to them. No one has been following him. Of that he is certain. He has made a mistake abandoning his sled. But that is not his concern. Right now what matters more is the absence of the animals. Sometimes he hears a soft hushing fall of snow when an unseen bird alights on a bough. Without it he would think himself crossed over into the country of the dead.

After three days he has eaten almost all of the meat they dried at the last fire. He has a little left but he knows he needs soon to come upon some game. When he does he will have to risk a gunshot in the still air. And will Matonabbee come then like a *pâkahkos* to seek him out? He will be ready. He will shoot him if necessary.

Walking in this way with fear at his back and with conflict in his heart is tiring. Matonabbee he feels could find him easily if he wished. Increasingly with every step he feels it was a mistake to abandon his sled. The snow has stopped falling. If Matonabbee wished to find him he could. He would do so with ease. The pink glow of the afternoon is fading to blue the deep purple shadows of the trees to black. He does not know what he will do without furs to trade. He has heard that there are hunters at the lake. Perhaps he can join with them. He needs people almost as much as he needs food. He would like to lie down. He would like to allow what will happen to happen but already the trees are flecked with stars and the moon when it rises tonight will be full. Already it is lifting from its bed. He can tell by the density of the dark. The walking will be good in this quiet still air when the moon lifts full and lights the world. A rippling green wind has begun in the upper sky. Even if there are no hunters left at the lake there will be fish. He chooses to walk on.

Athîkis has wandered from me in ever-increasing circles. He uses the knife I gave him to dig and scrape at the snow for moss. The griping pains in his belly never subside. They accompany him wherever he goes. They have become who he is. The child who hurts in his belly. The search for the moss is tedious but he is beginning to recognize the feel of it under the snow. When he finds a little he takes it back to where I lie and burrows quickly under the moosehide his face distorted with the pain in his guts until sleep releases him. He does not see the lame doe that comes cautiously in the dawn light to the scraped snow and snuffs there for lichen for herself. He wakes momentarily to what he believes to be a tree cracking apart in the frozen air.

The young man walks with his gun to the fallen doe and slits her throat. He kneels and puts his mouth to the jetting warmth drowning in its abundance. He slices her belly open and reaches deep inside the steaming cavity for the liver tearing it in a kind of ecstasy that even his teeth feel. When he looks up—still licking his hands preparing to reach behind the ribs for the heart—he sees not twenty paces off a small dark shape observing him. For a moment he believes himself in a dream rising to meet the doe's spirit.

Athîkis speaks. I cannot hear his words but I can see his face. I do not need to see more.

HISTORICAL NOTE

Into the Heart of the Country is a work of fiction based on real events. In its creation, historical figures have transformed into fictional characters obedient to the needs of the story. They are figments of my imagination, their true identities and natures folded between the lines of the historical record.

In recognition of the important work that is being done towards the revitalization of Aboriginal languages, the Cree and Dene names that appear in the book have been rendered for the most part in modern orthography. A few, like Matonabbee, have been left as they appear in the historical record. Samuel Hearne's account of Moses Norton's ancestry has been disputed by at least one historian. I have good reasons for choosing to follow Hearne. Moses' name for his daughter, Mary Norton, was Polly. She is my fictional Molly.

Her mother, Nêwositêkâpaw, appears in Moses Norton's will as Meo-see-ta-ka-pow. The origin of Matonabbee is unclear. It has been suggested that the name approximates "Crying Man."

ACKNOWLEDGEMENTS

My loving thanks go to Leo, my first, most necessary reader.

My grateful thanks to the researchers, librarians, and friends who gave me their generous help: Audrey McClellan, Arden Ogg, Jennifer Brown (*Strangers in Blood*), Sharon Walker, Bronwen Quarry, Denise Jones, Brian Wyvill, and Diana Davidson. Others, too, have been drawn into this web of support, and thanks are due to them also. Any historical inconsistencies are the result of my wilful allegiance to fiction.

Thank you, Hilary McMahon, for taking the book forward, and thank you, Jennifer Lambert, for bringing it to fruition. My thanks also to Alex Schultz, Noelle Zitzer, and everyone involved with its care.

Thank you, John, as always, as ever.

Numerous texts and documents have informed and inspired this work, including *A Journey from Prince of Wales's*

ACKNOWLEDGEMENTS

Fort in Hudson's Bay to the Northern Ocean in the Years 1769, 1770, 1771 and 1772 by Samuel Hearne, from which I quote parts of his letter of appointment. I am especially indebted to the wonderful Champlain Society publications and to the rich archives of the Hudson's Bay Company, as well as to the National Archives of the United Kingdom, which house the last will and testament of Moses Norton. For the disembodied voices that close Part III of the book, I am indebted to Louis Bird's beautiful story "The Wailing in the Clouds" (in *Voices from the Bay*).